King Stephen, the Silver Man, and Greta the Witch

King Stephen, the Silver Man, and Greta the Witch

Greta the Witch

Stephen Voller

AuthorHouse™ UK
1663 Liberty Drive
Bloomington, IN 47403 USA
www.authorhouse.co.uk
Phone: 0800.197.4150

Published by AuthorHouse 02/20/2015

ISBN: 978-1-5049-3824-2 (sc)
ISBN: 978-1-5049-3825-9 (hc)
ISBN: 978-1-5049-3826-6 (e)

Print information available on the last page.

This book is printed on acid-free paper.

CONTENTS

To Anne, who never proofread it … x

Prologue

JERUSALEM, AD 33

MIDDLE EAST: GOLGOTHA, ROMAN-OCCUPIED JERUSALEM, APRIL.

He was appalled by the barbaric nature of these people. The man the Roman soldiers had mistaken for himself was nailed to a wooden cross with their primitive metal spikes and left to bleed to death.

It was terrible to see.

He doubted these people could ever become fully civilized. He turned to go, disappointed that he was scheduled to return in about a thousand years to monitor how they had progressed.

Section 1

La Fete, England, 1136

"We'll make camp here," King Stephen called to his driver. "I am weary of traveling."

The caravan stopped, and Stephen's court and band of followers scrambled down from carriages and horses to set up camp on the road to Winchester. The king watched as his man, his Knight of the Garter and head man-at-arms, Sir Rupert of Ypres, took charge. Using his horsewhip liberally, and with shouts and curses, he cajoled the carriages into a defensive ring. The horses were relieved of their burdens and taken away by the grooms to forage. Rupert was brutal but efficient. He was the man you wanted on your side in a skirmish, and he had saved the king's neck more than once.

The king's tent was quickly put up in the center of the defensive circle. It was a practiced routine; they had been on the road for weeks. The tent was royal blue with his coat of arms embroidered in gold thread. The king's carriage was hung with blue curtains of the same color. As he descended from the carriage, his squire knelt and his footman bowed as he opened the tent flap for the king to enter. Both were dressed like himself in light armor and carried swords; however, his own armor and sword were much more ornate.

He threw his sword and body armor on a trunk and then removed his helmet. He turned as the flap of his tent was pulled aside, and she slipped elegantly through the flap, carrying a jug of water. She helped him remove his boots and then his heavy leather tunic.

Greta the Witch watched as the tall serving wench with the golden hair slyly pulled the flap aside and closed it discreetly behind her as she entered the king's tent. She was his current beau.

Greta had tucked her small frame into the corner of the carriage used to transport the king's tent. In this way, she could travel unnoticed. She had cut a small peephole in the wood at her eye level, and through it she could also see Rupert and his thugs bullying the camp into action. There were thumps as horsewhips found flesh and fists landed punches. The thumps were punctuated by cries of pain, running feet, and the sounds of the alarmed horses. The dogs that always followed the travelers barked, howled, and snarled. They knew the camp would soon be coming alive with food and tidbits, and they were sorting out their pack hierarchy.

Once the king's tent was fully in place and the king settled inside, the porters began putting up the smaller and less significant tents for the men-at-arms and the camp followers. Greta noticed they were also digging latrines; this meant they would probably be staying a few days, not just overnight. She was close enough to hear the giggles from the girl in the king's tent as he took his pleasure. She could smell the wood smoke as the cooking fires in camp kitchen came to life.

The cook and her serving wenches quickly assembled the trellis tables and laid out the jugs of ale. The servants knew that once Rupert and his thugs had settled down on stools with a drink in their hands and food in their bellies, the harassment would stop.

The king had traveled to France to visit his brother Henry. The court was returning to Winchester. With the late spring weather set fair and the game plentiful, Greta thought he had probably decided to rest a few days to hunt and take a break from war and politics. It was less than six months since he had ascended to the throne on the death of King Henry I. But England was ravaged by battles and petty disputes, with several powerful barons refusing to recognize him as their monarch. Even though they were not at war, Rupert has good reason for the defensive ring: the king had many enemies. Despite his viciousness, Greta admired the way Rupert set up the defenses. He was good at it.

Inside his tent, the king stood half-naked as the serving wench washed his body with water and then rubbed his skin with fragrant oils. She had good hands. She held open a fresh robe for him, and he lay down on the blankets, closing his eyes with pleasure.

La Fete was a pleasant place; he had come here as a boy to catch fish and hunt. It was sufficiently remote enough (some said uninteresting) that he could be anonymous here. Well, at least as anonymous as any king of England could ever be. By slow carriage, they were three days' travel to Winchester from here, so this was a good place for his plan. He knew of better places to hunt and fish, grand estates and forests, but this was an unpretentious way of life. In Royal Windsor or the New Forest, he had to take the elaborate court with him, but here he was able to relax and be more himself.

When he was planning the route the previous evening with his men-at-arms, Greta the Witch had appeared by his side and declared the place sacred. He doubted that. She said the site was on some sort of hallowed energy crossing point. His wife, Queen Matilda, who thankfully had gone on ahead, had surrounded herself by these witches and soothsayers. She said they could predict the future. Well, they had not been very accurate as yet, the king thought. He still hadn't won over the troublesome barons, as they had predicted.

His wife was important to him politically and financially, but in her middle age, she was quarrelsome and no pleasure in bed. They had not much in common, and he trusted her little. The queen had left Greta behind, because she said the old witch was too weary to travel. In truth, the king knew she was meant to spy on him. She knew he bedded the serving wenches when she was away, but she also suspected he was up to something. He knew Greta was probably watching him now from the carriage she traveled in. He grabbed the girl playfully to make her giggle, hoping Greta would hear.

Greta was a white-haired crone who smelt of strange herbs and rotting meat. She had the most striking yellow albino eyes, virtually no teeth, and fingernails that it was said could slash the skin of a full-grown bear. Of indeterminate age, she was as fit as a flea and could probably outrun and outride him in his fortieth year. She was known to be adept at defending herself and was especially fearsome when armed with the spear she carried strapped to her back. It was rumored that the tip was coated with poisonous snake venom.

As he lay back on his blankets, he could hear the raucous laughter of Rupert and his cronies as they drank their ale and flirted with the serving wenches. He could smell the delicious aromas of the meat roasting on the cooking fires and the bread baking in the pit ovens. His stomach rumbled with hunger. He enjoyed this life on the road much more than the endless rituals of the royal court. He hated the petty politics and bureaucracy of the monarchy, which he had to endure when he was back at Winchester. He was pleased that he had concocted a plan to delay his return to the royal court for a few more days.

He heard the cook ring a small bell, the signal that the food was ready. The girl went to fetch his supper, pulling back the flap of the tent; she led in the mini procession of serving wenches, who curtsied with difficulty before setting up a serving table, covered in a royal blue cloth, and then putting dishes of food and jugs of ale on the table. The king eyed each of the serving girls; he took particular note of the third one in line, who had a good figure. She glanced up as she placed a basket of bread on the table. She flushed red and quickly lowered her gaze. But in that fleeting moment, the king saw what he wanted.

When the food was served and the other serving wenches had left, he watched the girl use her elegant hands to tie the thin leather straps that closed and secured the tent flap. Now they would be alone for the night. Of course, the camp knew they were not to be disturbed. She knelt on the rug beside him and offered him some bread and roasted meat. The bread was still warm and absolutely delicious; the guinea fowl had been hung in the wagons for five days to mature and was then roasted with honey and wild herbs. It tasted wonderful. There was also a dish of salted swan and a plate of quinces. The cook knew these dishes were his favorite.

As darkness fell and the camp became quiet, Greta stepped down from the carriage and silently stood in the shadows. She wanted to ensure she was not observed. It was unlikely because everyone kept a distance from the king's tent after dark.

She knew that Rupert had posted sentries on the perimeter, so she moved carefully toward the cooking fires, taking a half loaf of bread and hunk of roasted meat from one of the tables. She put the loaf in her shoulder bag and chewed on the meat, holding it by the bone. She wasn't quite sure what type of meat it was; it was too dark to see. It tasted like either partridge or pheasant but could have been any sort of wild bird. Once she had eaten her fill, she tossed the bone under a carriage wheel. Immediately, three of the dogs pounced on the bone, barking and snarling, squabbling over the scraps. The sentry turned to see, and Greta slipped stealthily into the night beyond the outer ring of carriages.

She moved quickly into the tree line beyond the road and settled down to wait for the moon to rise. She could smell lavender and wild garlic in the woods, and she wanted to gather some. She tore a hunk of the bread from the half-loaf in her bag and chewed it slowly to pass the time. She closed her eyes so she could feel the presence of Queen Matilda and her sisters, the witches who were part of her mistress's sect. She felt their presence strongly over the distance to Winchester and sensed they were all warm and safe in their rooms in the castle. She could even smell the incense that her mistress favored in her room, even though she was thirty miles away.

However, here there was an even greater force that Greta could sense. She had not lied when she told the king that La Fete was a sacred place. It was where two energy lines crossed, and she wanted to go to the crossing point and deliberate. She could feel that something significant was about to happen, but she could not understand what. She hoped that going to the celestial crossing point on the night of a full moon would help her.

She opened her eyes and saw the moon had risen above the trees. She finished the last morsel of bread and set-off in her loping run, going first in the direction of the lavender smell. She cut some branches with her razor-sharp dagger and placed the lavender in her bag. It was a gift for her mistress. She then found the wild garlic and took a large clump. She loosened her upper garment and rubbed it on her skin. She also found some fresh fox dung and rubbed her shoes in the mess. It was these smells that kept the men away from her, part of her protection.

She tightened her clothing and set off to follow the energy line.

The next morning, the king was in a good mood. He had a plan for the day, and he had enjoyed his night with the girl.

He sat in his reserved place of honor at the larger trellis table outside the cook's wagon. As he ate his breakfast of freshly baked biscuits and cold roasted wild boar, his mood changed when he saw Greta approaching, in one of her animated states. She approached him directly, not waiting to be summoned forward. It was typical of her lack of respect. She wailed in her high-pitched voice as she came forward, shouting, "Woe is me, woe is me," in order to gain everyone's attention. She waved her stinking black cloak over her head like a flag, as she ran toward him in her strange sideways gait.

"Sire, we must leave immediately," she said in her high-pitched voice. Her white hair was loosened from its ties and wafted about her head in the breeze. "I have had a terrible vision."

The men-at-arms who were within earshot looked up in alarm. The superstitions around these witches were strong. Other members of the court drifted closer as the saw Greta's animated body language (staying far enough away so they could not smell her). In truth, Stephen knew she was a great actress who often raised her voice so many could hear.

She was also one of very few people who could approach the king without a bow or curtsey. Such a discourtesy would normally result in a nod from Rupert, and the unfortunate offender would soon be sprawling on the ground. If Stephen was in a foul temper, they would be taken away and given a savage beating. Some said Greta got away with it because she would put a curse on anyone who struck her.

Now that Greta had the camp's attention, she went on, without seeking royal approval.

"Sire, I have seen a vision of a flying object that will bring death and destruction to us all." She paused for effect, as there were horrified gasps from the courtiers and servants within earshot. "We must leave this place and head to Winchester with great haste."

She held her arms wide above her head in an elaborate gesture to emphasize the size of the flying object.

In truth, she had been genuinely confused and alarmed by this vision. Over the years, she had learned to survive by building on people's fear and loathing. They either feared her witchcraft or loathed the smell of her, so they would gladly pay to get rid of her. She invoked self-preservation by cajoling the less-intelligent and easily manipulated to believe that if she was killed or harmed, the perpetrators would carry a curse and go to hell. However, every so often, she did get a real vision. This one was very vivid, and she knew it to be true. She just couldn't explain it.

What Greta had actually seen in her vision was a silver flying saucer and a spaceman. The silver object was perfectly formed and made of a material she had never seen before. The curves of the object showed no signs of a blacksmith's hammer. It was larger than a house, too large to float, yet it appeared to not only rest on water but to hover over it and fly away in a perfect arc with incredible speed. It flew like a bird yet had no wings.

To Greta, the silver man was tall, muscular, and elegant. He carried himself like a nobleman. He did not have the misshapen limbs of a peasant who never had enough to eat in childhood. It seemed as if he were naked, because his suit fitted him tightly and fully enclosed his hands and feet. He carried no weapons or shield but had a domed helmet on his head made of the same silver material. His face was covered by a black mask, so she could not distinguish his features. The suit was shiny and showed no seams or joins. The material was like nothing she had ever seen.

In truth, she felt that the silver object and man in her vision offered no threat. She sensed that he was neither hostile nor aggressive, but neither was he open or friendly. This part of the vision she just couldn't explain, but what had really frightened her was the part of the vision that followed.

What Greta had actually foreseen was the future destruction of New York City. Of course, she would have no concept of a modern city with millions of people.

The vision showed many, many people lying dead. People just lay motionless as if asleep, with no marks on their bodies. She had seen battle scenes with the dismembered, maimed, and blood-covered corpses; it was not like that. She had seen plague victims with their bodies distorted in impossible angles from their mortal agony and their mouths and nostrils caked in vomit, but it was not like that either.

She saw more dead people than she could ever imagine. They were dressed in strange clothes, with skin colors and facial features she had never seen before. There were huge, wide, tall buildings with square windows; fast-moving objects bellowed smoke and flames. She felt connected to all of their deaths, as if she knew who these people were. But she could not recognize or relate to any aspects of their appearance. The feeling confused her.

She desperately wanted to discuss the vision with her mistress, Queen Matilda, and her fellow witches, her sisters. They would know what to do.

She wanted to persuade the king to resume the journey back to Winchester quickly and not stay too long in La Fete to hunt.

She knew this would be too much for the king and his men-of-arms to take in, so instead she said, “I have seen a great silver object falling from the sky; it will destroy La Fete. We must leave here today and make haste for Winchester.”

To add emphasis to her words, she sank to her knees before the king, letting her forehead touch the ground, imploring him to accept.

All eyes turned to Stephen, who sat impassively as he finished his breakfast. He took a long slug from his jug of ale and then stood up. The assembled camp knelt as he stood; those who were already seated bowed their heads in respect.

“We will leave tomorrow at first light for Winchester,” he declared. “Now, you lazy bastards, let’s go hunting.”

They rose from their prone positions and cheered him, clapping their hands and banging their metal plates and jugs of ale in approval. The king smiled with them, waved his hand to acknowledge their cheers, and raised his jug of ale in a toast. The truth was, this plan also suited his purpose.

Greta kept her head bowed low so no one could see her small smile of victory. Soon she would be with her mistress and her sisters. As the court dispersed, she rose from her prone position. There was dirt on her forehead, but she made no effort to remove it. No one noticed as she loped away to follow the king and his hunting party.

Stephen was dressed in his light hunting clothes. He was glad to be rid of his bulky armor and heavy helmet. Instead, he wore a wide brimmed hat of the same brown and green material as his hunting clothes. Both his hat and his clothes were embossed with his heraldic coat of arms, derived from the symbols of power and virility from the House of Blois. He always thought this coat of arms was strange; it featured a single mythical creature that combined the features of a centaur, man, griffin, and dragon. The horse-like body had dragon’s feet and featured a curled tail; the man’s torso had strong muscular arms and was about to shoot an arrow from a long bow. He wore a bandana around his long hair and had a trimmed beard; his features looked nothing like his own.

With him were his two most trusted lieutenants, Sir Rupert of Ypres and Henry of Gloucester. Both were also dressed in their lightweight hunting clothing of brown and green, designed to blend with the colors of the forest. He watched his groom make sure that everything on his horse was tightly strapped. Today they would hunt venison, and the flighty deer would take fright at the smallest sound, such as a loose metal buckle or flapping leather strap. He had chosen this prey so they could hunt as a small group. If they had chosen to hunt for wild boar, partridge, or pheasant, they would need a much larger group, with a line of beaters flushing the prey toward the huntsmen. Today, the small group suited the king, because his true purpose was not to hunt.

Henry of Gloucester was a short for a man-at-arms. He was known as the finest bowman in England. The muscles in his upper arms were thickened from years of using an English longbow (even more muscular than the arms of the man on the king's coat of arms). He was excellent in a deer hunt but even better in battle. He was second only to Rupert in the king's guard. Unlike Rupert, he was a quiet man, not full of bonhomie or lewd laughter around the camp fire. He preferred to sit quietly, whittling the feathers on his arrows so they flew far and straight. The points were honed to a needle-like point. Few could match him at wrestling or in a fistfight.

Although Henry went through the motions of preparing for the deer hunt, he knew that the real purpose today was a clandestine meeting with the king's cousin. Stephen wanted to discuss his reign with the pope but didn't want anyone in the court to know. He planned to change places with his cousin, a man of very similar build and stature.

Only Henry and Rupert were aware of this secret, so just the three of them would be on the hunt, along with two young squires. Henry was proud that he and Rupert were so trusted by the king. The two senior men-at-arms also made a formidable fighting unit, having proved themselves in battle many times. Just days before, on the way to the French coast, they had been set upon by bandits, attempting to capture one of the ladies in the party for ransom. This was relatively common in France, where a protocol existed amongst the aristocracy over the capture of high-ranking ladies. The location and time of these raids were often organized in advance. The captured ladies were expected to show great distress and surprise as they were sequestered away, to be treated by the French aristocracy as honored guests. Often the captor would throw elaborate parties, where the hostage was the guest of honor. Romantic collusions or scandalous affairs sometimes followed. Ransom negotiations would often be drawn out, as it was sometimes convenient to have a spouse out of the way for a while. These liaisons between noble families sometimes resulted in an arranged marriage: all very convenient, and it also made for delightful gossip at court.

Such an arrangement would have suited the king, as a way to get Queen Matilda out of the way for a while. However, while this sort of arranged kidnap was fine for the French aristocracy and minor lords and ladies of the English court, it was not acceptable for the queen of England.

The king had not been given any information about an arranged kidnapping, and he ordered a full attack. Rupert decapitated the leader of the bandits before he could offer to parley, and Henry shot and killed three of his accomplices before the leader's severed head hit the ground. The rest of the bandits fled. The travelers simply left the bodies beside the road and continued their journey to Calais. Henry had since heard gossip around the camp fire that the raiders were a mercenary group hired by the Baron of Wessex to assassinate the king.

The king enjoyed the banter with Rupert and Henry as they trotted toward the rendezvous. They rode ahead of the two squires, who followed at a discreet distance, keeping out of earshot. The squires led pack horses to bring back the meat and carried supplies for the hunt.

Before they reached the rendezvous point, Henry rode back and ordered the squires to wait by the road. This was normal, because the larger pack horses were more cumbersome and could spook the deer.

Henry rejoined the king and Rupert, and they rode to the rendezvous in Hertleye Wynteneye. The small hamlet was really just a clearing in the forest. Henry knew that the land was farmed by the loyal Winta family. Henry also knew that King Stephen had played here as a boy, where he learned to ride and hunt.

The king had a great affection for the place. On the ride to Hertleye Wynteneye, he had said he was planning to authorize a priory on the site. Knowing this was in the works, the Winta family had decided to make a pilgrimage to Canterbury and pay their respects to the archbishop. This way, they could not be accused of colluding with the king.

Greta's loping run had allowed her to just keep the horses in sight. The king and Rupert had been walking their mounts slowly to allow Henry to catch them up. She watched, hidden in the tree line, as Henry rejoined the king and Rupert, and then they rode up to the three men waiting in the clearing.

As the three horsemen approached, the waiting men all dropped to one knee and bowed their heads in respect to the king. When Stephen dismounted, the tallest of the waiting men came forward to embrace him. Greta noticed how alike these two men were in build and appearance; both were tall and thick-set, with similar beards and the same brown hair. They were also dressed in matching green and brown hunting clothes. She would not have been able to distinguish them, except the king's hat had his coat of arms embossed on it.

She crawled closer to the edge of the tree line and recognized the man as the king's half-cousin, William de Blois, one of Stephen's father's illegitimate offspring. William was a regular visitor to the court at Winchester. She could hear the men clearly from her hiding place; they made no attempt to talk quietly, and the clearing in the forest made a natural amphitheater.

"William," the king called, giving the man a hearty hug. "Cousin of mine, are you ready to become a king?"

"Of course," he said. "Always glad to aid my king."

Greta then watched in amazement as the king and William exchanged clothes. Their clothing was quite similar, they were both dressed for hunting, but now William had on the king's clothes embossed with his coat of arms. When William put the wide-brimmed hat on his head, the deception was very convincing. From this distance, Greta would have believed that William was the king.

While the men-at-arms took vittles around the camp fire, the king and his cousin strolled in the forest. They spoke in French, the language of their boyhood. Greta, who spoke fluent French, kept her distance, but she could clearly hear the booming male voices in the quiet of the forest.

The king began, "So, my cousin, I have a plan for you. You must travel to Winchester in my carriage so I may go and parley with the archbishop. I do not want the court to know I am gone. The deception should work well; you can remain in the carriage on the road, saying you have a fever.

But we must switch places again before you reach the court at Winchester, because I do not want our deception to be discovered."

"You mean that bitchy wife of yours will see I am better endowed than you?"

The king guffawed in denial and bragged, "Yes, she and the twenty serving wenches I have been bedding."

William said with good humor, "You better tell me, then, the ones you haven't had, so they won't see the improvement. Don't want to waste my time as king, especially if I'm going to be confined to my sickbed all the way to Winchester."

The king described in lewd tones one of the serving wenches he hadn't yet bedded. His cousin thought he would enjoy the trip to Winchester.

"Of course," Stephen added, "if she is not to your taste, you could always bed that witch Greta."

Greta had been disgusted by the male banter, but at the reference to herself, she almost stumbled and gave away her hiding place. With difficulty, she kept herself under control. She had heard enough and moved deeper into the forest as the king and his cousin continued to plan further details of the deception. She needed to vent her anger. She cut a supple willow branch as thick as her wrist and used it to thrash a clump of nettles, imagining the nettles were the king and his chauvinistic lackeys.

The king said to his cousin, "While I was in France, I learnt that my young brother, the bishop of Winchester, was planning to entertain the archbishop of Canterbury at Farnham Castle. I have sent word to my brother to wait for me there."

William knew that the archbishop, William de Corbeil, had conducted Stephen's coronation and was favored by the pope. He had stood up to many of the clergy who did not support Stephen's claim to the throne. William remarked, "I remember the archbishop as a pious man, who values money over the pleasures of the flesh, unlike most clergy, who want them both."

The king continued, "You are very perceptive, my cousin. I want to persuade the archbishop to travel to Rome and entreat Pope Eugene III for his blessing to my kingship. Once I have the pontiff's blessing, no baron in England would refuse to recognize me, for fear of excommunication."

William knew that normally, the king would instruct his men-at-arms to begin slicing ears, heads, and arms from the bishop's various wives, lovers, and children until the man agreed. In the case of the archbishop, it was simply a case of agreeing on a price. Of course, if the archbishop did have a weakness, a lover, for example, then she could be held hostage for good measure until he returned with the pope's blessing.

The king said, "Once we have persuaded the archbishop to travel to Rome, I will ride with him to Portsmouth so we can make sure he is not seen getting on the boat to France. If I do not catch up with you before you reach Winchester, you must order the carriage to turn toward the coast, saying that you need some sea air to aid your recovery. On no account must you reach Winchester before me."

The king paused, as he heard a thrashing noise in the distance. It sounded like someone chopping wood or clearing a section of undergrowth with great vigor. He steered his cousin back along the way they had come, toward the protection of his men-at-arms. They walked slowly, with their heads close together so their words did not carry to waiting men; the king went into further detail of the plan: "Once we reach Portsmouth, Rupert will travel to Rome with the archbishop and my brother. On their return with the pope's blessing, Rupert will be rewarded with a large estate."

William knew that once his cousin had control of the barons, he could oust them from their valued estates; he thought of one or two estates he wouldn't mind himself. William also realized that this persuasion had to be done while the real king was thought to be traveling to Winchester. If anything went wrong, the king could deny involvement. The archbishop was a stubborn man and might chose death instead of entreating the pope. The journey to Rome would be hazardous, and if they were captured, the story would come out. But the greater risk to Stephen was that the archbishop might not persuade the pope to recognize him as the rightful monarch. If this happened, England would fall into a full-scale civil war.

The king was confident that his cousin could carry off the deception. Stephen was known to like the pleasures of the flesh, and spending time in a covered wagon with a pretty serving wench was in character. The road to Winchester was one of the most used highways in England, ensuring that many travelers would pass the king's party and gossip at the next inn about his philandering. If it was necessary to buy time and head toward

Portsmouth supposedly to take in the sea air for his health, the king told William to return Greta and any other troublemakers to Winchester before continuing to the coast.

On the way to Hertleye Wynteneye, William's men had killed four fallow deer. After they had taken vittles with Rupert and Henry, the two huntsmen had rode back to William's household with instructions to keep silent on pain of death. They were good men, and William said they could be trusted.

While the king hid in the woods, Henry rode back to fetch the squires. The future knights loaded the deer carcasses onto the pack horses and returned to camp. To complete the deception, Henry told the squires that the king had ordered himself and Rupert to ride ahead to Winchester. They would leave immediately after they had escorted the king safely back to the camp at La Fete.

The squires watched as Rupert and Henry followed the galloping king's horse. They recognized the king's floppy hat with the royal crest and assumed that the monarch was anxious to get back to his beau. Just before the three men reached La Fete, the king and Henry held back while Rupert rode on ahead and bullied the camp into action in readiness for their arrival. As the king rode up, it was already turning dark, and Rupert was holding open the flap of the royal tent. William, with his hat pulled over his face, went straight inside. Rupert closed the flap behind him.

Meanwhile, Henry found the serving wench who had made eye contact with Stephen at last night's dinner and brought her to the king's tent. The girl was beside herself with fear, but the new king soon calmed her. In truth, she had never actually been close enough to the king to know if this was really him or not. The previous night was the only time she had ever looked at him, but the tent was in near darkness.

In the meantime, Rupert bullied and shouted, letting the travelers know that the king wanted everything ready for a departure before dawn tomorrow (this way, William could get safely behind the heavy curtains of his carriage in the darkness). He also announced that the king was feeling unwell after the hunt and should not be disturbed. Rupert appointed one his best men to oversee the departure and then said that he and Henry were leaving immediately for Winchester; they would ride through the night, which was not unusual for men-at-arms when the moon allowed night travel.

In the meantime, Henry located the king's current beau and led her out of the camp. She was a complication, so Rupert casually said that she may be carrying a sickness that had infected the king, and as a result, she was being sent back to her village. Once they were out of earshot, Henry expertly and silently sliced her throat, dragged her body well away from the path, and covered it with heavy branches.

When Henry returned to camp, he saw that the packing activity had already begun. He gave Rupert an almost imperceptible nod, letting him know that the girl had been disposed of. The two men-at-arms then made a show of leaving camp in the direction of Winchester. When they were well clear of prying eyes, they circled back to Hertleye Wynteneye to rendezvous with the king. It was easy to find the path, with the moon just a day from full.

Dressed in his cousin's hunting clothes, King Stephen was sitting by a small fire and eating the hunting rations that the squires had left behind. He could not remember the last time he had been alone, and he enjoyed it. No one to command, no one to watch him. He enjoyed listening to the animal sounds of the night and just sitting quietly in the still light of the moon. It was so good to be alone.

He heard the cantering horses approach and saw Rupert and Henry ride into the clearing. They greeted the king and settled down to eat before they turned in for the night. Henry took the first watch.

Greta observed it all from her hiding place in the forest. Her stomach growled from hunger as she smelt the food, but she dared not move.

The spacecraft approached the small star and its solar system of planets. The craft automatically woke him as it slowed down. He opened his eyes and watched the canopy of his sleeping capsule slowly rise. He awoke to a great thirst and reached for the nourishing drink the craft had automatically dispended next to his sleeping capsule. It took him a few moments to come to terms with his surroundings. He was in an interstellar spacecraft, traveling the cosmos alone. His purpose was to place sensors on planets of interest.

He checked the craft's position using the instrument console and saw they were on course to reach the third planet from the small star. Once he had cleansed himself and changed into a silver landing suit, he looked at the detail of this planet on the monitor. Progress of any civilization could be monitored by environmental changes, radio waves, and changes in background radiation. Indications showed that this water- and nitrogen-rich planet had less than a thousand orbits around its small star before a new carbon age would begin. It was the right time to place sensors on the planet and monitor activity. There were no indications of any life on any of the other planets in this solar system, just on this small blue and white one with a single moon.

His job was a vital one. His craft was one of an army that roamed the cosmos, sector by sector. His people had found that by constantly policing the planets that supported life, his people could prevent threats occurring. Over the millennia, they had discovered it was much easier to prevent conflict than to cure it by war. If a planet's civilization became too advanced too quickly, it could be eliminated or their progress slowed down. However, in most cases, they helped a society rather than just destroying it. His people promoted trade, and they searched the cosmos for planets that could provide minerals and food. They wanted life forms to grow and develop, to create economic activity. The trouble was this particular planet was too remote and too small to be of significant benefit, but if not monitored, its life forms could create trouble in the future.

The landing site was chosen because there was a good supply of water for refueling, and prevailing planetary winds would provide an ideal monitoring location. He had already placed sixteen other sensors around the planet; he had just one more to locate before beginning his journey to the next planet.

He had visited the planet a thousand orbits earlier, which was the last time he had been reborn. He remembered these people called an orbit a "year," and after check his console, he saw it had actually been 1,103 years. He also remembered the people called this planet "Earth." Time meant nothing to his people as he traveled the vast expanses of the cosmos, and they had developed a coping mechanism by regenerating their body tissues through a rebirth process. In effect, his mind remained, but his body died and was reborn as a baby. The baby took the form of whatever life form was encountered at the rebirth. While his body matured, he had stayed for about thirty Earth years.

He was ready to go back to his craft and get away from this planet. He remembered the barbaric nature of these people from his last visit, when he had seen them nail a man to a cross and let him bleed to death. He had doubted that they could ever be civilized. He also recalled how he had tried to help them by showing them how to synthesize food by simple chemical exfoliation and how to purify water. However, their minds did not seem to grasp these modest concepts. They were amazed when he expanded small amounts of food to feed so many, and they referred to the water he purified as "wine."

He ingratiated himself with the military commanders from the Roman army. A student of military history, he was fascinated by their tactics and primitive weapons. He spoke about how they could improve their tactics, trying to educate them, assuming he would be doing some good. But a group tried to assassinate him. To disguise himself, he had taken on the appearance of a man he met wearing a white robe, long hair, and a beard. They arrested the other man instead and barbarically nailed him to a structure cut from their trees, leaving him to die. Shortly after these terrible events, his rebirth was complete, and he left the planet in his craft.

This time, he would try to avoid such contact, but he was fascinated to see how this civilization had developed. He stepped out of his craft just as three people riding horses approached. They were not wearing the uniforms of the Roman soldiers, but he could tell they had a military bearing. He was immediately wary of their intent.

Rupert had taken the predawn watch and awoke the king before first light. They ate a cold breakfast and left the small hamlet of Hertleye Wynteneye just as the sun was rising. They walked their horses to preserve their strength, traveling in a protective formation; Rupert led, with Henry in the vanguard, and the king in the most secure position in the middle. He was anxious to proceed; if successful the king had promised him the Wessex estate, which would bring him untold wealth. It would also be sweet revenge for that attack on the road in France, when he had killed the leader of the bandits hired by the traitorous baron. Once he returned from Rome with the pope's blessing, Rupert expected to ride into Wessex with a letter of execution from the king, carrying out the death sentence on the baron personally. While they walked the horses through the forest toward Farnham, he pondered how he would kill him.

As they rounded a small wooded thicket and entered a clearing in the forest, his thoughts were brought back to the present. In the clearing stood a man dressed in a tight silver suit; behind him was a large silver object. Rupert saw no threat from the strange-looking man in the clearing. He held no weapons and was well within bowshot. Rupert knew that at this distance, Henry could send an arrow through the man's heart.

King Stephen had also been lost in his thoughts about how to persuade the archbishop to travel to Rome when they entered the clearing. His memory was pulled back into focus by the vision that Greta had spoken about. For here before him was a strange silver man and a strange silver object, just as she had described. The man's clothes were like nothing the king had ever seen. Stephen could tell from his build that he was strong and fit, but he did not have the upper body muscles of a swordsman or a bowman. The silver object behind him was also very strange. It was a perfectly formed domed structure.

But before he could take it in further, he was distracted by a terrible, high-pitched scream from the forest behind him, and then Greta charged from the tree line. She ran forward at a speed that seemed impossibly fast for her frail body. She held her notorious poisoned spear in her right hand as she ran directly at the silver man. Her lethal intentions were clear.

The silver man raised his right hand in an unhurried gesture, and then there was a blinding flash.

Section 2

Hartley Wintney, England. Thursday, March 1, 2012

Keith Maxwell never needed to set his alarm; Patch always woke him with a soft bark as soon as she heard the dawn chorus. Patch was a rescue dog, a cross between a springer spaniel and a Tibetan terrier, and they had been inseparable for five years. She was dark brown with white patches. At thirty-three, Keith lived with his widowed mother, Maud, in a Victorian terraced house in Hartley Wintney (the modern name for Hertleye Wynteneye). He quickly put on an old sweatshirt and jogging bottoms, and he and Patch were out the door before it was fully light. He loved this time, when he could walk in the open air with few people about. Patch led him on their familiar route to Hazeley Common, a vast open space of woods and bracken. She was soon busy sniffing for rabbits and pheasants, and Keith could focus his thoughts on his work. It was a lovely morning, unseasonably warm for early spring.

Keith was a senior research fellow at the UK government's prestigious Rutherford Appleton Laboratory near Oxford. Located about sixty miles west of London, the lab was a highly respected institution that had pioneered much of the leading work in nuclear physics. Keith had never married but was married to his work. He was considered one of the leading experts on detecting deep space radiation by using advanced satellites to look back in time to the birth of the universe: the Big Bang.

In fact, he looked every bit the boffin and the eccentric scientist. He was six feet four inches tall, with long gray hair and a beard, thick glasses, and a dress sense that just said techy or nerd. When he returned home, his mother had his breakfast waiting. She considered him incapable of making a cup of tea, let alone boiling an egg. She still treated him as if he were twelve years old; she cut up the toast into small strips that he could easily dip in his egg. She called this "soldiers."

"Did you have a nice walk, dear?" Maud asked, offering her cheek for a kiss.

For a moment, Keith wasn't certain if she was talking to him or the dog, but then he said, "Yes, thank you," and kissed his mother.

He sat down to begin consuming his egg. He glanced at the headlines in the *Daily Telegraph*; the main story was about a budget overspend on the upcoming London Olympics. He couldn't have cared less.

She turned to Patch and said, in the way that adults often talk to each other through their pets, "Here you are, Patch darling, here is your breakfast, while Keith eats his eggy and soldiers."

Patch wagged her tail as Maud put her bowl on the floor, filled with a mixture of dog biscuits and leftover meat from last night's dinner. She patted Patch affectionately as the dog ate it all up with lightning speed and then licked the bowl clean.

Keith said, "Honestly, Mother, I am not a child. It is egg and toast, not *eggy and soldiers*. Also, if you keep feeding Patch like that, she will get fatter than ever."

Maud pinched one of the toast soldiers from Keith's plate, bit it in half, and replied as she chewed, "Dr. Maxwell, if I want to treat you like a child I will, and if I want to feed up this gorgeous doggy, I will."

With that, she popped the other half of the soldier into Patch's upturned mouth. Patch wagged her tail, and Keith tried to frown but couldn't help smiling.

While Keith showered, his mother made his lunch and put the sandwiches in his office bag, placing the bag by his car keys so he wouldn't forget it. He came down the stairs at a run, patted the slumbering Patch, kissed his mother's cheek, grabbed his office bag, and left the house. As he drove the forty-five minutes to the lab, he listened to a recording of Tchaikovsky's *Swan Lake* on his iPhone through the car speaker system.

By 8:45, he was in his office, with a coffee in his favorite cup, a mug with the periodic table of elements printed on it. The beautiful ballet music was still playing in his head. As he began typing in his computer password, his boss, Professor Helen Collins, walked in. This was unusual, because Helen almost never came to his office. Most of the time, they communicated by email. It wasn't that they disliked each other, it was just that they had very little in common.

"Keith," she said, "have you got a minute?"

As usual, Helen was rather dismayed by Keith's appearance. His huge shoes were never cleaned, his jeans were always frayed at the bottom, and he had on a faded Oxford University sweatshirt. He was muscular, and she knew he worked out at the laboratory gym on his lunch hour, but he was a gentle giant. He was also incredibly clumsy.

"Yes, of course," he said automatically, pointing to a vacant chair. In fact, it was the only chair in his office that wasn't covered in books or papers. There was just a small office bag on it. Helen could tell by Keith's raised eyebrows that he was more than a little surprised to see her.

"No, don't get up," she said, not wanting him to have one of his clumsy moments and send his coffee mug flying. She put the bag on the floor and sat down, brushing the chair free of food crumbs before she sat.

Helen was a distinguished academic herself. She was not unattractive, even though she was the wrong side of forty. She was wearing a new business suit and had her hair done in a new style at the weekend. Unconsciously, she shook her hair as she sat and brushed her skirt flat, gestures that she hoped Keith would notice. But he failed to observe her hair or her clothes. Like Keith, Helen's intellect was much greater than her social graces or ability to make small talk. Talk about the weather or one's state of health was not considered important or relevant by these great scientific minds. Although Keith was drinking a coffee and Helen did not have one, it never occurred to Keith to offer her a cup, and it never occurred to Helen to ask for one.

"I have got something to ask you," she said without preamble. "I would like you to go to Zurich to present a paper on the detection of gamma particles. I have checked your diary, and you are free."

Helen said this as a statement, not as a question or request. She knew Keith wouldn't want to do it, but the advantage of electronic diaries was they were easy to check.

She added, "This is a commitment that the lab director had asked me to ensure that the lab covers." What she didn't say was that she didn't want to do it herself.

Keith got up from his desk, almost sending his coffee flying. He stood with his hands in his pockets and looked down at Helen.

"We have had this conversation before, Helen; detecting these types of particles is a total waste of time. I know it makes good publicity for the lab, but if the PR people just want to write another press release about the search for extra-terrestrial life, then can't you get someone else to do it? We both know that if you wanted to search for little green men, you don't look for gamma particles. It makes no scientific sense."

Helen had no answer, because she knew everything that Keith said was true. She usually took these trips, but she knew how incredulous the science was and didn't want her scientific reputation tarnished; she was up for a promotion soon.

Keith was a brilliant scientist but not a team player. She also knew that he hated traveling. He spent less on travel than anyone in her group. He didn't mind flying; he just hated being away from his routine, his work, and most of all, Patch, his dog. She glanced up as Keith's screensaver refreshed and a picture of Patch appeared on his computer.

Keith was still standing, and she didn't want to debate the point with him, so she looked at her watch, explained that she must run, and said as she disappeared down the corridor that she would email him the details, adding, "If you don't want to go, then find someone else to cover the presentation."

As her footsteps receded down the corridor, Keith decided he would wait for Helen's email and then see if he could fob the trip off on one of the research students at the lab.

Keith logged on to his computer and began the daily work; he soon forgot about Helen and the trip to Zurich, because the first results of a new set of tests were in. He had been working with a team at NASA's Kennedy Space Center (KSC) in Florida and the Fraunhofer Institute in Germany on a new sensor data simulation model. The idea was to look at many different (and apparently random) particles, radio waves, and background radiation effects to determine whether any patterns could be distinguished. These patterns could be monitored over time and could point to developments far out in the universe. Perversely, they may also detect life, but none of the researchers wanted to claim that because they knew the PR people would be all over it.

The data was also analyzed to look for concentrations of activity on Earth. In this way, it was hoped that meteorites and other space debris might be found. While Keith had slept, four of the world's most powerful supercomputers had crunched hundreds of terabytes of data derived from seven different satellites. In fact, one of the reasons NASA was involved was that some of the data was from satellites so secret that they didn't officially exist. All of this computing power was focused in the production of three graphs and a map of the world. As he printed out the email, he looked at the graphs and the map on his computer monitor. There were seventeen points of interest highlighted on the map; to his surprise, one was near his home in Hartley Wintney.

By typing the grid reference from the NASA data into Google Maps, he could pinpoint the site to within a few meters. He knew the area well; it was a nondescript section of Hazeley Common near where he had walked Patch that morning. His iPhone had a GPS app, so he stored the map reference. Later that afternoon, he locked his office and then drove the forty-five minutes home to walk his dog and have supper with his mother.

As he drove, Tchaikovsky's beautiful "Swan Theme Finale" was playing; Keith's thoughts turned to his father, who had died when he was a young boy. He didn't remember him, but his mother kept a shrine to him; his study was still as it was the day he died. His father had been a publisher of scientific books, and his mother said that Keith's love of science came from reading every volume in his father's study. Mr. Maxwell's scientific passion was game theory and the science of probability. Keith found out later that he had a secret life as a gambler and would often visit casinos to test his theories. His mother was tight lipped on the subject; she obviously had not approved of that part of his life. But he knew that his father had some books on the local history of Hazeley Common; he would read up on them to see if there could be any relevance to the site in question.

Keith took Patch for her evening walk up onto Hazeley Common. They passed the occasional horse rider, a few other people walking their dogs, and some kids on their bikes. It was a breezy evening, cool but not cold. It was good to be out in the fresh air. Patch ran ahead, sniffing, as she always did, nose to the ground, trotting in random directions, totally absorbed in her constant quest to find foxes, rabbits, squirrels, and pheasants.

She squatted on an area of short grass and did her business. Keith took a plastic bag from his pocket and deftly picked up the waste, and then he turned the bag back inside out and tied it so the solid was contained inside. He saw one of the plastic rubbish bins that the local council had placed at regular intervals across the common and threw the bag into it.

He then took out his iPhone and selected the GPS app, which showed he was a few hundred meters away from the stored location; it looked as if he was heading toward some old World War II workings. He had once attended a lecture at the local historical society, where he had been told that before D-Day, there had been a contingent of Canadian engineers based in the area. They had built a concrete ramp down a hill to test winches on trucks. At the top was a concrete structure, where the trucks were reversed in. The winches were then extended and attached to rail cars loaded with heavy pig iron. The Canadians tested the winches by pulling the rail cars up the concrete ramp. The strange concrete structures still survived seventy years later. He would check these facts later in his father's history books.

Within a few meters of the workings, his phone beeped, indicating he was exactly on the spot. He looked around. This open space was common land owned by the local council. There were no buildings and a few pine trees, but mainly it was brambles, bracken, and gorse. Footpaths stretched into the distance, ideal for dog walkers and horse riders. There were no distinguishing features where he stood. In fact, as he did a deliberate 360 degree circle, he saw no distinctive features of modern civilization. He could hear the distant sound of the M3 motorway and of light aircraft from the adjacent Blackbushe Airfield. The darkening sky was still blue, and he could see the vapor trails of the high altitude jets heading to Heathrow.

Disappointed but not surprised that there was nothing here of merit, he placed three stones on top of each other to mark the spot and walked Patch home for their supper.

The next day, Keith opened his email in his office. He didn't bother to read his supervisor's email about the trip to Zurich, he just forwarded it to some students he thought may like to go. He addressed the emails by looking at the department contact list chart stuck to his office wall. He was terrible at remembering names, but fortunately it included photographs. He sent it only to those he thought would be gullible enough to want to do it. His covering message simply said, "Anyone fancy an all-expenses-paid trip to Switzerland?"

That done, he ignored all his other messages, because he wanted to see if there was any more readings from the site on Hazeley Common. He looked at the new set of data from NASA; it included three new graphs and a map of showing where the points of detection had occurred. He zoomed in using the tracker ball on his computer mouse, and there it was again, a reading from exactly the same spot he had marked with the three stones.

Now all else was forgotten. He printed the graphs and the map using a large flat-bed plotter located on a different floor. He walked down a flight of stairs and retrieved the printouts. Back in his office, he cleared a small round table by pushing aside stacks of papers. Some fell on the floor, but he didn't care. He then spread out the graphs and map for detailed examination. The papers had a tendency to roll up at the edges, so he weighed them down with half-drunk cups of coffee, a stapler, and a hole punch.

He then spent the rest of the morning making detailed notes about the data in his laboratory notebook. He planned a thorough examination of the site the following day.

At noon, he called a colleague, a mathematician of some repute, for some advice on a particular calculation. While they had lunch together in the staff restaurant, Keith mentioned his project, and the colleague offered to lend him a very advanced Geiger counter, which measured background radiation levels to very high levels of accuracy. Keith promised to return the equipment on Monday.

Other than that, he interacted with no one else during the day. The lab closed early on Fridays, so he was home in good time for dinner.

On Saturdays, Patch knew she was in for a nice long walk. She knew because Keith had his weekend clothes on, not his normal work clothes.

They set off at their normal time, but today Keith carried a rucksack slung over one shoulder. The weather was still unseasonably warm, but he wore his trusty Barbour green wax jacket. When he arrived at the spot where he had left the three stones, he put the rucksack on the ground and opened it up. Patch came over, sniffing hopefully, thinking Keith had brought a snack with him, but she went away disappointed when what emerged was just a foldable spade and the Geiger counter. Patch resumed her sniffing for rabbits.

Keith took out his iPhone and verified with the GPS app that the data received yesterday from NASA showed that this was still the right spot. Indeed it was. He put his iPhone back in his jacket pocket and picked up the Geiger counter. His colleague had given him a detailed demonstration on how to use it. The mathematician was very proud of the Geiger counter; it was the very latest model and had cost him a considerable proportion of his department budget to buy it. The unit looked like a supermarket scanner. Keith switched it on, and a red light glowed. The Geiger counter let out a series of low beeps and clicks as Keith set it to check the background radiation.

He walked in a wide circle with the Geiger counter switched on and tried different settings and variables. There were no abnormal readings at the higher radiation settings. He switched the instrument to a more sensitive detection setting. As he approached the pile of three stones, the radiation levels rose, not to a dangerous level, but enough to be detected by the highly sensitive instrument. He held the Geiger counter close to the three stones, and the needle went off the scale. He picked up each stone in turn and held them next to the instrument, but it wasn't the stones that were emitting the radiation; it was something under the ground. He discarded the stones and began to dig.

Patch thought this was great fun and began to dig too, thinking that at last, Keith was digging for rabbits: very sensible. In fact, Keith didn't know what he was looking for. He shooed Patch away, and she went off toward the old World War II installations to sniff in peace.

He dug carefully, gingerly, because he didn't want to damage anything under the ground. After about fifteen minutes, he had dug through the top turf and cleared a hole large enough to stand in up to his calves. It was hard work; the grass and vegetation had deep roots, and the soil was dry and hard from the warm weather.

He ran the detector again. The sensitive instrument still showed a high reading. Whatever was pinging the instrument, it was deeper. He took off his jacket, wearing only his shirt and cricket sweater in the early morning sun. Fortunately, few people were out walking, so nobody came to challenge him. It would be odd for a man to be digging a hole on the common.

He soon enlarged the hole down to his knees. Still nothing was distinguishable in the rocks and the earth, but the reading remained high. He stood up for a breather, and as he climbed out of the hole, he caught his trousers on the thorny branch, and a bramble scratched his skin. He felt the fabric of his trousers snag and rip a little. He was wearing his smart new corduroys that his mother had bought him for his birthday, not the scruffy jeans he wore to work.

"Blast!" he swore under his breath, at both the tear in his new trousers and the pain from the scratches.

Hearing her master's voice, Patch came trotting toward him. In his anger and frustration, he lifted the spade high and thrust it deep into the ground. A flash of light sent him backward, and he landed on his backside several meters from the hole. At first, he thought he must have ruptured an electricity cable. But then several things happened all at once. Three mounted horsemen in fancy dress appeared, along with a white-haired old lady. The old lady carried a spear, poised to attack. With an angry scream, she hurled it at Patch.

The spear impaled the poor dog, and Keith ran to her instinctively, horrified.

Greta was mystified. Just as she was about to throw the spear at the silver man, there was large flash, in fact, two flashes in quick succession, and instead of killing the silver man, the arrow had impaled a dog. A strange man was sitting where the silver object had been; he was dressed in strange clothes and ran over to the bleeding dog. The forest had also changed. The trees were not as tall and no longer as densely packed. There were wide open spaces where there had been none before. There was also a strange burning smell to the air.

King Stephen was equally mystified. He struggled to keep his horse under control after the two flashes. His mounted companions were having equal difficulty. The king's horse threw him, and he landed badly on his side.

Suddenly, two more horses and riders appeared, just as the king lay prostrate and vulnerable on the ground. In fact, they were just a mother and daughter out for a Saturday morning ride on the common. But Henry and

Rupert were disorientated after the flashes, and thinking they were under attack, Henry felled the first rider with an arrow to the chest, and Rupert decapitated the second. When the severed head rolled to the ground, it became clear that the riders were women; they wore strange, tight-fitting clothes. The horses came to halt as their riders fell to the ground. Instinctively, Rupert went to round up the stray horses, including the king's mount, and check the perimeter in case there were more attackers.

Keith sat on the ground, cradling the dying Patch. He had tears rolling down his cheeks, and his shoulders were heaving with his sobs. With the rage of battle still in him, Henry was about to send an arrow through Keith's body when the king recovered from his prone position and put a hand on his cross bow to stop him. Keith pulled the spear from Patch's body and tried to stop the blood with his bare hands. He watched, helpless, as Patch closed her brown eyes for the last time, and Keith let his head drop onto her soft body, beside himself with grief.

Keith didn't know it, but his spade had snapped the sensor placed by the silver man almost a thousand years ago. It was a million-to-one chance. If he had carried on digging in his gentle way and moved the sensor, it would have gone immediately into stealth mode.

The sensor was in a thin tube about the size of a ballpoint pen, but with its own nuclear-powered battery. The minute radiation from the battery was being detected by the highly sensitive Geiger counter. The NASA data had detected the blast of data being sent. As Keith had plunged his spade in frustration after snagging his trousers on the bramble, he snapped the sensor. The short sharp burst of radiation was sufficient to unmask the four people and three horses that had been held in molecular stagnation since the twelfth century.

While Keith sat cradling Patch's body, in a remote part of the cosmos, the silver man was analyzing the data from the sensors he had placed on Earth in the twelfth century. The sensors showed an alarming increase in planetary activity; human civilization had developed much quicker than had been predicted, especially as he had doubted when he first visited Earth some two thousand years ago that human beings would ever become civilized. Projecting the data forward, he could see that within another fifty star rotations, or fifty Earth years, there was an 85 percent probability of detection. This could not be allowed to happen, and this data analysis would trigger an automatic response from his people.

A different traveler was dispatched. These craft contained the elimination capsules. Sensor travelers like the silver man were not permitted to carry elimination capsules for fear of action without considered council. It would take about five Earth years for the elimination capsules to reach the planet, after which 99 percent of all life would be destroyed. The elimination capsules were not designed to create Armageddon, but to take the life forms back to a point in their development where there was no threat of detection.

However, five Earth years was more than enough time for the silver man to reach the planet for one last look. He was curious.

Keith Maxwell awoke with a pain on his left side, a headache, and his hands tied.

He hadn't appreciated it then but as veterans of many skirmishes and battles, Rupert and Henry had acted as a very efficient defensive military unit to protect their king. After they murdered the two innocent riders, Rupert knocked Keith unconscious with a single blow of his sword butt. Keith had been so overcome by the death of his beloved Patch, he didn't care about the pain to his head.

Greta watched as Rupert threw Keith's limp body over one of the captured horses, like a sack of potatoes. Even though Keith was a tall man, Rupert was immensely strong. The head man-at-arms would have slit Keith's throat, but King Stephen stopped him so they could question him. They were convinced this was some form of attack to stop the king reaching his rendezvous with the archbishop.

Greta was still mystified about the transition from a silver man and the strange object to the tall stranger and a dog. She rode the other spare horse as Rupert led them deeper in the forest to set up camp. The king had fallen heavily, and they needed to time to rest and determine who may have betrayed them.

Greta listened impassively to the banter between the king and the men-at-arms as they walked the horses through the woods. She pretended not to understand the context of the conversation. She didn't want him to know she had been spying on them.

Rupert selected the campsite with care. None of them knew this part of the country well, so they had no concept that the landscape was different from the twelfth-century locale. However, she did notice a strange burnt smell to the air, as if there was something bad in it. She could also hear sounds that were unfamiliar to her. These were the rumblings of flying aircraft and distant traffic. The camp had good grazing for the horses, with a stream nearby. It was in a good defensive position and offered several avenues of escape. The king was clearly pleased with Rupert's selection.

The two horses they had captured were considerably larger, taller, and better nourished than their own horses. After they arrived at camp, the king selected one as his mount, Rupert the other. Henry kept his horse, and Greta chose the king's horse as her mount. The saddles and the bridles on the captured horse were also much better.

The king was propped against a tree. Greta made an herbal mix of calamine and nettles, which she mixed with soft mud from the stream and rubbed it on the king's bruises. She also made him a broth from the bark of a willow tree, to help ease the pain.

As he examined one of the saddles from the captured horses, he said, "Look at the craftsmanship on the pummel; I shall have to show the royal blacksmith when I get back to Winchester."

Henry said, "Sire, look at that binding, it is of a cloth I have never seen."

Greta saddled her horse, the king's old mount, and called down, "Sire, I am going into the forest to fetch some more healing herbs for you. They will take the pain away and help you sleep better."

The king gave a disinterested wave and continued to examine the new saddle with Henry, while Rupert kept watch. The truth was Greta wanted a little time on her own to think. She walked her horse through the woods to a clearing on the other side. She dismounted and let the horse nibble the grass while she sat on a fallen log and examined the sky.

She could see silver objects in the sky that looked as if they had wings and left a white trail in the blue sky. Sometimes there were two lines, and sometimes four. The white trails seemed to spread like smoke in the wind. She wondered if this was the burning odor she smelled in the air.

The trees were also strange; they seemed thinner and less developed. There was also a strange rumbling sound in the distance she could not explain. She decided to go back to camp and ask the tall stranger for an explanation. She found another willow tree on her way back to the camp and cut some bark with her dagger. She took it back to the camp and boiled it in some water from the stream. The broth, a natural aspirin, would help ease the king's pain. She also thought she would give some to the tall stranger when he woke, because he would be hurting from the blow Rupert had given him.

She could sense something important and significant about this tall stranger, as if meeting him was part of her destiny. But this was also something that she couldn't explain.

Keith was slumped on the ground, where he had been dragged from the horse. His hands and feet were bound with ivy that Rupert had cut from a tree. Before he realized what was happening, Greta cut the ivy away from Keith's hands. She then helped him to prop his back against a tree and offered him some of the broth she had prepared. He drank a few sips and then, without a word, slumped back into unconsciousness.

They hadn't seen any game in the woods, so Greta butchered the carcass of the dog and roasted it on an open fire for dinner. The dog had been well nourished, and there was a reasonable amount of meat. The king had the pick of the carcass, with Rupert and Henry picking next. Greta ended up with the scraps.

Keith woke when he smelt the roasting meat. He saw the three men eating from the bones and at first wondered what meat it was. He then noticed the brown and white fur of his beloved Patch left next to the fire and began to wretched uncontrollably.

Maud Maxwell, Keith's mother, became worried when he had not returned for his lunch. He usually came back from his walk for his coffee and biscuits by eleven o'clock.

She waited until 1:15 before she called his cell phone, leaving a curt message on his voicemail that his sandwich had gone cold. They were always punctual, a routine she and Keith had established ever since he was a boy. They always had toasted sandwiches for lunch on Saturday, and they were promptly on the table at one o'clock. She had eaten hers and left Keith's to go cold.

Around two o'clock, she left another voicemail, much more conciliatory and asking him to call her because she was worried. At three o'clock, she called again but hung up without leaving another message. Then she called her sister, who lived a few miles away in Basingstoke. After discussing the situation at some length, the consensus was to call him one more time, and if he didn't answer, to call the police. Maud thought this was very uncharacteristic of Keith and there was probably something seriously wrong, but her sister knew her nephew was absent-minded and thought he had probably just got sidetracked by one of his madcap science schemes. After she had hung up, Maud tried his cell one more time, and then she called the police.

Maud was not used to calling the police. In fact, she had never done it before. She called 999 and was asked which emergency service she wanted. She hesitated and said, "It is to report a missing person."

The efficient voice on the line asked her to call a different number for nonemergency police matters. Maud wrote the number on a notepad. She hung up and dialed the new number, and after a few minutes, a call center operative answered.

"Hampshire Police, how can I help you?" the operator asked in a broad Liverpool accent. Clearly she wasn't in Hampshire.

Maud said, "I would like to report my son missing."

The operator took the details efficiently and promised that a police officer would contact her within two hours; if they did not, she should call back.

At this point, Maud was more angry than concerned. She thought it more likely Keith had forgotten it was Saturday and gone off somewhere, than anything bad had really happened. He liked routine, but he was equally absent-minded. She felt slightly foolish calling the police. She sat down with a cup of tea and tried to distract herself by doing the *Telegraph* crossword.

A little while later, there was a knock on the door. Two uniformed policewomen stood there, and as they asked her name, one look at their facial expressions was enough for Maud's knees to collapse under her.

The policewomen put Maud gently in an armchair and gave her a glass of water. They also called an ambulance. A police car and then an ambulance outside of her modest three-bedroom end-of-terrace house caused the neighbors' curtains to twitch. Within forty minutes of the policewomen arriving, the first journalists arrived. The policewomen called for backup, more vehicles arrived, and soon the press circus outside the house was in full swing.

What was at first a simple missing persons call turned quickly into a murder enquiry. A young woman walking her dog on the common had found the bodies of the riders and called the police on her cell phone. They had found Keith's jacket at the scene, with his phone in the pocket. There were three unanswered calls on his phone. They traced the calls back to Maud Maxwell.

The story was now the headline on the BBC News. Maud watched in disbelief, and she sat on the sofa with her sister, who had driven over from Basingstoke (at the police's suggestion). The report featured a live video image from a helicopter flying over Maud's house. They could hear the helicopter overhead; she even recognized the neighbors' parked cars.

The murder of the two women was the lead story on the news bulletin, ahead of the continued political bickering about overspending on the London Olympic Games. Maud covered her mouth in horror as an image of Keith appeared on the screen and the reporter said, "Dr. Keith Maxwell, an eminent space scientist, is wanted for questioning in connection with the murders."

Maud could hardly believe her ears and buried her face into her sister's shoulder, sobbing.

Detective Amit Chakrabarti was born in the UK, from Indian parents. He had transferred from his native Birmingham eighteen months ago to take up a promotion in the Hampshire force.

This was his second murder enquiry. The previous one had been a gang dispute in Birmingham; the victim had been zipped inside a body bag before he arrived at the scene, so he never saw the blood-stained body. The nineteen-year-old killer had bragged about the shooting on Twitter, and within hours, the police arrested him, with the gun still hidden inside his jacket. He was in jail on remand, awaiting trial. As a result, Amit's record showed a rapid clear-up rate of serious crime. The Hampshire force had few officers from the ethnic minorities, so here he was on Hazeley Common, seriously out of his depth.

Like most police officers, he had never seen a dead body before, let alone a headless corpse or a body with an arrow impaled through the heart. There was a surprisingly large amount of blood. The victim with the arrow sticking out of its back lay with her legs twisted under her at an impossible angle. The police pathologist said the arrow had killed her, not the fall, and the arrow had been shot at close range.

However, this was nothing compared to the woman who had been beheaded. Bone and body parts were visible on both the severed head and the torso. There were lumps of flesh in the pools of blood beneath the severed neck. This was not the clean death often shown in the movies. The woman's head lay with eyes open about twenty feet from her torso. Bizarrely, her riding helmet had remained in place. Her mouth was slightly open, as if she were about to speak. She had been an attractive woman, and her makeup was still unspoiled, but this contrasted to the horrific mess of her severed neck that showed bone, flesh, and cartilage. The torso appeared to be relatively undamaged, apart from the neck area. Her clothes were soaked in her blood. A cloud of flies buzzed over the corpse, and insects crawled in the blood and gore. The pathologist said that death had been instant.

Amit fought down the nausea, not wanting to show weakness in front of his colleagues. He was still the new boy and wanted to make an impression. So far, they had managed to keep these gruesome details out of the press, but the names of the two riders had been released. They were a mother and daughter who stabled their horses at a local farm.

Protective tents had been erected over the murder scene. These covered a large area because the bodies, and body parts, were dispersed, and also, the police wanted to examine the foot and hoof prints for evidence. Extensive photographs were being taken. Forensic teams were meticulously examining the scene for evidence, some using brushes as they moved slowly along the ground.

Blood had been found in another area and was being sent for analysis. There were several hoof prints, but it was not clear if these were from the two horses the murder victims had been riding or from other horses. A horse expert had been called but had not arrived yet. There was no sign of the horses the mother and daughter were riding, but their description was provided by the distraught owners of the local farm.

Amit's cell phone rang; he looked at the display, which showed an unclassified number. He didn't want to answer it in case it was a journalist, but he pressed the green button on his phone and said, "Chakrabarti."

"Detective, this is Chief Constable Hamilton; what is going on?"

Amit was surprised. He didn't realize that the chief constable of the Hampshire Constabulary would even know who he was, let alone have his number. Then he remembered that his supervisor was on holiday. He recognized the chief constable's distinctive Welsh accent; he had heard him speak on several occasions. Amit had been introduced at a line-up once and shaken his hand, but he didn't think he would remember him.

Amit was keen to make a good impression, so he flipped out his notebook and began speaking rapidly, saying, "Well sir, we have a suspect in Dr. Keith Maxwell, a scientist; his green Barbour wax jacket had been found on the ground nearby. It contained his wallet, cell phone, and keys. There was £115 in cash in the wallet, with his credit cards, works ID card, and driver's license. The motive was clearly not robbery. His mother has confirmed he is missing. A hole had recently been dug, and there was a foldable spade, backpack, and scientific instrument on the ground."

The chief constable interrupted, "What type of scientific instrument?"

"We don't yet know that, sir; it has been taken back to Basingstoke Police Station for identification. There were several fingerprints on it, but they did not know if they were Maxwell's, because his are not on record. He has never been involved in a crime."

"What was the hole for?"

Amit didn't want to sound as if he was not in control, but he didn't know, so he decided honesty was the best policy: "We don't know what the hole was for; it could be that he was looking for buried treasure, or perhaps digging a grave. It was an odd shape for a grave, though."

The chief constable interjected, "Spare me your speculation, Detective. I am at the golf club, and this line is far from secure. Now write this number down and call me if you have any problems with the press."

Amit awkwardly stuck the phone under his chin and wrote down the number in his notebook, and then the chief constable hung up.

Amit put the phone back in his pocket and reflected that he had spoken too much—his habit when he got nervous. He leaned against a tree and flicked through his notes. The policewoman who had spoken to Mrs. Maxwell had said that Keith was out walking his dog. So, he realized, they may be looking for a man and a dog. He took out his phone to call the policewoman back; he wanted a photograph of the dog.

After he spoke to the policewoman, he decided to go and talk to Maud Maxwell himself. Also, there was little more that he could do on Hazeley Common until the forensic investigation had concluded. It would be dark soon; they would remove the bodies under the cover of darkness to avoid any photos by the press. The Police Dog Section would start at first light to try and follow Keith Maxwell's trail; there was little point starting in darkness. Amit knew he would have to be back at first light, so he decided to go home after he had talked to Maxwell's mother and grab an early night.

He found the head of the forensic team, who was on his hands and knees, taking blood samples next to the severed head. Amit tried not to stare at the macabre scene as he told the forensic officer his plan to see Maud Maxwell and then return first thing in the morning. The forensic officer just grunted in acknowledgment as he carried on gathering samples, blood and dirt staining his blue plastic gloves.

Amit walked back toward his unmarked police car. A group of journalists and curious onlookers had gathered in the car park. Two uniformed officers had stretched blue and white tape with "*POLICE LINE. DO NOT CROSS*" written on it across the path that led from the car park onto the open space of the common. Amit realized this was a surreal situation, because the common was such a massive area, any journalist could simply go a little way up the road and walk onto the common anyway. What held them there was the herd mentality of the crowd and the fear that they might miss something.

One of the uniformed officers lifted the police tape so Amit could easily duck underneath. As he did so, the detective inspector was pounced on by a swarm of reporters. He could hear camera shutters, a light came on, and a film crew stood in his path. He stood like a rabbit caught in the headlights, trying to clear his brain to think, as a barrage of questions were fired at him.

"How were these women killed?"

"Have you found Keith Maxwell?"

"What is happening?"

Amit thought quickly. He fell back on his police training; he had learned at Hendon how to handle the press.

He cleared his throat and said, "At this stage, we are pursuing a number of lines of enquiry and will issue a statement soon. I'm sorry, that is all I have to say."

Amit then forced his way through the crowd to his car, unlocked the driver's door, and drove away. Camera flashes illuminated the interior of the vehicle, and the journalists fired questions at him like bullets.

"What lines of enquiry?"

"Will you be making an arrest soon?"

"Have you found the horses?"

One of the reporters took a picture of Amit and emailed it to his office. Within minutes, an email came back with Detective Inspector Amit Chakrabarti's bio. Ten minutes later, a news flash appeared on the BBC website, with a picture of Amit from the *Birmingham Post,* when they had reported of the gang murderer. The headline on the BBC website read, "Murder Detective at Hazeley Common."

The chief constable had just finished his round of golf and read the newsflash on his phone.

Amit drove the short distance to Maud Maxwell's address. He was dismayed to see more journalists at the house. A uniformed policewomen was standing outside. He could hear a helicopter flying overhead, but it appeared to be moving away. It was just getting dark, so he concluded they had taken all the pictures they could at this stage.

A reporter stuck a microphone in his face as he got out of his car.

"Detective Inspector Chakrabarti, you are live on Sky News. Have you found out how the women were murdered?"

Amit again looked like a rabbit in the headlights and said the first thing that came into his head: "I am here to see Maud Maxwell, Keith Maxwell's mother."

It was an innocent remark, intended to be a factual statement of why he was there. His morbid expression, which was in fact nervousness, was taken as one of grief. He walked away from the reporter, nodded briefly at the policewomen at the gate, and then knocked on Maud's door. The door was opened by the policewoman he had spoken to on the phone earlier. She closed the door behind him, and he walked into a living room, where two elderly women sat on a floral sofa, watching Sky News on a large TV set.

Before he could introduce himself, he heard the Sky News reporter's voice on the television say, "Detective Inspector Chakrabarti has just entered Dr. Keith Maxwell's house to see his elderly mother; there is speculation that Keith Maxwell is dead."

With that, two things happened almost together: first, one of the women on the sofa let out a wail of horror, and then, his cell phone rang. While Maud's sister and the policewoman tried to calm the distraught mother, Amit had his head torn off by the chief constable, who said, "Listen, boyo, I am on my way. Do not speak to another sodding journalist until I get there."

So much for his early night.

Meanwhile, just five miles away in Fleet (the modern name for La Fete), Ellen Baker, a modern-day witch, was on the phone with her lover, Carla Jones (another witch). They were discussing the arrangements for Sunday market the next morning. Ellen was at home in La Fete, and Carla was at her mother's house in Surbiton, about thirty-five miles away.

Carla said, "Lover, I'll pick you up in the morning about 7:30; we need to get an early start."

Ellen replied, "So you are not going to come and screw me tonight then?"

Actually, Ellen didn't want Carla to come back to her house that night, because she had other plans. It was impossible for one witch to lie to another, but Ellen knew that Carla's powers were more limited than her own, and she would not be able to detect the lie over the phone.

Carla purred back, "Sorry, sweetie, you know I have to take Mother to this bore of a concert, but I'll make it up to you tomorrow night if we sell loads on the stall."

"I'll take that as a promise."

"It's a promise. See you in the morning; gotta go and get ready. Love you."

Ellen said, "Love you too," blew a kiss into the receiver, and hung up.

As she spoke, she felt a stir in the alternative earth plane, as if something significant was about to happen. Her pet cats felt it too, and the three of them came awake as one and looked at her expectantly. But she buried the thought quickly, because she was excited about the visit of her next clients. She went to get ready, and the cats followed her up the stairs to her bedroom.

She took off her jeans and t-shirt and admired her body in the full-length mirror. Ellen couldn't have looked less like the stereotypical witch. She was almost six feet tall, with bright red hair and green eyes, and she smiled easily. She also had what most men would describe as fantastic tits. She emanated a sensuality that made her attractive to both sexes, something she enjoyed and exploited wherever she could. She showered and put on a tight-fitting dress that exaggerated her cleavage.

Her gift was handed down from her mother. For as long as she could remember, she had been able to see the alternative earth plane and the souls who inhabited it. She had never been frightened about it, but as she entered her teenage years and her mother's cancer worsened, she had accepted she was different.

She left school as early as she could, partly because she hated it, but also because she needed to care for her mother. She knew that her teachers tolerated her absences because they knew she cared for her mother, but they also were frightened of "that arrogant, tall girl in the fifth form." They were glad to be rid of her.

Her mother ran a psychic business from home. Fleet was an affluent area, and the aging population consisted of many widows with money. They came on a regular basis to talk to their dead husbands and relatives through her mother and to receive tea and symphony. Ellen sat in many of these sessions and could also hear the conversation from the other side of the earth plane, which the clients never could. On more than one occasion, she had to stifle a laugh as her mother told a client an edited version of what the dead relative had said. Ellen realized this was one of the tricks of the trade: Tell the clients what they wanted to hear. So when a dead husband said, "She nagged me incessantly, and I'm glad to be rid of her," her mother would say something like, "He misses you dearly."

Her mother never advertised, but the phone rang regularly for appointments from new clients. Her business all came from reputation.

By the time Ellen was fifteen, the mortgage on their house had been paid in full.

Her father had been a traveling salesman that her mother had an affair with. He disappeared, and according to her mother, it was good riddance. As the cancer took hold and the morphine worked into her mother's mind, she spoke more and more lucidly to her daughter. She talked about her life and her experiences, and that education from mother to daughter was beyond anything that could be taught at school.

As time went on, Ellen participated more and more in sessions with her mother's clients. Her powers grew even stronger, and as her mother's illness weakened her, so Ellen grew in strength.

When Ellen was nineteen, her mother lost her fight with cancer, and she became the sole owner of their house in Fleet, estimated to have a value of £1 million. She had no qualifications and no job but a steady stream of clients. Regulars who had come to see her mother took to her daughter readily. Ellen now had a regular clientele.

She went to night school and learnt HTML, the computer language used to design websites. She set up her own website, and soon the trickle of clients became a steady stream, and she was able to earn a secure income.

She hired an accountant to keep her books and pay her taxes.

Witches could sense each other, and she formed close friendships with her sisters who shared the gift. This was not a psychic group that advertised on the Internet; they didn't have to.

Ellen and her sisters also met regularly at psychic fairs, where they could earn good money and attract new clients. Ellen had met Carla at one of these fairs. Unfortunately, these events were also attended by those who only pretended to have the gift. The sisters took a dim view of this and often took steps to expose these fraudsters. Sometimes it got pretty heated, and on more than one occasion, the police had been called.

Ellen enjoyed these fairs, and tomorrow's Sunday market would also be fun; it got her out of the house. However, the best thing that had happened since she had set up her website was she had a regular stream of younger clients who not only wanted her mind but also her body; the images of her on the website were deliberately provocative. She offered a range of services from pregnancy testing, eating disorders, and sexual therapy to contacting the dead. The fees for her physic readings were understood to include a lot more than the obvious. Ellen was what some called a sex addict, but it was an addiction for which she wanted no cure. She was in her voluptuous prime and wanted to enjoy it.

Tonight was special; a married couple from Nigeria wanted a baby, but she was having difficulty falling pregnant. He was a diplomat, six feet four inches tall, and with an air of dignity that made the diplomatic service a natural for him. She was an African beauty with perfect teeth and dark eyes; she had been Miss Nigeria.

Originally, they had come to her for psychic advice, recommended by a knowing friend, a sister who knew of Ellen's skill, but also the special location of Ellen's house.

Ellen's mother had chosen the house carefully. On the face, it was what estate agents described as a desirable family residence, a four-bedroom detached house with a large garden situated close to local amenities and in a highly desirable part of Fleet, known as the Golden Triangle. This was an area of large individual houses, enclosed by three intersecting main roads. On the edge was a Chinese restaurant, which was the favorite of many a late night reveler. The restaurant's prominent neon sign had given the area its nickname, but it was not officially on any map.

Ellen's mother chose the home with care. It was built on a unique east/west, north/south crossing point of two powerful celestial energy lines in southern England. The garden had been laid out over the years to contain all the plants necessary to accentuate the witch's craft, but a casual observer would never recognize the alder, lavender, witch-hazel, holly, and willow for what they were. This was a witch's house and garden.

When a couple like the diplomat and his wife entered the house, the power that enveloped them changed them, but they were not aware of the fact.

Ellen sat them down in the dining room; it was the center of the house and where the energy levels were concentrated. There was no crystal ball on a table or tarot cards; the furnishings were modern, the room bright and airy, and the décor designed to make people relax.

She offered them tea; wine was available to other clients, but this couple were Muslim and did not drink.

The husband wore a smart pin-striped suit, tailored in Seville Row. His wife wore a blue dress that clung to her body.

When tea was served, they dispensed with the small talk and got down to business. The husband spoke for them both, the dominant male, in the African way.

"We have abstained for a week," he said, "and my wife has not entered my bed."

Ellen opened an adjoining door, which led to a downstairs bedroom, where the curtains were already drawn. The room featured a large bed, which was actually two double beds pushed together. To the side was an ensuite bathroom.

"You must make love to your wife now," she said.

They had both anticipated this and were looking forward to making love. The couple entered the bedroom, hand in hand, and began to undress. Ellen had laid out chairs and a clothes stand, so they could hang their clothes neatly. She wore expensive lingerie under her dress; he wore boxer shorts, and the bulge of his excited penis was clearly visible. There was also a wet patch on the fabric of his pants.

They found it normal that Ellen remained with them. But to the couple's surprise, Ellen undressed as well and lay on the bed with them. Her white skin and freckled complexion were a contrast to the dark ebony skin of the diplomat and his wife.

But Ellen wasn't here to just watch, she was there to join in. The diplomat's wife had a beautiful body, like Naomi Campbell, the super model. She kissed the girl on the lips and took hold of the diplomat's penis through the thin fabric of his boxers.

Afterwards, the diplomat and his wife refreshed themselves in the bathroom, dressed, paid her in cash, and left. As Ellen hugged the diplomat's wife, she whispered in her ear, "You are pregnant with a boy." Ellen could see this with certainty with her psychic powers. The woman squeezed her hand in recognition but said nothing to her husband.

They both got back into their chauffeur-driven car, as if they had just attended a business meeting, their African dignity intact. Ellen never saw them again.

Ellen slept soundly that night, and the next morning, Carla picked her up in her trusty Volvo. The car was packed with boxes of the charms, mineral stones, and dream catchers they would be selling at the fair.

Hazeley Common, Hampshire

Deep in the common, but just seven miles as the crow flies from Maud Maxwell's house, Greta awoke before first light. She noticed the birds singing, but she could hear strange sounds as well. She lay with her eyes open, adjusting to the strengthening light.

The witch was deeply troubled. She could no longer feel the presence of her mistress or her sisters. She'd had the gift from as long as she could remember, where one witch could always feel the presence of another witch sister. It was a feeling that transcended the normal senses. She knew that Queen Matilda, her mistress, and her witch sisters had traveled to Winchester, just thirty miles or three days' horse ride away, but even at that distance, she should have felt their aura, and it would give her comfort. She could not believe they were all dead. For comfort, she felt in her bag for the lavender she had cut as a gift for her mistress. To her surprise, the lavender seemed to have wilted to dust—very strange.

When she first realized she could no longer feel the presence of her mistress and her sisters, she thought she must have lost her gift. But now she could feel the presence of new sisters; they were quite close, but she didn't know who they were. Her one crumb of comfort was she could still feel the energy lines that intersected in this part of the country.

There were also other things she could not explain. There was a smell in the air, of burning. Not as if something was on fire, but the air itself smelt dirty and contaminated. There were noises, loud rumbling noises both from the ground in the distance and overhead. She did not know this area of the woods well, but yesterday they had seen wide, straight paths that appeared to be covered with a solid black material. She was sure they had not been there before. There also seemed to be fewer trees and more open spaces; the plants were of a different shade of green, and there was virtually no wildlife. There were also those strange clouds, long white lines in the sky, as if they had been painted by the gods.

Ideally, she would have discussed these strange things with the people she trusted most: her mistress and her sisters. The king did not have the intellect to understand these discernments, and Rupert and Henry were just thugs. Who else could she talk to? Maybe the tall stranger could help.

She rose from her sleeping mat and walked a discreet distance into the woods to urinate away from the king and his two henchmen. The king and

Rupert were still asleep on the ground, while Henry dozed with his back against a tree. He was clearly on the last watch of the night. She wanted to do this before Rupert awoke, because he was quite likely to kick and punch Keith into a state of unconsciousness when the king began to question him. She crept over to Keith and put a hand over his mouth to keep him from crying out. Then she gently shook him awake. He was lying on the ground, still with his legs tied.

She whispered, just loud enough in his ear so only he could hear her, "Do you need to piss?"

She had a strange accent and a gravelly voice; it almost sounded as if she was French but speaking English, so although he understood, he said, "Sorry, I don't follow," so he could hear her accent again.

Greta made a gesture with her hand, mimicking a penis peeing, and repeated her question, which sounded to Keith like, "Do u ned to pizz?"

He said, "Yes," and for good measure added, "Oui."

He struggled to a sitting position. He wasn't sure what she was going to do; surely she wasn't going to watch him? Instead, she waved to Henry and made the same pissing gesture, as if she were holding a penis with her hand. He waved back, and Greta slit the ivy binding Keith's ankles with her dagger. Henry rose to his feet and notched an arrow in his bow. Keith had seen the power of that bow yesterday, when Henry had killed that horse rider. He stood up warily, rubbing his back, which was stiff from sleeping on the ground. Greta gestured toward a tree, and he turned his back toward her and Henry while he undid his zip and tried to concentrate.

Despite his need to urinate, he couldn't focus. Having a strange woman watch him and knowing an arrow could pierce his spine any second didn't make it easy. He often found it difficult to pee in public, especially in a crowded urinal with other men close to him. As he was taller than most, his eye level meant he could see too much. He did what he always did in these circumstances and tried to think of the numerical constant pi; he used to know it by heart to a hundred decimal places: 3.14159265359 … and he urinated on the ground with great relief.

To his surprise, Greta didn't tie him back up; instead, she gestured for him to sit opposite her on the ground near the fire. Keith was glad of the warmth; although the weather was unseasonably warm, it was cold in the early morning. He could still see the remnants of Patch's bones in the embers and felt a lump of terrible sadness rise in his throat.

Greta watched the tall stranger as he sat by the fire. He had on strange-looking clothes and shoes. The clothes were tight fitting and appeared very well made. The fabrics were different from those worn by the dead horsewomen but also new to her. He was as tall as Rupert, but although he looked fit, he did not have the muscular physique of a trained man-at-arms. He was clearly not a military man.

Without preamble, Greta asked, "What is your name?"

Keith found it hard to find his voice, he was still so upset. This was the woman who had skinned, cooked, and then eaten his dog. He croaked, "Keith Maxwell."

"I am Greta the Witch. Where are we?"

Keith could not place her accent. She was a striking-looking woman, short and wiry, probably not even five foot tall; her teeth were bad and her white hair a mess. She smelt terrible, as though she slept rough all the time. He couldn't quite place the smell; it was like a weird combination of animal dung and garlic. He could still smell her hand from when she had put it over his mouth. He wanted her to speak again so he could place her accent, so he said, "Excuse me?"

Greta thought he had answered his question and said, "'Excuse Me' is not a name of a place I have heard of; is it near La Fete?"

Keith's brain began to clear, and he realized that Greta was speaking with a slight French accent. He also realized she didn't understand the term "excuse me," and although it had not registered the first time, he was sure she had said she was a witch. If he hadn't seen the two women murdered yesterday, he may have thought this was an elaborate joke.

He said, "I am not sure exactly where we are, but we are somewhere near Hazeley Common."

Greta didn't recognize this name either, although it sounded familiar.

"Hazeley Common?" she repeated. "I have not heard of that place; is it near Hertleye Wynteneye?"

Keith was taken aback by the old French name for Hartley Wintney. He had read it in one of his father's history books but had never heard it spoken. He now realized Greta's earlier reference to La Fete was probably to Fleet, which was the nearest large town.

He asked Greta, "Are you from France?"

"No, I am from England. Have you not heard of Hertleye Wynteneye?"

"Yes, but most people call it Hartley Wintney."

Greta had never heard that name either. This was strange, because she thought she had known about all the people who knew Hertleye Wynteneye. It was a very small place after all, with just one family living there.

She said, "I have never heard the Winta family call it thus."

Greta did not ask Keith if he knew the Winta family. As far as she was concerned, this was such a small community, everyone would know the Winta family.

Keith said, "I don't think I know the Winta family. Where in Hartley Wintney do they live?"

To Greta, this was a very strange question, since there was only one house of any consequence in the village. But she let the question pass and instead switched to a different subject.

"What is that noise I hear in the distance?"

Keith listened for a moment, because any traffic noise was slight this early on a Sunday morning. He said, "It is probably some traffic on the M3."

"What is traffic? What is M3?"

Now Keith was confused. Perhaps this woman was playing with him. Was this a joke? Despite her disheveled appearance, her yellow eyes were bright and showed a hidden intelligence. There was no trace of a smile or humor in her expression. She was serious; perhaps she was foreign after all. Keith's tired and muddled brain now began to return to his scientific training, and he began to analyze the situation logically. He answered Greta's question slowly, to give him time to think.

"The M3 is the main London-to-Winchester motorway, and the traffic is made up of cars and trucks, mostly heading toward London."

He was now using logic to change parameters in his mind. If she didn't know that place, perhaps she was suffering from memory loss. He decided to ask a question to test her. So before Greta could pose a further question, he asked, "Do you know who the queen of England is?"

To Keith, this was a logical question to test where Greta was from. After all, Queen Elizabeth II had been on the throne for more than sixty years; if she knew anything about England at all, she would know who the queen was.

But to Greta, this was a shocking and treasonable question. She stood with a gasp, covering her mouth in shock, and Henry, who had been half-dozing, listening to the conversation, strode over and kicked Keith in the ribs. He immediately let out a groan and doubled over in agony. His cry of pain woke Rupert and the king.

Despite her shock at Keith's question, Greta's intuition as a witch told her that Keith was not being malicious. She realized he must not have known he had touched a very sensitive nerve. She recalled that one of the greatest challenges to Stephen's right to be king was from the Empress Matilda, his cousin (who had the same name as Stephen's wife, her beloved mistress); many said she was the rightful heir to the throne. She had heard that Henry I had made an oath to appoint Matilda his successor. It was said that he had rescinded this oath on his deathbed and appointed Stephen instead. Many disputed this, and it was the cause of the friction with the barons.

Keith had no idea why his question had provoked such a violent reaction from Henry. His ribs hurt where he had been kicked, and he curled up in a fetal position on the ground to protect that area of his body from further punishment.

He heard Henry say, "Sire, this man does not recognize your kingship."

Before the king could reply, Rupert drew his sword and approached Keith with violent intent.

Greta wanted to question Keith further. She needed to act quickly to stop the situation from escalating. She knew that the one person Rupert feared was her beloved mistress. Matilda had a very distinctive voice that was low-pitched for a woman, and she spoke English with a distinct French accent. Greta often amused her sisters with her talent to mimic her mistress.

Now she turned to Rupert and spoke sharply the voice of Queen Matilda herself:

"Hold hard. I want this servant alive. I, Queen Matilda, command it."

Rupert froze, with his hand about to draw his sword. The king also stopped mid-stride. Henry had notched an arrow but lowered his bow.

Greta switched to her own voice and spoke in a much more conciliatory tone.

"Let me question this man further, and then he will lead us to some breakfast."

After a short pause, the king said, "Very well, saddle the horses."

Reluctantly, Rupert sheathed his sword and Henry un-notched his arrow.

Even in his distress, confusion, and fear, Keith could appreciate the skill of these people. Their clothes appeared unsophisticated, and their simple leather boots certainly were drab. But the clever part was that when one of them moved into the trees, they became almost invisible. Even though he knew where they were, he lost sight of both Rupert and the king as they moved amongst the trees.

Keith noticed that they appeared to carry very few possessions, yet everything that they did carry had its purpose. Nothing was wasted or superfluous. They could make a smokeless fire; find shelter, food, and water; and keep themselves warm, all with a few items they carried on their horses. He had seen Henry use a flint stone to light the fire, with dry glass and wood he scavenged. The horse blankets and saddles doubled as bedding.

Keith shivered. Although he had on a warm shirt, his cricket pullover, and his thick corduroy trousers, he had left his coat behind (along with his cell phone). The fire had been extinguished, and he could do with his trusty Barbour now in the early morning chill. So far, he hadn't really felt the cold, and he knew the high adrenalin in his blood stream was causing his heart to beat a little faster, keeping him warmer.

They put Keith up on Rupert's tall horse and then tied his hands. The king and Rupert were riding the two new horses they had captured. Henry rode his own horse, and Greta was on the king's old horse. The embers of the fire had been hidden and all obvious traces of the camp erased, and the king said, "Now, Witch, get this rogue to lead us to breakfast."

Keith had not ridden since he was a child, but at walking pace, it was relatively easy to stay on. He gripped the front of the saddle with his tied hands, pushing his fingers under the saddle. The horse's body warmed his hands. The saddle appeared to be made of very crude leather, and he wondered if it would support his weight. Henry led Keith's horse by tying a rope to his own mount. When Keith saw how strange the king and Rupert looked, with the modern saddlery and archaic clothes, the penny dropped. He asked himself, almost speaking loud, *Could these people be from a different time?*

Keith put the thought aside. He was tasked with finding them some food. If he didn't, he would probably get another kick in the ribs (or worse). He didn't want to head toward a store or a restaurant; it would be hopeless with these people on horseback. Then in the distance, he heard the faint sounds of aircraft taking off. Of course: Blackbushe Airfield. Keith remembered that every Sunday, there was a large open air market at the airport, which was located on the edge of the common.

"This way," he said, gesturing enthusiastically with his head and tied hands. He pointed toward the airfield, and Rupert led the horses in that direction.

Meanwhile, on the other side of the common, the Police Dog Section had arrived. There was a police training college nearby, and most of the handlers were familiar with the common. They allowed the dogs to sniff Keith's jacket and a toy that had belonged to Patch; Amit had borrowed the toy from Maud Maxwell's house. The handlers held on to the extended leads as the dogs took the scent and headed off across the common.

The Hampshire Police chief constable had called in a special unit from the Metropolitan Police (the Met, as they were known in London). The Met officers were trained marksman, and their job was to follow the dogs.

Amit sat in a control vehicle with the Hampshire chief constable. He had been up all night, grabbing a few hours' sleep in his car. It was soon clear that the police dogs could not pick up any strong sent. Instead, the police teams divided the common in a grid pattern and began a search by walking in lines abreast, looking for any clues. It was going to be a long, drawn-out process; Hazeley Common was a large area.

Amit was still smarting from his dressing down by the chief constable after his off-the-cuff remark to the press about Keith Maxwell, which had caused speculation that the scientist was dead. The chief constable had been forced to hold a press conference last night to clarify the situation, but the story about the beheading had leaked, and the chief constable suspected that may be down to Amit as well. The detective was keen to make a good impression, and he looked at his notes to analyze the information that had come back from the police labs overnight.

The strange scientific instrument had been identified as an advanced Geiger counter. It had been borrowed by Keith Maxwell from his work place, but nobody they had spoken to knew what he wanted it for. One of his coworkers, who knew how to operate the instrument, was on his way. They wanted to check in case there was some radiation on the common. However, this seemed unlikely. The coworker had told Keith how to operate the unit, but Keith had only mentioned that he needed it for a project he had been working on with NASA.

The additional blood on the ground that forensics could not identify initially had come from a dog. Amit speculated that it was Patch's blood but was waiting to hear from the Maxwells' vet, to see if they could get a match. They now had photographs of Patch and the horses the two women had been riding. He ticked these items in his notebook.

The only other significant lead came from the arrow that had killed one of the women. The pathologist said it had come from the Middle Ages; it was clearly an antique, and it was being taken to the Royal Armories in Leeds to be examined by an expert in historic armaments. There were fingerprints on the arrow, but they did not match any on record. This had led to speculation that the weapon used for the decapitation was also an ancient weapon. From examining the injuries, the pathologist had described the weapon as very sharp, like a large sword.

After his discussion with Maud Maxwell and her sister last night, Amit had deduced that Keith was not involved with archery or swords or any form of weaponry. He could see no motive for Keith to carry out these brutal murders.

The morning news showed the police dogs and their handlers setting off across the common. A Sky News TV helicopter was in the air, but after some frantic phone calls, Amit had convinced them to leave the area. He didn't want it advertising the positions of the dogs, but he could not prevent the constant buzzing of light aircraft over the common. The airfield was popular with amateur pilots looking to keep their flying hours up to date. The pilots had something new to look at for a change. The large white tents covering the murder site, with "Hampshire Police" emblazoned on their roofs in large letters, were easy to pick out from a low-flying plane.

The chief constable had now taken personal charge of the operation and held a press conference for the major news networks. He was a distinguished man in his fifties and wore a dark blue uniform with an impressive row of medals on his breast. On his head was a cap with gold braiding.

He said, in his distinctive Welsh accent, "First, our sympathies go out to the families of the victims. We are using all resources at our disposal to ascertain what happened yesterday morning on Hazeley Common. We have also been given every assistance by the Metropolitan Police. Search teams are now out probing the common and have been doing so since first light. We ask the public to stay away from the search area until further notice. We wish to question Dr. Keith Maxwell in connection with these murders, but we are also following other lines of enquiry. If anyone sees Dr. Maxwell, they should contact the police immediately. No one should approach him; he may be dangerous."

Maud Maxwell had not slept well and now sat with her sister on the sofa, watching the broadcast live. The idea that Keith was dangerous brought a renewed bout of sobbing from his mother.

A BBC reporter was the first to catch the chief constable's eye and asked the question that was on everyone's lips:

"Chief, do you believe Keith Maxwell killed the two women?"

The chief constable frustrated them all with his answer: "At this time, I have nothing further to say, but I will brief you again when we have made progress with our enquiries. Thank you and good morning."

With that, he walked away. Maud's sister turned the TV set off and helped her sister upstairs to get dressed.

Amit's phone vibrated in his pocket. It was a call from the constable who had driven the arrow to Leeds. The young officer was so excited that Amit couldn't register what he was saying, so he asked him to repeat what he had just said: "Professor Templer, who is a specialist in arrows from the Middle Ages, confirms that the arrow is from the eleventh or twelfth centuries. He will confirm the date tomorrow when they have completed some carbon dating tests."

Amit wrote the information in his notebook but couldn't register any connection. He decided to ask the investigation team to check the records to see if any arrows had recently been stolen from collectors or museums.

The fine weather had drawn a large crowd to the Sunday morning market. The market was laid out in canvas-covered stalls that ran the length of the runway of the adjacent airfield. The market regularly attracted ten thousand people, but on a mild spring day like today, it might attract double that.

The chief constable sent Amit to have a word with the control tower at Blackbushe. He wanted to stop the light aircraft from overflying the police search area on the common. It was a sign of the chief constable's displeasure with Amit that he was assigned such a trivial task, which was normally performed by a junior officer.

It took Amit quite a while to reach the control tower, because he was delayed by the traffic heading for the Sunday market. The market sold everything from antiques and groceries to jeans, t-shirts, DVDs, TVs, and computers. Amit knew from the chatter in the canteen back at the police station in Basingstoke that the market was notorious for selling counterfeit or stolen goods. As was often said, stuff that fell of the back of a lorry. Trading Standards Officers raided the market on a regular basis.

He stopped in an area away from the market, where pilots and passengers of the light aircraft parked. Thankfully, there was no sign of any press. But there was a café next to the control tower, and he saw one of the satellite trucks parked outside. He thought that the TV technicians were probably inside, grabbing some breakfast.

He took the steps leading up to the control tower. The door was open to let in the warm spring air, and inside was a spotty youth, probably about nineteen, and an older man. Both were sitting behind a desk with two large monitors and a microphone.

They looked up from the desk as Amit walked in and held out his police ID card. The control tower gave a good view of both runways and the thousands of people now milling around the rows of covered stalls at the market. The parked cars shimmered in the early morning sun as the heat reflected from their metal body work. The parking area began on the other side of the airfield perimeter fence and stretched the length of the runway. Stewards wearing orange jackets could be seen directing the traffic into parking places. The whole area was a hive of activity. Smoke rose from the multiple burger vans and hot food stalls scattered around the market.

The older man was busy giving take-off instructions to one of the aircraft, and the youth stood up to examine Amit's ID card. Amit waited until the older man had finished speaking into the microphone and then said, "I am Detective Inspector Amit Chakrabarti from Hampshire Police. Are you in charge here?"

The older man stood up to introduce himself as Brian Paton, explaining that the youth was his son, Damien. He pointed at an empty seat, inviting the detective to sit down. Father and son were both dressed casually in jeans and t-shirts.

A pilot's voice could be heard through the speakers in the control tower: "Blackbushe Control, this is Golf November Alpha Tango One, requesting clearance for take-off."

Brian pressed a button on the microphone in front of him and said, "Golf November Alpha Tango One, this is Blackbushe Control, clear for take-off."

Brian clearly knew the pilot, because the next message over the speaker was, "Thank you, Brian, see you later. Tango One out."

Brian answered, "Thank you, Alan, have fun. Control out."

Brian seemed slightly embarrassed at the lack of formal radio protocol, and he motioned for Damien to take over so he could speak to the policeman. He added, "Things are pretty informal here on Sunday. The regulars are making use of the fine weather to keep up their flying hours or to earn a few quid giving lessons."

Brian paused as he listened to Damien giving instruction to a pilot. The pause gave Amit the chance to watch an aircraft land and immediately taxi around to join the queue of aircraft on the other runway, who were waiting to take off.

"Anyway," Brian continued, clearly satisfied with Damien's instruction, "what can I do for you?"

"We have an operation in progress on Hazeley Common to investigate the murders yesterday of two women," Amit said. "You may have read about it in the papers."

Brain nodded and said, "Terrible business," at the same time continuing to listen to his son.

"I have been asked by the chief constable to make sure aircraft do not overfly Hazeley Common while the operation is in progress."

"Detective, was one of the women really beheaded?"

Amit shook his head and said, "I am afraid I cannot go into any details about the case."

Brian rose from his seat and leaned over his son, who remained seated at the control desk. Brian pressed the transmit button on the microphone.

"This is Blackbushe Control to all aircraft. I have a message from Hampshire Police: please do not overfly Hazeley Common today, as there is a police operation in progress. Repeat: do not overfly Hazeley Common. Control out."

Amit shook hands with both Brian and Damien as he left, thanking them for their help. Brian said that he would repeat the message at regular intervals. They were obviously pleased to help.

Amit stepped out on the balcony of the control tower and took a last look at the crowds milling around the Sunday market. His stomach rumbled, and he remembered he had not eaten breakfast. He looked at the inviting sight of the aircraft café below him; as he looked on, the door opened, and three men walked out. They climbed into the satellite relay truck and drove off. Amit was pleased; the chief constable's roasting was still fresh in his mind, and he didn't want a brush with any journalists, even if they were only technicians.

He was about to descend the steps when something unusual caught his eye. On the far side of the airfield, he saw a group of horses tethered to some trees. His hunger forgotten, he reached for his phone.

As Rupert led them in the direction of the Sunday market, a delicious smell enveloped them. It was the odor of onions frying in hot fat, the characteristic smell of a Sunday morning market. Burger vans were selling hot dogs, sausages, bacon sandwiches, and beef burgers with onions, all sizzling in cooking fat. After the dog they had eaten last night, this was an exceedingly mouth-watering smell.

Keith had not eaten since breakfast the previous day, and he had vomited the contents of his stomach in his anguish over Patch. His stomach rumbled at the inviting cooking smells. Despite his hunger and distress, he found the ride across the common quite relaxing. Even though his hands were tied, he had a good grip on the front of the saddle, and the gentle walking motion of the horse was soothing. The sky was blue and the weather warm, and apart from the light aircraft flying overhead, it was very quiet. Although he knew this area of the common well from his countless walks with Patch, his elevated position on the horse gave him a new perspective, and he took in the view with new interest.

The journey also gave Keith the chance to study his captors. While Rupert walked his horse ahead, and Henry held back with the line attached to his own horse, Greta and the king rode close together. They were in deep conversation. They stopped at first every time an aircraft flew over, staring at the sky in surprise, as if they had not seen a plane before. However, after several had flown over, they seemed to lose interest in them.

They stopped every time they came across some object on the common. One of the first was a wooden signpost directing people to the footpath or bridleway. Keith watched the earnest discussion about the signpost, as they examined the quality of the woodwork and the clarity of the writing. To Keith, it was just a weathered old signpost; it had probably been there for more than ten years.

He made no comment, and they began to move forward again. Next they came across a plastic rubbish bin with a wooden surround. There was a black plastic bag inside the bin, obviously to make emptying the bin easier. Inside the bin, Keith could see metal cans, chocolate wrappers, plastic bags of dog waste, and cigarette cartons. They stopped, and the king and Greta dismounted to examine the bin and the rubbish inside. Keith could overhear their conversation.

"What is this, Witch?"

"Looks like a vessel of some kind, Sire." Greta put her hand in the bin and took out a can that had been slightly crushed. There was some Coke left inside, and the stale brown liquid spilled out, soaking her hand. She dropped the can back in the bin and then smelled her dripping hand.

"It seems to be a metal container with something wet inside, Sire."

The king drew his sword and lifted one of the plastic bags that had been tied up, probably with dog waste inside. He moved it on the tip of his sword toward his nose, recoiled at the smell, and dropped the bag back in the bin. Keith had to suppress a smile. The king put his sword back in its scabbard and mounted his horse. He had seen enough. Greta wiped her wet hand on the grass, stood up, and began to mount her horse, but suddenly, she froze.

She turned her head so she could see the can she had tossed back into the bin. On the side of the can, she could see some writing. The quality of the writing and the workmanship on the metal object was like nothing she had ever seen. In that fraction of a section, the reality of her situation hit her. She realized that this was a different time, a more advanced age. She didn't know how or why it had happened, but it explained her feelings that something significant was about to happen. She thought of the strange flying objects, the change in the landscape, the burnt smell in the air, the fine horses they had captured, and the tall stranger with his unusual clothes. This explained why she could no longer sense her mistress and her sisters; indeed, this meant that they were all long dead. At this dreadful thought, her eyes filled with tears, and her knees buckled. She had to cling to her horse to keep from falling. She forced herself to hold back her tears; she didn't want to show weakness in front of the men. With difficulty, she mounted her horse.

She turned toward the tall stranger and was about to ask him about the red metal object with the liquid inside, when she was distracted by two pheasants that broke cover from the undergrowth behind them. The brightly colored birds flapped their stubby wings rapidly to gain height.

In a blink of an eye, Henry shot both birds.

The king shouted, "Bravo," and he dismounted once again to help Henry dispatch the still twitching pheasants. Henry retrieved his arrows by putting his foot on each carcass and pulling the shaft out, and then he placed the birds in a bag attached to his saddle. Keith watched blood drip from the bag; it was obviously designed for the job.

Greta used the distraction to move her horse closer to Keith and ask, "What is this strange vessel?"

"It is a rubbish bin," he explained. "People walking on the common put their rubbish in it."

Greta understood some of these words, but they made no sense. To test her theory further, she asked one more question: "What was that red metal object?"

Keith paused before he answered. He could not believe she had not seen Coca-Cola before, but then the penny also dropped with him. He answered slowly and carefully, using his words deliberately, "You were holding a can of Coca-Cola, a soft drink people have been drinking for about a hundred years."

Greta looked into Keith's eyes and asked, "What year is it?"

"2012."

Greta whispered back in shocked realization, "No, it is 1136." But she spoke without conviction, because she realized that the tall stranger was right.

Keith did not reply; he could not find the words. He was convinced this was not an act; these people really did behave as if they were from the twelfth century.

Greta continued to stare at Keith in shock until the king commanded her to follow.

Meanwhile, forty miles away in London, Cathy Murphy was alone in her tenth-floor luxury apartment in London's Canary Wharf. She was sitting in bed, still in her Harrods silk pajamas. The widescreen television in her bedroom was showing a live Sky News report from Hazeley Common in Hampshire.

Cathy was a journalist at the *Daily* and *Sunday Chronicle*, Britain's largest selling newspaper. She was thirty-four, single, and in love with her job. Today, she was feeling very pleased with herself. Her scoop was now the talk of the town. That morning, the *Sunday Chronicle* had been able to publish the gruesome details of the double murder on Hazeley Common.

Her king-size bed was strewn with copies of all the Sunday papers, but her front-page story sat in the center of her bed, folded neatly to expose the headline:

Beheading in Hampshire

Cathy lowered the volume of the television as she Skyped with her assistant, Martha, using her Apple laptop. She finished the last bite of her toasted crumpet with honey, her Sunday morning breakfast-in-bed treat, and reached for her mug of tea. As she did so, Martha reached for her own mug of coffee, and the two women toasted each other through their video link.

"You did it, girl," Martha said. The tinny loudspeakers clearly relayed her Scottish accent. Martha was also single and lived in a much more modest flat than Cathy's up-market apartment. She was Cathy's mentor when she joined the *Chronicle* some eleven years ago, after completing her master's degree at Imperial College London. Now Martha was Cathy's assistant.

Martha was in her early fifties, just five feet two inches tall; she had a stocky build and looked like everyone's ideal grandmother. She reminded many of the hacks around the office of Mrs. Doubtfire. To Cathy, Martha was not only her best friend, but also in many ways the mother figure she craved. Both her parents were dead, and she rarely saw her elder brother. To Martha, Cathy was the daughter she never had. Martha had never married; there had been someone once, but it had not worked out, and as she often put it now, she was too old to bother.

Cathy said into her webcam, "I have got Sky News on, and they are talking about the beheading now."

Martha replied, "Yes, I saw the Hampshire chief constable earlier, and he avoided the question when asked about it. Seems the police are still a bit upset that the news got out."

Cathy chuckled.

The reason the two women were still in their respective abodes at this relatively late hour was because they were lying low. Exposing the beheading story had taken some doing, and all their cunning and ingenuity. Not to mention a little sailing close to the wind, legally and ethically. Martha's matronly grandmother appearance meant that she couldn't have looked less like a typical journalist. They had used this to maximum effect, in what they called a "tea and symphony" mission.

When the news broke yesterday afternoon about the murders, the *Chronicle's* editor had assigned Cathy the story. The *Sunday Chronicle* was the biggest selling edition of the paper of the week, and Saturday afternoon was the busiest time of the week. A cub reporter had been sent to Hazeley Common on a fast motorbike, and Martha had been driven to Hampshire in a car. The cub reporter's job was to relay back all the facts he could find out from the police operation at Hazeley Common, direct to Cathy in the *Chronicle's* office in Wapping, London. This included the name of the unfortunate young girl who had discovered the bodies of the murdered women.

Within minutes of her details arriving, the research team at Wapping had prepared a full profile of the girl. Martha read the profile on her phone while she waited outside Basingstoke Police Station. Her name was Abby Painter, and she was nineteen years old; she lived with her parents in Hartley Wintney. There were several pictures of her, mostly from Facebook. She was a pretty girl with short blonde hair.

When the girl emerged from the front of the police station, Martha stepped out of the car and walked up to the girl, placing a motherly arm around her shoulders.

She said, in her believable Scottish drawl, "Abby, I am sure that was a horrible experience. I have a car to take you home to Hartley Wintney."

The girl was too frightened, confused, and upset to resist. She assumed that this kindly lady was part of the police operation and was here to take her home. She knew her name and where she wanted to go, after all. The driver held the door for them, and they got into the back seat. There was water and snacks inside; she had never been in a car this posh before.

Martha introduced herself and explained that the driver already knew her address. She said, "Drive on, Constable" (using her colleague's last name instead of his initials).

This was a clever ruse. The driver's name was, in fact, John Constable, and he was an ex-police officer. But the tired and emotional girl just assumed that he was a serving police officer. It was a thin line, because it is criminal offense to impersonate a police officer.

The state-of-the-art microphones captured all of the conversation in the car and relayed it back to Cathy. With the aid of a sympathetic hand, a cool drink of water, and some Kleenex, the details of the arrow and decapitation emerged during the twenty-minute car journey.

Martha said, "It must have been awful to find those bodies like that."

Abby said, "There was like blood everywhere, it was like pools of it, especially from her neck. Her head was like lying in a puddle of it."

Two thoughts hit Cathy as the same time as she listened in: first, this was clearly a very gruesome murder, worthy of the front page, and second, it was irritating how today's teenagers used the word "like" all the time.

Martha hid her shock at the revelation about the head and then prompted Abby to continue by saying, "How horrible; what did you do?"

"Well, like the head was like miles from the body, and her neck was just like gross, with bone and guts and like blood everywhere. I didn't know what to do, I called my mum but she was like out, so I called 999 and like the police came."

Abby began to sob, and Martha cuddled her, supplying tissues and telling her she had done very well.

Cathy realized she had the headline and began framing the story as she listened in to the rest of the conversation in the car.

They arrived at the Abby's address, and JC parked outside. It was a nondescript street of suburban houses. As they pulled up, a woman appeared at the front door. JC stepped out of the car and waved at the woman, who waved back; she assumed this was an official car bringing Abby home. Expensive cars like this were rarely seen on this street.

As the girl was about to step out of the car, Martha produced a neat bundle of £20 notes. She said, "Here's a little something for helping us. Would you mind signing a receipt? I do get in such trouble with my boss if I don't do the proper paperwork."

Abby was over the moon to be given money, so she signed without question—and without bothering to read the legal small print on the receipt. Abby ran up to her mother, clearly relieved to be home. JC pulled away swiftly, not wanting Abby or her mother to ask any more questions. Martha waved good-bye from the back seat, but Abby was too engrossed in a conversation with her mother to look in the direction of the car. She held the bank notes in her hand and was showing her mother the money.

Cathy had been listening throughout from her desk in London. She smiled wryly at Martha's "boss and paperwork" line. It had been delivered so sweetly. The enhanced sound quality meant she could hear the bank notes being handed over. The £200 was well spent, she thought.

Cathy hummed an Elton John song as she typed the headline and the story for her editor to review:

Beheading in Hampshire

Gory details have emerged of the double murder in Hampshire yesterday. One victim was beheaded while the other had an arrow in her heart …

The editor of the *Daily Chronicle* had been appointed to the Royal Commission to review press behavior following the tragic death of Lady Diana, the Princess of Wales. The inquest into the horrific car crash in a Paris underpass that had caused Diana's death concluded that press intrusion had contributed to the accident. It had emerged that her Mercedes was being chased at high speed by scores of paparazzi on motor bikes and scooters.

Later, it emerged that the press had hacked into the voicemails and cell phones of the royal family. The *Daily Chronicle* was not the worst offender but had been cited in more than one incident of hacking. The editor kept her job, but it meant she wasn't going to break the rules again.

However, she knew a damn good story when she saw one. She liked Cathy and knew the gifted journalist would go far, but she also knew that in her enthusiasm for a story, Cathy often bent the rules. The editor wanted verification of the story and sent her a carefully worded email that would form the basis of an audit trail later. Cathy understood the game.

At 7:32 p.m., Cathy placed a call from her office phone to the head of pathology at Hampshire Constabulary. She placed it on her office phone because all calls were recorded, and she also knew that the time would be recorded accurately to one thousandth of a second.

Cathy politely apologized for calling so late, but said she was on deadline and needed clarification of a story for her editor. She used her practiced honey tones and was slightly provocative and flirtatious in her language, which she knew worked well on most men. It also meant the official would be less willing to have the audio recording of the call made public later.

Cathy said in her little-girl voice, "This really is quite difficult for me; I'm not used to calling men of such experience as you, but are there any special details of the murder yesterday that we should know? I'm afraid my editor has had to go out to an important dinner at the palace, and I have to ask these questions."

"Well, I cannot comment at all on the murder enquiry; my job is to examine the bodies for evidence."

"I see, but did you find anything unusual? I hate the idea of dead bodies, all that blood and stuff."

"This is certainly one of the most gruesome double murders I have seen in a long time."

"Gruesome? Sounds like something out of the Middle Ages. How horrible."

Cathy hoped that her reference to the Middle Ages would lead the pathologist to open up.

"It certainly is horrible," he said. "I have never seen anything like it."

"Like what?"

"I can't tell you that."

"Was it like one of those Middle Age horror stories, like being shot with an arrow, or having your head chopped off with an axe?"

"Something like that, but I can say no more."

"Thank you," said Cathy. "You have been most helpful."

After she hung up, Martha put down her headset. Cathy stood and gave her a high five.

"Result!"

The editor listened to the tape and sanctioned the next step of the operation, which was to send a transcript of the article to Hampshire Constabulary for comment. The story would now include a double denial from the pathologist, effectively saying they did not deny these incidents happened.

At 8:55, the story was emailed together with an Internet link to the sound track of the taped phone conversation with the pathologist.

The timing was significant, because this gave Hampshire Police just one hour to seek an injunction to stop the story from being published. If no injunction was received, the presses would begin to roll at 10:30. At midnight, the newspapers sales team would begin to syndicate the story around the world, which could well appear in the later editions of the other British Sunday morning papers. In any case, the *Daily Chronicle's* website would be live with the story, which would be syndicated around the world.

Hampshire Police had just one hour and five minutes to keep the genie in the bottle. They failed.

Despite learning that they were in the year 2012 and not 1136, Greta made no attempt to explain this to the king. She just didn't know how to begin to explain it. She kept silent, absorbed in her thoughts, as they walked the horses across the common.

As they neared the Sunday market, the sound of light aircraft taking off and landing became louder and louder. She kept quiet as the king and the two thugs discussed these flying objects. They all ducked involuntarily as they flew over.

Keith's hands were still tied. Although he had had no more significant conversations with his captors, he was able to observe them in a new light. He watched as Greta looked closely at every man-made object they encountered on their ride. She dismounted when they came to a chain-link fence and examined the metal work in detail, pulling on the fence to test its strength. The king, Rupert, and Henry rode on, disinterested. She rode over to every litter bin they passed, examining the contents from the elevated position on her horse.

When they reached the fence, Rupert dragged Keith from his horse, and he was commanded to give an explanation of the fair. Keith realized that if he said it was a car-boot-sale and Sunday market, he would just get another punch in the torso from Rupert. He could see that both men were hungry and impatient to get something to eat.

So he said, "It's the Sunday fair; let me go and get you something to eat."

Greta and Henry had tethered the horses so they could graze on some long grass by the side of the fence; now they joined the other three. The king looked at Rupert and said, "You go with him."

Greta untied Keith's hands, and he pointed at the closest burger van, which had a large sign saying "Big Tasty." Smoke and steam was billowing from a short metal chimney. Even from the distance of a few hundred meters, the smell of the frying onions was so inviting. Rupert kept his dagger pressed against Keith's ribs and held the back of his trouser belt as they walked the short distance across to the burger van. Although he was shorter than Keith, Rupert was much stronger than him.

There was a blackboard to the side of the van, with a menu written in large characters. The first item on the menu was "Jumbo hot dog with onions: £3.90."

Keith knew he had a £20 note, so he ordered five jumbo dogs from the girl, who looked down at him from the van. She had spiky green hair, a ring through her nose, and several tattoos. Keith wasn't sure who looked more strange, her or Rupert. The bizarre thing was that at the Sunday market, where English eccentricity reigned supreme, nobody gave Rupert a second glance. Yes, he was dressed a bit weird, but then who wasn't? In the short walk over to the burger van, they had passed two guys in motorbike leathers, two Goths dressed in black with a chain linking them, and an overweight man who was clearly making the most of the warm weather by wearing his shorts and a vest. Even Rupert stared at his pudgy white flesh and faded tattoos. There was also a Ren faire troupe dressed in multicolored clothes, performing as they strolled around the market.

Keith handed over the crumpled £20 note to the green-haired girl. Rupert looked on suspiciously as the girl handed Keith back his 50p change. She said, "Sauce over there," pointing to a table, where he could see ketchup and mustard. This was a concept too difficult to explain to Rupert. He was about to ask Rupert what he wanted to drink, but looking back at the blackboard, he realized that his 50p wasn't enough to buy a cup of tea or a can of Coke.

He carried the steaming hot dogs back to where the king, Henry, and Greta waited by the horses. Each was wrapped in a paper napkin.

He handed one first to the king and then to Henry and Rupert, and finally to Greta. Each snatched their food up without thanking him. He noticed that Greta examined the paper napkin with interest. She held onto the paper as if it were a precious thing, while the three men carelessly dropped their napkins on the ground.

Greta remarked, "This bread looks fresh and is surprisingly light in color."

Rupert said he didn't know what part of the animal the meat was from, but it smelt good. Keith was about to explain when both Greta and Henry let out a howl of pain. Clearly, they were not used to piping-hot food in the Middle Ages. In their hunger, they had both taken large bites of sausage, which was still sizzling in hot fat, and burnt their mouths. Cursing and swearing, yet desperate for the fabulous-smelling food, neither was prepared to spit out the hot sausage.

While Henry and Rupert continued to keep a wary eye on Keith, the king and Greta sat a little apart from the other three. While they ate, Greta decided to try and explain to the king what she had learnt from the tall stranger. She started hesitantly, choosing her words carefully so the king may understand.

"Sire, I have learnt something important from talking to the tall stranger. These people are from a different time. In the way that your father and his father lived in very different times many years ago, these people come from a time in the future."

Stephen looked at Greta incredulously. He wondered at first if this was one of her clever ploys, but he could see no malice or cunning in her expression.

"Swear on Queen Matilda's life that what you say is true," he demanded.

The king knew that Greta was totally loyal to his wife and would not take such an oath lightly.

Without hesitation and holding the king's gaze with her own yellow eyes, she said, "I swear this is true on Queen Matilda's life."

The king was open mouthed, trying to take in what Greta had just told him. With a half-chewed hot dog clearly visible in his open mouth, he demanded, "Why do you know such things, Witch?"

"Do you remember that red metal object we found earlier? Have you ever seen anything so well made from metal? Did you see the craftsmanship in that vessel? Have you ever see anything like that?"

The king had no answers. He stared at Greta. Sitting still for a period of time made her feel uncomfortable. She realized he could order Rupert to cut her throat at any time, and he would obey without question.

Suddenly he stood and beckoned for Rupert to follow him. He meandered over to the stalls and began looking at the items for sale with undisguised curiosity. "50p for that, gov," the clerk said as the king examined a polished red soda siphon. Henry went for his dagger, as if to protect the king from the insult, but Stephen restrained him. The metallic red spherical metalwork shone brightly in the early morning sun; the witch was right, he had never seen anything of this quality.

"Tell me, what is this object for?"

"Well, you haven't lived much, 'ave you, guv? You put a soda capsule in here, and you get your soda for ya whisky and drinks." The man lifted the metal flap at the back of the siphon. "This is where you put the fizz in, you insert ya cylinder of gas to produce ya bubbles."

The king only understood the word "drinks" and said to Rupert, "I'll take it." Rupert snatched the soda siphon from the man, who objected, "Hold up, what about my money?"

Keith gave him the change from the hot dogs, the 50p coin from his pocket.

Meanwhile, across the airfield, standing on the platform of the Blackbushe Airfield control tower, Detective Inspector Amit Chakrabarti watched through his binoculars as Dr. Keith Maxwell walked across to a burger van. Amit recognized the tall, lanky figure from the photographs.

Another man was walking next to him. He saw them purchase some food from the van and take it back to where the horses were tethered. Standing next to Amit were two police photographers. One filmed the suspects in high definition video, while the other clicked away on a camera fitted with a long telephoto lens.

The chief constable was on his way but had spoken briefly to Amit on the phone, telling him that his priority was to arrest Maxwell. Amit had not been given any instructions about any accomplices.

His police radio crackled into life. Two teams of plainclothes officers were now in position on either side of the field. Their job was to move in and arrest Maxwell. Both sets of officers were armed; Maxwell was wanted for a double murder, and they were not going to take any chances. However, with the large number of people around, they were keen not to begin shooting unless they had to.

Greta could sense one of the new sisters was quite close. She wanted to talk to her, to confirm her theories. The king had walked away after their brief conversation, and she was not sure if he had grasped the idea that they were in a different time or not.

With the men at a distance, she walked away from the horses toward the throng of people around the stalls. Every so often, there would be terrific roar as one of the huge flying machines lifted into the sky. She ducked involuntarily every time they did, and she was slightly amused to see the king, Rupert, and Henry all duck in unison.

But her desire to speak to a sister overcame her fear, and she pressed on through the crowds.

She could also see several of the horseless vehicles moving rapidly along the solid road. Some were parked in the field. They smelt like the food she had just eaten. It had a burnt, charcoal-like taste. The people she passed were all tall, dressed in strange clothes, and some carried small objects next to their ears that they were speaking into. Some were looking anxiously at these strange objects or smiling at them and touching them rapidly with their fingers.

As she passed, people gave her a wide berth. Many made comments about her smell. She also looked so strange with her long white hair and strange clothes. She approached a stall that was selling wind chimes; a sign above read "Fortunes." She noticed two women at the stall and realized that these were both the sisters she had sensed.

Despite their varying appearance, she could tell immediately that they were lovers. The give-away was in the sensual nature of their body language as they brushed against each other in the close confines of the stall. One sister was tall, as tall as the king, with curly red hair, and the other was short, with long dark hair. Both were busy with customers as she approached, but the tall sister must have sensed her presence and turned in her direction. Greta realized that she was the more powerful of the two witches.

Then all of a sudden, everything around her turned to pandemonium.

Several men began shouting from two different directions, and people ran screaming, one woman almost knocking Greta over in her terror. She could now distinguish the shouts:

"Armed police! Lay down, lay down, on the ground."

The people who were running by were shouting, "Guns … Police … Get away … Move."

Some were screaming in terror. Greta didn't know what "guns" or "police" meant, but she knew it wasn't good; people were clearly in a panic. As the crowd cleared, she took in the scene before her.

The men were shouting at the king, Rupert, Henry, and the tall stranger. Rupert still had hold of the stranger's belt; he shielded Stephen with his bulk as he raised his sword. Henry was notching an arrow and at the same time raising his bow to aim at one of the four men, who were crouched on a knee and pointing a small metallic object at the group. Greta knew that in a split-second, an arrow would kill one of the crouching men. Time seemed to stand still as the tall stranger raised his hands above his head and shouted, "Don't shoot, don't shoot."

One of the four crouching men was now shouting, "Lay down your weapon and you won't be hurt. Now! Do it now."

Greta couldn't believe her ears. These four men weren't carrying swords or bows, but they were telling the king to disarm. A crowd had gathered a short distance away and were all now pointing their handheld square objects in their direction; some were talking into them in an agitated manner.

Predictably, Henry released his arrow with deadly effect. She had seen him kill many men in battle before, and he knew exactly where to aim; the bloody point emerged from the back of the man's skull. He collapsed in a heap, bleeding profusely from the fatal wound. His body twitched in his death throes.

With lightning dexterity, Henry notched and fired a second arrow, which flew toward the chest of the next police officer. The officer had time to move to one side, but the arrow struck his upper arm, and he screamed in agony. Normally, in close-quarters fighting like this, Rupert would have charged as Henry's arrows flew, and the two remaining police officers would be dead. But Rupert remained in front of his king, protecting him.

The other police officers fired now within a split-second of each other. The powerful bullets tore into Henry's chest. Greta involuntarily covered her ears at the loud sound of the gunshots and saw Henry fall to the ground, blood splattering from his fatal wounds.

The king and Rupert were startled by the loud explosion from the small handheld objects. They watched, open-mouthed, as Henry's body collapsed under their powerful destruction. Henry's body lay contorted at an impossible angle. An amazingly large amount of blood spread quickly across the ground.

However, the loud noise also spurred Rupert into action. Greta watched as he grabbed Stephen and led the king and Keith away from the explosions. Almost immediately, they were lost in the crowd of running, panicking men, women, and children. Greta followed the fleeing men as they pushed and shoved their way through the crowds. She watched as they reached the horses and then, leading the spare horses behind them, disappeared into the woods. Even in their haste, Greta could see the king struggling; the exertion had clearly aggravated the injuries from when he had fallen from his horse.

Greta was unsure whether she should follow. She dithered, letting the crowds swirl around her. The noise of the aircraft was now drowned by a new sound. It was like a child screaming, but much, much louder (she had never hear police sirens before). She saw horseless carriages approaching at high speed with blue lights flashing on their roofs. The Sunday market crowds instinctively turned away from the loud noises and the flashing lights, and Greta was swept up in the crowd, as mass panic took over and everyone pushed toward the exit.

Within minutes, the first video footage of the incident was posted on YouTube. Over four hundred video clips and photographs were uploaded onto the Internet in the next three hours.

Sir Geoffrey Milton, known as Milt to his friends, had the job that most people would know as "M" in the James Bond movies. He was head of MI6, the British Secret Service. Milt was dressed for his Sunday morning round of golf and enjoying a breakfast of poached eggs and bacon with his wife at his home in Hampstead, North London. His Blackberry buzzed. He answered, "Yes, Charles?"

It was his personal private secretary, speaking in his clipped Etonian accent: "Sorry to disturb, bit of a flap on with the Americans. Cultural liaison wants urgent meeting at office this AM, bit of a bore, but given absolute priority. Car on its way."

"Any idea what it's all about?"

"Sorry, he wouldn't say on phone. Bye."

The maid came in and announced that his car was waiting.

Milt kissed his wife and asked her to cancel his golf date this morning, saying he hoped to be back for lunch. She looked up from the *Sunday Times*, offered her cheek for a kiss, and said she would, forcing a smile. It was often like this.

His wife was holding the broadsheet newspaper open and reading something inside, so he could clearly see the front page headline:

Double Murder in Hampshire

He wondered if this meeting with the Americans had something to do with that. Charles had used the words "absolute priority," which were not used lightly. They meant this was something the Americans were treating with the utmost seriousness. His driver opened the rear door of the unmarked Jaguar; several newspapers were neatly laid on the back seat.

Milt got in, and the driver closed the reinforced steel door with its double thick bulletproof glass behind him.

Milt saw immediately that the headline in this edition of the *Sunday Times* had changed. The headline now read:

Woman Beheaded in Hampshire

Now Milt understood what "absolute priority" meant. He wondered whether this was a terrorist incident related to Islamic extremists.

He called Charles and said, "Please ask Ahmed to join us."

"Already here, see you in ten, bye."

When Milt arrived at his office, Charles was already seated at the conference table with Ahmed. Ahmed Ipicki was the head of Islamic affairs at MI6. They were drinking coffee with two American visitors. One he recognized as Wayne DiBello, the head of the CIA in Britain (his official title was "cultural liaison"). The other man he did not recognize, but he was obviously American. He was a tall, good-looking black man who stood and shook hands with a very firm handshake, introducing himself as Mat.

Without asking, Charles poured coffee for Milt, added milk and sugar, and stirred. Both Americans wore business suits with open-necked shirts, while Charles and Ahmed were casually dressed in polo shirts and jeans. Milt was still in his golf clothes.

"Milt, I'm sorry to drag you in on a Sunday," Wayne DiBello began, "but we have a situation we need your help on.

"I have read the morning papers," he continued, emphasizing his point by pulling a *Sunday Chronicle* from his briefcase and indicated the beheading headline, "so I can understand why you invited Dr. Ipicki to the meeting. But this has nothing to do with this incident, and on a need-to-know basis, I would request that he be excused."

It was not at all subtle, Milt thought, but Ahmed got the hint; he stood up and took his coffee, saying politely, "I'll leave you gentlemen to it," then closing the door behind him. Milt noticed that he had not shaken hands with the Americans before he left. Now this was intriguing, he thought; nothing to do with the beheading and nothing to do with Islamic extremists, obviously.

Wayne continued, "We have been tracking some unusual activity and have reason to believe that an unusual event happened about the time of those murders yesterday."

Wayne looked across at his colleague as a prompt for him to begin speaking. Mat cleared his throat and then began, "NASA has been working with Dr. Keith Maxwell on a project to monitor some activity from deep space. We believe that yesterday, at the time and place of the murder incident, something happened that we cannot yet explain."

Charles was the first to react (his highly active brain worked much faster than most people); he said, "So you have assets monitoring UK airspace?"

Milt had been thinking the same thing; this meant the Americans were actually monitoring activity in the UK from space. However, this was not the time to bring this up; to smooth over the situation, he interjected, "What exactly happened?"

Mat continued smoothly, ignoring Charles's comment, "There was a short burst of radiation, which seemed to occur on the exact spot at Hazeley Common where the murders took place yesterday."

Charles shuffled some notes he kept in a folder he carried and said, "Oh, yes, the police reports say they found a scientific instrument at the murder scene; apparently it was a Geiger counter for measuring radiation." Charles typed on his iPad and put the tablet on the table so everyone could see a picture of the unit. Next to the image was a label saying "Hampshire Police X555-866-A23." Charles said grandly, "I understand that this is a particularly sophisticated Geiger counter."

Mat replied a little more smugly than was really necessary, "Geiger counters are used on Earth; the radiation we are talking about can only be detected from space assets" (implying "We have them, you don't, Brit"). Mat locked Charles with a hostile stare.

Wayne continued, in a much more conciliatory tone, "The work that Dr. Maxwell had been doing with NASA is vital; we would like to speak with him and examine the site at Hazeley Common. We know nothing about the murders, but we have no reason to believe that the two incidents are connected."

Wayne and Mat drained the last of their coffee and stood up to leave. The four men stood to shake hands.

Charles said, "We'll keep you informed," as he shook hands with Mat.

Wayne looked at Milt's golf club sweater and said, "Sorry about your round of golf; we must play eighteen holes one day."

Milt replied, "Yes, I'd like that." He thought it would be a good opportunity to ask about those space assets monitoring the UK.

As Charles escorted the Americans out of the building, Milt was left alone in his office. He poured himself another cup of coffee and reached for the copy of the *Sunday Chronicle* that Wayne had left behind. He read the article by Cathy Murphy and made a mental note to check her file.

He was startled by Charles opening the office door. Charles had a way with doors; he opened them like he spoke: he just sort of crashed through them in a rapid manner, as if opening them wasted valuable time. He glanced across at Milt as he sat reading the newspaper, and as usual, he was three steps ahead of him.

"Pulled Cathy Murphy's file this morning, no previous, worked at *Chronicle* for about ten years, rising star, expected to be winner of journalistic prize this year." In Charles's machine gun delivery, Milt's brain registered that "no previous" had meant she had no previous convictions (MI6 kept routine tabs on all leading journalists).

Charles continued, "Put in call to the Met CC; will call you on secure in five." With that Charles, crashed back out the door, closing it with gusto behind him.

A few minutes later, the chief constable of the Metropolitan Police was speaking to Milt on a secure private line.

Milt said, "We have an interest in that double murder in Hampshire."

The word "interest" used by the head of MI6 told the UK's most senior policeman that there was a national security issue involved in the case. It meant that all noncriminal matters would be handed over to MI6. The call was polite, businesslike, and brief. After the chief constable hung up, Milt heard a second click as Charles, listening in the next room, also hung up.

Two minutes later, the Met CC called back and was immediately put through by Charles.

He said to Milt, "I have informed the Hampshire chief constable of your interest." The chief emphasized the word "interest." "You are to contact Detective Inspector Amit Chakrabarti, who is in charge of the murder enquiry." Again the call was polite and brief.

When the call ended, Milt was expecting the second click, but instead, Charles's voice came on the line: "Detective Amit Chakrabarti, recently promoted to detective inspector, joined from West Midlands Police about two months ago. No previous. On my way to meet. Enjoy rest of Sunday."

Milt heard the phone line click and then a door slam as Charles left the adjacent office.

On his arrival in Hampshire, Charles went to the tented murder scene on Hazeley Common. The site still had several specialists at work, dressed in white and blue boiler suits. However, most of the team had been moved to Blackbushe to examine the recent shootings. He found Detective Inspector Amit Chakrabarti and showed him his MI6 ID card. The chief constable had ordered Amit to go back to Hazeley Common to meet the MI6 officer. Amit thought this odd on two counts: first, the priority was clearly now at Blackbushe after the killing of one police officer and the serious wounding of a second; second, why would MI6 be interested in these murders? Charles thought Amit looked done in and said kindly as they shook hands, "How about a spot of lunch?"

Amit drove Charles in his unmarked police car to a pub on the Hazeley Common. The Shepherd and Flock was busy with locals and people who had obviously been attending the Sunday market. They were gossiping openly about the Blackbushe shootings, and the TV in the pub was showing live pictures from the scene. As they waited at the bar to order their food and drinks, the news channel broadcast a video clip of the incident that had been recorded on a cell phone. The image was enlarged and freeze framed, and three men were shown at the scene. Despite the poor quality of the enlargement, Amit immediately recognized one of the men as Maxwell.

Amit worried that someone in the pub may recognize him from his TV appearance, but nobody spoke to him. They ordered roast lamb; Charles ordered a pint of London Pride bitter and Amit orange juice. They found a corner table where they would not be overheard, and Charles began asking Amit for details of the case. Amit hadn't realized how hungry he was and polished off the roast dinner, which was delicious. Charles ate sparingly, pushing what he considered to be overcooked vegetables to one side of his plate.

Amit drove Charles back to the site at Hazeley Common. When they arrived, Charles explained that he would be bringing along a couple of assistants, but they would try not to get in the way. Amit left him to it.

A few minutes later, Mat and a colleague arrived in a Jeep Cherokee. They couldn't have looked more American if they tried. They unloaded some equipment and began to scan the area. Amit didn't know what they were looking for, but he knew better than to ask. After all, MI6 were now in charge, and he had clear orders to fully cooperate from the Hampshire chief constable.

After the shootings at the Sunday market, Ellen and Carla had packed up the car and driven to a local pub, the Crown and Cushion at Minley. After lunch, they had gone home and spent the afternoon watching the news bulletins about the shootings, going to bed early.

Ellen awoke in the middle of the night, around two o'clock.

The cats had gathered. They had felt it too. A disturbance in the alternative earth plane. No, not just a disturbance, something new and significant. It was the same feeling she had felt on Saturday afternoon, when she had hung up from Carla.

She felt the presence of a new and powerful sister at the market yesterday, but when the awful incident with the police shooting occurred, she had forgotten all about it. Thinking about it, she had sensed the new sister's aura a day or so previously. The cats had been restless since Saturday morning, but she had other things on her mind, such as the visit by the diplomat and his wife.

Lying next to her in the large double bed, Carla also awoke. She sat up and put on her bedside light. She asked groggily, "What time is it?"

Ellen said, "Two o'clock. I feel her presence; she is reaching out to us and needs to talk."

Carla closed her eyes and focused. She also felt the presence of the new sister and said, "Then we best get dressed and make her welcome, my love."

Ellen stretched out an arm and switched off the bedside light, saying, "It's okay, she won't be here for a while." She hugged Carla's warm body to her own and closed her eyes.

Ellen could sense Carla's feelings. Carla was not as powerful a witch as Ellen and was fiercely jealous of any other witch who got close to Ellen. She occasionally allowed a man in their bed, because she knew Ellen enjoyed men as well as women. But Carla would never allow another woman in their bed. They both sensed that this new sister was a very powerful witch, possibly more powerful than Ellen. Carla was jealous already.

Greta followed the energy line toward the witches' presence. She could sense that she was getting closer. The presence of another witch was like a physical pull in her stomach. She was hungry and thirsty but ignored these feeling. As she followed the energy line, she could feel a tingling in her hands.

She had slept for a few hours in an abandoned building, but now as morning began to break, she felt the two sisters were together and quickened her pace as she continued along the energy line.

She continued to pass many strange objects on her journey. There was a long straight area protected by tall fences, which appeared to have metal strips attached to the ground. The roads had names like Long Acre, but they weren't long and not as big as an acre. White Oak had no Oak trees. The horseless chariots seemed to be everywhere; many were stationary but some were moving. They had bright lights. There were also lights above on tall poles that seemed to burn without fire. She followed the paved roads but tried to keep out of the lights. Her loping walk carried her easily over the distance.

There were so many houses. Streets and streets of them. The houses were strange, built of solid materials. There was no wood or straw, and little smoke from any fires. She wondered how these people cooked or kept warm.

She turned a corner as it was getting light and saw the house. It was no different from any of the others nearby, but it was situated exactly where the energy lines intersected.

As she walked up the driveway, the front door opened, and the redheaded sister opened her arms to embrace her. Greta ran into them gratefully.

"Welcome, sister," Ellen said. "We have felt your presence."

"Thank you, thank you, my sister. I am Greta."

"I am Ellen, and this is Carla."

Carla came forward and grudgingly embraced Ellen.

Ellen said, "Greta, you must have traveled far, let's get you a hot bath and some breakfast."

Behind Greta's back, and so only Ellen could see, Carla pinched her nose at the smell and mimed with two fingers pointing at her mouth, mimicked a vomiting action.

While Ellen went to make tea, Carla took Greta into the bathroom next to the downstairs bedroom. Carla noticed that the sheets on the bed had been changed, and there were fresh towels in the bathroom.

Carla began to run a bath, but Greta stood in the doorway, puzzled. "What am I to do in this room, sister?"

"You are to wash, of course; would you like a bath?"

"But I don't want to … bath."

"Would you prefer a shower?" Carla asked, ignoring the awkward phrasing.

"What is a shower?" Greta asked.

Ellen came back in, carrying a tray of tea with three mugs, milk, and sugar. She put the tray on a table by the bed and assumed that Greta had asked where the shower was.

"Greta, you can use the shower in my bathroom if you wish."

Greta didn't really understand what this meant but simply said, "Thank you, Ellen." She could sense the hostility in Carla.

Carla gave Ellen another look. The shower in Ellen's bedroom was special to them. They often showered together in there and kept certain toys in there for their mutual pleasure. It was an expensive walk-in shower that Ellen had custom built.

Ellen picked up the tray of tea and carried it upstairs. Greta followed, looking with childlike curiosity at all of the pictures on the walls and objects in the house. Carla followed at a distance, so the smell wasn't so bad. She took a perfume bottle from her bag and sprayed it around liberally. Ellen gave her a look of disapproval.

Ellen put down the tray of tea for the second time and asked Greta if she wanted milk and sugar. Greta said yes to both but didn't really know what the question meant. Ellen handed her the steaming mug, turning it so Greta could take it by the handle.

She indicated the shower to Greta, as Carla added milk to her own mug. Ellen had not bothered to add the milk for Carla, a sign of her annoyance with her at her discourtesy to their guest.

There was no door on the shower; there was a drying area near the door with a door to a toilet, and two wash basins with wide shelves, covered in Ellen and Carla's toiletries and makeup.

As Greta entered the bathroom, a movement sensor automatically turned on a light. Startled, Greta looked up at the lights, wondering how this could have happened. As she circled around, looking up, she stumbled down the single step leading into the shower area. Another movement sensor started the shower, and Greta gasped as finely sprayed water soaked her. She nearly dropped her mug of tea in shock but managed to keep a grip, although she spilled most of the tea.

In her surprise and panic, she moved the wrong way, and instead of stepping out of the shower, she moved further in, where an even more vigorous jet of water started automatically. Jets of water sprayed her from the side as well as from above. Greta was now in full panic, screaming and screeching.

Ellen hit a button on the outside of the shower, which stopped the flow of water. But the effect was gradual rather than sudden; the vigorous spray became a mist, then a trickle, and then it stopped.

The bathroom was finished in black tiles that when wet acted as a perfect mirror. Greta saw her reflection in them. She stood there in complete disarray. Her clothes were soaked; she still held the mug, now filled to the brim with shower water. It was a comical sight, and all three witches were soon laughing uncontrollably.

After Greta took off her wet clothes, Ellen stripped to her underwear and washed Greta's hair in the shower. Ellen was so tall and Greta so short and thin, they looked like a mother and daughter.

Ellen was amazed at the dirt that came out of Greta's hair. The blonde hair turned almost white afterwards. Ellen showed Greta how to wash her body with a soapy sponge. Carla looked on in jealous rage and refused Ellen's invitation to join them. Carla thought Greta looked like a teenage girl, with tiny plump breasts and a finely muscled body. Ellen flirted with

Greta, not because she found her attractive; she just couldn't resist making Carla more jealous. Greta realized the game they were playing and flirted back.

Greta was mesmerized by her own reflection in the tiles. The contrast in their bodies was striking. Ellen was tall and broad shouldered, with enormous breasts, while Greta was good head and shoulders shorter. She was the tallest woman Greta had ever seen, almost as tall as that vicious brute Rupert.

Carla took Greta's sodden clothes downstairs and put them in the washing machine. She noticed some sheets and used towels in the laundry basket that were ready to be washed. She saw the male stain on the sheets and smelled another woman's perfume. She made a mental note to ask Ellen about that later. She took some deep breaths and told herself not to jump to conclusions, because she knew how possessive she got. Instead, she decided to make some tea and toast.

As Carla walked back up the stairs, carrying the tray of tea and toast, she could hear Ellen and Greta chatting and laughing over the sound of a hair dryer. When she walked into the room, all her self-control evaporated, and she nearly dropped the breakfast tray. Greta was sitting on the stool in front of the dressing table, and Ellen was blow-drying her hair. There was a mirror on the dressing table, and Greta's yellow eyes shifted from staring at her own reflection to focusing on Carla. Carla could also see her reflection in the mirror, and her face turned to thunder as she took in the scene.

Both Ellen and Greta wore dressing gowns. Greta was wearing Carla's pink gown, while Ellen had her green one on. They had been Christmas presents to each other last year. Carla would sit on the stool in her dressing gown, and Ellen would dry her hair; it was something they did for each other.

Carla put the tray down with thump and walked out without a word. Ellen carried on drying Greta's hair, but even over the noise of the hair dryer, Ellen could hear the front door slam before Carla roared away in her car. Greta felt the brush in Ellen's hand jump when the door slammed.

Greta was highly sensitive and was aware of all of the feelings between the two sisters, but she said nothing. She wanted time with Ellen; she had been right: she was by far the more powerful of the two sisters. She had so many questions, and she felt Ellen could help resolve them. Privately, she was glad Carla had gone.

Ellen made small talk as they ate the toast and drank the tea. Ellen found Greta some clothes in Carla's closet, because hers were too big. Ellen chose older clothes that she hoped Carla wouldn't be too upset about. Shoes were a problem, because Greta had such tiny feet. Clogs seemed to be the only thing. These were new; Carla was very possessive about shoes. She hoped that she wouldn't be too upset. She would buy her some new ones.

They went down to the kitchen, which had a large wooden table. Ellen began cooking bacon and eggs. She began making more tea, and then Greta said she needed to go outside.

At first Ellen didn't understand, but from the kitchen window, she saw Greta look around the garden and then squat next to a tree, pulling up her denim skirt and lowering her tights as she peed.

She watched in disbelief. Greta then dressed herself and came back into the house, taking her seat and resuming the conversation as if nothing unusual had happened.

Before they sat down to eat, Ellen showed Greta how to use the toilet. Not to put too fine a point on it, she peed while Greta stood in the doorway. Greta was fascinated by the whole experience and used the toilet herself in front of Ellen.

Ellen was amazed by how hungry Greta was, and she cooked her more eggs and bacon. Greta ate in a very primitive way with an open mouth, mainly with her fingers, using her knife and fork only sparingly.

As she ate, she told Ellen her story.

"My mistress is the Lady Matilda, Countess of Boulogne and Queen of England. I was ordered by my mistress to spy on the king and his men-at-arms. She had gone on ahead to Winchester. While she was gone, I had a terrible premonition about a silver man and buildings I did not recognize, with many dead people."

Greta paused, and Ellen could see her struggling with the emotion of the vision.

Witches cannot lie to one another. Sisters instinctively know if another witch is being untrue, and Ellen knew that Greta believed every word she said. The trouble was the story was so fanciful, it did not make sense; for one thing, obviously, Matilda wasn't the queen of England. But Ellen wanted her to continue, so she put a comforting hand on her arm and said nothing.

"I followed the king and his henchmen to a clearing in the woods, and the silver man I saw in my vision appeared. I don't know what came over me, but I knew I had to kill him. I charged at him with my spear."

Greta stood and raised her arm, mimicking a stabbing motion; Ellen could see the hatred in her face.

Ellen's iPhone buzzed, making Greta jump.

It was a text from Carla, being bitchy: "Did she come?"

Ellen texted back, "I have been silly; come home, it is important x."

Greta went on with her story.

"Suddenly there was a blinding flash, and instead of killing the silver man, I had killed a dog."

Ellen didn't know why but she felt pain, not of the dog, but someone else that she didn't know. It was strange, but she put the thoughts aside.

Greta went on with her story, and about half an hour later, Carla walked sheepishly back into the kitchen. Ellen was making cheese on toast with Worcester sauce, Carla's favorite. Ellen and Greta feigned surprise, but they both knew Carla was on her way; there were few secrets between witches.

Ellen made a fuss over Carla, kissing and hugging her as if they had been apart for ages. Greta though this must be a polite thing to do, and to Carla's surprise, she emulated Ellen's enthusiastic welcome. Then to the amusement of Carla, she said, "Ellen showed me how to toilet."

Ellen sat Carla in her favorite chair and put a plate of cheese on toast and a cup of hot chocolate in her Prince Harry mug in front of her. She put the same in front of Greta. But Greta's hot chocolate was in a Prince William mug.

She sat down with her own tea and said, "Greta, tell Carla your story."

Greta began hesitantly, but it was getting dark by the time she finished her story. As Ellen stood to open a second bottle of wine, Greta's head slumped forward, and she fell asleep at the table.

They carried her into the downstairs bedroom and took off her shoes, skirt, and cardigan. Carla recognized her own clothes and shoes, but she was so enthralled by Greta's story that she kept her mouth shut. As they closed the door, they heard Greta snoring contentedly.

The two modern witches got into bed and took out their tablet computers. This required some research.

Through Wikipedia, they quickly verified that King Stephen had reigned between 1135 and 1141. There was record of Fleet being called La Fete and of Hartley Wintney being called Hertleye Wynteneye. It was said that King Stephen was buried at Faversham Abbey, so if that story was true, then whoever was buried there was not King Stephen.

But the really startling fact was that if Greta's story was true, she was more than a thousand years old.

The next morning, Greta marched into Ellen and Carla's bedroom without knocking and announced that she had used the toilet. She was still dressed in the tights and top she had slept in; she had not bothered to put on the rest of her clothes. The cats followed her in.

She said she would shower and, without being invited, removed her clothes and walked into the shower. Carla noticed she was using her best shampoo but said nothing.

Over breakfast, Greta asked about the pictures on the mugs. She had failed to recognize any of the current British royal family.

Carla then showed Greta several pictures on her computer tablet to see if she knew any of them. Unless Greta was the best actress in the world, she failed to recognize Elvis Presley, the Beatles, and the current and previous presidents of the United States. She also did not know Margaret Thatcher, Saddam Hussein, Michael Jackson, Princess Diana, Charlie Chaplin, Gandhi, or Queen Elizabeth II (although she did hesitate when she saw Diana's picture).

Greta was not lying; as witches, both Carla and Ellen knew that, but was she suffering from some form of memory loss? Or was it an elaborate hoax, like the woman who claimed to be Grand Duchess Anastasia of Russia, the youngest daughter of the last tsar and tsarina? Or was she suffering from delusions of grandeur?

They asked her to explain how King Stephen had come to the throne, and as Carla checked the facts on her tablet, she accurately described Stephen's accession following Henry I.

Ellen decided to throw in a curve ball and asked, "How many wives did Henry VIII have?"

Greta thought for a moment and then said, "I don't know, I don't know Henry VIII."

Ellen put a sympathetic hand on top of Greta's and said soothingly, "That is all right; he wasn't born until 1491."

Greta looked confused.

They were distracted by a noise, a thump from the hallway as the newspaper was put through the letter box. Carla picked it up and looked at the front page. She put the newspaper on the kitchen table in front of Ellen, pointing to the date at the top of the paper. Tuesday, March 6, 2012.

Greta said, "But the year is 1136," and her voice trailed off.

At that moment, all three witches realized that Greta was from a different time.

They were brought out of their shocked silence by a knock on the door. Ellen went to open it, and Carla and Greta followed her.

Outside were two uniformed policewomen. One said, "Morning, madam; we are conducting door-to-door enquiries, because the fugitives from Hazeley Common are still at large. Did you hear about the murders yesterday?"

Ellen replied, "Yes, we were at the market yesterday when the shooting happened, terrible business."

"What were you doing at the market?"

Carla had been behind Ellen when she opened the door but quickly retreated back into the kitchen when she recognized one of the policewomen; the officer had cautioned her during a particularly violent confrontation with some of the fake witches at a psychic fair in Wokingham the previous year. She grabbed Greta's hand and took her with her.

As they returned to the kitchen, she could hear Ellen saying, "We have a stall at the market; I heard the shots but didn't see anything of the actual shooting."

After a few more questions, the policewomen gave Ellen a business card and asked her to call if she remembered anything else.

Ellen closed the door, put the card on the table in the hall, and went back in the kitchen. Carla and Greta were both sitting in shocked silence, each wondering what to say next.

Ellen decided that this was getting them nowhere; to break the mood, she said, "Let's go shopping."

They took Greta to the large Marks & Spencer superstore near Camberley. As Carla drove them in her old Volvo, Greta screamed in excitement at being driven in a horseless carriage at such speed. Ellen and Carla both laughed.

Greta behaved outrageously in the shop. She rushed between racks of clothes and shoes, having never seen such abundance, such opulence, and such vivid colors. Her behavior was noticed on the CCTV cameras, and security were called. Ellen was holding new clothes over her existing clothes and then rushing to the next rack for more.

The two security guards were ex-Gurkhas from Nepal. They had handsome Asian features, and Greta stared at them in open-mouthed wonder, attempting to touch their faces as they escorted her from the store. Carla stood outside with Greta, while Ellen apologized to the store supervisor and bought £250 worth of clothes and shoes for Greta on her credit card.

Ellen's phone rang as she was leaving the store. It was a regular client, a dear old lady who came to her regularly for a reading. Ellen arranged for her to visit the next day. *Well*, she thought, *her £100 would go some way to paying for Greta's new things.*

She then suggested to Carla that they go into town and get their nails done. Greta's nails were unbelievably bad.

Greta embraced a thousand years of progress fast. She came home with a new hairstyle, fantastic-looking nails, and a makeover. She felt wonderful. Ellen also said she had booked a cosmetic dentist the next day. Carla mouthed behind Greta's back, "Who is paying?"

Excitedly, Greta tried on her new clothes, and even Carla was swept away in her enthusiasm. That night, Carla cooked her specialty, toad-in-the-hole, which is sausages cooked in batter. It was impossible to explain to Greta that it contained no toads; she still didn't understand what bit of the animal that sausages were. Carla and Ellen were doubled up with laughter.

After dinner, they sat down to watch TV together. Television was another new concept for Greta, but there were so many new things that she had given up asking questions. She just hoped it would all become clear later. However, like a small child, she had secretly looked behind the TV to see where the images came from.

The lead news story was still the search for Dr. Keith Maxwell and accomplices unknown, centered on the Fleet and Hartley Wintney areas. They had been responsible for two murders, and their fourth accomplice, who was still unidentified, had killed one police officer and seriously wounded a second with his bow and arrow before being shot dead.

The story used video clips of varying quality. Most had been taken at the scene by members of the public on their cell phones. Carla and Ellen had heard the shots but hadn't seen more than the backs of the heads of a crowd of people.

Ellen remembered feeling Greta's presence when she was serving on the stall, but she didn't remember seeing her in the crowd.

An image of a man's face appeared on Ellen's large plasma screen. It was a very life-like color sketch of the man the police had shot and killed on Sunday.

Greta pointed at the screen and said, "That is Henry of Gloucester, the finest bowman in England."

Carla and Ellen exchanged a look. Both realized at that point that they may have something to contribute. Ellen remembered the card the policewoman had left her. It was still on the hall table, but she said nothing in front of Greta.

In bed that night, Carla and Ellen discussed what they should do. Carla thought they should call the police first thing in the morning, but Ellen was not so sure.

"What would we say," she asked. "We have a witch staying with us from a thousand years ago? They will lock us in the funny farm and throw away the key."

"We could just say we have some information that may help with their enquiries. You don't even have to give your name these days."

"But that would be betraying a sister; we cannot do that."

They couldn't agree and eventually fell asleep, back to back.

The next morning, they still couldn't agree. Ellen took Greta to the dentist in her car, while Carla drove to Surbiton to see her mother.

In the waiting room, Ellen read the magazines and newspapers. There was a newspaper there she didn't normally read, the *Daily Chronicle*. Inside, there was a picture of a very sexy reporter, Cathy Murphy, who was pictured clutching an award, dressed in a low-cut evening dress. She had won an award the previous night, and the story went on about her recent achievements, including being the first to reveal the horrific beheading story in Hampshire.

On a whim, Ellen used her phone to find the *Daily Chronicle's* website and sent this reporter an email, asking her to call because she had information about the murders in Hampshire.

At the *Daily Chronicle's* offices, Martha was at her desk, nursing a killer hangover. Cathy had not yet arrived in. They had both got royally pissed after Cathy had won her award. JC had driven them both home, but Martha didn't remember getting into bed.

Martha read all Cathy's emails from the website. Most were from timewasters and nutcases. All got an autoreply, thanking them for their email and promising it would receive Cathy's careful attention in due course, but they received so many that it was impossible to reply individually. They changed the text of the autoreply from time to time, but the gist was the same.

Martha went through this morning's emails one by one, hitting the Delete key on most of them. Most were nutcases. Some were from men of a certain age, after Cathy's body.

She saw Ellen's email, noting it was about the murders in Hampshire, but after seeing the return address with the prefix "white.witch@", she hit the Delete key without opening the message. Probably a nutter. She went to get another mug of strong coffee.

Ellen received the autoreply from her email to Cathy Murphy just as Greta returned to the waiting room from the dentist's surgery. For some reason, the dentist came out with her; he was clearly excited.

He said, "I have never seen a set of teeth like Greta's, fantastic."

Greta obviously took this as a compliment, but Ellen found this curious, because her teeth were clearly in a terrible state. He nodded to Ellen and handed the receptionist a buff folder with writing on the front.

The receptionist smiled with radiant white teeth. She said, "Your estimated treatment cost is £3,000; after a deposit of £1,000, I will book your next appointment."

Ellen took out her credit card reluctantly, trying to think what she would tell Carla. But before she handed over her credit card, she asked the receptionist if she could have a quick word with the dentist. The receptionist said of course and touched a button on the keypad. She assumed that Ellen was about to query the bill, so she said, "Michael, a patient out here has a query."

The dentist emerged and said politely, "May I help you?"

"Yes, what did you mean when you said that you had never seen teeth like Greta's before?"

Relieved that this wasn't a complaint about the cost, Michael smiled his whitest dentist smile and said, "I mean they are truly unique, as if they are from a different time. There is no evidence of modern fillings or fluorine, and I cannot explain it. I have reduced my bill accordingly, because I am so fascinated by her case."

"Thank you," said Ellen. "That is very kind." She punched her PIN code into the credit card machine.

The receptionist removed the card with a flourish and smiled. Ellen thanked her, and Greta followed her out.

When Carla arrived home for dinner, Ellen told her about her call to Cathy Murphy. She had also showed her Cathy's picture at the award ceremony on her tablet computer. Carla saw why Ellen had called her; she was very sexy.

After a good dinner, a few glasses of wine, and some special "Ellen and Carla time" in the shower before bed, Carla agreed that this was better than calling the police.

As she still had no reply to her email the next day, Ellen called Cathy's office and got Martha's voicemail. She left a message, saying she had emailed the previous day.

She called again after lunch, as Martha was away from her desk. Cathy took the call and was immediately intrigued.

Cathy hit the Record button on her tape machine and spoke to Ellen for fifteen minutes. They arranged to meet, but Ellen had set a condition.

The condition that Ellen set was that Cathy meet her, alone, at the Surbiton railway station. A slender, dark-haired woman met her at the station exit, introducing herself as Carla. Carla was polite as she greeted Cathy, but more business-like than friendly.

They drove in Carla's Volvo a short distance and parked outside a restaurant called Zizzi. Carla had suggested it, partly because it had high-backed booths, where they could talk discreetly, but also if Greta misbehaved and they could never go back, it would be no great loss.

Carla explained they would meet her friends in the restaurant. Cathy went into the bathroom before going to the table. As she sat on the stall, she sent a text to Martha with the registration number of Carla's Volvo. Martha knew where she was, because they used a simple tracking app on their smartphones.

Martha texted back, "JC is with you." Martha then sent a text containing Carla's full name and address, date of birth, value of the car, and that she had no known criminal convictions. Her credit rating was average. She also recommended the spaghetti carbonara, as it had the best reviews on the TimeOut website.

Cathy texted back, "Smart arse xx."

JC, their chauffer and ex-police officer, had followed Carla's Volvo from the station to the restaurant, but Cathy had not spotted him. He would have been surprised (and mortified) if she had.

Cathy was introduced to Ellen and Greta; they shook hands. They had already ordered white wine, and Ellen poured herself and Carla a glass. Cathy ordered a bottle of the most expensive red wine on the menu. She also asked for some sparkling water.

It was a bit of squeeze in the booth; Ellen was a big girl, but Carla didn't seem to mind being close to her. Ellen sat on one end, Cathy the other, and Greta sat next to Cathy. Cathy was reminded of the story of the three bears: Daddy Bear, Mummy Bear, and Baby Bear. Greta had a childlike physique.

Cathy asked if she could record the interview; that way, she wouldn't have to take notes. They said they didn't mind, and she placed a recorder on the table in front of Greta and pressed Record. Greta had no idea what she was talking about. In fact, the device was also a radio transmitter.

Martha listened live in her office in London, while JC listened in his car outside the restaurant. To pass the time, JC and Martha sent text messages to each other, making sarcastic comments on the food choices Cathy made:

Not sure I fancy that starter
No, I would have gone for brioche
I see she went for the carbonara

Listening on the live link, both Martha and JC heard the laughter from Ellen and Carla when Greta asked the young waiter if they had any toad-in-the-hole. In the end, Greta just said she would have the same as Ellen: Parma ham with melon, followed by lasagne. JC and Martha were a little confused when they heard Greta add, "Whatever that is."

Cathy had often been in these situations and knew how to entice people to talk. She was an astute and clever listener and was able to steer a conversation to quickly get to the salient facts. She was also a past master of keeping other people's glasses charged but drinking little herself.

She had expected that the dinner would last just an hour or so, and then she would be back on the train home. She had already filed her story for tomorrow, a profile interview with Michel Devereau, the deputy director of the European Space Agency (ESA), and she was looking forward to an early night after the excesses of the awards ceremony. She drank more of the sparkling water than wine, but the three witches had finished the white and were now on the red.

Cathy ordered more wine. She was completely unprepared for Greta and her story; she didn't know what to say when Ellen claimed she was actually from the past.

Between mouthfuls of melon and ham, Ellen said, "We have a stall at Blackbushe market and were there last Sunday when the police shootings happened. I felt Greta's presence but never met her until she arrived at my house the day after."

Greta interjected, "I followed the energy lines to Ellen's house, where I also met Carla. I recognized Henry of Gloucester's picture on the television."

The witches were falling over themselves in their enthusiasm to tell their story.

Cathy asked, "So how can you be sure that Greta is from a different time?"

Carla had finished her starter, so she took over the story to allow time for Ellen and Greta to eat theirs. "We showed her a variety of pictures of well-known figures from recent years, like Elvis, the queen, and the pope, and she failed to recognize anyone. Also, Ellen took her to a dentist, who said he had never seen teeth like hers in modern times."

Cathy asked, "What is the name of the dentist?"

Ellen answered, "Camberley Cosmetic Dentistry."

Cathy made a show of making a note on a pad but knew that Martha would already be searching for it on Google.

As the conversation continued, Cathy's excitement built from a possible feature story, to a headline tomorrow, to another scoop for Sunday. Her tiredness and early night forgotten, she excused herself and called Martha on her cell.

She said excitedly, "Are you getting this? Are you fucking getting this?"

Martha said, "Do you want me to book them in at the Ritz? Should JC break cover?"

"Yes and yes," she answered. "Let the good times roll, let's do it."

As Cathy sat back down in the restaurant booth, a tall, handsome man in a dark business suit appeared at their table, and Cathy introduced John Constable. By this time, there were three empty wine bottles in the ice bucket. Greta thought she had never seen a more handsome man. Ellen thought he probably had a nice cock, and Carla ignored him and put her hand higher on Ellen's thigh.

To "book someone in at the Ritz" was journalistic code for making someone an offer they couldn't refuse for an exclusive on their story. JC was now discussing with the three women the terms of an offer where the *Daily Chronicle* would pay them £100,000 if they did not speak to any other journalist about this story until next Monday. He produced a contract from his pocket; their names and addresses were already written in.

Carla was a little surprised at this, and as the most sober of the three witches, she said half-heartedly that they really should show it to a lawyer before they signed. JC and Cathy went into a well-practiced dialogue about why showing it to a solicitor was a bad idea; it would delay things and end up reducing their fee. Besides, what did they have to lose?

Cathy ordered a bottle of champagne, and they signed the contract.

Cathy got a taxi back to the station. By now, Carla had drunk too much to drive; she left her old Volvo parked outside the restaurant while JC drove the three women back to Fleet.

He asked if he could stay the night, so he could take them to their hotel in the morning. This was actually a ruse to obey Cathy's last whispered instruction to him: "Don't let them out of your sight, big boy."

They didn't use the Ritz Hotel anymore, they used the Dorchester. Ellen and Carla were very excited when they found out. As usual, Greta had no idea what they were talking about, and as Ellen and Carla were talking excitedly about what they would bring with them, she interrupted their enthusiastic tirade by saying, "JC can sleep with me," pulling him into the downstairs bedroom and slamming the door behind her with a kick of her Marks & Spencer shoe.

Ellen and Carla looked at each other after the door slammed shut and then roared with suppressed laughter. They had to hold on to each other to make it up the stairs.

Greta had always known she would meet JC. She had visualized him ever since she was a child. He was her perfect man.

She didn't know it would take her a journey of a thousand years to find him. But that explained why she could never feel his presence before. She lay now as she had always known she would, against the warmth of his chest. His arms around her, she felt safe and secure for the first time in her life as he told her his story.

He had been brought up in a rough part of London, the Isle of Dogs.

Greta thought it must be rough to live on an island full of dogs, but she didn't interrupt. In fact, there were many parts of JC's story that she didn't understand, but she resolved to ask him about it later. She knew they would have lots of time.

In fact, JC said he now had a company flat in London Docklands that was close to the *Daily Chronicle's* offices in Wapping, not far from where he grew up. The area was being redeveloped for the London Olympic Games. The Isle of Dogs was now quite an up-market area, and if he didn't have the company flat, he couldn't afford to live there.

He had never married and lived alone. But Greta already knew that: a woman's instinct, a witch's intuition.

From an early age, his father had taken him and his younger brother to the local boxing club. His father said they needed to be toughened up, but his mother didn't approve. His younger brother was the bright one at school and soon dropped out of boxing, but JC went on to become the London Schools champion at fifteen.

He struggled at school and joined the army a year later.

After his basic training, his tall stature singled him out for the Guards, and he saw service in Northern Ireland and then Iraq, where he was wounded.

After he was declared fit to return to service, he was promoted to captain and assigned to the Police Special Branch, which oversees all royal protection duties.

He was part of the team that traveled with Charles, the Prince of Wales, and Lady Diana, Princess of Wales, and later, he protected the young princes, William and Harry.

He was in India when the famous picture of Diana was taken, sitting alone outside the beautiful Taj Mahal. He had stood behind the photographer when he took the picture.

He was in the backup car following behind Diana's limousine when she was tragically killed in Paris. The driver of Diana's armored Mercedes was an experienced man, but he pushed his luck a little too far that night. He was trying to outrun a group of paparazzi following the car at high speed on motorbikes and scooters. The Mercedes clipped a concrete pillar in an underpass at over 100 MPH. The car cartwheeled, spinning out of control, and smashed into a concrete wall. He was one of the last people to see Diana alive; he had tried to give her CPR. But he knew from his time of trying to help fallen colleagues in Northern Ireland and Iraq that she wouldn't make it.

After he returned to London, he met Spiers Clarkson, who was then editor of the *Daily Chronicle*. He gave Spiers his story about Diana's death on the condition that his name didn't appear, and Spiers kept his word.

A few months afterwards, he went to a charity dinner where the Countess of Wessex was speaking. There was one other Special Branch officer on duty that night other than himself. The countess, who was married to Prince Edward, was one of the more junior members of the royal family and only warranted a small protection detail.

The occasion was a memorial fundraising dinner at the upmarket Grosvenor House Hotel on London's Park Lane. Princess Diana had been patron of this children's cancer charity, and it was a dinner to honor her and to raise funds. A three-course meal without wine was £250 a head.

There were large pictures of Diana around the room, and the video tribute to her charity work with children brought a tear to every eye in the room, including his own.

Some three hundred guests sat down to dinner, and Spiers was the guest speaker; his job was to introduce the countess, who was taking over as patron of the charity. The choice of Spiers was quite contentious, because there was still quite a lot of antipress feeling in the country. Many people felt that Diana's death was caused in no small part by her constant hounding by the press. "Press intrusion" was now a phrase on everyone's lips.

Spiers made a good speech and then introduced the countess. She spoke reverently of Diana and praised the work of the charity. She sat down to thunderous applause, and coffee and liqueurs were served.

At an event of this size, London hotels employed an army of temporary staff to wait at tables. It is impossible to vet everyone, and one of the staff turned out to be a psychotic woman who had been obsessed with Diana.

JC saw the way she lifted her arm to strike before he saw the razor sharp butcher's knife clutched in her fist. He lunged and knocked her to the ground, with the blade just an inch from the back of Spiers's neck. He disarmed her easily, and the incident was hushed up. She was detained indefinitely under the Mental Health Act, and as far as JC knew, she was still in a mental institution.

Afterwards, Spiers made JC an offer he couldn't refuse, and he had worked for the *Daily Chronicle* ever since.

Spiers had left his job at the *Daily Chronicle* to follow a career in television; he was now a celebrity TV talk show host in the United States. JC still drove him whenever he came to London.

The editor of the *Daily Chronicle* had assigned JC to Cathy Murphy, who she described as a "brilliant young hack that needed protecting from herself."

As they drifted off to sleep, Greta recounted JC's story in her head and made a mental note to question him about some aspects she didn't understand.

But one thing Greta did know was what Princess Diana looked like. Carla had showed her the picture on her tablet. She was sorry the elegant woman was dead; she had been a powerful sister, and she would have loved to have met her.

The Dorchester Hotel, London

Looking back, the journey to the Dorchester was the beginning of Greta's rise to international celebrity. Ellen and Carla (and especially Greta herself) were completely unprepared for the rapid turn of events that would follow.

JC pulled up to the Dorchester in the relatively unimpressive black Mercedes, given the two Rolls-Royces, Aston Martins, Bentleys, Ferraris, and Lamborghinis that were parked outside. The uniformed doormen recognized JC and made a show of opening the doors for the ladies and taking in their luggage.

Two bellmen escorted the ladies and JC to a waiting elevator. There was no need to check in; the suite had already been paid for.

On the green outside, there were two photographers who used the Dorchester as their regular spot. Their digital cameras captured images of all three women as they emerged from the car. The images were sent electronically to a studio in Ealing, but facial recognition software failed to get a match with any celebrity. The images were stored anyway.

Earlier that morning, the photographers had taken pictures of both Beyoncé and Sting and their respective entourages, who were also staying at the hotel. Beyoncé was playing a concert at the O2 Arena, and Sting was selling out at the Royal Albert Hall. These pictures were now being marketed to the highest bidders.

The suite in the Dorchester was like nothing Ellen or Carla had ever experienced. The rooms were luxurious beyond measure, with antique furnishings and a view across the park. Greta just went into overdrive in her excitement, flicking light switches, turning on taps, opening cupboard doors, and squealing with delight. There were two bedrooms, two bathrooms, and a sitting room. In the sitting room, Martha was waiting with a photographer and a lady she introduced as a makeover artist. Both were dressed all in black. There was water, soft drinks, coffee, tea, and pastries on a side table.

Over coffee, Martha explained what would happen.

First they wanted some pictures. The makeover artist, whose name was Zoe, and Bryan, the photographer, would recommend an approach to dresses, makeup, and hair. They would then do the shoot here in the suite. This evening, they had been booked in to the West End show *Les Miserables*, have dinner at Roules in Covent Garden, and then be brought back here by JC.

Zoe now began to assess the sizes of each of the women. She knew most by a practiced eye, but in Ellen's case, she checked bra and shoe size. She wandered into the next room, where she barked a series of figures to someone on her cell phone. Greta had still had no understanding of these gadgets, despite exhaustive explanation from Ellen and Carla.

Within ten minutes, the doorbell to the suite rang, and four young women, dressed in the same black outfits as Bryan and Zoe, wheeled in hanging rails. They then removed the covers to reveal a glory of clothes of every imaginable style and color. There were neatly arranged racks with shoes, boots, hats, belts, bags, and accessories. It was couture of unimaginable quality and every girl's dream. Ellen clapped her hands with delight, and Carla hugged her in her excitement. Greta jumped up and down like a little schoolgirl.

The four young women stood back at a discreet distance. With an expert eye, Zoe picked out an outfit for each of the women. Ellen liked hers immediately and went to try it on. Carla was less sure about hers and chose another one as well as the selection that Zoe had made. Greta squealed in delight when Zoe handed her a black and teal dress and matching boots. Now as each of the witches peeled away in turn to the bedrooms to try on their outfits, the first three of the girls in line moved forward in a practiced line, as if in the military, to assist each of the women with their outfits.

In the end, Carla chose the outfit Zoe had first picked for her, but with different shoes. She did so only after trying on three others. It was a beautifully embroidered claret-wine colored dress, with an elegant bodice.

Zoe had carefully selected an outfit to emphasize Ellen's large breasts. She had on a low-cut lacy blouse and tight pencil skirt with a slit up the side. High heels were very tarty and sexy.

The women were positioned on a chaise longue with an elegant stone fireplace in the background. Bryan took some pictures, which he described as "rushes," and Martha, Zoe, and Bryan viewed them on a monitor. They discussed the images, altered the position of the lights, and moved some of the items in the background.

They repeated the process and then asked the witches to change position on the chaise longue and gave Greta a black hat to wear.

Now they were happy. There were nods and slaps on shoulders as they viewed the rushes on the monitor.

The girls in black now took each of their charges back into the bedroom, where their outfits were carefully hung up. Zoe snapped orders, instructing that various garments were to be ironed or brushed immediately.

Now dressed in their underwear and fleecy Dorchester dressing gowns, they were led to a discreet elevator that the four black-clad assistant had waiting. They were taken to the basement of the hotel, where three adjoining chairs awaited in the hairdressing salon and spa.

Salon assistants came and washed each witch's hair. Greta nearly punched the young girl who tried to force her head backwards over the sink, but Ellen calmed her just in time.

Zoe and Bryan were now in deep and earnest discussion with another man, who was clearly the head stylist. Ellen watched in the mirror as each used their hands to describe in an animated and exaggerated way the style they obviously wanted for each of the women.

The head stylist now described to each of the women the style they would like to use. Predictably, Carla was the only one who was unhappy, and after some discussion, they compromised. Zoe was getting the measure of her.

Greta had her long wet hair straightened, with teal highlights added to match her dress. Ellen's red hair was made even redder and fluffed out. Carla had her hair in a bun on the top of her head, with diamond-encrusted hair sticks through it. She looked very elegant.

When the hair was done, then came the makeup. Greta's was subtle apart from her eyes, where black mascara was used extensively. Ellen's was tarty: bright red glossy lipstick and green eye shadow to enhance her green eyes. Carla's was elegant, to emphasize her high cheek bones.

The witches were given a lunch of fruit, pumpkin soup, and smoked salmon while they were pampered. Then they were taken back up to the suite. The assistants helped them put on their freshly pressed clothes and polished footwear, and they were carefully positioned by Bryan back on the chaise longue.

Twenty minutes later, after several different poses, hand positions, and facial expressions, they were done. The champagne was opened. The black-clad girls left, rolling out the racks of clothes with them in perfect practiced precision.

JC arrived to take them to the show and then to dinner; the witches went dressed as they were. Martha joined them in the back of the Rolls-Royce, which took them first to the Theatre Royal in Drury Lane to watch *Les Miserables* and then later to Covent Garden. Flash bulbs seemed to follow them everywhere. Bryan was already at each venue when they arrived and took more pictures as they went in. Bryan's assistants took more pictures while they were inside the theatre and the restaurant, and more pictures as they left.

That night, Ellen and Carla made love in one of the sumptuous beds, and Greta ravaged JC in the other. Ellen and Carla could hear their grunts and groans of pleasure. Ellen hoped to join them for a bit of foursome fun, but Carla didn't want to.

The witches and JC were woken by a phone call around eight o'clock, and a sumptuous room service breakfast arrived. None of them were that hungry after last night's huge dinner, except JC, who piled his plate with sausages, bacon, and eggs.

Much to Ellen and Carla's amusement, they tried to explain to Greta how sausages were made and why they tasted so good.

Amazingly, by Sunday morning, the witches' outfits had been copied and replaced with new matching ones. Another trip to the salon for their hair and makeup, and then they were dressed in their new outfits, which were fitted with military precision by the girls in black. They were now ready for the media frenzy to come.

The *Sunday Chronicle's* headline was:

The Witches of Hampshire

The front page was simply a large picture of the three women in an unsmiling, elegant pose. Greta sat with her arms wide apart, as if casting a spell. Her tall black hat and long white hair made her look like a witch. Ellen sat forward, legs crossed, which emphasized the split in her skirt and her ample bosom. Carla stood at the back with one hand on Ellen's shoulder and the other raised, as if casting a spell.

Bryan had edited the picture using digital enhancement software. Their eyes had been made a little larger and in a way more evil. Ellen's cleavage was slightly deeper, and Greta's hat was more pointed. Carla's expression was made even more demur.

The effect was stunning. Three real live witches living in the UK, and one who claimed to be a thousand years old. Inside there were several more pictures, some taken at the theatre, others at the restaurant. Mostly they were of Greta, then of Ellen, and Carla was just in one other.

The clever people who had syndicated Cathy's beheading story now syndicated this new story to more news agencies with even more vigor. Cathy's reputation as a journalist was growing. It was a media frenzy, with Greta and Ellen receiving all the attention. Carla was especially hurt when she overheard one of the assistants say, "They all want Greta and the sexy one with the big tits, but nobody wants to talk to the stuck-up one at the back."

Cathy's article had been brilliantly written. It mentioned that Greta may have a link with the murders in Hampshire, but there was nothing that suggested anything on the wrong side of the law.

After an exhausting day of media interviews, on Sunday evening, they were taken to dinner at the stylish Savoy Grill. At the Savoy, as if by coincidence, Martha introduced them to Larry Spindler, a talent agent.

Larry promised to handle the witches' affairs; apparently, there was already a clause in the contract the witches had signed to give the *Daily Chronicle* exclusivity.

They thought no more of it. Instead, they drank more champagne, ate fantastic food, and spotted a number of celebrities in the Savoy Grill. They were amazed when Larry brought Rod Stewart to their table to introduce them; he also handled Rod's affairs.

By Monday afternoon, they were all exhausted. Ellen wanted a hot bath and to take off the killer heals. Carla wanted to go home. Greta was being interviewed live on Sky News, which Larry said was being syndicated by CNN.

They were already the lead story on most of the Internet news wires. Larry was doing everything he could, of course, to stoke the fire. Bryan's pictures were syndicated throughout the world.

What was really compelling and popular were the live interviews that both Greta and Ellen gave. Neither was media savvy, least of all Greta, so what people saw was a raw interview with a real personality. The viewers loved it.

Ellen was able to use her extraordinary powers to spook the reporters. In the middle of an interview, she would mention some personal matter connected with the reporter interviewing her. It was so natural to Ellen; she could see a lost relative not on the earth plane and asked the reporter about the person, just as if she was at home doing her normal work. It made for a great interview.

Greta was even more characteristic. She looked like a witch and behaved outrageously in front of the camera, drinking tea from a saucer, using outrageous gestures, even grabbing the groin of a female interviewer, who she thought was a man. In fact, she used to be a man. The ratings soared.

JC had pulled a favor with Spiers, and the executive producer of his hugely popular US talk show had worked out a deal with Larry to pay Greta $1 million to appear on his show on Wednesday night.

New York City

Greta and JC flew first class to New York, taking British Airways from London Heathrow to La Guardia Airport.

Throughout the journey, JC tried to explain what was happening to Greta. But in the end, he gave up; he couldn't explain it all, so they just drank glass after glass of champagne.

As they began to descend, JC opened the window blinds. The brightening dawn light illuminated the Manhattan skyline, and Greta became very agitated. Initially, JC thought she was afraid of flying and sought to sooth her concerns. But when they were in the back of the stretch limousine being driven to their hotel, Greta told him about her vision.

She described how she had seen many tall buildings like these, adding that she had seen thousands of dead people. She had not understood why her vision had upset her so much at the time, but now she knew why. At the time, she did not know that she would actually be in this strange city with her perfect man. Now he too was at risk.

They held hands in the back of the limo, staring into each other's eyes and whispering to each other. The driver watched discreetly in the rear view mirror and thought how romantic it was. He had known JC for a long time and was glad he had found his gal.

That night, Greta was interviewed on Clarkson's show, and she was a sensation. It was not just what she said but the way she said it. She was so different from the polished, typical media pundit. Her answers were so outrageous and so unexpected.

It began conventionally enough, with makeup. Greta wore a plain black dress from Marks & Spencer and a simple pearl necklace. The necklace was the same color as her long hair, which was beautifully combed. The dressing room had a TV monitor showing a live feed of the show, and as Spiers spoke with a politician who was championing a change to US gun laws, there was a knock on the door, and a voice called, "Greta, five minutes please."

JC led Greta up some steps to the studio and listened as Spiers read an introduction: "Now we have something very different. I am delighted to welcome someone few of you have seen before. She has traveled here today especially for this show from London. She claims to be a thousand years old. Ladies and gentlemen, please welcome Greta the Witch."

The studio manager waiting in the wings motioned for Greta to walk on, and JC applauded with the rest of the studio audience as she went over and shook hands with Spiers.

Spiers began by asking, "So what was life like a thousand years ago?"

Greta answered in her distinctive gravelly voice, "We had no department stores, no decent shoes, and no sausages, but the air didn't smell burnt."

Spiers smiled and asked, "What do you mean, the air smells burnt?"

"JC tells me it is pollution from your horseless carriages, I mean motor cars."

Spiers received an instruction in his earpiece and steered the questioning to a more logical topic: "That is fascinating, Greta, but tell me where you were born."

"I am not sure where I was born, but it was somewhere in southern England. I do not remember my mother and father. I was brought up by my witch sisters, and we had to regularly hide from the men who came in the night."

Spiers interjected, "What about these men?"

"They would rape and kill my sisters, by burning them alive. I can still hear the screams in the night."

While Greta spoke, you could have heard a pin drop in the studio. Everyone hung on every word. In the end, they ran out of time; the producer had to run the studio credits while Greta was still talking. The interview was the lead story the next morning on every news program: the real-life witch from a thousand years ago. The interview went viral on the Internet and was so popular, it caused servers around the world to crash. She had become an overnight celebrity.

But what really stoked the fire of the story was that after Greta's appearance, she dropped out of sight.

Once she finished Spiers's show, Greta was exhausted. She had been tired before the show from the jet-lag and the worry about her vision. JC also found that she was suffering from a severe cold.

JC was a practical man. He understood that if she really was from the Middle Ages, she would not have the common immunities of people today.

He knew that American doctors would do almost anything for money, so he took Greta to a private New York hospital, where he had once taken a celebrity who had overdosed. The hospital was used to discretion.

He filled out some papers, produced his gold American Express card, and explained that they needed to see a doctor who specialized in common childhood diseases like measles, mumps, and rubella. When the doctor appeared, he explained that Greta had grown up on a remote island in the Indian Ocean and had never been immunized as a child.

Greta was so unwell with her cold that she didn't really register what was happening to her. But they made her swallow a variety of pills and gave her several injections. She was checked into a private room for the night, given copious amounts of vitamin C, and slept for fourteen hours.

JC slept in her room on the couch, and when she awoke, he ordered breakfast of fresh fruit followed by eggs Benedict.

The nurse who brought in the breakfast tray also brought in the newspapers. The staff here were well used to celebrities, but when she saw Greta sitting up in bed, she took a double-take at the front page of *USA Today* and beamed with recognition. Greta, who was still a little groggy from her cold, smiled back and thanked her. She was starving, and before the girl was out the door, she began attacking her food with gusto.

JC had seen the girl glance at the paper and looked at the front page, which displayed a full-color picture of Greta during her interview with Spiers. The headline read:

Greta, the 1,000-Year-Old Witch

JC turned on the television and was amazed to see a reporter from Fox News on the steps of the hospital. He pulled back the drapes and could see a throng of TV trucks in the street below. He could even pick out the reporter, who wore a bright red coat as she was giving her live report. There was a police cordon holding back a crowd, and he could see a large banner being held up that said "Greta, we love you. Get well soon."

JC had switched off his Blackberry the night before, so it would not awake Greta. When he switched it back on, he saw he had hundreds of unread messages and a string of missed calls and voicemails.

The hospital was well used to fending off hordes of media. They had a well-practiced procedure for keeping patients from being bothered. JC saw that many of the missed calls had been from their agent, Larry Spindler. He hit Redial, and Larry answered on the second ring.

"JC, thank God, how is Greta?"

"Greta is fine, she is just recovering from a heavy cold."

"Good, I mean, I'm glad she is recovering. We got a big story here, JC."

"Larry, I know, I can see the press outside the hospital. You gotta get us out."

"Relax, JC, I got it all planned. Here is what we are going to do. I am going to create a distraction and then send a car in the back way. There is an underground exit at the back that comes out in the next block. Can you be ready in an hour?"

JC looked up as Greta was munching through her eggs Benedict, oblivious of any of the press activity outside. Instead of using a knife and fork, she had picked up the half-bun and was eating the ham and poached egg like a sandwich, with small, bird-like bites. At the same time, she was flicking through the pages of *Vogue*, looking at the fashions. She looked innocent and childlike in the large hospital bed. JC's heart went out to her in that moment, and his affection for her spilled over into total dedication. He wanted to love and protect her forever. He was silent in his thoughts, and Larry's voice came over the Blackberry he still held to his ear: "Is an hour good, JC? Are you still there?"

"Larry, better make it ninety minutes."

As a distraction, Larry arranged for another of his clients to exit through the front door of the hospital. His other client was the son of a Hollywood film star, who had checked himself into rehab because his first solo rock album had flopped. *Rolling Stone* magazine had described the album as "total unabashed garbage, without a single lyric or bar of music worthy of mention." Larry privately agreed with the review, but he had sent the young man specific instructions on what to do. He exited the front door of the hospital to a flurry of flash photography, wearing sunglasses, a black tee shirt with "GARBAGE" written on it, in reference to the *Rolling Stone* review. There was a hastily applied bandage to his wrist, as if he had tried to cut it with a razor blade. In fact, he had not cut himself at all, but the hospital agreed to comply. They sent a bill for their trouble to Larry, whose office added 25 percent markup, and the film star paid it without question.

JC helped Greta into the back of a nondescript delivery van, holding her hand as they drove out of the back entrance of the hospital.

To JC's surprise, Greta was never sick again, for the rest of her life.

Greta knew both how to stand out in a crowd and how to hide in one. She pulled her dark hood over her head to hide her hair and ran with the loping stride of a young boy. To the casual observer, she looked like an average teenager in a hoodie. She moved with purpose toward the aura she sensed from the two sisters she had seen at the fair. She also felt that they were welcoming her to them (well, at least one of them was).

As she loped along, she observed this strange new world around her. In her own mind, she had accepted the theory of the tall stranger called Keith.

She had not told him, but she suspected that the silver man had performed the miracle that had brought them to a different time. It also explained to her why she could not feel the aura of her sisters from the past. This made her sad, because if all this were true, they were long dead. Her sisters were the only family she had ever known.

She couldn't remember her childhood as such. As long as she could remember, she had been surviving. She didn't know if her mother and father were alive; well, they certainly wouldn't be now. She had no memory of them. Her earliest recollection was of growing up with her sisters in a hamlet where the witches lived. She remembered nights of terror, where armed men came into hamlet with flaming torches, setting the huts alight. She had run for her life, learning to survive in the woods on her wits and her cunning. She had never trusted men but knew that one day, she would meet a special man she could rely on. In her visualization of this man, she could not see his face, but she knew he would be tall and strong. She had wondered at first if it was the tall stranger Keith, but her instincts told her that it wasn't him.

Now she took in her new surroundings. Horseless carriages sped along the hard, straight roads. They produced the burnt smell she had first become aware of. There were strange signs in bright colors with symbols on them. The signs were mounted on sturdy metal posts and positioned so the people in the horseless carriages could read them. Some were just colored shapes, some had writing on them, but they made no sense: "Dual carriageway," "30 KPH Limit," and "Do not litter."

Other signs showed her the direction of towns. She was walking toward Hartley Wintney and turned toward Fleet. From her conversation with Keith, she knew these were the modern names for Hertleye Wynteneye and La Fete. She realized that the new sisters must live in Fleet, because she was sensing them from that direction.

She could also sense the strong energy lines, which she had followed to their crossing point the night before she had followed the king on his hunting trip. Greta thought it no coincidence that these new sisters would live close to the crossing point.

Whenever she could, she traveled in a straight line, toward the new sisters' aura. But sometimes, she found her way blocked by fences or other barriers. She had to double back several times and walk along the road.

She tried to keep as far back as she could, because the noise of the horseless carriages was deafening and the burnt smell they emitted, horrible.

Fleet Railway Station, Late Sunday Evening, March 4, 2012

Carol's train went from London Waterloo to Basingstoke. It stopped at Clapham Junction, Surbiton, Woking, Brookwood, and Farnborough before reaching Fleet, her station. She was thirty-five and divorced; her mother was at home, looking after the kids. They would all be asleep by the time she got home.

She wore a nondescript coat and hat, not the latest fashion but passable. It was designed to not draw attention. She hid her long auburn hair under a plain scarf and wore flat shoes. In her bag, she had her high-heel stilettos, not uncommon amongst city girls. You saw many walking to work in flat shoes or trainers these days, changing into their work shoes at the office. Of course, Carol's reason was a little different. She was going to meet a regular client on this Sunday night. He was a Middle East businessman, she assumed; he always paid cash. Before she arrived at his hotel room, she always changed into her stilettos.

Her mother thought she worked as a legal secretary in London. This was what she had done before she was made redundant. She explained she had to work at nights and weekends, when urgent documents needed to be prepared. The pay was good, she said: double-time on Sundays. Of course, her pay as an escort was much better than that of a legal secretary, even at double-time. The agency she used advertised her as an "experienced, mature legal secretary"; they claimed she would accompany male clients to dinner or the theatre, but they often wanted more, and for this they paid extra.

The legal secretary ruse worked with her mother, so she could dress to both please her clients and keep the façade with her mother that she had a legitimate job. She was looking forward to getting home, having a hot bath, and cleaning his smell off her.

The night was unseasonably warm as the train began its final run into Fleet station. As it began to slow, it passed a wooded area by the lake adjacent to the station, and she could see what she thought was a small fire in the woods. Unusual, she thought.

Fleet station was long and narrow, with a large car park for commuters adjacent to the track. The station entrance was at one end of the platform, at the front of her train. The regulars to Fleet always walked up the train to disembark, so there were several clustered around the doors as the train pulled into the station, keen to get home. Some had obviously been to the theatre or West End in London; they seemed a little drunk but good natured.

The station car park filled up in the morning from the end near the entrance backwards, with the early commuters taking the prime parking spaces close to the entrance. As it was a Sunday, the car park wasn't full, but by the time Carol had arrived, late afternoon, the only parking bays available were in the back. To reach her car, she now had to walk back along the track. The car park was dimly lit, probably to save money or reduce carbon emissions, she thought.

As Carol walked through the car park, the half dozen or so commuters who had also disembarked got into their respective cars and drove off. By the time she was halfway to her car, she was alone. The car park's dim lighting made her feel uncomfortably vulnerable as she approached her car. She pressed the unlock button on her remote, and her car's lights came on, giving her comfort and renewed purpose. She quickened her pace along the rows of neatly parked cars.

Unexpectedly, she saw movement in the next line of cars. She gasped in disbelief. It was a horse and rider, coming directly toward her. Immediately, she realized that the rider would reach her before she got to her car. There was something about the deliberate movement toward her that made her feel uneasy. She quickened her pace and then began to run.

She heard the rider shout, "Come 'ere, wench," and she felt hands grab the back of her coat and pull her over the horse, expertly holding her down. Her alarm turned to panic, but she was held firmly. It all happened so quickly that she was unable to protest or cry out. She was not sure that anyone would be around to help her anyway.

But as the she felt the horse quicken its pace and canter toward the woods, she regained some of her composure, found her voice, and began to scream and shout. The horseman, without breaking stride, deftly slapped her across the face. She was so shocked she fell silent, clutching her jaw, tears of fear and pain swelling in her eyes.

Rupert thought, *This one has spirit; the king will be pleased.*

Rutherford Appleton Laboratory, Monday, March 5, 2012

At the Rutherford Appleton Laboratory, where Keith Maxwell worked, there was a crisis meeting going on.

The lab had been besieged by the media since the news of Keith's disappearance and the murders in Hampshire. It was normally a sleepy backwater of academic efficiency, and this level of press interest was unprecedented. For this reason, John Bennington, the lab director, had summoned Professor Helen Collins, Keith's supervisor, and Dr. David Thomas, the head of marketing communications, to his office.

Helen was on the phone to Zurich, explaining that Keith was unable to attend the conference today and present his paper on gamma particles. She apologized once again, citing circumstances beyond their control, and hung up.

There was a large conference table in Professor Bennington's spacious office, and spread out on the table were copies of that morning's papers and the previous day's Sunday editions. There were also printouts from the leading on-line news sites that carried the story, including CNN and Huffington Post.

All featured the Keith Maxwell disappearance and details of the terrible murders in Hampshire, plus the shooting of the two police officers. Thomas picked up a copy of the *Daily Mail* and read the headline:

Eminent Scientist Wanted in Murder Hunt

Thomas was middle aged with dyed black hair and a fake tan. His skin had an orange tinge. He had a slight New Zealand accent, although he had lived in the UK for fifteen years. He began to read the story out loud:

> *Police are searching for eminent space scientist Dr. Keith Maxwell from the Rutherford Appleton Laboratory near Oxford. Dr. Maxwell is wanted in connection with the murder of two women found on common land near his home in Hampshire.*

As Helen looked over his shoulder as he read, she got a whiff of his cheap cologne; she also noticed the photograph of Keith in a white lab coat, smiling at the camera. It had been downloaded from the publicity section of the lab's own website, which contained biographies of the lab's leading scientists and researchers.

Thomas looked up from the newspaper and said, "This is typical of what is being said. I have arranged a press conference for later this morning; the journalists are gathering already."

He turned to Professor Bennington, a political appointee not used to these types of media gatherings. Helen knew he was good at running the science side of the lab, but he was out of his depth when it came to nonacademic matters. He was already sweating nervously. Discreetly, Thomas asked if he would like him to handle the press conference, knowing Bennington would be way out of his comfort zone. Unsurprisingly, and with great relief, the lab director agreed and promptly left the office.

While the exchange was going on, Helen read the second article, which was from the website of the *Weekly World News*:

NASA Scientist Beamed Up by Aliens

> *Police in Europe are mystified by a report of a scientist with close connections to NASA being beamed up by aliens. The incident happened in a remote part of southern England where alien activity had been reported many times, and not far from the site of the mysterious Stonehenge. Rumors are that a large hole was found nearby.*

Thomas turned to Helen and said, "We had better get ready. I have prepared a statement for you to read out." He handed her a single sheet of A4 paper.

As Helen read it, she was surprised that Thomas wanted her on the platform. He was well known for hogging the limelight for himself. Not usually vain, Helen now went through the checklist of clothes, hair, and makeup. She realized she would need some time to get ready.

Bennington's office was on the top of a four-story building, the tallest building on the site. As Helen looked out of the office window, she had a good view of the whole complex, which occupied an area of more than a square mile. From this position, it looked like a bit like a university campus, but when you looked closely, there were some unusually shaped buildings that looked more like industrial complexes. Some had smoke or steam coming from them. Helen saw Bennington hurrying across a courtyard to the Diamond Light Source building, which looked like a giant silver doughnut. She guessed he was heading for refuge in the locked building, so as to get away from the limelight.

She was torn from her thoughts by a long line of vehicles moving along the main road into the site. The convoy was being led by one of the lab's Land Rovers, which had a blue light flashing on the roof. The other vehicles had the names of the various press, TV, and radio stations on their sides. Some trucks had folded satellite dishes on their roofs. The trucks and cars parked in a line outside the largest building on the site, which housed the staff canteen. There was frantic activity as technicians emerged from the vehicles and began unloading equipment, cables, lights, and camera equipment.

She had never seen so much press activity, and she felt the butterflies of nervousness in her stomach. She got a whiff of cheap cologne again as David came and stood next to her to watch the press convoy.

He said, "Looks like we are in for a good turnout."

She saw he was smiling, obviously relishing the prospect of this press conference.

She found that disgusting and left the office to finish getting ready.

Helen's previous experience of press conferences at the lab were sedate affairs, where frankly it was a struggle to fill a small room. By contrast, today was a media zoo. More than a hundred journalists and reporters had arrived. David had told her that both Sky News and the BBC were relaying the press conference live, and there were also live feeds on the Internet.

To accommodate everyone, they held the conference in the largest room on the site: the staff restaurant. The rows of neatly aligned dining tables had been moved against the walls, and a table at the front held placards for Helen and Thomas.

In front of the table was a bank of microphones, some with the logos of the various news and media companies attached. Extra lights had been set up, so the room was hot. Canteen staff and a crowd of curious lab workers were seated at the back of the room to watch the spectacle. The top table had been carefully placed so that the background displayed the circular x-ray building, which looked a bit like a flying saucer. Helen realized that David had done this deliberately to maximize the publicity. She was a little overwhelmed by it all.

A few minutes after the scheduled time, David led Helen up to the top table. He seated her with elaborate courtesy, pulling her chair out for her to signify to the watching journalists that this was an important person. Helen noticed that he had changed into a fresh suit and had applied a little makeup. She'd had little time to do much to her appearance, only brushing her hair and applying some lipstick. She felt underdressed and underprepared.

David brought the room to attention by tapping the microphone and saying, "Ladies and gentlemen, ladies and gentlemen, may I have your attention? Thank you."

The room fell silent as a TV producer wearing a set of headphones approached the top table, counted down from ten, and then pointed at David deliberately, signifying that they were live and he should begin. On cue, David began reading a prepared statement:

"Ladies and gentlemen, welcome to the Rutherford Appleton Laboratory. My name is Dr. David Thomas, and I am head of communications here at the lab. I regret that I have to welcome you here under such sad circumstances, because of the disappearance of one of our most eminent and respected scientists, Dr. Keith Maxwell.

"With me today is Dr. Maxwell's supervisor, Professor Helen Collins. Professor Collins will read a short statement before we open up the floor for questions.

"Professor Collins, over to you."

There was some coughing and shuffling around as cameras and microphones were repositioned on Helen. She spoke slowly, nervously, reading from the prepared statement:

"I have had the pleasure of supervising Dr. Maxwell in his work at the Rutherford Appleton Laboratory for the last three years. He has published over 180 scientific papers on sensing technologies and is named on fourteen patents that the lab has produced. He has worked at the lab since 1998 and is a highly respected member of staff.

"Dr. Maxwell's work on deep space radiation is respected the world over, and we hope that he will be able to return to work soon. Thank you."

There was a moment's silence, and then David stood and said, "We'll take your questions now."

A reporter in the front row caught David's attention. She stood and said, "Cathy Murphy, *Daily Chronicle*. Is it true that Dr. Maxwell was looking for aliens?"

The place descended into chaos.

Maryland, USA

Near the National Security Agency (NSA) headquarters at Fort Meade, Maryland, the lights had been on all night in the nondescript office a few miles from the base. Three people in the room watched the press conference from the Rutherford Appleton Laboratory on a live Internet feed. The large HD screen clearly showed the despair on the British PR man's face. As the press conference descended into chaos, the sweat dripped down his face and smeared the poorly applied makeup into his dyed hair.

Dr. Ali Palaszwaski, a NASA scientist and one of Keith's collaborators, was one of those watching the broadcast. A private jet had flown him from Florida to Fort Meade as soon as the news broke. His father was Russian, his mother Egyptian, and in adulthood, he had become a short, stocky man with a balding pate. His dark eyes darted left and right incessantly as he spoke. The words tumbled out of him as if his brain was racing ahead of his ability to communicate.

Also flown in some eight hours ago was Dr. Mary Morrell, a scientist from NASA's Marshall Space Flight Center in Huntsville, Alabama. Mary was a specialist in deep space particles. She was of African-Caribbean descent and was one of the fattest people Ali had ever met, and he had met some large people. The table in front of them was strewn with empty coffee cups, soda cans, and food wrappers. They had been in the room since lunch the previous day. Mary was eating from a large bag of potato chips as she watched the screen.

The high-definition screen showed tears on Professor Collins's face; she was now sitting in her chair, weeping openly. The PR man with the obviously fake tan was trying to bring control to the situation, asking if there were any questions he could answer that did not involve aliens.

"This is utter chaos," Ali said, pointing at the screen and looking at the man seated at the head of the conference table.

This was Admiral Gerald Smythe, a tall, good-looking man with a dark suit and crisp white shirt. His hair was short, befitting a military man, and the dark stubble of his beard showed through his tanned skin.

"I agree," Smythe said. "We are learning nothing here." He pressed a button on a remote control to switch off the screen.

He rose and poured himself a cup of ice water. He removed his jacket, placed it carefully over the back of a vacant chair, and then looked at each of them in turn. Mary put down her half-eaten bag of potato chips and wiped her chubby hands on a paper napkin. Ali sat straighter in his chair. When the admiral looked at you with those clear blue eyes, you knew it was time to listen; it wasn't a good time to eat potato chips.

Ali could see by looking at the two digital clocks on the wall that it was 11:01 in the UK, site of the press conference, and 6:01 there in Fort Meade. The room they were in had no external windows, so it was difficult to sense if it was day or night. The admiral looked surprisingly cool and dignified, despite being awake all night. Ali felt tired. He looked across the table at Mary and saw that her face was drawn with fatigue. Ali thought that he probably looked like that as well. Ali knew the admiral had to brief the NSA director at eight o'clock, and he wanted to clarify what he was going to say to him before they stopped for the night.

Smythe put his cup down on the table on a precisely arranged paper napkin and looked at his notes.

He said, "Let's go over what we know so far, and then I need to meet the NSA director. We know there was some concentrated activity of interstellar particles at the exact point and time in the UK where Dr. Keith Maxwell apparently disappeared on Saturday. There is no indication that this was a result of any manmade activity."

He paused to look up at each of the scientists. Ali nodded his assent vehemently and was relieved that Mary also nodded her agreement. Ali hoped that Mary would not say anything to disagree with the admiral and thereby delay their break; he needed a shower, a hot breakfast, and some sleep. Smythe looked down at his notes once again and continued to read:

"We know that this spot was one of seventeen locations where we had previously recorded this interstellar particle activity, but this event was at a higher reading than previously recorded."

Ali saw Mary wince at the scientific oversimplification of this statement and look at him for moral support. Ali shrugged, caught in a dilemma between wanting to correct the statement and his desire for some sleep. His gesture, he realized, was a coward's way out, a neutral gesture, so Mary could decide if she wanted to correct it or not.

The admiral noticed the look passing between the scientists and asked, "Mary, do you have a concern with that statement?"

"Well, it's sort of, kinda correct, Adm'ral," she said in her heavily accented Alabama drawl. "It was a higher reading in some areas of the spectrum but not in others. All we really know is the reading was different from the previous ones. What I would really like to do is run the data through the supercomputers again and set some new parameters."

The admiral looked at Ali, prompting him to speak.

Ali said, somewhat reluctantly, "Mary's point is that the higher reading may not mean anything; it could be explained by other variables, so we really need to look at all the spectrums to see if the instruments failed or something else is the cause."

Smythe stood up and stretched his hand out. Ali stopped speaking in midsentence.

"Okay," the admiral said. "Enough. Go get some rest, I'll meet you back here at two o'clock." He put on his jacket and walked out.

Mary and Ali looked at each other in dismay. Ali was hoping go home to Florida; he didn't want another day with the admiral. However, before he could say anything to Mary, there was a knock on the door, and four serious-looking Marines filed in. One said, "We are here to escort you to your quarters."

At two o'clock, the same Marines escorted the NASA scientists back to the conference room. The admiral was already seated, watching a recording of a BBC news bulletin. The broadcast featured live video of the site where Keith Maxwell had disappeared and showed a large police operation in full swing.

The conference room had been cleared of last night's debris. When he saw the trolley laid out with fresh food and drinks, Ali's first thought was, *Oh no, this is going to be another long session.* There was freshly brewed coffee, sodas, and food laid out neatly. Mary picked up a bag of potato chips and two large sandwiches before sitting back in the same seat she had vacated earlier in the day. Ali took a Diet Coke and a sandwich and also returned to his same seat.

Ali noticed that the admiral looked as smart as ever; he had on a crisp white shirt and tie and another very smart business suit. Ali had found new underwear and a shirt in his size in the room where they had stayed in the Fort Meade complex. The room had no telephone or Internet connection, and his mobile phone was taken from him when he arrived at the building yesterday, so he had not been able to call his wife. He had chatted to Mary on the short walk over to the conference room, and he knew she had not been able to call home either.

Ali was trying to think of a discreet way of addressing the issue because the admiral did not do small talk, but then Smythe said, "I expect you would like to call home; here are your mobile phones."

He handed a phone to each scientist. The admiral continued, "The NSA director has asked me to pass on his sincere thanks for your help and support. There are a number of matters he has asked me to work through with you this afternoon. I have arranged for your flight home this evening at six o'clock. Now please go make your calls."

Ali and Mary thanked him and went into the corridor to call home. As they spoke, their calls were recorded by specialist equipment in a building a few miles away.

When they came back into the conference room, Smythe explained that while they had been resting, the NSA had run the data again through its supercomputers.

He handed Ali a laptop and gave a pile of printouts to Mary, saying, "I will leave you to look over the results and come back later for a report."

What was immediately apparent to Ali was that these reports were different from the ones they had seen yesterday. In fact, the previous set had been run on both NASA's supercomputers and supercomputers at the Fraunhofer Institute in Germany.

Unknown to the scientists, the NSA director had raised the security status of this enquiry, and this new data was run only on the NSA computers. The computers were not necessarily better; it was just that the

NSA didn't want the results known by people at NASA or in Germany. In fact, if you asked the admiral privately who he trusted the most, he would probably say the Germans.

Ali immediately saw a pattern in the new data, something that had not been apparent before.

"Mary, look," he said excitedly. "See that spike? Looks as if the gamma particles went off the scale. But there's no real change in the other spectrums."

She looked up from the printout that she had been reading as Ali pointed at the graph on the laptop screen.

"Mmm," she said, tapping the printout with a finger greasy from her potato chips, "but what is strange is there has been no activity from the site since; the other sites seem to be showing similar activity as before."

The silver man also noticed the loss of data from the sensor. The other sensors appeared to be working as normal. Sensor failures were rare; they had been perfected over the millennia. The half-life of the radioactive battery was not an issue, so he decided to investigate. Although the destruction capsule had been launched, it would be easy for him to visit the planet before they were activated. He was also curious to see how these life forms had developed.

He set the coordinates, and his craft accelerated toward the distant blue plant, the third one in from the small star.

Bend, Oregon

The admiral assembled a SWAT team of Marines led by a colonel he trusted totally. Their job was to investigate the sixteen sites identified by the NASA scientists. Only one was within the United States, in a remote part of Oregon, about fifteen miles south of the town of Bend.

The SWAT team set off for the site, which was well hidden from the nearest highway. They spent two days and nights, working around the clock under spotlights, digging a hole thirty feet deep and just as wide, on the exact coordinates they had been given. The ground was dug with their heavy equipment, and all the dirt and rocks were sorted and analyzed.

There were no Geiger counter readings of any significance. The Marines were not in the loop and were just ordered to dig. They didn't know what they were looking for. The soldiers thought their superiors had really lost their minds this time, asking them to dig a hole, run the dirt through a sieve, and then fill the hole back in again. The bored and bewildered Marines found nothing, filled in the hole, and left.

While they were on their way to the second site in Argentina, the NASA scientists detected another blip in the data from the site in Oregon. The SWAT team was ordered to turn their transport planes around and head back. They dug up the same earth again but still found nothing, even with the admiral supervising the operation himself. The Marines doing the digging were in complete disbelief, but the big-shot officers had arrived, so they did what good soldiers did: followed orders. They filled in the hole again and headed to Argentina. The data blip resumed once more from the site in Oregon after the team left for South America. When they arrived in Argentina, they dug a similar hole but again found nothing.

But now the smart people at Fort Meade began to see a pattern. While they were digging, there was no blip; when they stopped digging, the blip returned. However, bored and bewildered soldiers with mobile Internet connections usually find something to do, and this team was no exception. A few days later, the headline in the *Weekly World News* was:

US Marines Find Alien Spaceship

> *A crack unit of US Marines has been drafted to recover the remains of an alien spaceship that crash landed in Bend, Oregon. The US military returned twice to the remote site. A military spokesman denied the Marines were looking for aliens, saying they were on a routine training exercise.*

The sensors had a stealth mode to avoid detection that was invoked automatically by activity around them. During his journey to the planet, the silver man noted that this mode had been invoked twice in a short period of time. In stealth mode, the sensors shrank to the size of a pebble and were indistinguishable from the soil around them. The sensors could remain that way indefinitely, but at random intervals, they would poll their surroundings to see if it was safe to resume normal operations. In their stealth mode form, the sensors were virtually undetectable.

The moment Henry fell to the ground, fatally wounded, Rupert's instinct was to protect the king. Men-at-arms were expendable; it was their duty to protect the sovereign at all costs.

He didn't know what the weapon was that had killed the finest bowman in England so easily, but he also knew that his sword was ineffective against it. The three men ran toward the horses. He used his body as a human shield, positioning himself between that fearsome weapon and the king. Keith had no choice but to follow. Even in their haste, Rupert still held onto his belt.

The crowds parted as they rushed away.

Rupert was a fearsome site, brandishing his sword. It was impossible for the police to fire, for fear of hitting innocent bystanders. Besides, their priority was their dead and wounded colleagues.

When they reached the horses, without warning, Rupert hit Keith another glancing blow on the temple, which knocked him out cold. He was a strong man and picked up Keith's inert body, laying it like a sack of potatoes across his horse. The king and Rupert rode off, Rupert pulling both the horse carrying Keith and a spare horse behind him. The king also led a spare horse. Horses were valuable; you didn't leave them behind, even in a life-and-death situation.

They quickly found cover in the woods, where nobody could creep up on them unnoticed. Rupert knew how to hide in a wood; he had hidden the king many times.

Rupert knew that his priority was to give the king's wounds time to heal; they also needed to find food and water. He considered killing the tall stranger when he woke, but he thought it a good idea to question him first.

He made the thicket as comfortable for the king as he could. They would rest here until nightfall.

Detective Inspector Amit Chakrabarti realized that this case had now escalated beyond his pay-grade. He was relieved when the Hampshire chief constable said he would be taking personal charge of it. The operation now shifted into another gear, and a major incident room was set up at Blackbushe Airfield.

A police helicopter arrived and began a systematic search of the area, using infrared, heat-seeking cameras. These could detect bodies hiding in the woods. Simultaneously, police dog handlers began to search the area. Help was requested from the army. The Royal Engineers had a base nearby at Minley, and they provided six powerful Land Rovers with searchlights.

This took some hours to organize. As it grew dark, the Land Rovers flipped on their searchlights, and the diesel engines roared like lions as the drivers navigated the soft ground. They couldn't have advertised their position better if they tried.

Rupert led the king and the horses through the woods, away from the noise and lights of the horseless carriages. He was unconcerned about the tall stranger; he was beginning to wake up but was still lying across the back of the horse. If he fell off, he no longer cared.

As the night drew on, the noise from the horseless cars subsided. They had water, they had rested, but they were still hungry. They needed food. Rupert had not seen any real game; he decided to have the tall stranger find them some more food.

They came to another one of those paved roads, and across it was a small building that looked similar to the one where Keith had gotten the hot dogs that morning. In fact, it was a late-night kebab van. There was a glorious smell of cooking coming from it, and Rupert's stomach rumbled.

He halted the horses beyond the tree line besides the road. There was little traffic at this time of night. He shook Keith and helped him to his feet. While the king waited, he grabbed Keith's belt and was about to march him across the road to the van, as he did before, but Keith resisted, explaining that he had no money.

Rupert just marched Keith across the deserted road with even more gusto. The kebab van owners grew suspicious when they spotted the two men walking up to the van. They assumed they were drunks because they staggered, trying to hold on to each other. Drunks on foot usually meant trouble; cars were preferable. Under the counter, they kept a couple of baseball bats for such occasions.

As Rupert and Keith approached, one called out, "How can we help, lads?"

Keith replied, "Three kebabs please."

"Okay, that will be £15."

Neither of the kebab stall holders had moved toward preparing the food; they wanted to be sure that these two were going to pay first. Also, asking for three kebabs when there were only two of them was a little odd.

Keith didn't know what to do next, but Rupert did. He drew his sword and, in a practiced motion, held it against the cheek of one of the cooks. There was little room on the raised dais of the van, and the cook was forced back against the far wall of kitchen cabinets.

The two cooks were brothers, originally from Turkey. The older brother, who was pinned against the wall by the sword, said, "Steady on, mate, it's only a kebab." He raised his hands in mock surrender.

Rupert said, "Give me the food, or I'll run you through." There was no mistaking the malice in his voice.

The younger brother was now spurred into action. He nervously cut the meat and filled the pita bread with salad. He said unnecessarily, "Chili sauce?"

Not knowing what he meant, Rupert looked at Keith, who said, "No thanks, just give us three Diet Cokes." Keith felt terribly guilty stealing food and drink from the two men, but he was as hungry as Rupert. As Rupert marched him away, Keith turned back toward the brothers and shouted an apology, promising to come back and repay them later.

After returning to the king, Rupert put the food and drinks in his saddlebag, and they trotted the horses deeper into the forest to find cover, so they could stop and eat. Keith thought about running, but Rupert would just ride him down. He hadn't ridden a horse since he was a boy but somehow managed to mount up and follow Rupert and the king. Good job he did, because as he caught up with them, Rupert was about to stab the can of Coke with his dagger. Keith pulled the tabs to open their cans. They drank and coughed immediately; they had never drunk fizzy drinks before.

Although there were frequent police vehicles on the road as part of the murder enquiry, the two Turkish brothers didn't report the incident. Even though some of the police officers frequented the kebab van, they wanted no trouble from the law; their immigration papers were not exactly in order.

After they had eaten, the three horsemen moved on and presently came to Fleet Pond, which is near the railway station. It was a Sunday night, and there was very little traffic about. They set up a camp where there was good grazing for the horses. Keith was no longer tied up and could have run away, but he knew it was pointless. Rupert would catch him, knock him unconscious, or worst still run him through with his sword.

Besides, he was becoming fascinated by their behavior. Were they really from a different time? Could that be possible? He slept as best he could. It was cold out in the open. He wanted to call his mother to let her know he was all right, but he had left his cell phone behind.

Rupert left the camp on foot, but the king was awake. Keith figured he was probably as adept with his sword as Rupert. He didn't know where Rupert went, but he was gone for half an hour or so.

He came back, leading a woman at knife point and grinning luridly at the king.

To Keith's horror, they began to assault her, but he was too scared to interfere. He felt ashamed and disgusted as Rupert knocked the woman to the ground and restrained her while the king ripped away her clothes and got on top of her. When he was done, Rupert also raped her, but by this time, her cries had become a whimper, and she just lay on the ground, unresisting, while Rupert raped her.

Eventually, after their lust was sated, they let the woman up, and she ran away, sobbing, her clothes in disarray. The king lay on the ground and began to snore, while Rupert sat against a tree, sharpening his dagger. His look dared Keith to try and run.

Less than a mile away, Ellen shot up in bed. She had sensed the girl's distress when she was captured by Rupert. Then the distress calmed. Ellen also sensed someone else close by, a special man, but for Carla's sake, she ignored these feelings. Soon, she fell back to sleep.

By first light on Monday morning, it was clear to the Hampshire Police chief constable that the search was going nowhere. He had scheduled a press conference and needed some results. He needed help.

Using the secure phone in his chauffeur-driven car on the way to Blackbushe Airfield, he called the personal assistant to the chief constable of the Metropolitan Police. She in turn used a secure line to call the Special Air Services (or SAS) regiment's headquarters in Hereford, near the Welsh border.

A little after noon, four of the British military's elite SAS men disembarked from their helicopter at Blackbushe. The helicopter did not switch off its engines; it immediately took off back to Hereford. The four men were dressed in dark military combat uniforms and carried large backpacks.

The press photographers camped along the perimeter fence of the airfield took copious pictures. Sky and BBC News showed the helicopter landing live. Speculation was rife.

The four SAS men were from a special search and destroy (S&D) unit. They had just returned from Somalia, where they had caught a gang of pirates who were responsible for millions of dollars of losses to shipping companies. The pirates used high-speed boats to attack the slow-moving cargo ships. They boarded them at sea and held the crews at gunpoint, often planting explosives they could detonate by remote control.

The pirates knew that these valuable cargoes needed to be delivered on time, and the shipping companies would pay large ransoms to avoid delay.

One gang had hijacked a supertanker full of compressed natural gas from Oman, demanding a huge ransom. The sultan of Oman had been educated at Cambridge University in the UK and then attended the military training academy at Sandhurst. The Royal Navy had a forward operating base (FOB) in Oman, and the senior naval officer in charge of the base had been a friend of the sultan when he was at Cambridge.

The Royal Navy dispatched a Type 45 destroyer to the area, along with a nuclear submarine. They tracked the pirates from over the horizon and under the sea. By arrangement, the Oman authorities paid the ransom.

The SAS S&D unit went ashore from the destroyer and tracked the gang to a remote farm house. They planted a radio targeting device on one of the buildings. The destroyer launched a missile from its position in international waters. The explosion killed the entire gang.

The incident was never reported, but soon after, the Oman Navy placed a £4 billion order for four Type 45 destroyers.

When the four SAS men got out of the helicopter, the chief constable met them and shook their hands. He could tell by their eyes that these men were all trained killers. He had arrested many men during his time as a policeman, and in some of the more hardened criminals, he saw the same look.

The leader of the unit was a black man called Soji (not his real name). He wore no insignia of rank, but his body language said he was in command.

They drank tea from paper cups, as they looked at a large-scale map of the area that had been pinned to a table; the chief briefed the SAS men on everything he knew.

After some discussion, Soji suggested that the chief constable remove his people from the area and block access to the common.

The common was a public right of way, and many people walked their dogs or rode horses in the area. The chief constable agreed to restrict access on the main pathways in the common.

The SAS men then asked to be taken to the spot where the three horsemen had mounted up and ridden away the previous day.

One of the men in the team began to search the area. He came back to the group and spoke briefly to the leader, who walked over to the chief constable and explained what was going on.

"Chief Constable, my colleague here is a specialist tracker. He believes we can follow the trail of the horses. Is there somewhere we can stow some of our gear?"

In fact, the tracker was a Maasai tribesman from Tanzania. He was a legend in the SAS. The people in Hereford boasted that he could find a single grain of sand on a beach. Nobody could pronounce the tracker's Tanzanian name, so he was known as Trev, which was short for Trevor the Tracker.

Trev had tracked the pirate gang in Somalia and would now track the horsemen on Hazeley Common.

After the SAS team ate a meal in the police canteen, they stowed their equipment and headed out at a fast walk, with Trev moving ahead of the rest of the team, like a sniffer dog.

After about an hour, they came to the camp in the woods. The modern junk food had obviously played havoc with the king's and Rupert's stomachs, and they found the evidence. Keith, on the other hand, was so tense, he had not been able to go since his capture.

What impressed Trev was that this group was clearly skilled in the art of concealment. They doubled back occasionally to check if they were being followed. They walked on hard ground, not soft, and were careful not to break branches. They moved their horses so the grazing was not obvious. They walked in single file to confuse anyone following.

They found more empty fast food containers and drinks cans. Trev began to follow the trail again.

By the time the silver man reached the planet, three more of the sensors had experienced stealth activity. He did not go to the site where he had put the three men on horses, and the woman who tried to attack him, into molecular stagnation. Since then, his instruments told him, the planet had completed a thousand orbits around the small star.

Instead, he went to the site where the sensor had invoked its stealth mode twice in a short period of time. This was because his scan of the planet had shown that this site was free of activity, while the other site was not.

The silver man landed his craft and set it up to refuel from a large water supply nearby. He saw immediately that the ground on the site had been disturbed, so he retrieved the sensor using an extendable probe he had carried from the craft.

On his arrival, the silver man was taken aback by just how fast these life forms had developed. He had sensed orbiting spacecraft, and there were many vehicles capable of flight. The volume of electronic communications was impressive. Of course, they were still a long way from interstellar space travel and could not yet communicate beyond their galaxy. It was a shame that the destruction was necessary; it would be interesting to see how far they would develop. His craft needed a little more time to refuel, so he decided to move toward the nearest town and observe more. He would then travel to the other sensor sites.

However, he would not take too long. There was still plenty of time before the destruction capsules arrived, but there was another reason to hurry. He was due to be reborn soon and didn't want to get caught on the planet again when it happened. He needed somewhere more remote. The rebirth process regenerated his body tissues. It was a process his people had evolved over the millennia. They were not immortal; one day, he would no longer be able to be reborn. Regenerating their body tissues allowed them to travel the vast distances across the cosmos. The rebirth process had lasted twenty revolutions of the planet's star, or twenty Earth years. This was a slow rebirth; his next rebirth would be quicker, but he wanted to be away from the planet before it happened.

The techs at Fort Meade had run a number of computer simulations about the origins and threats of the sensors: they concluded that they may be able to entice whoever planted the sensors to return. While the US military conducted an elaborate military exercise near the other sensor sites to create a distraction, the admiral was waiting in Oregon. In fact, he was with three other men: his trusted Marine colonel and two hand-picked Navy SEALs.

This operation required the utmost discretion, and the NSA director was getting increasingly nervous about the leaks to the *Weekly World News*, so he ordered Admiral Smythe to lead it himself. The admiral did not understand the science, but the techs at Fort Meade had equipped them with some of the latest equipment for the job. They were camped under a tent lined with graphene, a new type of antidetection material, and they had blankets and clothing made of the same material. The admiral had been told that graphene was a special type of advanced carbon, really thin, and inside it, they were undetectable, invisible—or at least the techs claimed this. It was strange, because the blankets were ultra-thin and lightweight; you could see through them, and they appeared to offer no protection at all. The fine material resembled a spider web.

It was a little after three in the morning and still dark. The Navy SEAL on watch had woken Admiral Smythe when a silver object had appeared by the Deschutes River. From their elevated position above the dig site, they watched through night vision goggles as a silver-clad figure moved in their direction. The object near the river had not moved since it had first appeared. It was too distant from their position to see it clearly.

The silver figure drifted toward them. To say he walked was not quite right; his silver boots floated a few inches above the ground, but he did not actually move his feet. Their orders were clear. They were to observe any activity, capture any intruders if they could, but they were not destroy anyone. In fact, the Navy SEALs were equipped with a number of nonlethal weapons. In truth, the admiral had no idea what they were up against.

The silver man passed about a hundred yards from their positions, moving toward the town of Bend. The admiral gave a prearranged hand signal, and he began to follow the silver man with one of the Navy SEALs, while the colonel and the other SEAL began moving toward the silver object.

Once they had crawled over a low ridge and were out of sight of the silver man, the colonel stood up and wrapped his stealth blanket around his neck like cloak; the SEAL did likewise, and the two fit men covered the mile or so distance to the silver object in a little under eight minutes. The colonel grunted with satisfaction when he looked at his watch. Not bad for a forty-two-year-old man, carrying full kit and over sandy terrain.

About a hundred meters from the silver object, the colonel called a halt behind a rock. The two men stopped to catch their breath and check their weapons. The colonel took out his night vision binoculars and examined the object. It was clearly a vehicle or craft of some kind. It appeared to be taking in water from the river through a long tube. There was a blue glow to the spherical craft. It had several triangular-shaped struts protruding from it, like aircraft wings. It appeared to be floating slightly above the ground.

The colonel pointed at the Navy SEAL's helmet-cam, and both men pressed a small red button clipped to their jackets. This started their helmet-cams. The units were capable of transmitting live pictures back to Fort Meade, but the techs thought any form of communication could be detected, so there was a blackout on all comms. The recorders had limited memory and battery life, so they were to be used only when necessary. The colonel pointed left and then right; the SEAL nodded and set off to one side of the craft, while the colonel went the other way.

The purpose now was to observe the object and capture as much information as they could on the helmet-cams. The colonel had chosen the side where the tube went down to the river. He could hear the water being pumped along the pipe and then realized it was going both ways. Water was being taken in and then returned to the river. The pipe was transparent; as he got closer, he could see two halves to the pipe, separated by a membrane inside. He went closer so his helmet-cam could get a clear picture; he figured the techs would be interested in that.

As he leaned over to get a clear view, a gust of wind blew his stealth blanket against the pipe, just the slightest feather touch from the lightweight material. Then, faster than he could blink, the pipe retracted into the craft, which then vanished, leaving only a small impression in the dirt on the river bank, where the water pipe had been.

The colonel and the Navy SEAL now stared at each other over the empty space where the craft had been, cameras still rolling.

The silver man was almost to the small town when he received the signal from the craft. It had been touched by an advanced carbon material that it diagnosed was a weapon. It was hard to believe that these people had already developed advanced carbons, but he immediately turned back and returned to the craft's landing site as fast as he could go.

The admiral and the SEAL followed the silver man at a distance. They, too, had tied their stealth cloaks around their necks. Since they had no comms, they did not know that the craft had disappeared.

Suddenly, the silver man turned and raced back toward them. The admiral thought they must have been detected, and he gestured toward the ground. He dropped to the dirt and saw from the corner of his eye that the SEAL had also fallen to the ground, with his weapon ready. The silver man came directly toward their position. The ground on either side was flat, rocky terrain that offered no real cover, so he lay as flat as possible and covered himself with the protective cloak. As the silver man approached them, he pressed his Record button and tapped his helmet; the SEAL tapped his helmet, signifying he had understood the command to begin recording.

He lay as still as he could and tried to regulate his breathing. Now just a few meters away, it was clear that the silver man would collide with the Navy SEAL. It must have taken all his training and an incredible amount of self-control for the SEAL to remain completely still while the silver man came straight toward him.

Just then, they collided; the silver man literally bumped into him but did not respond aggressively. He just kept going as if he didn't see him. In fact, the silver man had not seen the Navy SEAL, because his camouflaged uniform blended in with the ground. But as the minor collision happened, the blanket was dislodged, and the graphene blanket brushed against a sensor in the silver man's suit.

The silver man stopped and looked down at the SEAL. But his surprise was not so much at the man lying on the ground, but the fact that this was confirmation that these people had developed advanced carbons; just then, everything went black.

The admiral had moved like a cat toward the silver man and pulled the trigger on his taser, sending 100,000 volts into the silver man's back; he collapsed to the ground.

"Now let's see who the fuck you are," Admiral Smythe said.

Headline in *Weekly World News*:

> *US Marines Capture Alien and Search for Missing Spaceship*
> *US Marines have set up a large operation in Bend, Oregon, to interrogate a captured alien and search for the alien's spaceship. A US military spokesman denied the Marines were looking for aliens, saying they were on a routine training exercise.*

At first light, the site near the river looked like a war zone. The Marines brought in an entire division and set up a forward operating base camp. The admiral had ordered the colonel to do whatever it took to find that craft.

Now some thirty hours since they had captured the silver man, the admiral was in his command tent by the river, talking on a secure satellite link to General Alexander, his direct superior.

"How the hell do these stories leak?" General Alexander asked.

"We've got a thousand people down here in Oregon, sir, and they all have Internet-activated cell phones," Admiral Smythe said.

"Good job nobody believes this shit," General Alexander said, "or I'd be fired in a minute."

The previous evening, the admiral had given all the Marine commanders a severe dressing down about security leaks. They had confiscated all of the soldiers' personal phones, tablets, and laptops, but somehow the stories kept getting out.

After they tasered the silver man, the admiral had called in a casualty evacuation (CASEVAC) helicopter. The CASEVAC had been on stand-by at the nearby Gopher Gulch Airstrip and arrived with an advanced contingent of Marines, who immediately began the process of setting up the FOB. The NSA followed a prearranged contingency plan in the case of capturing an alien, flying the silver man directly to a site in Colorado, where a secret bunker complex was hidden deep inside a mountain. The NSA then hastily arranged transportation for a special team from NASA's Johnson Space Center in Houston, who had been trained to deal with the eventuality of a captured alien. Although Admiral Smythe knew this team had never actually seen one, they had rehearsed the possibility with dummies, and the NSA director said they were the best people for the job.

The admiral flew in the CASEVAC to Colorado to supervise the transportation of the silver man's inert body. The Marines in the helicopter had two tasers fully charged, just in case he woke up. They also cuffed his hands and feet.

What the admiral didn't know was that the high-voltage electric shock from the taser had caused two things to happen.

First, it had blocked the silver man's distress call. If this had got through, a rescue mission would have been launched and the elimination capsules would have been delayed. In time, the lack of contact from the traveler would trigger a search and rescue mission. But that period of time had not yet passed.

Second, the electric shock caused the silver man's body to go into rebirth. This was not dangerous, but it meant that he would remain unconscious for several weeks, while his body tissues regenerated.

The skeleton crew of Marines assigned to the Colorado complex were on hand to meet the CASEVAC. They wheeled out an old-fashioned hospital gurney, and the silver man's body was lifted out of the helicopter and laid on his back. Two Marines then wheeled the gurney into the mountain complex, while the admiral followed closely, leading the two Marines with the tasers. They meandered through a maze of corridors, entering several sets of double doors before stopping in an operating theatre.

The complex had been built in the 1960s during the Cold War and was designed to house the president and key staff during a nuclear attack. Admiral Smythe had seen enough field hospitals to know that this operating theatre contained very little modern equipment. It was like a 1960s time warp, with an outdated yellow and blue color scheme. The walls were decorated with different colored ceramic tiles. The gurney that the silver man body lay upon and the other furniture in the room was all made of the heavy chrome steel, polished wood, and Bakelite plastic of the era. If Beatles music were playing, the illusion would have been complete.

After the end of the Cold War, there were no funds for improvements. Captured aliens weren't considered a vote winner, so they were not a funding priority.

Dr. Ali Palaszwaski and Dr. Mary Morrell had been invited to join the Johnson Space Center team. However, "invited" wasn't quite the word that Mary would have used. She had been called at home at four in the morning, and an NSA operator told her that Admiral Gerald Smythe was sending a helicopter to collect her in one hour. She knew it wasn't a request; you didn't say no to the admiral.

As she drove to NASA's Marshall Space Center in Huntsville to meet the helicopter, she assumed this was a going to be just like the session with Ali Palaszwaski and the admiral. This time, she had thrown some extra underwear into her holdall. She cleared base security and then parked her car as close to the helicopter as she could. She didn't like to walk any farther than she had to. The dark green helicopter was illuminated by the lights of the helipad. As she locked her car, a Marine stepped out of the helicopter and approached her. He was a tall, thin man, and Mary thought he looked too young to fly a helicopter. The engines had been switched on, ready for take-off, and so the young soldier had to shout so Mary could hear him: "Dr. Mary Morrell?"

She nodded vigorously and shouted, "Yes, yes."

"ID please?"

She held up her NASA ID badge so the Marine could read it in the reflected light of the helipad.

He stooped to read it and then gave a thumbs-up to her and motioned toward the helicopter; she saw a helmeted figure through the cockpit window return the signal. The pilot then took her holdall and set off at a sprint toward the waiting machine. The rotor blades were now spinning, and Mary followed at a much more sedate pace, holding down her jacket and ID badge in the back wind. She knew from experience that the

ID badge had a habit of whipping up on its cord, and the hard plastic laminated edges could scratch her face. The smell of aviation fuel was overwhelming, as was the noise. She ducked as she approached the rear door, which was held open for her by the tall Marine. He stooped to duck his head and helped her into the back seat. It was two-person seat, but she only just fit into it, and the seat belts had to be extended to their full extent to fit around her. Conversation was impossible over the engine noise, but after he handed her a headset, she asked over the noise where they were going.

She got a polite, "Sorry ma'am, just need to make sure you are strapped in, okay?"

He gave her a thumbs-up, which she half-heartedly returned, and then she heard another voice over the headset, saying, "Corporal, load up, we are cleared for take-off."

She tried again: "So how long will it take to get there, Corporal?"

But there was no reply. She gave up, found a bag of potato chips and a can of soda in her holdall, and made herself as comfortable as she could. She could see from the direction of the sunrise that there weren't heading toward Washington.

After a long, uncomfortable flight, the helicopter began to descend toward a military base in the mountains. She saw from the air that there was a road leading up to a guard post; there were some military vehicles around but no buildings of any significance. As they touched down, Mary realized why there were no buildings: a set of huge hangar doors opened to reveal an illuminated cavern inside the mountain. Mary still didn't know where she was. There was no signage anywhere.

They landed with a bump, but the engines were not turned off. The soldier opened the side door and helped her disembark, and handed her over to another Marine, who drove up in a Jeep to collect her. The vehicle was so old it looked like it had been used in World War II. Almost immediately, the helicopter took off, but Mary could hear the driver grinding the gears of the old Jeep even over the roar of the chopper blades.

The Marine said nothing on the journey, and Mary thought that there was no point in trying another one-way conversation, so she kept silent. She held onto her ID badge again as the driver accelerated and raced through the open hanger doors. The illuminated roadway inside was curved and wide enough for two-way traffic. There was storage area at the front of the cave, where a contingent of Marines were moving crates on forklift trucks.

After a few hundred yards, the Marine slowed the Jeep and parked alongside a number of other military vehicles. He grabbed Mary's holdall and led her though an unmarked doorway into a windowless room. There were cheap plastic chairs arranged around square wooden tables and a reception counter that looked as if it dated from about the same era as the Jeep. A female Marine officer sat at the counter; behind her was a clock on the wall. She stood up, saluted, and held out her hand to shake Mary's.

"Dr. Morrell, welcome to Camp Cody. Let me show you to your quarters."

With that, she grabbed Mary's holdall and set off at a fast pace through an adjacent door. Mary followed, having to hurry to keep woman in sight as she hurried through a maze of corridors. As she panted along, she thought, *These Marines don't seem to want to say much, do they?*

Mary arrived, slightly breathless, at a door held open for her by the woman Marine. Inside was a small bedroom with a single bed, a wash basin, and a threadbare gray towel folded over it. Apart from a small mirror above the basin, there were no fixtures or pictures on the whitewashed brick walls. Other than the single bed, the only other furniture in the room was a writing desk with a hard plastic chair. There was a small closet attached to the desk.

Mary said nothing as she looked at the single bed, but the soldier saw the direction of her gaze. It was obvious to them both that Mary wasn't going to fit on the bed.

She was distracted from her thoughts by a familiar voice from behind her, saying, "Mary, good of you to join us." She turned to see the familiar face of Dr. Bob Cabana. Bob was a short man with a Hollywood smile, and if he could have embraced Mary's bulk, he would have. Instead, he took her hand in a warm, double-handed shake.

"Bob, great to see you," Mary said. "What are you doing here? I thought you had retired."

Mary knew Bob as a NASA veteran; she had known him for twenty-five years, and he was highly respected as the outgoing director of the John F. Kennedy Space Center in Florida.

"No, I step down next month. I'm here in charge of my last mission."

Bob waved his arms in sarcasm at the bleak surroundings. The female Marine had disappeared, Mary hoped, to find her a room with a bigger bed.

"Anyway, Mary, great to have you aboard; come and meet the rest of the team."

Mary could have done with freshening up, but she followed Bob like a puppy. He had always had an infectious boyish enthusiasm about him, and in his early sixties, it had not left him. He led her into a conference room, with a large table and the same cheap plastic chairs around it. Apart from a clock on the wall, there were no pictures. However, she was pleased to see that on a side table there was a good supply of coffee and doughnuts.

There were ten other people in the room. She recognized Ali Palaszwaski immediately, as well as several old NASA colleagues. She went around the room, greeting old colleagues and introducing herself to new ones. During the introductions, it became clear that these people were all members of the Alien Life Form Support Team (ALFST). They all assumed this was just another briefing; apparently, this sort of exercise happened all the time.

After Mary was given time to visit the rest room, Bob called the meeting to order, and everyone took a seat. Mary sat next to Ali.

"Ladies and gentlemen," Bob began, "thank you for coming. I realize that it would have not been your first choice to fly out at short notice to this remote outpost in Colorado, but believe me, what I am about to tell you will make it all worthwhile."

Mary whispered to Ali, "So that's where we are, Colorado."

Bob continued, "This facility was built in 1964 as a refuge for the president and his staff during a nuclear attack. I am glad to say, it has never been used, but it is also a designated site for the ALFST. You are all fully briefed members of ALFST, with the exception of Dr. Mary Morrell and Dr. Ali Palaszwaski, who were invited to join us upon the special request of the NSA."

Ali glanced at Mary and rolled his eyes to the ceiling at the word "invited."

Bob turned to a side table, where there was a stack of thick manuals. He picked up the top copy and held it up for the group. Mary could see the embossed NASA logo on the cover, and the words "TOP SECRET" were written in inch-high letters.

"Most of you are familiar with this document, because you helped write it." Bob turned the document so he could read the title out loud; it was written in bold capital letters:

"PROCEDURE TO ANALYZE AN ALIEN LIFE FORM"

Bob handed around copies of the 235-page document. There was a buzz of conversation as he did so. He then continued with a statement that brought an immediate halt to the small talk around the room: "Ladies and gentlemen, this is not a drill." He paused for effect. "Yesterday, a Special Forces operation captured what is believed to be an alien life form near Bend, Oregon. The life form is here in this facility now, and it is our job to find out as much as we can about it. But first let me show you a video of the capture."

With that, Bob opened the conference room door, and the female Marine who had showed Mary to her quarters wheeled in an old-fashioned TV set on a large trolley. There was a DVD player on the trolley, attached to the TV with cables. She plugged in the units into the wall, pressed a few buttons on a remote control, and then handed the remote to Bob. There was a nod of thanks, and then she walked over to Mary, placing a key on the desk in front of her. "Your new room key, Dr. Morrell."

Mary was impressed.

Several people in the room had used the interruption to grab drinks and more coffee; Mary did the same. Bob then called them back to order.

"This video was shot at night by four different operatives using helmet-cams. It has been edited by the folks at Langley and lasts about three minutes. I am going to play it once without interruption, and then I will replay it section by section, so you can ask questions."

Bob pressed a button on the remote, and an NSA Classified logo appeared on the TV screen. The screen went black, and then an image appeared of a silver object by a river. There appeared to be a tube extending from the object into the water. The object appeared to be taking in water from the river. The image was jerky, obviously because the cameras were mounted on the heads of men who were moving. Occasionally, another soldier could be seen in full battle dress, weapon ready, with the helmet-cam clearly visible. The soldier was wearing a strange cloak.

There was no sound, and Bob was fiddling with the remote, trying to get the sound to work. Suddenly, he pressed the right button, and there was a blast of sound from the TV speakers that startled everyone in the room. One of the soldiers said, "Where did it go?" As Bob hastily lowered the volume, they could hear the soldier's footsteps as he moved quickly, obviously searching for the silver object, which had vanished.

The screen went black, and when the pictures resumed after a few seconds, there was a different view, with the river now in the distance. There was little sound, apart from the exerted breathing of the soldier wearing the helmet-cam. By the position of the ground and the steadiness of the picture, it looked as if the video was being recorded while the soldier was lying down. Bob pointed at the screen, and everyone noticed the faint image of the silver man. Again there was a stunned silence of disbelief as they watched the silver man float into view, and then they saw the rapid movement as the admiral put the taser against his back; the last sound was the vicious electric shock of the weapon. Then Mary heard a familiar voice say, "Now let's see who the fuck you are." The NSA logo appeared again, and the screen went black.

Several of the people in the room had shown strong emotion when the silver figure was brought down with the taser. Mary was amongst them; she had placed a hand over her mouth and let out a scream of shocked horror at the sound of the electric shock. A doctor who specialized in children's medicine wept openly. Mary hugged her; her name was Anne Davis. Other people were standing; one had knocked over his plastic chair. He picked it up, embarrassed. Ali placed a comforting hand on Mary's arm and mouthed silently, "That was the admiral." She nodded.

Bob called them to order again, saying, "I am sorry if the video has upset some of you, but I wanted you to see what we have. Now let me take you through the video, step by step, if I can use this damn remote."

A few people laughed, a release of tension.

Bob started the video from the beginning and then paused on a view of the silver object with the tube going down to the river. He looked down at some notes. "The techs at Langley interviewed the soldiers on the mission and believe this to be some form of spacecraft," he said. "It had struts that looked a little like wings, and this tube appeared to be taking in water from the river. Comments?"

Several people now stood so they could get a closer view of the screen. Ali touched the screen and said, "Yes, I can see one of the triangular struts."

A bearded man Mary had not met before said, "If it were a craft, it would have some form of propulsion system, but none seemed to be visible. Bob, do you have any still photographs of the object?"

"Sorry Carl, I don't, but I'll see if I can get some screen shots for you."

Bob made a note on a pad. The discussion went on for another hour as Bob stepped through the video. He then called a halt for lunch. It was one o'clock in Colorado, but Mary's stomach was still on Alabama time and told her it was getting on for dinner time. After a passable lunch of chicken salad sandwiches, they were all back in the conference room forty minutes later. Mary had time to check out her new room and found it was just like the previous one, but bigger, so that two single bunks could be pushed together to make a larger bed.

Bob again held up the 235-page manual he had handed out earlier and brought them all back to attention. "Okay, ladies and gentlemen, you have seen the video; we are now going to go and see the silver man. But before we do, let me talk you through the procedure we are going to follow."

For the next twenty-five minutes, Bob went over the safety and environmental procedures from the manual. It was clear from what he was saying that there were no going to be any short-cuts. It turned out that the manual laid out a soups-to-nuts procedure to deal with this process, and Bob had told them all that they would follow it to the letter.

They would begin at the beginning of the fifteen-step process. Step 1 was to record every detail of the body. The first thing that was necessary was for them all to dress in bio-protective clothing. This involved surgically scrubbing like a doctor entering an operating theatre. Men and women were segregated into different dressing rooms, and given disposable surgical clothes, followed by an outer green plastic boiler suit, and then green rubber boots. Mary was relieved that the female Marine was on hand to help them dress. She had obviously found a large enough suit to fit Mary.

Before they dressed, the women were instructed to remove makeup and jewelry, and then they washed their hands and faces in the disinfectant soap. The boiler suits had hoods, which they pulled over their hair. As they stepped out of the dressing room, a spray washed their suits in disinfectant. They also walked through a disinfectant foot bath to clean their rubber surgical boots.

The men, all dressed in the same green suits and boots, joined up with the women, and Bob led them along a corridor in single file. They squelched along in their rubber boots, wet from the foot bath, leaving a damp trail behind them. The flickering strip lighting reflected off their wet green suits. Bob led them into a viewing area, where a floor-to-ceiling window overlooked an old-fashioned operating theatre in the next room. The silver man they had seen in the video was lying motionless in the center of the room on an operating table. The operating theatre was brightly lit, and there was an instrument panel on the wall opposite the viewing window so the temperature, humidity, and radiation levels in the room could be monitored by anyone looking through the viewing window. There was also an old-fashioned digital clock, accurate to the second.

When she saw the clock, Mary looked at her wrist to check her watch's accuracy. But then she remembered she had left it in the changing room with the rest of her jewelry. The clock read 14.13.47, or thirteen minutes past two.

Bob asked for volunteers, and most of the men put their hands up. Bob selected Carl Lancaster and Ali to go into the room to begin Step 1 of the operation. The two men put on breathing apparatus, entered an air lock, and went into the room. Mary and the others sat on plastic chairs in their uncomfortable plastic suits and listened to the voices of Carl and Ali through loudspeakers in the viewing gallery; the radios in their breathing apparatus transmitted their muffled voices. They measured and photographed every inch and dimension of the silver man. As they did so, one of team members typed all the data into a laptop.

The silver man still wore a helmet, so his face was not visible. He had the build of a man; his suit was tight and the shoulders were broad. There was a bulge at his crotch. He still wore silver boots and silver gloves, so none of his skin was visible.

They watched as Carl and Ali operated a weighing machine that was integrated into the operating table; as they called out the measurements, she could hear the tapping of the keyboard as the data was typed in. Bob then pressed a button on an intercom and told Ali and Carl to come out of the room. Apparently, their air supplies were about to expire.

They entered the air lock, and after the door closed on the operating theatre side, there was an automatic blast of disinfectant spray that startled everyone. They inner air lock door opened, and Ali and Carl came back into the viewing area, their suits still dripping. They removed their breathing apparatus, and after a debriefing, Bob dismissed them. The women returned to their dressing room, where the lady Marine instructed them to shower and wash their hair. The water was clearly mixed with a disinfectant, and it made Mary's eyes sting.

A reasonable dinner of pork chops with baked potatoes and vegetables was served promptly at six o'clock. The conversation over dinner was excitable, with many of the ALFST team members clearly enthralled by this scientific breakthrough. There was also an informed and intelligent debate about the ethical issues and the implications of a real-life alien life form here on Earth.

Carl said, "One of the scenarios we modeled was the implications on financial markets around the world. It could significantly affect technology and energy stocks if investors felt that those companies could be undermined by new technology, but could significantly enhance the value of companies in the food, commodity, and defense sectors."

Bob interjected, "This is the one of the reasons we insisted on a complete comms blackout. On no circumstances must you communicate with anyone out of this complex."

Ali said, "Bob, we understand that, but from a moral point of view, shouldn't the United States inform its closest allies about the existence of the silver man?"

Bob replied, "That is the president's call, but for now, our instructions are clear."

Mary found the conversation enthralling but found she couldn't concentrate. She was tired from the time difference and her interrupted sleep the night before, so she made her excuses and had an early night. She slept well, despite the fact that she had to straddle the gap between the two single mattresses.

After breakfast the next day, they went through the same process to dress in the rubber suits. Overnight, a body scanner and an x-ray machine had been brought into the operating theatre. This must have taken some effort, and Mary could still see the disinfectant dripping from the outer parts of the equipment.

Two other members of the team entered the operating theatre. They had been trained on this equipment and had a medical background. After some initial excitement, there was great disappointment when the images showed nothing more than the external silver suit. At first, they thought the equipment was faulty, but after double-checking them, it was clear that both pieces of equipment were working perfectly.

The medics in the team attached every form of monitoring device they could to the silver man. However, they failed to get any real data; he was obviously dead. He did not respond to any stimuli. He was not breathing, there was no heartbeat, and there was no body warmth; there was nothing detectable at all. Nonetheless, the data was recorded and suitably backed up.

They also tried to take some blood using a syringe, but none of the needles they used could penetrate the silver suit.

The scientists analyzed every form of particle they could. The operating theatre became so full of electrical equipment that they ran out of wall sockets to plug it all in.

Brian Fellows, the anthropologist in the team, in close cooperation with Dr. Anne Davis, felt the silver man's body from head to toe using his gloved hands so he could estimate his bone and organ structure. Neither Brian nor Anne detected anything out of the ordinary; they estimated that he was in his late twenties or early thirties. There was no indication of any bones that were broken but could not tell anything about his head, hands, or feet because they could not feel through his helmet, gloves, or boots.

After ten days, Dr. Cabana authorized them to move on to the Step 2, which was to take a small sample for analysis.

This was harder than it should have been. Nothing about the silver man was superfluous or could be removed. There was no opening in his clothing or anything that could be removed. Neither his helmet nor his boots could be removed, and nothing they tried could cut the material of his outer garments.

In the end, they decided to focus on the heel of one of his boots, which looked like it was made out of plastic. The previous day, they had tried a number of different tools to get a sample of the material and analyze it. Scalpels and traditional surgical instruments were ineffective. They finally tried a diamond drill; Mary watched as Brian Fellows and another medic powered up the drill inside the operating theatre. She listened to them speaking over the loud speaker system:

"I will hold the ankle and toe, and you try and shave something from the heel."

"Okay," Brian said. "Hold on then."

The drill had been fitted with a diamond cutting disc, and the gems sparkled in the operating theatre lights. There was a crackle over the speakers as the drill started, and Mary could hear the motor clearly through the viewing area glass. It must have been very loud inside the operating theatre.

The watching team leaned in closer to the glass to get a better view, as Brian pressed the cutting disc slowly and gently against the heel of the boot. There was clearly no effect on the boot from the drill.

He said in frustration, "This is a very hard material. I am going to try more pressure."

Mary watched as he knelt upon the gurney table so he could push down with his upper body on the drill, but despite his obvious exertions, still nothing happened.

They had placed a tray under the heel of the boot to capture any fragments, but when they two men emerged from the operating theatre, it was clear that no fragments were visible inside the tray.

Around four o'clock in the afternoon, Dr. Cabana called a halt. He told them to meet at eight o'clock the next morning to brainstorm on what to do.

This week in the *Weekly World News*

NASA Scientists Try to Save Dying Alien

> *Leading NASA scientists are performing lifesaving surgery on a dying alien. The team has been rushed to a secret underground bunker below the Colorado mountains to work in a race against time. The team is being led by former Shuttle Commander Dr. Bob Cabana. A NASA spokesman denied that Dr. Cabana was in Colorado and said he was on a family vacation in Europe.*

An eleven-year-old boy wrote on a blog on the *Weekly News* website:

> *"If this alien is really dying, he should be given electric shock treatment like they do in the movies."*

Mary Morrell, who read the blog entry on the Internet while eating her last bag of potato chips before bed, decided to take the idea to the brainstorming session the next morning.

The group met for breakfast the next morning at eight. Bob took them through a summary of what they had achieved the previous day and then presented an overview of the objectives for the coming day. They then brainstormed ideas on how best to achieve the day's objectives. Bob was a great team player and reinforced the mantra that there were no bad ideas. There was also no blame culture, so Lancaster, who had suggested using the diamond drill, was not blamed for its failure to cut the heel of the silver man's boot; in fact, Bob made a point of saying it was a great suggestion.

Brian Fellows said, "I put all of my strength into trying to cut that material yesterday, and the drill was completely ineffective. By rights, it should have sliced through plastic like a hot knife through butter. I don't think we have anything else that could cut into it. We should look at more radical and unconventional approaches."

Mary said, "I was looking at some of the Internet blogs last night, and someone suggested we use electric shock treatment."

Bob turned and wrote "electric shock treatment" on the flip chart as one of the ideas that they could try.

Although there was some challenging glances at Mary after her suggestion, nobody questioned it. By the end of the brainstorming session, the list also included the use of lasers, explosives, rifles, plasma, acid burning, and nitrogen freezing.

After the ideas were exhausted, Bob formed the team of twelve scientists and medics into two groups of six. The purpose was to brainstorm how they could implement the different ideas on the flipchart; each group would present their ideas to the other. This way, the team as a whole could choose the best of the best ideas. The two groups moved chairs to different parts of the breakfast room, and after an hour, Bob brought them back together.

Ali was elected spokesman of his group and went through his list. The second group, which included Mary, had elected Brian as their spokesman.

After some heated debate, a list the most promising ideas emerged. Some were rejected as being too difficult to conduct safely in the operating theatre environment, for example, the rifle shot.

However, the one possibility that had some consensus was Mary's idea of the electric shock treatment, so this was added to the list, but as the last thing to try. Electric shock treatment would not enable them to collect a sample to analyze, but it could make the silver man respond to some external stimuli.

They tried all the other ideas: tearing, scraping, cutting, sawing, grinding, sandpaper, chemicals, micro-needles … but none worked.

Mary could see that the team was becoming very frustrated that none of their attempts produced any result. Each new idea required significant effort to implement. First, the equipment was specified and then brought in. The equipment had to be disinfected and then used by team members dressed in the surgical suits. This took time, and team members sat around for hours with little to do.

During the daily brainstorming meetings, Mary could see that Bob was finding it increasingly difficult to keep a sense of professional and rational debate. The team's frustration boiled over into petty arguments, and Bob often had to call a time-out to allow people to calm down.

That morning, there had been a stand-up row between Brian and Carl over the proposed use of the cardiac resuscitation machine, which had been brought in to administer the electric shock treatment. Brian insisted that the equipment should not be used, as it could destroy the silver man's internal organs and prevent them from being used for further analysis.

Brian said, "Dr. Lancaster's cavalier and irresponsible actions may well rob medical science of the most important breakthrough ever."

Mary noticed that when academics and scientists became upset, instead of using someone's first name, they reverted to their more formal titles.

So Carl retorted, "Dr. Fellows is simply afraid of losing income from his next book; he simply can't wait to publish another crackpot work, this time bragging about how he analyzed the internal organs of an alien life form."

Bob eventually calmed them all down, and that afternoon, the medics set up the cardiac resuscitation machine and prepared to place the two electric paddles over the silver man's heart. The positioning of the paddles had caused some more heated discussion amongst the team, because nobody knew where the heart of the silver man was (or indeed if he *had* a heart). In the end, Bob had intervened and decided they would place the paddles where the heart was on a human. He also decided to start by using the lowest power setting on the machine.

The medic shouted, "Clear," which was standard procedure but completely unnecessary, because the other team member in the operating theatre was standing back as far as possible, fearful of this drastic procedure.

The medic touched the paddles to the silver man's chest, and there was a small pop. Nothing else happened. The body lying on the table remained completely still.

The medic looked up at Bob, who said, "Increase the power."

The power was increased, but still nothing happened.

The power was increased again to the maximum, but still nothing happened.

Bob called a halt to the day's proceedings, and that night the group was very despondent over dinner.

After dinner, using a secure video link, Bob had a conference with General Alexander and Admiral Smythe.

The discussion was necessary because all of the ideas on their original list had now been tried, and they were no closer to knowing anything about the silver man.

Bob began, "Gentlemen, for the last seven days, we have attempted to complete stages 1 and 2 of the NASA Procedure to Analyze an Alien Life Form. Stage 1 involved taking comprehensive measurements, which we completed and documented. Stage 2 involves taking a small sample for analysis. Although we have tried every known method of cutting a sample from the silver man's clothing, nothing has worked. We have now reached a point where a much more radical approach is required. Therefore, I need your authorization to use heavy cutting equipment."

General Alexander asked, "Do you have any idea whether the alien is still alive?"

Bob replied, "Sir, we have not been able to detect any breathing or heartbeat or any indication at all that he is still alive. We even tried some electric shock treatment, but it produced no response."

Admiral Smythe interjected, "Dr. Cabana, in your opinion, is he alive or dead?"

"Admiral, I would have to say at this point that I believe he is dead."

General Alexander asked, "What is involved in this heavy cutting equipment?"

"Sir, we literally cut the silver man limb from limb. It is the equivalent of a magician's act of sawing someone in half, except this is no trick."

Admiral Smythe said, "Well, if he's dead, then this is no problem."

General Alexander said, "I agree, cut him up."

With that, the NSA director cut the connection, and Bob was left staring at the NSA logo.

Supplies for the secret operation were usually brought in at night by helicopter. Mary could hear the double-bladed machines approaching by their characteristic whoop-whoop sound, even in the confines of her bunk deep inside the mountain. The sound was amplified by the mountainous terrain and cold mountain air.

The noise often woke the scientists. They would wander outside in track suits and nightwear, clutching steaming Styrofoam cups of coffee to watch the helicopters land, curious about the cargo they carried. That night, Mary joined the small group outside in the cool night air under a cloudless sky. She watched the teams of Marines as they unloaded more than just the doughnuts for the team's breakfast. The forklift trucks unloaded heavy wooden crates they all assumed contained the heavy laser cutters.

The Marines efficiently unloaded the helicopters, which then took off into the night sky. The outside landing lights were extinguished, and the stars shone brightly in the clear mountain air. The small group of onlookers dispersed, and Mary and Ali sat down in one of the old-fashioned Jeeps.

They were alone, and they had a magnificent view of the stars in the night sky. Mary looked up at the three stars on the belt of the constellation of Orion, the Hunter, and said, "I wonder if that is where the silver man came from."

In the seat beside her, Ali shrugged. "Maybe," he said, tracing with his cup the broad swath of the Milky Way and the billions of stars. "But maybe from there; who knows?"

They sat for a few minutes in silence.

The discussion after dinner had been about Bob's decision to use the heavy cutting equipment. Mary was disappointed at that decision but could see no other way. If they cut him up, however, they might never get the answers about him.

She said quietly to Ali, "If we cut him up tomorrow, we may never know where he is from."

Ali took some time to answer, and when he did, Mary realized he was very emotional, almost in tears; he said, "I know, it feels as if we are killing him."

Mary put her hand on Ali's shoulder and said, "I feel the same, but there's nothing else to do. Come on, let's get some sleep."

As they walked back into the mountain bunker complex, there was a sharp contrast to the peace and tranquility outside. Inside, it was a hive of activity. The Marines sweated and strained as they unpacked and installed the heavy equipment, so the scientific and medical teams could use it the next morning.

Inside the operating theatre, where the silver man lay inert on the operating theatre table, it was calm and still. The room was brightly lit, the temperature and humidity were carefully controlled, and four HD CCTV cameras recorded every activity in the room 24/7, with a secure video link to Fort Meade.

Then something totally unexpected happened. Suddenly and without warning, the silver man's suit began to deflate. It was as if a balloon had a slow leak, and the air had escaped slowly. The fabric gently came to rest on the table, with only his shoes and helmet still remaining intact.

The movement of the suit was so gradual that it didn't trigger any of the multiple monitoring systems in the room. Initially, the deflation went unnoticed by the bored operators at Fort Meade on the graveyard shift.

About twenty minutes later, an operative at Fort Meade returned from a bathroom break and took a fresh look at the image of the silver man on the monitor. They had been viewing the same image now for two weeks, and it dawned on him that there was something different. He rewound the recording and watched the suit deflate.

As instructed, he called the admiral, who answered on the second ring and ordered Bob Cabana and the team to return to the viewing gallery. Most were dressed in yesterday's clothes and were still groggy from the lack of sleep.

Like every day, the team went through their practiced routine to enter the operating theatre area where the silver man lay. They were now suitably scrubbed and dressed in their surgical suits; they sat on their stools around the perimeter of viewing gallery, looking through the glass into the operating theatre, where the silver man lay with his deflated suit.

Most were wishing they were allowed to bring coffee in, but food and drink were forbidden in the viewing area. Mary's mind was on the unopened tray of doughnuts and pastries in the break room next door. She was wishing she could peel back the shrink-wrap and bite into that soft sugary confection.

However, her sugar craving was soon forgotten as she watched the video recording of the silver man's suit deflating; the video was played several times, first in real time, then in slow-motion, and then frame by frame. Bob asked for suggestions. Some stifled yawns; not everyone was as interested in this development as Mary.

"Could be some form of rapid chemical decay," Carl suggested.

Ali said, "Carl could be right; if so, we should set up some gas detection and chemical analysis equipment."

Bob made a note on a legal pad.

After a few more minutes, Bob adjourned the meeting so the gas detection and chemical analysis equipment could be set up in the operating theatre.

Everyone agreed with this course of action; it not only made scientific sense, it also gave everybody a chance to get to the coffee and doughnuts while the equipment was set up.

Then just as the team was about to file out of the viewing area, Ali pointed and said, "Look, the helmet is moving."

Sure enough, as the team stopped, Mary saw the visor on the silver man's helmet pop open. Over the speakers, they all heard the distinctive cry of a newborn baby. The team fell silent; everyone turned toward the sound, not sure if they could believe their ears.

Mary moved with a mother's instinct. Breaking all the rules, she barged her way through the double air lock, hitting the buttons so the second door opened before the first closed. She then stepped into the operating theatre without wearing breathing apparatus, with her hood pulled down to expose her face and leaving both doors open.

It had been impossible for the diamond saw to move the silver man's helmet before, but she simply pulled aside the helmet, removed her gloves, and lifted out a beautiful newborn baby boy, perfect in every way. She may have been mistaken, but she thought she saw his skin color change to match her own. In her eyes, he was now even more beautiful.

She spoke instinctively, the words forming without thought: "A beautiful baby, thank the Lord, thank Jesus."

The name of Jesus stuck.

It took time for the traveler's body tissues to regenerate, and during that period, they were dependent on the support of any host life form they encountered. Long ago, they had evolved a defense mechanism designed to protect them during this vulnerable phase. During rebirth, the traveler assumed the appearance of whatever life form they encountered (in this case, human beings). They also emitted a special chemical that immediately compelled the host life form to protect them. The chemical was an enhancement to the natural instinct that compels any human parent to protect their child.

For this reason, the team of rational and distinguished medical staff and scientists forgot all their discipline and training; they followed Mary into the operating theatre in blatant disregard of the air lock and quarantine rules. They burst into spontaneous applause as Mary held the baby up in her arms. Her face was wet with tears of joy. The women cooed around the child and wept openly, and there was more than one man with a tear in his eye.

Mary took one of sterile white linen towels that were neatly stacked in the operating theatre, ready to absorb any plasma or chemical spillage, and swaddled the baby Jesus with an instinctive easy motion that came from raising four children of her own.

Now the mothers, fathers, and grandparents in the room began a tirade of advice about feeding and so on. They lined up to take turns to hold the new baby. Even Bob Cabana, a proud grandfather himself, joined in.

Two of the women went to a computer screen in the corner and began typing out an inventory of supplies they would need for the baby.

Admiral Smythe, who was watching from Fort Meade, was outraged by the lack of protocol. He dialed the secure telephone in the operating theatre, but the ringing could not be heard over the hubbub of excited conversation over the baby Jesus.

In addition to the medical, scientific, and security personnel, there was a large logistics and administrative operation supporting Dr. Cabana and the team at the bunker complex. These people were tasked with procuring all the special medical equipment they needed. Staff Sergeant Sandra Makepeace was a logistics officer on the early morning shift, and she looked at the latest procurement request on her screen with a raised eyebrow.

The procurement team were always being given impossible deadlines to find all sorts of items, from the body scanners to the diamond drills. The project had so far racked up over $28 million in costs. The logistics team had been told that this operation had no budget limit, so they just kept on spending.

But these new items were even more bizarre. The list included a crib, baby formula, baby wipes, and diapers.

Everything on the list was designated "UOR," short for "Urgent Operational Requirement." A UOR meant it was needed within four hours. This was not unusual; almost everything requested for this operation was UOR. So far the procurement team's performance against the UOR target was poor; how could you source special medical equipment like micro-needles within four hours?

Sandra clicked her mouse to print the UOR list, muttering to herself that these people were crazy, wanting baby things in a secret bunker at 4:30 in the morning on UOR; surely if there was a mother in the team, she already had these things with her.

However, she was there to follow orders, and she wanted to get the performance target up. She headed for the parking lot and then drove to the nearest twenty-four-hour Wal-Mart.

It was not unusual for a female soldier from the local military base to be buying baby things at Wal-Mart at five o'clock in the morning. But the tired mother of four on the cash register realized that this soldier was not a mother. She could tell by the things she bought, all in the wrong pack sizes. She also didn't look like she had just given birth; she was way too relaxed, and there were no bags under her eyes. She almost said something about the diapers being for a newborn and the baby grows for a one-year-old, but the cashiers were trained not to comment on customer purchases.

So she used her smartphone to take a sneaky picture of the soldier; on her break, she emailed it to the *Weekly World News.* She got a reply the next day thanking her, followed by a check in the mail for $250.

In the next edition of *Weekly World News*

Alien Newborn Baby Shops at Wal-Mart

> *An alien baby born in a secret location in Colorado has been given a new crib and diapers purchased at Wal-Mart. This US Army soldier (pictured) bought the baby equipment in the middle of the night to try and avoid suspicion.*

Bob Cabana and his team now lost all self-restraint. There had been a comms black-out on the mission. Although the team was allowed to call home, they could not discuss any aspect of the mission or even say where they were.

But now they called family and loved ones just to tell them about the wonderful new baby. Some used discreet references, but others, including Mary, named the baby Jesus. The techs at Fort Meade intercepted Mary's phone messages and managed to block an email of Jesus' picture reaching the outside world.

Ali was a Muslim. He was not that devout; he had the occasional beer or glass of wine, he ate hot dogs, but he went to the mosque on holy days. He had been brought up with the teachings of the Koran and brought his children up with the same disciplines, and now he saw before him a new prophet.

He couldn't resist talking about it. The admiral listened to a taped recording of Ali speaking to his wife. The bug they had planted in his cell phone enhanced the sound quality, so it was as if they were both in the room with him.

Ali was saying, "It was amazing, the body lay absolutely still for weeks; we couldn't even open the suit, and then this amazing thing happened: a baby came out."

Then Ali's wife asked, "You mean a man gave birth to a baby?"

"No, he didn't give birth, as such; his helmet opened and the baby was just there. Not just any baby, but a beautiful black baby boy. Oh, you should see him, honey, he is absolutely gorgeous."

"You gotta send me some pictures."

"Will do, but what we think happened was when he got tasered with the electric shock, he went into some sort of regeneration process. They have named him Jesus. I tell you, honey, this boy is special. I think he is the Prophet."

The female voice said, "Ali Palaszwaski, just listen to you; you are talking nonsense."

The admiral hit the stop button; he had heard enough. He called his assistant and ordered a flight to take him to Colorado immediately. He needed to get out there to restore discipline.

While he was in the air, the latest *Weekly World News* story broke:

New Messiah Is Born in Colorado

> *A baby born in Colorado is being hailed by leading doctors as the new Messiah. The new Jesus was born at 4:35 a.m. and weighed nine pounds, two ounces.*

The editorial staff at *Weekly World News* were largely used to their stories being parodied, lampooned, or ignored, but this time, the story went viral on the Internet. Word spread at lightning speed around the world, and this issue became the largest selling edition of the paper ever.

In Colorado, the crowds began gathering.

Within two days, the Marines estimated that the crowd outside the Colorado bunker complex was 20,000. They called for reinforcements.

Another 15,000 people were being held back at road blocks by the National Guard. The highway to the site was closed. But overnight, more people had headed cross-country on foot, in 4x4s, and in RVs.

A number of news helicopters hovered over the site, broadcasting live pictures and giving a clear direction to the people who wanted to believe in the new messiah. The NSA rushed a court injunction through the Colorado courts, and the helicopters were prohibited from overflying the bunker on the grounds of national security. But the news story would not go away.

There were many weirdos and the zealots, but there were normal people as well, from all the religious groups: Christians, Muslims, Jews, Hindus, Buddhists, and Sikhs; they all hoped that this was the second coming, the new messiah, or whatever they called him. In countless TV interviews, the followers in Colorado came over as idealists, who wanted hope, something new that they could believe in.

Admiral Smythe and General Alexander met with the president, and the White House Press Office (PO) went into full swing.

First there were denials, but the momentum on the story continued to build.

The PO issued more denials, and the momentum built further.

The vice president went on record to deny the story. Sally Carmichael, head of the White House Press Office, advised the president not to comment.

Privately, they briefed world leaders.

Sally wanted specialist help and contacted Malcolm Packer, a retired British PR consultant, who had been involved in covering the birth of Prince William and Prince Harry, the children of Princess Diana and Prince Charles. He was considered a world expert on managing the PR on celebrity babies. *Manna from heaven,* he thought when the White House called and offered him a three-month consulting contract at twice his previous salary.

Malcolm's advice was to take the responsible press inside and allow them full access, in return for leaving the story alone afterwards. This was a deal that the British royal family had struck with the press many times, and it was a formula that worked. In any case, he advised, once the story was out and splashed on every front page, TV news program, and Internet site, people would soon be bored of it.

Admiral Smythe and the NSA director partially took his advice. But they also had plans of their own. They brought in an unknown actress and found an orphaned white baby to use as a decoy. At the same time, Mary and the black baby Jesus would be smuggled out of the complex to a secret location. Sally, Admiral Smythe, and General Alexander figured that while there had been a black US president, the world wasn't yet ready for a black baby Jesus.

The actress's name was Jenny Able (actually, that was her stage name; her real name was Jennifer Clarke). She had a peaches-and-cream complexion, with dark hair, brown eyes, and not much of a figure. The PR people had suggested that she not be seen as too sexy.

She had had a boob job, supposedly to help her acting career, but given the right bra and costume, it would look as if she was producing milk for a newborn baby. Makeup was applied skillfully, and a screen test given. The girl thought she was auditioning to play Mary in a religious movie.

An elaborate operation was set up to ensure that the decoy-baby was well cared for, and a team of caregivers were brought in at the NSA's expense. The president ordered this operation filmed 24/7, because he didn't want any claim that the baby had been harmed in any way, if it all leaked later on.

A psychologist was assigned to help Jenny play the part, not just to act it but to believe in what she was doing. She had to be convincing.

The White House PO went into high gear twenty-four hours before the press conference was scheduled, with a specific plan to target thirty-six journalists they felt represented the best national and international reach for this story. It included international correspondents from leading news agencies around the world, including the BBC, China's *People's Daily*, and Al Jazeera.

TV cameras and tape recorders were banned, but HD video footage would be made available after the event, which would not be broadcast live. The NSA considered that too risky. The journalists were told only that they were being invited to a special briefing by the president on the story about the baby born in Colorado.

The White House also began confidential briefings to world leaders. The president spoke with some leaders himself, while ambassadors and the secretary of state spoke to others.

US forces were put on a heightened state of alert, and US embassies were told to invoke a lock-down procedure, just in case.

Admiral Smythe and General Alexander briefed the president on the evening before the press conference. The president told them the news had brought a very positive response from the world leaders he had spoken to. All politicians liked a good news story. The president also said he was now more optimistic for peace talks in the Middle East.

General Alexander and Admiral Smythe were deeply concerned about possible leaks. With the number of people who now knew, it was inevitable that the story would get out.

The secretary-general of the United Nations would be joining the president on the platform at the press conference tomorrow. The journalists didn't know this as yet. It was hoped that this would be an unexpected surprise and give additional credibility to the proceedings.

However, just in case anyone was in any doubt, the president spelled out for the record, in a room where he knew the cameras were recording everything he said, that on the advice of the NSA, he was about to lie to the director-general of the UN, the assembled press, the American people, and America's closest allies. They were all going to be led to believe that the baby they were to see tomorrow, the white baby boy, was an alien baby, possibly the new Messiah.

The president continued for the benefit of the recording, "The real baby Jesus is being well cared for by a team of trained nurses dedicated to his every need, supervised by a distinguished scientist from NASA, Dr. Mary Morrell, who had been significantly involved with the silver man since he was taken to the Colorado bunker."

The president paused in his monologue; he thought for the first time about the significance of Mary's name as well as the baby Jesus. He had not thought about that before. He could see the NSA director wanted to speak but waved him to silence so he could continue.

"The real baby Jesus has been taken to a secure location on a Caribbean Island. He has arrived safely."

Nobody was going to sleep well tonight, thought the president. His makeup team were going to be challenged to make him look fresh at the press conference tomorrow.

The following twelve hours were a hive of intense international diplomatic activity.

Every world leader wanted to share the platform when the president introduced the new baby. Each country had a solid reason why they should be there; Israel was one of the most passionate. On top of this, the Washington envoy to the Vatican had requested a meeting with the president, on the basis that the pope himself would fly in.

On the advice of the secretary of state, they turned down Israel's heartfelt requests, because if that happened, they would have to balance with the Arab countries. This would mean the Israelis sharing the platform with Jordanians or Syrians, which of course was out of the question.

Nobody said no to the pope, so instead, the secretary of state played a waiting game, delaying and putting off a decision until he knew it would be too late for the elderly pontiff to reach Washington in time.

The British prime minister wanted to be there, and his plane was already in the air. After all, it was a British scientist's work that led to the capture of the silver man, and Britain was America's greatest ally. After several long telephone calls, the prime minister's plane was diverted to Alberta, and he paid an unofficial and unexpected visit to the Canadian prime minister. Of course, the intensive use of satellite phones alerted the listening posts all over the world. The conversations caused mild hilarity in basement offices in Pyongyang, Tehran, Moscow, Berlin, Paris, and Beijing. Nothing much remained secret anymore; the information just never went public.

Representatives of the Hindu and Sikh religions in India, and the Buddhists in Tibet, all wanted in. The Chinese government was suddenly very pro-Tibet. The other countries where sensors had been discovered were Argentina, Australia, Brazil, Canada, Mexico, Russia, Finland, New Zealand, New Guinea, South Africa, Chad, Morocco, Denmark, Malaysia, Germany, Japan, and Indonesia.

In the end, they decided that only the UN would take part. Even the NSA director acknowledged that sometimes the UN had its uses.

At ten o'clock the next morning, thirty-five expectant journalists sat in the White House briefing room, surrounded by Secret Service personnel and White House staff.

One journalist from the *Washington Post*, who actually had the shortest distance to travel, had not been able to make it at the last minute, because her young daughter had been taken ill. Sally refused to let her send a colleague as a replacement, and when the editor of the *Washington Post* heard this, he was not in a positive frame of mind toward the White House; he said, with no disguised threat of malice, that he was "itching to write his editorial once I know what the fuck this was all about."

The journalists who were regulars at White House briefings were surprised, because the normal form was to find a prepared statement on their seats, along with relevant notes. Today, their chairs were empty.

As the clock in the White House anteroom struck ten, the vice president, NSA director, head of the White House Press Office, secretary of state, heads of the Joint Chiefs of Staff, and the director of NASA walked in and took their assigned seats in the front row.

There was a stirring amongst the journalists. This was an unusually auspicious gathering. Then someone announced, "Ladies and gentlemen, the president of the United States and the director-general of the United Nations."

As was custom, everyone stood, and on cue, the White House staff and Secret Service personnel applauded enthusiastically. The president could see many familiar faces in the room, and he noticed that they were totally thrown by the presence of the UN secretary-general; although they applauded politely, their own applause was less than enthusiastic. In fact, it was a very rare event for the UN secretary-general to share a platform with a serving US president, especially this one, because he disliked the man intently, and the White House had continually clashed with the UN all the time he had been in office.

Jamaica

Near the eastern coast of Jamaica was a remote place where the tourists hardly ever visited, called Williams Field.

In the late 1990s, an Internet billionaire built a mansion up in the hills. Shortly after it was finished, the market crashed, and it became an asset that he had to liquidate as quickly as possible.

Through an obscure Cayman Islands corporation, the CIA bought the mansion for a knocked-down price and used it as one of their safe houses in the region. What had brought the property to the CIA's attention was the state-of-the-art communications system and self-contained power supply.

The safe house was staffed by a husband and wife team, Jed and Lisa Jackson, who lived in a cottage on the grounds. Jed tended the gardens and took care of any routine maintenance, while Lisa cleaned and kept everything ready for their occasional visitors. If they needed extra staff when guests stayed, they were brought in from the local village.

As far as Jed and Lisa were concerned, the mansion was a vacation home for executives from the Cayman Islands bank that owned it. Most of the time, the big house was empty, but they got paid, they had a good life, and as they often said to each other in private, "Ain't nobody was going to spoil it."

Lisa would have given everything for the thing she wanted most in the world, a baby. But doctors told her that was not possible, so she was content with her life with Jed.

The mansion was called Jacobs Creek. It had eight bedrooms, each with their own en-suite bathrooms, a large outdoor pool, a fully equipped gym, and a suite of offices. On top of the office building, which was separate from the main house, there was a full-size helicopter landing pad.

Jed had an email from the office manager in the Cayman Islands, saying that they should expect visitors at the weekend. He told Lisa over breakfast that some executives were flying down there with their families, and they were to make everything ready. It was not their place to ask who the people were or how long they were planning to stay. Lisa was delighted at the word "families"; she hoped some children would be coming.

Rather than a chore, they preferred to have visitors. It gave them a purpose, and it was interesting to meet different people. Previous visitors had always been polite and courteous, and there was rarely any trouble.

Jed and Lisa went into a practiced routine. They had a contingent of regular staff they called in when they had visitors, who were all glad of the work. Jed went to collect the small group of cooks, housekeepers, and serving staff.

When they arrived back at Jacobs Creek, there was small fleet of delivery trucks in the drive, delivering the supplies of food, drink, and fresh flowers that Lisa had ordered. Nobody ever questioned the bills.

Everyone fell into a familiar routine: the bedrooms were made ready with fresh linen and towels; the bars, fridges, and freezers were freshly stocked; the pool was cleaned; and the garden tidied.

In his email reply to the bank, Jed had asked whether he needed to pick up the guests; he assumed they would be flying in, as most did. He was told that some guest would arrive on Saturday by rental car and then more would arrive the following day by helicopter. Attached to the email was a list of additional items the guests required. Lisa was very excited when she looked at the printout of the list, because on it were some baby things.

Oh joy! She loved it when children were there, but she especially loved having babies on the grounds.

She gathered together the other female staff, and they clucked and cooed with enthusiasm over the list.

She called her sister, who worked in Kingston. After a long conversation, she asked her sister to pick up the things for her and drive them up to Jacobs Creek.

Knowing Lisa's calls to her sister where never short, Jed had taken his yard brush and gone to sweep the helipad; it hadn't been used for a few months. Sure enough, when he finished his sweeping, Lisa was still on the phone.

The following day, a young black couple arrived in a rental car. The household all turned out to meet new visitors, and Lisa found it hard to hide her disappointment when she saw that the car had no child seat. The couple shook hands with everyone, introducing themselves as Mat and Jessica.

They handed Jed their credentials, and he showed them to the bedrooms. He told them they could take their pick, as they were the first to arrive. Jessica made a show of viewing each of the eight bedrooms, but they had already selected which one they would use from the CIA plans of the building. With apparent indifference, they chose the corner suite, which had the best view of the entrance gate. Their bags were brought up, and Mat looked out to watch as the rental car was driven into a shaded parking lot under the helipad.

Claiming tiredness after an exhausting journey, they said they would get a few hours' sleep before dinner. Mat was tall and good looking; he gave Jed a discreet wink when Jessica's back was turned. Jed got the message and tapped the side of his nose twice, giving Mat a man-to-man secret grin.

Mat explained that the other guests would be arriving the next day by helicopter. He said that he and Jessica would be down for dinner about seven o'clock.

Jed said sarcastically, "Enjoy your *rest*," and went to find Lisa.

As soon as they saw Jed saunter over to the cottage where they lived, Mat and Jessica began a well-practiced operation to sweep the house. From a hidden compartment below the bottom lining of their suitcases, they took out the tools of their trade and made a thorough electronic search of the entire complex, using the latest sensors.

As expected, nothing was found, and Mat sent a text message to a Cayman Islands number:

"Arrived safely, all quiet."

A few minutes later, his cell phone beeped and the reply read:

"4 + 1 @ 4 Bluebird."

The text meant that four people plus the baby would arrive at four o'clock. Mat showed the screen of his phone to Jessica so she could read the message. She nodded her understanding but said nothing aloud. Jed deleted all the messages from his phone. He then took out the SIM card and replaced it with a new one. He cut the old SIM card into small fragments, put half the fragments in a tissue, and flushed them down the lavatory; the other half he put in an empty soda can and tossed it in the trash.

Around six o'clock, Mat and Jessica used the gym and swam in the pool, and then they had dinner, all without fuss. They went to bed early. All the staff had an early night.

Mat and Jessica were awake by 3:30. In the dark, they checked all around to ensure that everything was in order. Just before four, they heard the helicopter rotors and watched as a powerful searchlight from the aircraft swept over the mansion. The agents knew that the helicopter was chartered from a local company; it had been flown in from the USS *Ross,* a Navy warship that was over the horizon and in international waters. The warship had carried the four passengers and the baby at full speed since they had embarked off the eastern seaboard near Virginia. The classified operation was carried out in the utmost secrecy and with the superb efficiency of the US Navy. The USS *Ross's* captain had been Admiral Smythe's roommate when they attended the Naval Academy almost thirty years ago, and they had been close friends ever since.

The pilot landed the helicopter gently, illuminating the helipad on the descent with a powerful landing light. As soon as the aircraft touched down, the rear doors opened, and four people emerged from the helicopter. The rotors continued to turn on full power.

As Mat and Jessica watched through the darkened windows of their bedroom suite, they could tell that there were two men and two women in the group, but it was too dark to see who was who. However, a movement sensor soon turned the lights on, because the helipad was now illuminated, and they could now see the faces of the group. They watched the women descend from the helipad by the rear steps, keeping their heads low. One of the women was carrying a small holdall, and the other woman carried the baby. Mat and Jessica immediately recognized her from the intelligence they had been given as the NASA scientist, Dr. Mary Morrell. The woman with the holdall led, walking almost backwards to assist the second woman carrying the baby as best she could. The agents knew the second woman was Dr. Anne Davis, who specialized in child medicine. They assumed the holdall contained her medical kit and essentials for the baby.

The other two male passengers unloaded bags from the helicopter luggage hold, slammed the rear doors, and dropped to one knee as the helicopter took off. They waved to the pilot, who saluted. The helicopter roared away in the direction it had come, leaving a silence behind. Shortly, the sounds of the night, the sounds of the insects and the birds of Jamaica, returned.

Lights now illuminated the mansion complex. As Mat and Jessica watched, they saw a flustered Jed and Lisa, still in their nightclothes, and an entourage of the other servants of the household, also in their night attire, rush out to greet their new guests. This was the signal for Mat and Jessica to go down; they had to appear as if they were also unaware of the helicopter's arrival, so they also remained in their nightclothes. They needn't have worried, because the two CIA agents went almost unnoticed; everyone was fussing over the baby, who was the immediate center of attention.

"My, my, look at you, aren't you the most fabulous?" Lisa cooed over the baby; she was thrilled when she learnt that his name was Jesus.

Lisa was beside herself with pleasure when Mary allowed her to carry the baby to their suite; it had already been prepared with the crib and other baby things. The male servants carried the bags of the new arrivals up to the bedroom suits, and the cooks trailed off to prepare an early breakfast for everyone. Mat could hear Jed saying, "If you had let us know what time you were arriving, we would have been dressed and ready for you."

The fuss over the baby gave Mat and Jessica a few minutes alone with the two male arrivals. Matt shook hands first with the bearded one and said, "Hi, I'm Mat."

"Hi Mat, I'm Carl Lancaster. I must say you aren't dressed as I expected." Carl looked down at Mat's night attire, clearly not what most people think a CIA operative would wear.

As he was shaking hands with Brian Fellows, the second passenger, Mat, said quietly, "Please, gentlemen, remember that you are bank executives on vacation."

Jessica added, "I should say a family vacation, because we have to remember our priority here is the baby."

With the greetings done, they headed up to the house so the arrivals could unpack in their assigned suites.

Before the mission started, Admiral Smythe had briefed the agents personally on the team he had selected to travel to Jamaica. The operation was given a code name, Silver Testament, and had the highest security classification used by the NSA and CIA. Silver Testament carried the same security classification as assassination attempts on world leaders or threats to the president. The operation was only known to a handful of people, including the president, the NSA director, and the admiral. The last time this level of security was used was for the operation to assassinate Osama bin Laden.

At his briefing with Admiral Smythe, Mat asked where the name of the operation had come from; the admiral had said that it was inspired by an article he had read about the construction of the troubled silver line on the Washington Metro. It also seemed appropriate to the admiral, as the baby had been referred to as the silver man.

Mat also remembered from the briefing that Mary and her husband were estranged, although not actually divorced. They lived separate lives and rarely saw each other. Their kids were both in college and knew that their mother was "married to her work at NASA"; they saw nothing strange in her long absences from home. They kept in touch by Skype and by email.

Dr. Carl Lancaster was an educational psychologist, and Dr. Brian Fellows was a distinguished anthropologist. Both were life-long respected academics, and according to the intelligence reports, they both saw this assignment as a route to a Nobel Prize. Mat didn't know how the intel people would know that but kept the thought to himself.

Dr. Davis had been selected for the mission as a respected specialist in children's medicine, but also because she was Jewish, and the president thought this may be a useful political factor.

Jessica held back from the three men as they walked up to the bedroom suites, a chance to be alone with her thoughts. She was excited; it was as if her whole life had led to this one moment. She didn't know if the intelligence reports about the baby Jesus were right or not, but even if he wasn't the new Messiah, he was the first alien life form known on Earth. Either way, this was pretty significant, the sort of moment she had joined the CIA to experience. Mat was an ardent professional, here to do the job he was assigned to do. She had no sense he felt any more significance to this assignment than a drug bust or resolving a kidnapping, but she felt differently. This was special.

By sun-up, everyone was showered, dressed, and eating a good breakfast. Now a new sound could be heard over the insects and the birds of Jamaica, a wonderful sound that gave all the adults an extra spring in their step and a broader smile on their faces: it was the cry and laughter of a newborn baby.

John F. Kennedy Space Center, Florida

While Mary was having breakfast in Jamaica, Ali Palaszwaski returned to work at John F. Kennedy Space Center. KSC had a proud history; it was where the Apollo missions were launched. From KSC, Neil Armstrong left Earth and became the first man to walk on the moon. All the space shuttles were launched from KSC. The KSC visitor complex still attracted thousands of visitors every year. Visitors could walk around the huge Apollo rocket, walk inside a space shuttle, and even touch a moon rock.

From his office window, Ali could see Tower 39, where the space shuttles were launched. He could also see the enormous assembly building where the space shuttle was hoisted vertically so the huge liquid hydrogen tank and rocket boosters could be attached. These amazing feats of engineering would send the shuttle into orbit in nine minutes. A shuttle launch literally made the ground shake for miles around.

He could also see the building where most of the International Space Station (ISS) was built. The ISS was the size of a football field and has orbited the Earth since November 2000.

But all of these achievements were in the past, and these days, Kennedy was a sad place, a bit stuck in the past. Most of the buildings were built in the 1960s and 1970s; they reminded visitors of a high school, with that characteristic and uniform floor and wall finish and exposed pipes and plumbing. The low-rise buildings had long, windowless corridors with many doorways, which had obscure and impersonal numbers and letters on them, such as COSH Lab 17 or ISS S Detail 44.

Many of Ali's colleagues had left over the previous two years. They had been given early retirement or simply let go. When Congress refused to fund the shuttle follow-on program, KSC no longer had a mission. NASA had its budget slashed, and costs were cut.

Ali's department was one of the few areas of activity left. The team joked it was easy to get a parking slot close to the building, and there was no longer a long line at lunch, but most of the NASA employees of Ali's generation wished the old days were back.

The state of Florida and NASA had set up some agencies to assist ex-NASA employees to find a new career. Many workers joined NASA soon after graduation, and now in their late forties or early fifties, they were too young to retire but too old to just walk into another job.

One such agency, Space Florida, had an incubator unit just outside the security gate to help ex-NASA employees set up new businesses. The building had once been inside the security perimeter, but as the number of employees had shrunk, so did the security perimeter, and unused NASA buildings were leased or demolished.

Ali was entering the incubator now to meet an old colleague and friend, Dr. Frank Perusich. Frank and Ali had joined NASA about the same time, and both had an interest in the study of deep space particles.

Frank was a larger-than-life character, with a loud voice and an even louder belly laugh. Frank and another colleague had set up a consulting company to investigate mineral deposits in space.

The two-man company, somewhat grandly called Space Precious Metals Mining Inc., had a brass sign outside a small office suite on the second floor. Frank had emailed Ali a couple of days ago and invited him to drop by because he had something interesting to discuss.

Ali decided to drop in on his way into KSC that morning. They were both early birds by habit, and he arrived just after 7:30 in the morning; the building was largely deserted. Frank had bought a tray of pastries and coffee at Dunkin' Donuts on the way in, so they sat at a small meeting table in the office, talked about old times and their families, and had their morning fix of sugar, carbohydrates, and caffeine.

After a few minutes of chit-chat, Ali finished his last mouthful of cherry Danish and said, "You said you had something interesting to show me."

"Yes, I do." Frank turned his swivel chair, wiped his hands on a paper napkin, and grabbed a printout from his desk. "We have been working on a consulting contract with Elon Musk's Space X to look for evidence of rare minerals on asteroids."

Ali knew that Frank's company looked for certain spectrums in data from old space missions. This data had been accumulated by the Hubble Space Telescope and other deep space satellites that were mapping the asteroid belt, between Mars and Jupiter. It was thought that many of these asteroids could contain valuable minerals like gold, platinum, and lithium, or even precious stones like diamonds. Musk, the billionaire behind Tesla electric cars and the Space X commercial space missions, hoped to one day send a manned mission to an asteroid to collect these precious metals. Ali thought this was unrealistic but said nothing.

Frank flicked through the printouts and pointed to a graph on the page.

"When we look for the minerals, we normally see a peak in this part of the spectrum here." Frank pointed with a sugary finger at a small range of peaks on the graph and then turned the page. "However, what we found here was not what we expected at all."

Frank's sticky finger was pointing at a second graph that showed a much higher peak in a different part of the spectrum.

Ali said, "What's the anomaly?" It was a reasonable question from one scientist to another to see if there was a flaw in the data.

Frank had obviously anticipated the question and pushed the printout to Ali. "See for yourself."

The rest of the printouts were pages of similar readings showing the same peak on different days, but from different satellites. Clearly, there was a consistency in the data.

When he arrived at his office twenty minutes later, Ali closed his office door and called the admiral on his cell phone.

Admiral Smythe answered on the second ring with a curt, "Yes?"

"Admiral, this is Ali Palaszwaski at KSC. How are you doing?"

"Fine, what can I help you with?"

"I have come across some new data that I would like to discuss with you."

"How significant is it?"

"Admiral, it could be very significant. I would really like Mary Morrell to also have—"

"Ali, Mary cannot be reached just now," the admiral interrupted. "I'll send a plane for you this afternoon." Then he hung up.

Ali emailed his boss that he had to go to Washington for a few days, and then he went home to tell his wife he needed his overnight bag.

Two hours later, Ali arrived at Fort Meade and was shown into a meeting room with a view of the parking lot. He was offered something to drink and told that the admiral would be with him shortly.

A few minutes later, Admiral Smythe walked in, looking as immaculate as ever in his tailored suit. They shook hands, and the admiral got down to business.

"So what have you got to tell me?"

Ali reached into his briefcase for the sheaf of papers that Perusich had given him and went through a similar explanation of the graphical peaks.

The admiral sat straighter in his chair and said, "So what?"

Ali said, in clear and measured tones, "I think it's a beacon for alien visitors."

"What do you mean, a beacon?"

"To guide them in, a bit like the way commercial airliners navigate their way across the globe. They lock on to radar tracking beacons in certain locations."

"You mean there are more of them coming?"

"I don't know that, Admiral, and I cannot be 100 percent certain that what I am saying is correct, but I believe …"

The admiral interrupted, "Why aren't you 100 percent certain?"

"I need to verify some data with colleagues, and the best person to do that is Mary Morrell. I called her cell phone, but it's no longer connected, and she hasn't replied to my email."

The admiral sat in silence for a few minutes, staring directly at the scientist. Ali knew when to shut up.

Suddenly, the admiral stood up, said, "Wait here," and left, closing the door behind him. An orderly came in and asked Ali if he would like something else to drink. Ali asked for coffee. He knew it would be a long night.

Ali awoke in a helicopter. It was dark, and he realized they were about to make a landing. He could see a few lights in the distance, but otherwise no distinguishable features. He was slumped on the rear seat next to a man he had never seen before. In the front seat next to the pilot sat the admiral.

Ali blinked and tried to focus. His mouth felt dry, and he was bursting to pee. He could not remember how he had got here, and then he remembered the coffee. They must have put something in it, he thought. He had probably been drugged.

The tall, handsome black man next to him said, "Dr. Palaszwaski, I am pleased to meet you; my name is Mat."

Ali shook his hand unwillingly and asked, "Where are we going?"

Mat tugged on Ali's seatbelt to check he was strapped in and said evasively, "You'll find out soon enough."

With that, he clicked a switch on his headphones and spoke to the admiral, who turned and acknowledged Ali was awake. Ali realized he was being shut out and decided instead to watch the lights below to see if he could work out where they were.

He watched the ground come up to meet them, and then the helicopter touched down with a slight bump. Doors were opened by people outside, and Ali, the admiral, and Mat all disembarked. Ali noted that Mat carried Ali's briefcase and his overnight bag.

They were led down a staircase and into a large house, which was surrounded by magnificent tropical gardens and a large pool. He didn't know where he was, but he knew better than to ask. Besides, he felt tired and groggy, and he just wanted to find a bathroom and then get some rest. But in the short distance to the house, he sensed that it was warm; it felt like he was back in southern Florida or possibly in the Caribbean.

Ali was shown to a bedroom and told to get a few hours' sleep. He had a headache, and after going to the bathroom, he showered, took some headache tablets, and slumped into bed.

He awoke to blazing sunshine and a discreet knock at the door. In his shorts and t-shirt, he opened the door to find a uniformed maid with a breakfast tray, which she placed on the table. He went to find his wallet, expecting to have to tip her, but she had already left, shutting the door behind her.

He was hungry. He thought it may be a side effect of the sleeping drug they had given him. He ate the fruit, eggs, and bagels but didn't touch the coffee. "Once bitten, twice shy," he mused.

He showered and dressed, and just as he was tying his shoelaces, there was a loud knock on the door. He looked up as the admiral barged into the room, looking resplendent in a smart tropical suit. He stood to one side and was followed in by Mary Morrell, who in contrast made a much less aggressive entrance.

As Ali stood up in surprise, with one shoe still untied. Ali and Mary hugged warmly. The admiral said, "Dr. Palaszwaski, I apologize for bringing you here in the middle of the night, but it was necessary for the security of this operation."

Ali was quite relieved when Mary released him from her hug; she said, "Ali, we have some exciting news to share. There is someone I would like you to meet." She was clearly enthusiastic and grabbed his hand, pulling him to follow her.

Not known for his small talk, the admiral had already left the room. Ali released his hand, quickly tied his shoe lace, and caught up with her.

He was still a little groggy from the sleeping drug. He followed Mary to an office suite in an adjacent building, and they sat down in a comfortable meeting room with a good view of the gardens. He saw children's toys in the garden but thought nothing of it. He assumed this was some sort of US government facility. Like most scientists, he was not impressed by large houses or wealth. He knew it was fruitless to ask too many questions about this facility. For now, he was content to know they were somewhere in Jamaica. He thought he should tell his wife but then realized that she probably thought he was still at Langley.

The meeting room table was covered in printouts, and there was a laptop connected to a large screen that displayed the NSA logo. On the wall was a large whiteboard that was covered in notes and calculations, written in Mary's distinctive rounded script. Mary sat down at the laptop; Ali saw her type a few characters on the keyboard, and the large screen changed to display a map of the solar system and a graph similar to the one he had seen in Frank Perusich's office.

As Mary began an explanation, she opened a can of soda and a bag of potato chips. "I have been analyzing the data provided by Perusich at Kennedy, and we are seeing a distinctive pattern in this sector of the solar system." She moved the mouse on the computer and highlighted an area on the computer screen. She munched another few chips while she continued, "We are seeing a distinctive and regular pattern of activity that seems to indicate some form of transmission or some form of beacon."

Ali stood and examined the graph on the screen more closely so he could see the regular and uniform blips on the graph.

As he did so, he heard the admiral's voice from behind him, saying, "I agree with Mary. I think it's a beacon or some sort of homing device."

Ali turned to see Admiral Smythe enter the room, leading a young black boy of four or five by the hand. Mary beamed as she saw the boy; he instinctively ran to her embrace. The boy said, "Mama, it is a beacon."

Mary kissed the boy's hair and said, "Jesus, I want you to meet a good friend of mine, one of the most brilliant scientists at NASA. Jesus, this is Dr. Ali Palaszwaski."

Ali said, "I'm pleased to meet you, Jesus."

But inside, he was shocked; if this was the baby he had seen born a few weeks earlier in the Colorado bunker, he had grown up unbelievably fast.

Jesus looked at Ali with highly intelligent eyes, and Mary said, "Ali, I know what you are thinking: Jesus has developed very fast. After just a few weeks, he has the body of a five-year-old."

Jesus then stunned Ali by saying, "Dr. Palaszwaski, I just read your paper on space debris and found the conclusion very interesting indeed."

Ali sat down in shock; he couldn't believe that a child of five could have read a scientific paper.

Mary was clearly proud of her protégé. She smiled at Ali's obvious shock and amazement at Jesus's comment. But before she could say anything, the admiral interjected in his characteristic, no-nonsense way, "Jesus, what did you mean when you said that it is a beacon?"

The child said, "The spectrum on your charts are similar to the Wow! signal detected about forty of your sun's revolutions ago. My people use a frequency about 1420MHz, to hide where hydrogen resonates."

Jesus laughed as if he had made a joke, and Mary laughed with him. The admiral sat stone faced. Ali was so shocked by the lucid scientific explanation that he failed to laugh, but he did manage a weak smile.

Mary provided a brief technical explanation for the admiral's benefit: "The Wow! signal caused great excitement amongst radio astronomers in 1977. Scientists in Ohio were working on the Search for Extra-Terrestrial Intelligence project, SETI for short. They detected a pattern in a radio signal that they thought emanated from an intelligent life form in outer space. It lasted just seventy-two seconds and was never detected again. The frequency of the Wow! signal is very similar to the frequency that hydrogen resonates, and as the universe is largely made up of hydrogen, it is easy to confuse it, like looking for the proverbial needle in a haystack."

Mary's explanation had given Ali time to recover from his initial shock, so he asked Jesus, "So please tell us, why would you want to hide in the hydrogen spectrum?"

"To avoid detection, of course, silly; they don't want the homing beacons discovered."

Mary ruffled Jesus's hair at the slightly disrespectful reply, but before she could reprimand him, Ali persisted, "But why don't they want their homing beacons discovered?"

"So the elimination capsules cannot be detected and destroyed."

Now Mary took over the line of questioning.

"Jesus, sweetie, we have talked about these elimination capsules before; now tell these two gentlemen what you know about them."

"My people monitor the cosmos; my mission here was to plant sensors on your planet. The sensors showed an extraordinary rapid progress in this civilization, so to prevent you from becoming a threat to them, they are sending elimination capsules here."

"Jesus, sweetie, what will happen when the elimination capsules arrive?"

Jesus replied with a childlike honesty, as if relating a trivial fact without realizing the seriousness of his words, "They will eliminate 99 percent of known life, returning evolution back to a point where it is no longer a threat."

The admiral let out a gasp. Mary covered her face with her hand in shock.

Ali sat impassively and asked, "How do the elimination capsules work?"

"They contain an organic virus that is 99 percent effective against all life forms."

Admiral Smythe asked, "When will the elimination capsules arrive?"

Jesus thought for a moment and moved his lips as if performing a mental calculation, and then he said in his clear, confident child's voice, "616 days, 6 hours, 14 minutes, and 27 seconds."

Back in Washington, the president and the NSA director watched a recording of the conversation with Jesus.

Admiral Smythe said what they were all thinking: "If the boy is right, we've got about eighteen months left."

Silver Shield, August 12, 2012, 616 Days to Go

That day, the Silver Shield operation was sanctioned by the NSA director, with the same security classification as Silver Testament. The goal was to destroy the elimination capsules before they could reach Earth. The admiral took personal charge of the operation and appointed Ali as his special scientific advisor. He was given a spacious office at Fort Meade, just down the hall from the admiral's.

Admiral Smythe also introduced Ali to a weapons expert he had assigned to the team. His name was Lance Lord. General Lord was a tall, broad-shouldered man, with gray hair and a handsome tanned face. He had retired from the Air Force and lived on a yacht in California. Previously he had run the Star Wars project, which developed space weapons to destroy enemy satellites and protect US satellites from electronic and physical attack. Ali discovered that Lance had a very firm and painful handshake.

Ali's first job was to assemble a scientific team to help him. He opened PowerPoint on his computer and began typing what he knew. He did this often, as a way of analyzing complex information and finding a way forward.

First he typed:

- *Homing beacon found on asteroid.*
- *Elimination capsules en route to Earth from place unknown.*
- *Estimated time of arrival: December 25, 2014, 9:37 EDT*

The thought hadn't struck him until then, but that was Christmas Day, next year.

He opened a new slide and typed:

Objectives:

1. *Prevent elimination capsules reaching Earth*
2. *If Objective 1 fails, plan to minimize destruction*

Ali had a scientific and logical mind. He was trained to look at the facts, analyze the situation, and then come up with a solution. He was not conditioned to think of the emotional destruction around this, but he did give some thought to the PR consequences if this story leaked.

He thought of the movie *Men in Black,* where a secret government agency continually dealt with extra-terrestrials and threats to destroy the planet, while the general population knew nothing about it. He now wished there was such an agency. He could have just called them and job done. He looked at the framed picture of his wife and kids on his desk and felt icy sweat on his neck. Unfortunately, there were no men in black, but if he failed, it would be the end for his family and billions of people on Earth.

Over the next few days, Ali and Lance brought in their respective teams, and the skeleton plans were fleshed out. Silver Shield expanded to occupy an entire floor in the Fort Meade complex. A digital clock was installed that ominously counted down the time to impact. The admiral had no need to exert his dogmatic management style on the teams; the clock gave them all the focus they needed.

Ali's skeleton objectives became the two key objectives of the mission, but Admiral Smythe added a third: about press leakage. So under the digital clock, there was a large printed notice that read:

Silver Shield: Objectives

1. Prevent impact
2. Minimize effect
3. Stop PR

Ali thought this typical of the admiral, to shorten everything so it was as brief as possible. Lance's team were working around the clock, because given the timescale that Jesus had given them, they had only a few weeks to launch a mission to reach the location of the homing beacon in time. Ali knew from his time at NASA just how big space was and how long it took to travel through the universe. Ali recalled that shortly after joining NASA as a trainee, he had watched the Voyager 2 lift off from Cape Canaveral, Florida, on August 20, 1977. He could always remember dates like that. But it was not until he had served a further twenty-two years at NASA before the spacecraft reached the planet Jupiter. Of course, they had learnt a lot since then, and spacecraft were faster, but they still had to travel a third of the distance to Jupiter in less than two years.

Nobody had ever deployed a space weapon in anger before, but several nations had drawn up plans and conducted tests, including the United States. Lance had disclosed during one of the regular three-way briefings with Ali and the admiral that during his time running the Star Wars program, America had secretly test-fired several space weapons. He said the weapons had deployed successfully, but at that point, the admiral had curtailed the conversation. Ali realized he was trusted to a certain extent, but certain information was not going to be disclosed to him. Secretly, he was glad; he knew that the United States (and, for that matter, other nations around the world) possessed terrible weapons of mass destruction, but as a pacifist, he preferred not to think about them too much.

Meanwhile, back in Jamaica, Mary was tasked with extracting as much information from Jesus as she could. They had compiled a small team of child psychologists, and a select team of specialists analyzed video footage of Jesus. His every movement was recorded, even his visits to the bathroom. They even filmed him in his sleep, in case he said something while he was dreaming, but he never had so far.

Every second was on tape, and a 24/7 operation was set up by the admiral to analyze all the footage. As each team of analysts finished their shift, they would send a summary email of anything significant from the tapes. But so far, it had yielded no further intelligence.

Each morning, Mary spoke on a secure line with the head of the analysts team, and they discussed a strategy for the day.

The previous day, they had tried to talk to Jesus about a mission to find the silver spacecraft and return home, but Jesus said this was out of the question until his rebirth was complete. But so far, he could give Mary no timescale for the process.

They asked him about destroying the homing beacons and the elimination capsules, but he just said that was impossible.

Working with the education psychologists, they began a program to educate Jesus about weapons that used electromagnetic pulses and even nuclear weapons, in the hope that he may say something that would link a possible destruction method. Although Jesus was a very quick learner, only so much could be done each day, and so far, there had been no significant breakthroughs.

It had just been a few weeks since Ali had been drugged and flown at night to Jamaica. When the admiral complained that progress was slow, Mary reminded them that Jesus was just a little boy.

A deep space mission such as this was usually ten years in the planning. For Silver Shield, they had just a few weeks.

Ali had been hugely impressed by Lance, and they now had a robust plan that had been conceived in such a short time. One major issue was maintaining secrecy of the mission, because if word got out, there could be absolute panic and anarchy in the streets. Launching a rocket was not a subtle thing, and unscheduled launches went around the newswires on the Internet like wildfire. So Lance had come up with the brilliant plan of using the cover of an existing scheduled NASA mission to Mars. This mission, called Mars Rover 2, had been planned to coincide with the red planet's orbit being closer to Earth.

Effectively, the NSA had pulled rank on the NASA mission and hijacked the launch vehicle, replacing the unmanned Rover 2 vehicle with their own payload of mass destruction. Ali knew that his scientific colleagues would be deeply upset by this; he knew some of the people working on the mission personally. He felt bad, because the admiral had ordered that none of the Mars Rover 2 team were to be told about the payload switch until after the mission reached Mars. Admiral Smythe reluctantly agreed that it would be necessary to tell them from this point on, because instead of landing on Mars, as originally planned, the Silver Shield rocket would slingshot around the planet and accelerate on toward the homing beacon on the asteroid.

On top of this, Lance and his team identified three other rockets that were capable of launching in time to reach the asteroid. One was a US rocket built by Boeing, the second was a Russian rocket that had been built but never launched because of funding cuts, and the third was a Chinese rocket that Lance found out about through his personal connections. It turned out that not even the CIA knew the Chinese had this particular rocket.

In an unprecedented level of speed and cooperation, within days, leading representatives of both the Chinese and Russian space programs had arrived at Fort Meade and were fully briefed. It was a huge risk to the secrecy of the mission, but the president realized the consequences and seriousness of the threat.

Lance now formed three teams of weapons experts. The Russian rocket could carry the heaviest payload and was to be loaded with nuclear weapons, with the sole aim of destroying the asteroid where the homing beacon was located. A contract was given to a Russian engineering company to build a vehicle to smash into the asteroid. They were told it was to analyze mineral samples. The company asked no questions; they were glad of the work.

They were even more delighted when they were asked to build a second identical vehicle. President Putin authorized the construction of a second Russian rocket, even though it would be too late to reach the asteroid by the deadline; it was a backup plan and his contribution to Silver Shield.

This was the riskiest launch. If the rocket exploded on the launch pad, and an uncomfortably large number of Russian rockets did, it would cause the largest nuclear explosion on Earth. Although the launch pad was in a remote part of Kazakhstan, the prevailing winds would mean large parts of Asia, including India, Korea, Indonesia, Malaysia, Singapore, and possibly Japan, could experience multiple casualties. The worst case scenario was billions of casualties.

While the Russian team was at Fort Meade, an unmarked buff folder was discreetly left on the main Russian rocket engineer's desk. It contained the classified designs of a new US thruster engine control valve. These valves had failed on several previous Russian missions. New valves were fitted to the Russian rocket within days. The US and Russian engineers considered the risk factors at launch now to be within an acceptable range. Both the US and Russian presidents then authorized the mission.

The US rocket would carry a pulse system that could emit a powerful burst of electromagnetic radiation (EMR). This was like a high-powered pulse of radio waves concentrated in the Wow! spectrum of hydrogen. This intelligence had been gained during Ali and Mary's discussion with Jesus.

This pulse would disrupt the communication from the homing beacon. In theory, the EMR pulse could be activated a reasonable distance from the asteroid, so it was hoped that the beacon could be neutralized sooner rather than later.

This rocket was already on a launch tower, located in the secure Air Force base at Kennedy. As soon as the payload was on board, the rocket was launched under the cover of darkness. The US Air Force press office announced the mission as a military satellite supply mission. The press release was largely ignored.

That morning, Lance announced, "Bird 2 has flown." The team cheered and celebrated with pizza at their desks at lunch.

Within weeks, a second Boeing rocket would be assembled at the launch tower. Again, this one was going to be too late, but they wanted to send another EMR-equipped vehicle as a backup. This was known as Bird 2A. The two Russian rockets were codenamed Bird 1 and Bird 1R.

The Chinese rocket had the most ambitious of the three plans. It was the slowest of the three and would be the last to reach the asteroid, but if Bird 1 and Bird 2 failed in their missions, then Bird 3 would be the only hope. The goal was to capture the beacon and then fly it directly into the planet Jupiter. To their great embarrassment, the Chinese could not produce a second rocket in time; there was no backup. The Chinese premier apologized to both the US president and the Russian president, explaining through an interpreter that "it was not a question of money, but nine women can't make a baby in one month."

The Chinese mission was also different because it would be a manned mission. In fact, the two-person crew would be martyrs. They would have to land on the asteroid, locate the beacon, and then fly their spacecraft directly at the planet Jupiter, destroying it.

The mission seemed fanciful, but it was a good chance for both the Americans and Russians to find out how good the Chinese space program really was.

There was a high probability that the Chinese crew would be dead by the time they reached Jupiter, killed by space radiation. Also, as Jupiter's gravitational pull caught them, they would accelerate to speeds way beyond what a human had traveled before. It was not clear if they would survive.

On top of this, they would arrive after Bird 1, which meant the asteroid could have been blown into millions of radioactive fragments. If the homing beacon was still active after this explosion, and the EMR pulses from Bird 2, then locating the beacon would not be a problem. But in doing so, the Chinese crew would expose themselves to deadly radiation.

There was also the not-insignificant challenge of landing a spacecraft on an asteroid, finding the homing beacon (nobody knew what it looked like), and then taking off again. They would also have a short window before Bird 1R, with its second nuclear payload, and Bird 2A arrived with its EMR. Both could prove lethal to the Chinese astronauts.

While the backup birds could be controlled and delayed, this would be a difficult decision at the time.

The Chinese rocket would then have just enough fuel to take off and head toward Jupiter before the massive planet's gravitational pull caught them and pulled them inexorably toward certain destruction. They would not have enough fuel to return to Earth.

Surprisingly, the Chinese said there were a large number of volunteers for this mission. A crew was selected in secret; the US team asked no questions.

The mathematicians gave Birds 1 and 2 a 60 percent chance of success and Bird 3 a 20 percent chance of success.

Admiral Smythe then ordered the Silver Shield team to split into two. Lance and the three rocket control teams relocated to Houston, while Ali, who was concentrating on what to do if the elimination capsules reached Earth, remained in Fort Meade.

November 12, 2013, 160 Days to Go

The large digital clock on the Fort Meade wall read 160 days, 8 hours, 10 minutes, 37 seconds.

Ali realized that his office trash bin contained remnants of last night's dinner, today's breakfast, and today's lunch. He had slept briefly in his desk chair and showered in the office washroom. He had not left the building for more than thirty-six hours.

He was running out of ideas, and the team around him was becoming fractious and ineffective. They had assembled an awesome group that included germ warfare experts from Britain, Russia, China, and North Korea. The North Koreans were known to be particularly advanced in this area.

They had ruled out vaccination early on. First, they didn't know what to vaccinate against, but even if they did, they probably couldn't make enough vaccine and administer it in time. Of course, there was the argument to protect just the great and the good, but even that required an impossibly large amount of an unknown remedy.

Next, they didn't know how many elimination capsules there were. Mary hadn't been able to clarify this with Jesus. Ali knew that the team of education psychologists and psychiatrists in Jamaica were trying to extract as much information from Jesus as they could, by associating different objects and methodologies. For example, they showed him a corked test tube and asked, in a round-about way, if this looked like an elimination capsule. But so far, they had learned nothing at all.

Ali was tired. He rubbed his eyes and looked up at the whiteboards on his office wall. One board was dedicated to considering the possibility that there was just one elimination capsule; could they isolate it and contain it in some way? Another board dealt with the possibility that there were multiple capsules; could they contain all or most of those?

They didn't know if the elimination capsules would be the size of a test tube or a truck or a large building. They didn't know if they would contain a gas, a liquid, or a solid. They didn't know if they would be animal, vegetable, or mineral. They knew zip.

Another whiteboard was dedicated to considering evacuating some of the human population to the moon or to Mars. The UN had set up a project to build such a craft. But it was only in the preplanning phase and could not be built for decades, let alone months.

Everyone associated with Silver Shield considered the risk too high to tell the UN any details of the threat, knowing how easily the information could leak and cause international panic. Ali concurred with this. But he felt desperate and alone; he missed his wife and family. He fell asleep at his desk, clutching the picture of his family.

The ringing of his desk phone woke him.

He picked up the handset and said sleepily, "Palaszwaski."

"Ali, glad I caught you. You are in early?"

Ali recognized Mary's distinct voice calling from Jamaica. He could tell by her voice that she was excited about something. He noticed the red light on his phone blink, indicating that this call was on a secure encrypted connection. He rubbed his eyes and noticed it was just getting light outside.

Mary went on, "Ali, I think we have a breakthrough."

Ali sat up immediately and grabbed a legal pad so he could make notes.

Mary went on, "One of the psychologists suggested we show Jesus some old science fiction movies and see if anything came of it. We started with *ET.* Jesus asked for a push bike, but he didn't make it fly. We then showed him all the *Star Wars* movies; he thought they were very funny and began mimicking the characteristic swoosh-swoosh sound of the Jedi lightsaber."

Over the phone, Ali could hear the sound of Mary sorting through the DVD boxes.

She continued, "We then tried the three *Men in Black* movies; he became bored and fell asleep. They showed him *Judgment Day*, *Armageddon*, and *Deep Impact* (about a giant asteroid destroying the Earth). After watching *Deep Impact*, Jesus became quite melancholy."

Ali interjected, "What do you mean, melancholy?"

"Well, upset really; I would like to play you a CCTV clip if you are on-line."

Ali moved his computer mouse and clicked an icon to give Mary permission to open a video clip on his computer. "Sure, go ahead."

This was practiced routine; they had spent many hours on video conferences in this way. Ali hung up the phone, and an image of Mary sitting in the office in Jamaica appeared in a window on his large PC screen. Her voice now came over the computer speakers.

"He went for a ride around the gardens on his bicycle," she said. "He came and sat with me in the nursery."

Ali now watched as a HD video opened on his computer screen of Mary and Jesus in the nursery in Jamaica. There was a date and time on the video, so Ali could see that the footage had been recorded yesterday evening, he assumed just before Jesus's bedtime.

Mary sat in one of large beanbag chairs in the nursery, and she had a protective arm around Jesus as she read a story to him. Remotely, Mary fast-forwarded the video footage, obviously moving it forward to a specific section that she wanted Ali to hear. She paused the video occasionally, and he recognized the story as *Oliver Twist* by Charles Dickens.

Mary then put the video on Play, and he heard Jesus's distinct, high-pitched voice ask, "Mama, that part of the movie where the big waves come and destroy those two people on the beach, could that happen to you?" He pointed at the ocean, which could be seen out the nursery window.

Ali remembered that in *Deep Impact*, the heroine, played by Tea Leoni, and her father, played by Maximilian Schell, hug each other on the beach as the giant wave from the asteroid's impact in the ocean overwhelms them, obviously drowning them instantly.

Mary said, "Well, sweetie, if an asteroid fell into the ocean of that size, we don't really know what would happen. It would cause a big wave, a tsunami, and it could reach up here. We would have to go higher up the mountain.

She asked, “Is that what the elimination capsules are like?”

“Well, they are different, depending on the planet. The exact form will be decided once the delivery craft is within range.”

“Do you mean when it reaches where the homing beacon is located?”

“Yes, and then the capsules travel the short distance to the planet on their own. Sometimes, they grow in flight so they are large enough to change the atmospheric conditions on the planet but not destroy it completely; other times, they use an organic virus.”

“What is an organic virus?”

“Mama, I'm not sure, it is not my area of specialty, but I know it makes life forms on the planet sick; most of them die.”

“Would the organic virus kill me?”

“If it reached the planet, yes, it would, Mama, and probably everyone here.”

“Would that include Mat, Jessica, Jed, and Lisa?”

Ali realized that Mary was playing on the boy's heartstrings. She must have felt bad doing it, because he was very fond of his adopted family and guardians at Jacobs Creek, especially Jed and Lisa, who treated him like the son they never had.

Jesus was silent for a while; he rubbed his eyes, as if wiping away a tear, and then over the computer speakers came the words that Ali so wanted to hear: “Mama, I think I know how to stop the elimination capsules.”

Mary had awoken Ali in his office a little after six o'clock, and by seven, he was back in his office, having showered and shaved. He was on his third cup of coffee and watching the CCTV footage of Mary's conversation with Jesus with the admiral; Lance viewed the footage via secure video link from Houston. The admiral had frowned at Ali's untidy office when he had walked in, looking as immaculate as ever; he kicked his overflowing waste bin with disdain and moved Ali's half-eaten bagel to the far side of his desk so he could sit down with a good view of the screen. He took out a clean handkerchief from his pocket and wiped the crumbs away from the desk in front of him.

Ali ignored all this, because he was excited that they had a plan and a purpose. Ali was impressed by how effectively Lance and the admiral went into an operational mode. Now that they knew the nature of the enemy they were fighting, their true military professionalism shone through.

Admiral Smythe was scheduled to meet with the president and General Alexander later that afternoon, to report on the progress of Silver Shield. This was opportune, because they faced a key operational dilemma. Bird 2 was now in range, which could send out a powerful EMR beam to override the signal from the homing beacon. However, the concern was that activating the EMR beam could alert the craft delivering the elimination capsules. Now that they knew how to destroy the elimination capsules, was it worth the risk to switch on an EMR signal? A tough call.

While Ali, Admiral Smythe, and Lance viewed the video, back in Jamaica, Jesus was throwing a Frisbee with Mat in the pool; it was one of the boy's favorite things to do.

Mary watched them from the nursery window. She could see Jesus laughing as he enjoyed the game. He splashed in the pool, and his ebony skin shone in the sunlight as he stretched to catch the Frisbee. He threw it back to Mat with great dexterity. Mat was a fit man, but Jesus matched him throw by throw.

Despite the happy-go-lucky scene, Mary had tears in her eyes. She realized just how dangerous destroying the elimination capsules would be for her baby. He would have to go back into space before his regeneration was complete. She sat down on a beanbag chair and picked up the Charles Dickens novel they had been reading.

It was the part where the boys drew lots to decide who would ask for more food; Oliver lost, and she read the famous line out loud: "Please, sir, I want some more." She reflected on how life was a lottery; how had she ended up here?

As she read, Jesus rushed in. He wore only his swimming shorts and carried a towel. He had the body of pre-pubescent boy now; the psychologists said he had the body of an eleven-year-old but the mind of a fully grown adult. His body had matured from a baby to the equivalent of an eleven-year-old human in less than a year. His mood changed from happiness and excitement from his game in the pool to immediate concern as he saw the look on Mary's face.

He rushed into her lap, dropping the towel on the floor, and Mary hugged him instinctively, ignoring the dampness on her clothes from his wet swimming shorts.

"Mama, don't be sad. It will be okay."

Although Jesus's voice was still high pitched like a boy, he spoke with the true concern of an adult.

"How can I not be worried?" she asked. "If you go into space, you may not be able to regenerate fully."

"Mama, I believe I will be okay. I must try. I estimate that my regeneration is halfway finished. If I keep the craft below sub-atomic speed, I will be able to complete the regeneration when I return."

Mary assumed that sub-atomic speed referred to some acceleration or high-speed maneuvering of the silver craft.

"But how can you be sure you can do that?"

"It is no great distance to the homing beacon, so I believe I can achieve well within the tolerances I have set."

Mary hugged Jesus. It was strange to hug a boy's body, to hear a boy speak, but to hear the seasoned argument of full-grown man.

"Come on," she said. "Let's go see what's for lunch."

The headline in *Weekly World News*:

Giant Asteroid on Course to Destroy Earth

> *Astronomers have confirmed that a giant asteroid is on a direct collision course with Earth and will destroy the planet on Christmas Day.*

Amateur astronomers are enthusiastic folk, and they love to exchange their observations on the Internet. As the elimination capsule grew in size, it became visible, and astronomer blogs began to fill with data and comment. As night fell around the globe, different astronomers in different countries began to track the object. The story was picked up by some of the scientific press.

Government agencies around the world also began tracking the object. Those countries that were outside of the Silver Shield community began to issue pictures and press releases.

TV stations and national newspapers picked up the story.

Sally Carmichael was briefing the president, the NSA director, and the admiral. She looked like a Hollywood actress, wearing a blue Chanel suit and white silk blouse. Her blonde hair was almost the color of her blouse, but not as white as her teeth. Her glossy lips were blood red.

"Mr. President," she began, "I recommend we let NASA issue a statement on the asteroid; otherwise, it will look suspicious. I suggest a headline like *NASA Says Giant Asteroid Will Miss Earth.* To say nothing will just allow speculation to build. If we issue the statement, it will be a headline for today and forgotten tomorrow."

The president looked at General Alexander, prompting him to speak.

The NSA director leaned forward in his seat and said quietly, "May I brief the president in private?" He looked sideways at Sally, who got the hint.

This was not unusual for sensitive national security matters, but Sally made a point of shuffling her briefing papers and closing the door behind her quite loudly. General Alexander noticed she left behind an aroma of expensive perfume.

When the three of them were alone, he said to the admiral, "Please brief the president on the latest developments."

"Sir, we know that the elimination capsule has been growing in size. It is detectable by amateur astronomers now, and there is a lot of comment about it on the Internet. We understand that Jesus intends to reverse this growth and then destroy the capsule by flying it into the sun. However, Mary believes doing so may cause irreparable harm to his regeneration process, and he may not return from space."

He continued, "We do not know how long it will take for the elimination capsule to shrink in size, and we do not have any way of communicating with Jesus once he leaves Earth. There is a significant risk that the elimination capsule may continue to grow in size before he reaches it. So I would suggest that we word any press comment now in such a way to reflect that."

General Alexander interjected, "Sir, we also need to brief our allies on Silver Shield. They too will be under pressure to say something about the object. It may be a better tactic to leave NASA out of it and allow some other nation's space agency to take the lead. This way, we can avoid any embarrassment for NASA."

The president asked, "Who do you suggest?"

"How about the ESA?"

"The European Space Agency? Didn't they refuse to cooperate on Silver Shield?"

"Exactly, sir; let them end up with egg on their face."

Sally was a little surprised when the president told her to brief ESA but not NASA on the story, but she did not question why. She was enjoying these one-on-one briefings with the president, and he was becoming increasingly flirtatious with her. She was flattered by his eyes following her long legs and ample breasts. He was just a man, after all. She wasn't sure where it would all lead but decided she would wear a lower cut blouse and silk stockings for their next encounter.

She contacted Michel Devereau, the deputy director of ESA, who was based in Brussels, Belgium. Michel was French and had an accent to die for, but he was short and fat in a Napoleonic way and not Sally's type.

Sally briefed Michel on the asteroid and asked if his press people would put out a statement saying it would get smaller. Michel agreed to send it to her for comment before it was released. He flirted with her outrageously on the phone for a few minutes, saying he would be coming to Washington next month for a conference, and they should have dinner and champagne. She said, "Of course. I would love to see you." As soon as they hung up, she made a note in her Blackberry diary to be out of town that week.

Michel's email arrived as she was eating her lunch at her desk. There were two kisses at the end and a link to his itinerary at the conference. She opened the attachment, read it quickly, and replied:

> *"Michel, Press release fine with me, thank you. Hope to see you next month. X"*

The ESA press release hit the news wires twenty minutes later.

Giant Asteroid Will Miss Earth

Brussels, Belgium: A giant asteroid between Mars and Jupiter is not on track to reach Earth and will soon shrink in size, ESA scientists have calculated …

The next day, the asteroid grew larger, and the story was featured on the front page of *Le Figaro* in France, the *Daily Telegraph* in the UK, *Der Spiegel* in Germany, and several other European national newspapers as "highly embarrassing" for ESA who had "obviously got it wrong again."

Michel got a dressing-down from the ESA chief executive, but when he called Sally for an explanation, his call went straight to her voicemail, and her assistant said she was meeting with the president and could not be disturbed.

That night, Sally was alone in her Washington apartment, working on her laptop. Evenings alone were rare, and she treasured them. Her life was a whirlwind of dinners, formal White House events, and less-formal meetings with key journalists and politicos. She sat on her large double sofa in a comfortable track suit. She sipped at a mineral water, glad to miss dinner and have a chance to detox.

She was looking at the latest economic data and preparing a briefing paper for the president. She paused to look up at the vase with a dozen beautiful red roses; they had been sent from the NSA Director, Kevin Alexander, along with a note. It read, "I apologize for excluding you, K."

Her Blackberry buzzed, and she saw a text message from him: "*Did you get all 12? K.*"

She looked up again at the roses. He was clearly smitten with her. She knew how to flirt and how to keep a man at bay. Hardly a day or a meeting went by without someone trying to get her into bed. She smiled to herself as her Blackberry beeped again, as another email from Michel Devereau arrived, asking her to call him. She noticed he only added one kiss this time.

She mused on Kevin Alexander, the NSA director. He was a tall, good-looking man, a strong candidate for the nomination when the president ended his second term. He was estranged from his second wife; she had never met her, but she was quite a feisty woman by all accounts. Kevin came from a banking family and was rumored to be worth over $100 million. He had chosen a military career rather than banking and had drifted into politics after serving as a military spokesman during the second Gulf War. Quite a catch, really.

She replied to his text, "*Yes, all 12 lovely, thanks S.*" She decided not to add an x for a kiss.

She returned her concentration back to the economic data, which was surprisingly positive. She noticed a comment from one of the analysts that linked the economic progress to the stories about the new Messiah.

A year had passed since she had orchestrated the White House campaign to reveal the false white baby and the actress to the world. During that time, stock markets around the world had risen to all-time highs, investment had grown to unprecedented levels, and world economic activity had surged. She flicked the page to look at several graphs, which all showed positive growth. The analysts also said there had been an increase in global conflicts being curtailed, truces were reached, and tensions had eased. Charities and not-for-profit organizations were reporting increased donations. In most of the developed world, the number of people getting married rose, the number of divorces fell, and the pregnancy rate increased.

The report also looked at crime statistics, which showed a decline in both violent and nonviolent crimes in most US cities since the news of the baby Jesus.

Sally opened a file on her laptop that monitored the press references to the story and saw clearly that after the initial flurry of press comment, the story had disappeared from the front pages. Few continued to follow the story, apart from the eccentric. The tactics by Malcolm Packer, the British PR expert, had worked. Although Sally knew that the execution of his strategy was somewhat altered by the White House, it was a gamble that had paid off.

The actress who had played Mary in the press conference had adopted the baby as her own; she then met a young man from Alabama, married him, and moved to his farm. They lived happily in wonderful isolation without an Internet connection or TV. But just in case, the FBI kept her under surveillance.

To all intents and purposes, the false white baby disappeared from public view.

Greta and JC were now inseparable: him, the six-foot two-inch, barrel-chested former policeman, she, the diminutive witch with a childlike physique. Her bright white hair was now highlighted in different colors to match her outfits. This soon became part of her trademark image.

Her new teeth were as white and as perfect as any Hollywood star's. To enhance her image further, her cosmetic dentist had elongated her incisors, giving her a vampire-like appearance.

Greta was now a celebrity. She and JC shared a huge penthouse apartment overlooking Central Park. JC no longer drove the limo, they had a chauffeur. JC was her business manager and coordinated her affairs with professional care.

Greta was one of the highest-paid celebrities on US television. Her biweekly talk show was syndicated around the world and achieved top ratings for the last three months.

Her eccentric style and frank questioning meant the show was for adults only. It went out live but with a thirty-second delay, just in case. Just as many celebrities had their careers destroyed by an appearance on her show as were helped. But every A list or wannabe celebrity who had a new movie, book, or political campaign to launch wanted to be on her show.

Greta the Witch Live was filmed in front of a live audience. What made the show so watchable was that Greta had no respect for anybody's reputation. The producers discovered early on that the ratings were highest when Greta was not briefed about the people she was interviewing. That way, she had no ideas about them or their reputation. It also meant that the audience knew more about the guests than she did.

On the last show, she was interviewing an aging actress who was promoting her new movie. Greta's first question to the woman was, "What have you done to your face?"

The HD cameras showed a close-up of the woman's face; the effects of her recent face-lift were clear, even though she was heavily made up. Normally, celebrities and their agents made arrangements with the producers of these shows to restrict the close-ups; they agree in advance on how the celebrity is filmed and what lighting effects should be used. But these arrangements were not followed on *Greta the Witch Live.* It was an anything-goes affair.

The actress tried to make light of it, admitting she had had a little work done and trying to steer the conversation back to her new movie.

But Greta was like a dog with a bone; her next comment to the poor woman was, "You look absolutely dreadful. If I were a man, I wouldn't want to fuck you. What does your husband say?"

Fortunately, the thirty-second delay allowed the director to bleep out the obscenity. Greta didn't know, but the celebrity magazines had been full of a story about the actress' third husband, who had just left her for a twenty-one-year-old model.

The poor actress tried to hold herself together but eventually ran from the set in tears. The ratings soared. The film studio was delighted; she couldn't have done more to promote her new movie than be humiliated on *Greta the Witch Live.*

Tonight's show was going to be special, because the NSA director had agreed to appear. General Kevin Alexander had a distinguished military career, and there was strong speculation that he was planning to run for president. In fact, he was relatively unknown to the American public, and this was a calculated gamble to kick-start his fledgling campaign.

As Greta rode in the stretch limousine to the studio, she held JC's hand on the wide back seat. Whenever she saw the New York skyscrapers, she was transformed back to her vision when she had seen the silver man and all those dead people around those huge tall buildings. The events since that time had played tricks with her memory, but she was still convinced it was the New York skyline that she had seen in her vision.

The only person she had ever told about her vision was JC. He always listened to her with great sensitivity but never gave an opinion. He assumed that riding in these cars made her nervous; he didn't understand about her deep anxiety. So far, every part of her vision had come true, except the one about the dead people.

They arrived at the studio, where there was the usual crowd of fans outside of the stage door. JC and the studio security detail kept a wary eye as Greta signed autographs, shook hands, posed with her characteristic incisor smile for photographs, kissed babies, and accepted bouquets of flowers.

Once inside, Greta went through the familiar routine of hair and makeup. Wardrobe brought in her designer outfit and shoes. JC and the studio went to great lengths to ensure that the interviewees never met Greta before the show. They had their own dressing rooms in a different part of the studio, with a different team of people to help them. Watching Greta's reaction when she first met her guests was always one of the highlights of the show.

As Greta got dressed, she could hear the warmup act on the set, getting the audience ready for the show. The idea was to prepare them to applaud spontaneously on cue.

As she walked on stage, the audience needed no prompting; they erupted spontaneously into an enthusiastic standing ovation. She curtsied in the way she used to curtsey to the king, a trademark move that audiences loved; she also blew kisses and waved a thank you to the audience. It took a full two minutes before the applause subsided and she could sit down in her chair.

Unlike other talk shows, Greta never introduced her guests. After the opening credits, the announcer said, "Tonight on *Greta the Witch Live*, Greta will interview Army General Kevin Alexander, the director of the National Security Agency."

At this point, General Alexander walked on stage, dressed in his military uniform. The audience applauded on cue, although there was no standing ovation, and the applause was distinctly less enthusiastic than it had been for Greta.

The general had not met Greta beforehand; he was told it part of the magic of the show, but he didn't like it. He waved to the audience, thanking them for their polite applause, and reached out to shake hands with Greta.

Greta did not rise from her chair and refused to take the general's hand. The applause from the audience faded quickly, and they audience sat in hushed silence, sensing this was going to be another "Greta moment." The studio director held the close-up image of Greta and then cleverly switched to show the bewildered look on the general's face. Everyone seemed to be holding their breath.

In the silence, Greta spoke softly, but her words were unmistakable; she asked, "Where is the silver man?"

The general was completely taken by surprise and sat down heavily in the chair opposite Greta, removing his military cap. The cameras clearly showed how his eyes flickered, taken completely aback by the question.

Nobody watching really understood Greta's question, but here was something amazing. One of the most important people in the US government, who reported directly to the president, had been ambushed by this outrageous woman.

Millions of people watching were glued to the drama; some wondered whether she would grab his crotch next (she was famous for doing that).

To everyone's surprise, Greta stood and began to pace around the studio. The show's director instructed the cameras to follow her as she walked around the set. The TV audience saw the parts of the set they didn't normally see: equipment, cables, cameras, lights, and the less polished parts of a TV studio.

General Alexander remained seated. He had been briefed to expect the unexpected but was told by the PR folks that whatever happened, he should remain calm and professional. He couldn't understand how she would know about something as secret and sensitive as the existence of the silver man.

Both he and Greta wore hidden earpieces that allowed the production team to pass instructions while they were on air. Behind the scenes, there was much confusion; the director instructed the video editor to be ready with an early commercial break if necessary. Her finger was poised over a button.

Suddenly, Greta turned and stared at the general, and then her body began to convulse. Her eyes showed just the whites as she spasmed and fell to the floor.

JC rushed in from the side of the studio as she began to faint. He caught her easily and carried her back to her studio chair. He knelt beside her, and then she seemed to come around.

She stood without aid from JC, pointed her right arm at General Alexander, and said, "You are a liar and a fool."

Now the director tapped the editor on the shoulder, and her finger hit the button to cut the live transmission and go to the commercial break.

The estimated sixty million viewers let out a sigh of frustration as a Toyota ad filled their screens. The Japanese automotive company couldn't have taken a more backward step in their brand respectability if they had tried.

But the editor had been a fraction of a second too late with her button. Sixty million viewers saw Greta take a step toward the NSA director, clench her hand into a fist, and go to strike him. Just in time, JC pulled her back.

While millions of viewers watched the car commercial, inside the TV studio, it was pandemonium. US Secret Service agents now rushed the stage. Greta and JC were overpowered and pinned to the ground. The NSA director was hastily escorted from the building and whisked away in a waiting car. This was all filmed by the cameras.

The commercial break was cut short, and then the recording of Greta and JC being pinned to the floor was shown on air. Greta's punch, however, was not.

The studio director was now showing live coverage of medical staff attending to Greta and JC. Neither had any injuries; the medical attention was unnecessary, but it made great TV. The studio announcer described the scene as "sensational" and "outrageous." Viewer figures were reaching unprecedented numbers. JC helped Greta to her feet, and she leaned theatrically against him for support. The studio audience gave them a loud standing ovation.

Sally immediately got on the phone, trying to mitigate the damage. The general's campaign for the presidential nomination was probably over before it had begun, but the real problem was the mention of the silver man.

The studio switchboard lit up with calls about Greta's show, and the video was now viral on the Internet. Silver-man conspiracy theories filled Internet bulletin boards.

As if this wasn't enough, the program had another thirty minutes to run. The director spoke to Greta in her earpiece, urging her to say something.

She tapped her ear twice, a signal to the studio staff that she had heard and understood. JC helped Greta back to her chair.

She sat very still, waiting for the hubbub in the studio to settle down and the audience to return to their seats. Greta looked directly at the camera. The set was cleared of everyone except JC, who sat in the chair where the general had sat. He held Greta's hand.

Greta began speaking:

"I have a vision, a terrible vision. It shows millions of dead people here in New York City and around the world. I do not know how or when it will occur, but the man who was just here knows the answers."

She stood, took JC's hand, and walked off the set. She leaned against him for theatrical effect, and once again the audience gave her a rapturous standing ovation.

The show still had thirty minutes to run, so after an extended commercial break, they ran the tape of the entire program again from start to finish, with the announcer adding an improvised commentary over the video images that further enhanced Greta's reputation as a psychic.

That night, there were riots in New York City and most of the major cities in America. The National Guard was deployed in fourteen states. The next morning, the president declared a state of emergency.

After the broadcast, JC took Greta home. They had a routine; their privacy was very important to them. Having been on the other side, so to speak, JC knew, how journalists snooped and how to thwart them.

The glass on the apartment windows was mirrored so no photographs were possible with telephoto lenses. Calls and Internet connections were encrypted. Deliveries came to the basement only; they were carried up only by trusted staff. Nobody got into the apartment without being vetted and nobody was ever left alone inside.

The building itself had twenty-four-hour security that JC had vetted personally. He employed a firm to test the effectiveness of the security from time to time. This kept them on their toes.

In addition to their driver, Greta and JC employed a full-time maid and cook. The staff had rooms in an apartment below, close enough to be on call, but they were not allowed in the apartment at night. Once they were inside the apartment, JC turned off his cell phone; Greta never carried one. The phone to the apartment was directed to automatic answer; the only way in or out now was through the staff apartment floor, and that was out of bounds. They were secure.

They opened a bottle of champagne; Greta insisted on Mumm, she liked the bottle's yellow label. JC made some thin wheat toast and spread it liberally with foie gras. Greta ran a bath, and they both lay in the tub, drinking champagne and eating their toast and pâté. They talked, made love in the bath, went to bed, and slept the sleep of the just.

At the White House, however, nobody was sleeping, least of all the president, who was meeting with General Alexander, Admiral Smythe, and Sally Carmichael.

They were in one of the situation rooms below the Oval Office, watching live footage of the rioting in New York, Washington, LA, Chicago, Detroit, and New Orleans. They were aware that other cities were also experiencing rioting, but they only had six screens.

Reluctantly, the NSA director and the admiral agreed to allow the president to brief Sally on the silver man. Now an insider, she spoke while the three men listened:

"If I had known about this, I never would have let the general appear live on this show. I know this was done to boost your presidential nomination, but with a security operation of this magnitude, it was far too dangerous."

The NSA director and the admiral shifted uncomfortably in their seats. They disliked being told the truth by a woman, albeit a very attractive woman, in front of their boss, the most powerful man in the world.

The president interjected, "Sally, it is all very well to be wise after the event, but we need a strategy to put the genie back in the bottle and bring some calm; what do we do?" He pointed at the TV screens, which showed burning buildings and ambulances taking wounded rioters and police officers to overflowing hospitals.

Gunshots could be heard, vehicles were being set on fire, and stores looted. Body bags were being lined up.

Sally paced the room; she had on a low-cut blouse and short skirt. Her heels were high, and the pacing was for maximum effect. At last she sat and faced the president directly. She crossed her long legs, which all the men in the room noticed.

"I think you need to go on live TV and say you have appointed a task force to investigate these claims, but in the meantime, everyone should remain calm. We then call in a favor with Fox News and get them to broadcast an interview with Greta to deny her claims."

"But what if she won't do that?" General Alexander asked.

Sally leaned forward so the president had maximum view of her cleavage and said, "Then you need to make her do it." She stood and added, "I'll set up the broadcast," and then she left.

JC awoke early and worked out in their private gym. While Greta remained asleep, he showered and made tea. They drank it in bed together.

He then went into his study. This was a secure room JC had built that was protected by an electronic Faraday cage; eavesdropping was impossible. He turned on his cell phone, checked his messages, and looked at his email. He made a note of each message in a moleskin notebook, numbering them. He then turned on the TV; Headline News on CNN which was dominated by the riots. He muted the volume on the TV and looked at BBC News on his computer, and as he did so, he also read the on-line edition of the *Daily Chronicle.*

He then took a separate sheet of thick monogrammed paper from a drawer in his desk and prioritized his actions and calls. He would shred this paper when he was finished with it and lock his moleskin notebook in a safe. There were no other papers or unlocked files in the study; he lived by a clean desk policy.

His first call was to Sally Carmichael, the White House press secretary, who had left a message, asking if Greta would do an interview with Fox News. It was now a little before 7:00 a.m., but Sally had left her cell phone number and said to call anytime.

JC and Greta had met Sally several times at different functions; she was a great networker. He remembered her as tall, attractive, and flirty, the sort of "PR bunny" he often came across. During his time with the *Daily Chronicle,* he had seen all the tricks of the trade, with many of these types offering almost anything to get the right story in the paper.

Today, though, Sally was very open and professional on the phone. She was not at all flirtatious, and JC realized that the call was probably being recorded.

She filled him in on the rioting and said that the president wanted Greta's help to restore calm. JC said he would talk to Greta and call her back.

He went back into the bedroom, Greta had taken a bath and was dressed in a silk dressing gown, applying makeup. She did so with little-girl enthusiasm, smiling at herself in the vanity mirror. He switched on the TV, and they watched a synopsis of the rioting. He explained what the White House wanted, and she said it would be fine, as long as Cathy Murphy did it.

JC called Sally back and said Greta would do an interview but with a journalist they chose, not Fox News. They haggled a little about the time and place, and Sally finally agreed. Then using his secure desk phone, JC called Murphy at the *Daily Chronicle* in London, where it was lunch-time.

Within two hours, a private jet lifted off from London City Airport en route to New York. On board was Cathy, Martha, and Bryan, her cameraman. As they lifted off, the *Chronicle* salespeople were already selling the rights; this was going to be the biggest story yet.

After she ended the phone call with JC, Sally typed out a short letter of resignation and sealed it in an envelope. She knew she would carry the blame for this situation, but she was going to jump before she was pushed. Worst still, now she'd never get to sleep with the president.

General Alexander realized his presidential campaign was over before it had started. He also typed out his resignation. *Perhaps*, he thought, *I can still screw that Sally Carmichael before I have to leave.*

The admiral realized that the NSA director's position was up for grabs; he decided to speak to the president. It was a great opportunity.

Four things happened the following night to indicate that the rioting was much reduced.

First, the president's broadcast had calmed things down; second, he had deployed the National Guard to support the police, and they were authorized to use maximum force to protect America's cities. This was followed by a PR campaign from Sally's office, making it clear that "maximum force," when spoken by the president, meant shoot to kill. An appeal went out for everyone to stay off the streets.

But the third thing that greatly reduced the violence was the weather; an unseasonably rainy night meant people just stayed indoors.

Allied to all this was the fourth reason: Greta was due to speak at breakfast the following morning, and the rain-sodden evening was full of fascinating TV coverage and speculation about what she may say.

A jet-lagged Cathy Murphy arrived at JC's and Greta's apartment. Bryan set up his camera in the spacious lounge, with a great view of Central Park and the skyscrapers of New York City in the background. Greta sat in an armchair, and Cathy was set at an angle to her, in a similar but slightly smaller chair. Greta was the star.

The ever meticulous Martha had selected a simple outfit for Greta. Nothing too outrageous; on this occasion, it would be the words that mattered, not her appearance. Greta wore a simple white dress. Her hair was uncolored, but she wore a prominent jade necklace and a gold Rolex watch (JC had negotiated placement rights with the jewelry and watch companies). Cathy wore a Chanel business suit in royal blue. Bryan carefully arranged the lighting to highlight the yellow in Greta's eyes.

The interview was largely recorded in one take, but Bryan did some editing after filming some reaction shots. Using JC's secure Internet connection, he uploaded the broadcast to an FTP server.

Job done, they opened the champagne, and JC cooked spaghetti bolognaise. They collapsed into bed around two o'clock. The number of empty wine bottles outnumbered the number of people who had eaten at the table.

Rupert had become excellent at what is now called bush-craft. His main role was as protector to the king. He had served Stephen even before he ascended to the throne and had been involved in countless battles and skirmishes, where one side or another would parley. They would fight if they had to, but it was much more effective amongst the nobility to pay, or better still be paid, than to fight. He was used to patient negotiations, clandestine meetings, staying hidden, foraging off the land, and staying alive. These skills saved time and money. Armies were time consuming to equip and move to where they were needed, and very expensive to feed, clothe, and equip. But Rupert knew the key thing about negotiating was to choose the time and place. So he was good at staying hidden.

The king tolerated Rupert's abject cruelty and lewd behavior at court, because he was excellent in these difficult situations. He trusted Rupert totally. He had kept him safely hidden in many hostile situations, even right under the enemy's nose.

One thousand years on, many of these skills had been lost, but the special SAS team tracked the king, Rupert, and Keith to their hiding place. By the time they got there, Trev was highly respectful of their quarry's subterfuge techniques. His reputation in the regiment was he had never lost a trail. But he came close today; high praise indeed.

Rupert had found a hiding place near Fleet Pond, the largest fresh water lake in Hampshire, covering more than fifty acres. Fleet Pond is about five miles from Blackbushe Airfield. Soji called the Hampshire chief constable on his personal cell phone. The senior policeman was about to ask how he got the number but stopped himself. Soji gave the coordinates where the king, Rupert, and Keith were hiding and waited until the police teams had moved into position. After a brief handshake from the chief constable, a police vehicle took the SAS team back to Blackbushe, and a helicopter whisked them back to Hereford.

Rupert was no fool; as they became surrounded by the police, he discussed their options with the king.

"Sire, your wounds still need time to mend, and we are now heavily outnumbered by many foes. I suggest we question the tall stranger about these people, and prepare to parley."

The king nodded his assent.

Keith had been sitting quietly, watching the distant police operation through a gap in the undergrowth. The relationship between Rupert and Keith had now reached a necessary tolerance. Rupert realized that killing Keith would mean losing their insight into this strange new land. Keith was no longer restrained by the ivy ropes, but he knew if he tried to run or move suddenly, that Rupert could overwhelm him within seconds. But in truth, Keith had really given up on his thoughts of escape; he had turned his captivity into an academic exercise. It was fascinating to study the character of Rupert and the king. He still didn't know if they were genuine time travelers or if this was an elaborate hoax, but he was determined to find out. Keith also realized that if he answered Rupert's questions directly, and in some cases lied or bent the truth so Rupert heard what he wanted to hear, he avoided being beaten. The king rarely addressed Keith directly, preferring to speak through Rupert.

Keith was still more than a little wary of Rupert's next move. Rupert was a brute and unpredictable; he still felt the effects of the blows to his head and his ribs. His legs and back ached from the horse riding and sleeping on the hard ground. He was cold from living out in the open and felt he could do with a shower and change of clothes, but otherwise, he felt okay.

Keith overheard Rupert's conversation with the king, so he was not surprised when Rupert beckoned him closer and asked, "What do you know of these people surrounding us and of their intentions?"

Keith answered using language he had heard them discussing: "These are police officers, who have the short banging weapons that killed Henry. They will talk to you if you show them you mean no harm."

The king sat on the ground, with his back against a tree, holding his injured ribs; to Keith's surprise, he spoke to him directly: "What if we refuse to parley? Will they charge us? Will they honor a bargain?"

Keith was a little taken aback by the direct question from the king; he knew nothing about police tactics except what he had seen in television police dramas. He was also no medical doctor, but he could tell by the gray pallor of the king's face that he needed medical attention.

Keith's reply was carefully phrased, copying Rupert's respectful form of address: "Sire, the police officers are honorable people and will listen to any arrangement you suggest."

Rupert interjected, "Will you stake your life on that?"

Keith produced a white handkerchief from his pocket and said, "If you allow me to walk out waving this, I believe the police will listen to you."

Rupert looked at the king. He didn't understand the white hanky. As far as he was concerned, the universal sign of a parley was to reverse your sword.

Keith pressed his point, saying, "Let me go out; if I get shot by those guns, I mean short banging weapons, so be it."

Just as the SAS team took off from Blackbushe to return to Hereford, Ellen had a premonition.

She and Carla were in the kitchen of their house in Fleet. They had just finished lunch, and Carla was playing a game on her iPad, still a little sulky after they had returned from their trip to the London Dorchester Hotel. She felt she was playing second fiddle to Ellen and Greta. Despite assurances from Ellen, she still felt inferior and was more than a little envious of how Greta had shot to fame. Privately, Ellen was getting fed up with Carla's moods and her possessiveness. She felt their relationship wasn't going anywhere. Moreover, she had new feelings for someone else.

Ellen's iPhone rang; the display showed JC's name.

"Hi, JC?" Ellen answered in a questioning way, because she sensed that it was Greta calling.

Without preamble, she heard Greta's distinctive gravelly voice in the receiver: "Ellen, you must go to him."

There was a slight hiss on the line, characteristic of trans-Atlantic phone calls.

Like Ellen, Greta was a powerful witch, and at times of danger or distress, their powers were enhanced. Carla had no sense of it; her powers were not as advanced. Greta and Ellen were seeing the same premonition and discussed it as if they were both looking at the same television show. They could visualize through their shared premonition the three men as their hiding place was scanned by the telescopic sights of the police marksmen.

Ellen could see all three men in her mind's eye, but it was the tallest of the three who had caused her heart to flutter. She did not know who the other two were. Greta sensed this, even over the distance of thousands of miles. She knew them.

Greta said, "The other two are the king and Rupert. Be careful of Rupert, the bigger one; he is a brute. You must hurry."

Ellen said, "I must go," and hung up the phone.

As Carla looked up to enquire who that was, Ellen grabbed her coat and called over her shoulder, "I have to go out." She offered no other explanation. Carla thought it strange but sulkily returned to her iPad.

Ellen jumped in her BMW; she knew exactly where to head. She had recognized the area from her premonition. Fleet Pond was just a few minutes' drive away. She knew the area well; some of her earliest and happiest childhood memories were feeding the ducks with her mother. Her mother's spirit came to her now and sat in the passenger seat. Her mother was smiling; she would be there to see her daughter meet this special person. Her mothers' presence gave Ellen comfort.

Gingerly, Keith emerged from the tree line, with his hands raised above his head and one hand waving his white handkerchief. Rupert and the King held back, thinking that Keith may be killed at any moment.

Rupert and the king were both startled when a voice boomed out:

"Dr. Keith Maxwell, please lie on the ground, and you will not be harmed."

Rupert drew his sword and moved protectively in front of the king.

The chief constable repeated his command and then lowered the loud hailer as the police marksmen kept the scientist in the crosshairs of their telescopic sights. He said quietly, so only the three marksmen next to him could hear, "What targets do you have?"

The marksmen were targeting left, center, and right.

As Keith lay down on the ground as instructed, the central marksmen said, "Target appears unarmed, obeying instructions, clean shot."

The marksman to his left said, "Movement in woods behind, no clear shot."

The third marksman, who was scanning the woods on the other side, said, "No target."

The chief constable was about to raise the loud hailer to his lips, when an extraordinary thing happened.

Rupert led the king out of the tree line, mimicking Keith's stance of his hands raised above his head, but with his sword in one hand with the blade reversed. They walked to where Keith lay, and Rupert sunk to his knees on the ground beside him. The king refused to kneel but bowed his head.

At this point, each of the three police marksmen said quietly, "Clear target."

The chief constable hesitated to ensure that the three men in the crosshairs of his marksmen were still and then lifted the loud hailer to his lips. His voice boomed out again, "Keep your hands above your heads, and stay where you are."

The chief constable now had life and death in his hands, but calmly and clearly, he spoke an order to the marksman beside him: "Safe weapons, please."

He waited until he heard each of the marksman say, "Weapon safe," and then lifted a whistle to his lips, which was on a cord around his neck. The whistle was the signal for the waiting police officers to move in and arrest the fugitives. He wanted no risk of his marksman shooting their own colleagues.

But before he could blow his whistle, another unexpected and extraordinary thing happened that took the chief constable and the watching police officers by surprise. A vehicle appeared from nowhere and drove at speed directly across the scrub land toward the fugitives.

Ellen only had eyes for the tall man with long hair and a beard. Unlike the other two, he was dressed in modern clothes. She had seen him emerge from the tree line, waving a white handkerchief over his head, followed by the two other figures.

She had known since she was a little girl that one day she would meet a man like him. Tall with an angelic grace, with long hair and a beard. It was strange, because she had never liked any other men with beards. She had kept the secret hidden in the recesses of her mind, especially from Carla.

As she accelerated toward the group of three men, she was aware of the sound of a loud hailer, but inside the vehicle, she could not hear the words clearly as her BMW bumped along the rough terrain. Her mother's spirit still sat in the passenger seat, smiling.

As she got closer, she could see he had a cut on his face; it looked as though somebody had struck him. On the one hand, she wanted to embrace him and gently tend his wound. On the other hand, she knew from the reports in the newspapers that this was Dr. Keith Maxwell, who was wanted for questioning for murder. But her heart told her that he was innocent.

She stopped the vehicle and went to him instinctively. She was hardly aware of the sound of someone shouting over a loud hailer and the shrill blows of whistle. The police caught her before she could get to Keith.

She watched helplessly as other policemen handcuffed him and led him away.

Ellen was questioned at the scene and then released with a caution.

As the news of the arrests broke, the media moved from Blackbushe to Basingstoke Police Station.

The small regional police station was located in a side street near the town center and had no facilities to host such a large gathering. So in the interests of public safety, the Hampshire chief constable asked the chief of the Metropolitan Police for help once more. The Hampshire chief constable also had an ulterior motive for contacting the most senior-ranking police officer in Britain; he expected some praise and recognition for the successful arrests.

The Metropolitan Police chief did indeed congratulate his colleague, but before the Hampshire chief constable could request assistance to deal with the overwhelming press interest in Basingstoke, he was told to move the prisoners to the high-security Paddington Green Police Station in central London. The Metropolitan Police chief didn't mention that Charles from MI6 had suggested such a move.

The chief constable issued a statement saying that the prisoners would be moved to Paddington Green, and a press conference would be held there the next morning at ten o'clock. The police hoped this would send the hordes of press away from Basingstoke back to London. Instead, it had the opposite effect. Since Paddington Green was where the UK detained terrorist suspects, the media put two and two together and made five, and it led to speculation that the murders were linked to terrorist activity.

On arrival at Basingstoke Police Station, Keith had a hot shower and some beans on toast. The humble meal had never tasted so good, and he asked for another portion.

After seeing his arrest and learning where he was being taken, Maud had sent some clean clothes with a note written in her characteristic hand. The envelope had been opened before he received it. In the note, she had said he had been on the BBC News, and she was very proud of him. She also said that the nice policewoman who had stayed with her said he could phone her from the police station. He did so at the first opportunity.

"Hello, Mother," he said when she answered.

"Oh Keith, thank goodness," she said. "I have been so worried; are you all right?"

Keith almost wept with joy on hearing her familiar voice, but to keep his emotions in check, he resorted to his scientific thought process: "Yes, I'm fine. It is good to hear your voice; I am at Basingstoke Police Station, and they have given me something to eat. I have had a hot shower."

"That's nice, dear."

"I explained that I didn't kill those women and hope they will release me soon."

"That's nice dear." She carried on speaking to him as if he were still nine years old. "Now, Keith dear, you tell the police the whole truth, and I'm sure it will be all right."

"I will," he replied.

There was an awkward silence. Neither could bring themselves to discuss the death of Patch, which was just too upsetting.

His mother's voice on the line broke the silence: "I have a nice surprise waiting when you get got home," she said.

The police officer sitting next to Keith in the telephone cubicle tapped his watch, indicating that Keith should end his call.

He said, "Sorry, Mother, I must go now. I'll call you again when I can."

She said, "Take care, my son," which was the closest she would ever get to saying she loved him.

As Maud put down the phone, she patted the puppy sleeping on her lap. She had found a breeder on the Internet and selected a replacement for Patch. Keith was going to be delighted.

Keith's interrogation took place in a cell with a solicitor present. Detective Inspector Amit Chakrabarti took his statement. Since the event at the car boot sale, it was quite clear that the horsewoman who had been shot with the bow and arrow had been killed by the now-deceased Henry of Gloucester, and the most likely assailant of the decapitated horsewoman was Rupert.

There was a string of minor charges that could have been thrown at Keith, such as aiding and abetting a petty theft (when they stole the kebabs), but as this had never been reported as a crime in the first place, it was not really worth the paperwork.

Keith confessed to it all, and Amit was getting fed up with the scientist's incredible attention to detail by the time he finished.

He considered releasing Keith on bail, providing he surrendered his passport, but then there was the matter of the rape. Keith clearly wasn't party to it, but he had witnessed it.

Amit took the statement to the chief constable, who was just en route to another media interview and so was not pleased to be delayed. The chief constable decided to allow Keith's bail; he didn't want details of a rape tarnishing his moment of glory, justifying it on the basis that no crime had been reported. He didn't tell Amit, but another reason for allowing the bail was that the chief constable's office of the Metropolitan Police said that the Security Services no longer had an interest in Keith Maxwell. This was code for MI6 weren't interested in him anymore on national security grounds.

Keith went home to his mother; he was indeed delighted with his new puppy, which he named Strudel. It was a German shepherd, and strudel was his mother's favorite desert. After Keith had a long soak in the bath, they had chicken chasseur for dinner with apple strudel and custard for pudding. Keith let Strudel lick the custard in his bowl. His mother chastised him but then let Strudel lick her own bowl clean.

Keith went to bed around nine o'clock and slept until ten the next morning. When he awoke, his first thought was to search for Patch on his bed, but then it all came back to him.

Strudel was too young to go out for walks; she hadn't yet had all her injections. So the next morning, Keith played with her in the garden and then read all the newspaper cuttings about the murders that his mother had diligently compiled. He also watched some of the TV news coverage she had recorded.

His mother had gone to get her hair done, and then she said she was going shopping at the local supermarket. So he was able to spread the cuttings out on the dining room table and compare them.

He couldn't believe how wide of the mark some of the journalism was. Some of it was just fiction, total fabrication.

He watched the recording of the press conference fiasco at the lab, where Professor Collins and that PR dork he never liked, David Thomas, had been torn to shreds. He realized he should email his boss.

Keith was fascinated by the story about the three witches. He watched the TV footage of them over and over and stared at the pictures of them in the paper. He could not deny it to himself that he was especially attracted to the tall, red-haired woman named Ellen. He was sure it was her who had mysteriously driven up just before the police had arrested them at Fleet Pond. But she had not been dressed like she was on the TV. Wow!

As he let the recording of the BBC News bulletin of the SAS helicopter landing at Blackbushe play in the background, he found his laptop and turned it on. He noted he had 317 unread emails in his Inbox. He ignored them and emailed Helen to say he was back at home and would be returning to work next week. He got an instant "Out of Office" reply; apparently, she was on long-term sick leave. He found out later this was due to the stress that had started after the press conference.

He was about to close the lid on his laptop when the television showed an extraordinary clip of an interview with the yellow-eyed witch on Spiers Clarkson's chat show. He had the TV volume turned down, but he vaguely remembered a story about Clarkson leaving his job at the *Daily Chronicle* under a cloud. Anyway it hadn't done him any harm; he was doing well now.

The TV footage cut to a clip of the three witches stepping out of a Rolls-Royce and attending a West End show. There was close-up of Ellen. He grabbed the remote control and froze her picture on the screen; she was extraordinary. Her eyes seemed to reach out of the television and stare through him. He gave a shiver, and goose bumps rose on his forearms. He had never experienced such an emotion.

At that very moment, less than two miles away, Ellen felt a twinge. The two cats under her desk also stirred. She was going through her emails and checking her schedule for the coming week. Carla had gone to Surbiton to stay with her mother; they had had a row, and she didn't know when (or if) she would come back.

Ellen had thought a lot about Keith since seeing him near Fleet Pond. She knew it was her destiny to meet him, and now she could sense he was thinking of her. Carla was out; a perfect time.

A Google search took her instantly to three Maxwells listed in the Hartley Wintney phone book. It wasn't obvious which one was correct, so she closed her eyes and held her index finger against each of the numbers on the screen; she felt a tingle as her finger hovered over one of them. This must be his number. He answered on the second ring.

"Hello Keith."

"Who is this?" he asked, but secretly he knew who the husky female voice belonged to.

His mother thought it very strange that he was going out to dinner with a woman he had never met. She told Keith she had bought something special from Waitrose for dinner, but then she added that it would keep. She had made him feel guilty.

Keith was excited and a little nervous. This was not his first date; he had dated several women at university and after he started working at the lab. They had all been fellow scientists, but he had never felt like he felt now after seeing Ellen's pictures and hearing her voice on the telephone.

Keith had put on his newest clothes and splashed on some aftershave (he didn't actually shave, but he did trim his beard). As he said good-bye, his mother reluctantly offered her cheek for a kiss and gave him one of her looks.

On leaving, he stroked the sleeping puppy and said, "Well, at least you will have this gorgeous creature to yourself all evening."

Strudel blinked briefly up at Keith before falling back to sleep.

His mother smiled at the puppy and then said, "Have a good time."

Keith walked to the curry house; it was just a few hundred yards away. Ellen was already waiting outside in her BMW; he recognized the car. He also recognized the shape of her bushy red hair and wide set of her shoulders sitting inside the vehicle.

He waved as he got closer and quickened his pace. He was worried; should he kiss her or just shake her hand? He saw her get out of the car, and then she came at him like a whirlwind, throwing herself into his arms, and they kissed. She fitted into his arms perfectly; he didn't want to let go. It was as if he had known her all his life. They kissed for a long time. Cars began honking as they went by, and then someone shouted, "Get a room," and they broke their kiss and laughed together like teenagers.

They walked arm in arm into the Indian restaurant. It was crowded, and they were shown to a table for two. The tables were positioned close together in the small restaurant, and their table was squashed in between a fire exit door and an adjacent table occupied by a family of four. There were two teenage children, who both looked bored, and sat fiddling with their mobile phones, while their parents tucked into a multitude of dishes covering the table.

The parents nodded to Keith and Ellen as they squeezed by, realizing that getting these two tall people into the neighboring table was going to be a challenge. The mother nudged the teenage boy next to her and motioned for him to pull in his chair. He reluctantly did so, never looking up from his phone.

In an act of chivalry, Keith pulled out the small table to allow Ellen to squeeze into the chair. As he did so, the small vase of flowers on it fell over. The spilt water ran over the sides of the table and onto Ellen's shoes. He was mortified and dropped to his knees and began mopping Ellen's shoes with a napkin. She said it didn't matter. The teenage boy now looked up laughed. He laughed in the exaggerated, overloud way that teenage boys do. His mother pulled on his arm and said, "Liam, don't point; it's rude." But she couldn't resist laughing herself. She covered her mouth with her hand to try and stifle her amusement. The teenage boy began filming Keith on his phone. Other heads began to turn to see what the commotion was all about. Keith felt himself blushing.

The waiter who had shown them to their table held back, because he couldn't move any nearer to the table. The space between the tables was always narrow, and it was now made even narrower because Keith had pulled the table out.

Ellen was also laughing at Keith, sprawling on the floor. She looked down at the crown of Keith's hair and could see a small bald patch appearing. Despite her mirth, she also looked at his clothes and realized she had some work to do.

As Keith stood, he caught his head on the underside of the table and groaned, saying, "Fiddlesticks," as he rubbed his bald patch to dull the pain. The vase then fell on the floor and smashed. This caused a momentary lull in conversation at the sound of breaking crockery, and then everyone applauded the breakage. The teenage boy laughed even louder and stood to get a better angle of the mess on his cell phone.

At the expression "fiddlesticks," the two teenage children and Ellen all began giggling. Keith laughed with Ellen, still rubbing his head.

Through his chuckles, Keith apologized to the waiter and said he would pay for the damage. The waiter prevented Keith from bending down again in the small space to pick up the pieces of the broken vase; he was like the proverbial bull in a china shop. The waiter moved them to a larger table in the opposite corner of the restaurant; Ellen was beside herself with laughter.

As they sat down, Keith made a show of steadying this table's vase with both hands, as if it were a priceless object. This caused renewed laughter from Ellen, and the diners on the adjacent table got the joke and laughed with them.

In fact, everyone in the restaurant smiled with them. These two people seemed so right for each other. Both tall, both confident. The women in the restaurant all noticed the way they looked at each other and wished their own partners and husbands looked at them that way. Most of the men in the restaurant had taken in Ellen's magnificent physique and thought Keith a lucky guy. But what really drew the glances toward Ellen and Keith was their open body language, the way they smiled at each other and held each other's gaze.

As they were leaving, the mother of the two teenage children whispered in her husband's ear, "I remember when you looked at me like that."

The waiter appeared again and took their order for drinks and starters. The restaurant had two beers on draft; Ellen ordered a Kingfisher and Keith a Cobra. They arrived in suitably branded glasses. From that day, their pet nicknames for each other became "Bird" and "Snake."

When the poppadums arrived with the pickle and chutney relishes, they were deep in conversation and had not even looked at their menus. The waiter asked politely if they were ready to order, and Keith said they needed a little more time. The waiter went away, unsurprised.

Keith was telling Ellen about his ordeal at Basingstoke Police Station: "I didn't realize how hungry I was. I had a shower and ..."

Ellen interjected, "I would like to have seen that." She pulled him to him and kissed him. Keith nearly knocked his beer over, blushed again, took a mouthful of poppadum to cover his embarrassment, and then continued.

"So as I was saying, I had a shower and then they put me in a cell. They brought me beans on toast. It was on that cheap white bread with margarine, instead of butter, but it never tasted so good. I had a second portion."

Ellen said, "Oh, I love it like that, but with a bit of Worcester sauce and cheese sprinkled on top." She lifted her hand and twitched her fingers, as if she were sprinkling the grated cheese.

This time, it was his turn to lean forward and kiss her. In doing so, Keith not only managed to put his sleeve in the mango pickle, he also knock over his beer. He stood up quickly, saying, “Oh fiddlesticks, sorry, sorry.”

The spilt beer soaked both the menus and dripped onto his trousers. The waiter rushed over with napkins to mop up the spilt beer and help Keith wipe the pickle from his sleeve and wet beer from his trousers. Ellen was now in mild hysterics. The waiter brought fresh menus and another beer for Keith. Ellen held her menu over her face, because she couldn’t contain herself as Keith ordered their food.

He asked her if she would like chicken or lamb, but all she could do was reach for her napkin to stifle the tears of laughter; she could not speak.

He asked again, “Does chicken balti sound okay?”

She just nodded.

When the waiter finished taking her order, she went to the ladies’ room to get herself back under control. She couldn’t remember when she had a better time.

When she came back from the restroom, she noticed that the waiter had relaid the table with a fresh new white tablecloth and brought new plates of poppadums and pickles, because the others were swimming in beer. She broke the plate-size crisps with the back of her spoon, filled her side plate with relishes and pickles, and then passed it to Keith. She then took Keith’s empty plate and put some pickles and relishes on that, which she now used as her own.

Keith was mightily impressed by her dexterity. If he had done it, the tablecloth would have been covered. Of course Ellen knew that, which is why she had served the sticky pickles. They both understood that, but words were not necessary.

They had moved on from the way they liked their beans on toast to be cooked and were now deep into conversation about the incident at the car boot sale when the warming plates arrived and were placed carefully in the center of the table. The waiter gingerly moved the vase of flowers to one side. This brought on a renewed bout of hysterical laughter from Ellen.

A trolley laden with sizzling silver dishes was wheeled up to the table. Their waiters held each dish up for inspection and announced its name with great reverence, ending with the word “please.” So it was “chicken balti, please” and “pillau rice, please,” and so on.

Keith and Ellen hardly missed a syllable of their conversation as the food was being served. They looked politely at the waiters as they said the name of each dish but moved around in their seats so they could continue talking as the waiters leaned across the table.

The second waiter picked up the gist of what they were saying.

He was, in fact, one of the owners of the restaurant, and his brother was Detective Amit Chakrabarti. His brother had told him some aspects of his latest case. So this was the "mad scientist" and the "witch with the red hair" he had described. Interesting.

Keith and Ellen continued their conversation, oblivious to all else in the restaurant. They ordered some fresh mango and ice cream for dessert, had coffee, and failed to notice that the restaurant had emptied.

It was after midnight, and the second waiter came over and introduced himself as Sandeep, asking if his wife could have a word with Ellen. Ellen noticed a handsome older woman dressed in traditional Indian garb sitting at a nearby table. Ellen agreed, of course, and stood up to take the hand of the woman as she approached. She introduced herself as Rani.

Keith was mystified as he saw Ellen's expression turn grave. She took Rani to a vacant table and sat down.

Keith asked Sandeep for the bill, but Sandeep said there was nothing to pay; it was on the house. Keith protested and took three twenty-pound notes from his wallet, offering them to Sandeep. Sandeep took one as a tip for his staff and insisted that that was all that was necessary.

He became distracted as he watched his wife; tears had come into her eyes as she spoke with Ellen, who clutched both of her hands and looked at her kindly.

Sandeep asked Keith, "Would you like anything else to drink? More coffee or a liqueur, perhaps, on the house, of course?"

Keith asked for some more coffee. Sandeep barked an order to the waiter who had served them first, and a pot of coffee and three brandies appeared. Sandeep poured coffee into Keith's cup and then refilled Ellen's, and then he poured himself a cup.

He picked up one of the schooners of brandy and toasted Keith. Keith selected a schooner, and they clinked glasses. Ellen and Rani came back to the table. Rani had regained her composure a little, and Sandeep poured her some coffee. To Keith's total amazement, Ellen now explained to Sandeep what she and Rani had discussed.

"Sandeep, your wife is not well," she said. "She lost her baby because there is something wrong inside. You must go to a doctor and see a gynecological specialist. But do not worry, because I can see a child for you in the future."

Sandeep took Rani's hand and smiled.

Ellen went on, "But now it is late, we must go."

They all stood. Ellen gave Rani her card and said she should call her if she wanted to talk again. The two women hugged, and they all shook hands.

Outside, Ellen led Keith to her car. Without saying a word, she drove to her house in Fleet, where she discovered to her delight why "Snake" was such an excellent nickname for Keith.

At the same time they were driving to Ellen's house in Fleet, about thirty miles away, the king and Rupert slept in separate cells in London's Paddington Green Police Station.

While Keith's questioning had been relatively routine, the interrogation of the king and Rupert was much more complex. The start of the process at Basingstoke Police Station should have been routine enough, but it began badly as the officers tried to fill out a simple form to register the prisoners; the first questions were name, address and date of birth.

Rupert answered first for the king, giving his name as "His Royal Highness King Stephen of Blois." The arresting officer ignored the royal name, assuming Rupert was taking the piss, but began by asking, "Is it 'Stephen' with a 'v' or a 'ph'?"

It went downhill from there.

Rupert was illiterate, so he looked at the King, who answered, "Ph."

"Sir, how do you spell 'Blois'?"

"B-l-o-i-s."

"Are you French?"

"No, I'm English, but my mother was French."

"What is your date of birth?"

"11 September 1096."

The officer wrote down September 11, 1966.

"Address?"

The king said, "I do not understand the question."

"Where do you live?"

"In one of my palaces, but usually at Winchester."

The arresting officer gave up with the king and instead turned to Rupert.

"Name?"

"Sir Rupert of Ypres."

The other police officers around the desk couldn't help but snigger. They were all reminded of the famous Monty Python movie sketch, when an actor with a French accent hurls insults at the king and his followers, standing below the castle walls. Thinly disguised whispers could be heard talking of hamsters and elderberries.

The arresting officer said sarcastically, "All right, all right, any of you know how to spell 'Ypres'?"

One of the junior officers said, "French p-r-i-c-k."

That is when Rupert threw the first punch. The arresting officer pressed an alarm button under the desk, and the area was soon full of writhing, struggling officers, who managed to get handcuffs on both the king and Rupert. After the scuffle had been calmed, Rupert and the king were taken to separate cells.

What was obvious to the police team was that these men had been sleeping rough for some time and needed a hot shower and a change of clothes. Their clothes looked as though they had come from a fancy dress shop. The priority, though, was to search the prisoners thoroughly for any concealed weapons and remove anything they may use to harm themselves.

They had set procedures to deal with drunks and all sorts of violent detainees, so they assembled the required team and set about their tasks.

The king thought it beneath his dignity to protest and did what the four burly police officers wanted. He removed his tunic and outer garments and stood only in his breaches. It was obvious that his bruises needed some medical attention, and a doctor was summoned. They could hear Rupert violently resisting in the next cell, and there were yelps of pain as he struggled with the officers (most of the yelps were from the policemen).

In the end, the police gave up trying to get either prisoner to remove their breaches and forced them into the hot shower with them on. At first, the king and Rupert resisted, but like Greta, they soon got the hang of the pleasure of hot soapy water from above and came out, if not sparkling, a lot cleaner than when they went in.

The doctor arrived and treated Rupert's cuts and bruises. He examined the king and said he should have a chest x-ray in case of fractured ribs. But otherwise, both prisoners were said to be in good health. He was particularly fascinated by their teeth. He offered the arresting officer some painkillers for the king to take and gave a look that said much about his suspicions of police brutality.

The police supplied the king and Rupert with a change of clothes. This consisted of prison gray tracksuits, underpants, socks, a t-shirt, and a pair of slip-on plimsolls. Their wet breaches were finally removed, and they emerged in their new gray attire.

Beans on toast was interesting. The police had never seen anyone eat quite like these two. They were glad when the unmarked van arrived to take them to Paddington Green, thankfully passing responsibility on to their Metropolitan Police colleagues.

On arrival at Paddington Green, the king and Rupert were taken directly to the well-equipped medical center inside the high-security police station. They had slept most of the way on the ninety-minute journey in the closed police van. Both were very tired after their weeklong excursion on Hazeley Common.

Charles, Sir Geoffrey Milton's assistant, had spoken directly to the arresting officer at Basingstoke and received a somewhat coy account of the prisoners' injuries. He had also spoken to the doctor who had examined them. Charles had noted the point about the chest x-ray.

The Met had handed the operation over to MI6, and MI6 was working inside Paddington Green in close cooperation with the American CIA in London. Both MI6 and the CIA had been sent copies of Keith's comprehensive statement at Basingstoke Police Station, and it was clear that this eminent scientist believed that the other two prisoners, who he called Rupert and the king, were from a different time. This seemed incredulous but also explained a lot. However, Rupert and the king were also accused of multiple murder and an unreported rape.

The medical center at Paddington Green was well equipped; it had been set up to deal with any major terrorist incident in the capital. The medical staff, as instructed, examined Rupert and the king thoroughly.

They both made amorous and outrageous advances to the female staff in their crisp white medical uniforms. In the end, Milt agreed they could be sedated so the medical examination could proceed without further sexual harassment.

After an hour or so, the doctor in charge came into the room where Milt, Charles, and Wayne DiBello, the head of the CIA in London, waited. She carried two clipboards holding the medical papers of each prisoner.

The doctor, Dame Ann Brightwell MD, sat down and began her report. Dr. Brightwell was head of the Medical School at University College London but also assisted MI6 whenever it was necessary. She was a handsome, well-built woman in her early sixties with bushy gray hair and red, half-moon spectacles. She was known for her quick wit.

She and Milt were good friends. Charles had briefed her on this case's unusual nature and asked if she could examine the men to see if they were truly from another time.

The first thing Dr. Brightwell said was, "There is no DNA, fingerprint, or retina match on the database, so whoever they are, they're not in the system."

She looked at Frank as she said this, so the meaning was clear that they had checked the CIA database as well as the usual Interpol and MI6.

"I'll say one thing though about these two," she added, "being groped at my age is quite flattering."

The men laughed.

She began flicking through the pages on one of the clipboards.

"The one called Stephen is probably in his forties; he has bruised ribs consistent with a fall a week or so ago, but they are not broken."

Ann held an x-ray image up to the light, which she had just unclipped from the sheath of papers.

"He will feel better in a few days. He has several old injuries and scars on his body, consistent with knife wounds."

She clipped the x-ray back to Stephen's board and began flicking through Rupert's chart.

"The one called Rupert is probably a little younger, in his mid-thirties. He has suffered several injuries in his time, again consistent with knife, puncture, or fracture wounds. Some have been crudely stitched, possibly by himself. We have treated an infection in one and restitched it."

She paused for effect and then went on.

"We found a number of characteristics of each subject that may be consistent with your theory of time travel. First is their teeth. Don't get me wrong, their teeth are not great, but they don't have any evidence of sugar decay or modern dentistry. They also have worms, which we have treated. This is consistent with a primitive diet. They both have lice in their hair, which we will treat with appropriate shampoo when they wake up. I would like to examine the clothes that they were found in."

Charles said, "Already sorted, Dame Ann, on the way, courtesy of Basingstoke's finest, together with weapons found when they were arrested. Be here in thirty."

There was a knock at the door, and a young doctor came in and handed Dr. Brightwell another piece of paper. Somewhat excited, he said, "Ma'am, it is as you suspected." The young doctor smiled, nodded, and left, shutting the door behind him.

"Yes," she said, scanning the notes on the paper in front of her, "this is very interesting. Both subjects have the clap."

DiBello looked at her, confused.

"They both have gonorrhea, a common sexually transmitted infection caused by a nasty bacterium, Neisseria gonorrhea. It is easily treated with antibiotics, but we had the particular strain analyzed and consulted a group at St. Mary's who specialize in historical medicine."

Again the distinguished medical practitioner paused for effect.

"It appears to be a strain that was eradicated more than seven hundred years ago—except for one case found a few days ago in a woman aged thirty-five, from Fleet."

Weekly World News

1,000-Year-Old Soldier Joins Elite Forces Unit

The British equivalent of the Navy SEALs has employed a thousand-year-old soldier to help revive old bush-craft skills . . .

Soji laughed as he read the on-line edition of the paper on his iPad. He was having breakfast with Trev the Track and Rupert in the officers' mess at Hereford. He said, "Fucking journos; we're much better than those Navy SEAL wankers."

They had just returned from Pakistan, where they had successfully tracked and captured two Taliban leaders who had been hiding out in the mountains on the Afghanistan border.

With them was Colonel Tom Shields from the US Navy SEALs. They had conducted the mission together and had the utmost respect for each other. Tom laughed at Soji's jibe and said, "Yes, but at least we don't have to ask permission from Her Majesty."

Arriving in the mess hall was a contingent of Navy SEALs and select SAS troops. Today, they had come to learn from a master of his trade. Their instructor was going to teach them how to stay undetected in enemy territory.

Soji banged the table with the end of a fork and called for silence. He respectfully introduced Colonel Shields, who welcomed the group. The Navy SEAL introduced the lead instructor.

Rupert stood and began to address the troops.

The king was much more difficult to deal with. Legally, if it were proven he was actually a crowned king of England, there could be a constitutional crisis. If they put him on a stand, there was a risk of show trial, which nobody wanted. Milt realized that a smart lawyer could actually get King Stephen crowned and force the current queen to abdicate. This was unthinkable.

Charles had called in a favor from one of his old tutors at Oxford University. Coincidentally, Charles had received his PhD in medieval English history, and his professor was Sir Peter Edwards. Sir Peter was, in Charles's opinion, the foremost living authority on English history. Sir Peter considered Charles one of his star pupils and treated him almost like a son. He knew, of course, about Charles's chosen profession; the University of Oxford was a prime recruitment ground for MI6, but they never spoke of it. Charles would just say he was a civil servant.

A longtime friend of Sir Peter's was Professor Rupert Soames from the Faculty of Law. He was a constitutional expert and was often consulted by the royal family and their advisors on matters about the monarchy and accession. Rupert appeared regularly on radio and television, whenever a birth or death occurred, and was considered an authority on who could or would be next in line for the throne.

Both professors were in their sixties and agreed to meet Charles and Milt for a "hypothetical conversation" in Sir Peter's study. Ironically, the study was in St. Peter's College; Sir Peter was fond of saying, "No relation," as an in-joke.

Sir Peter served dry sherry in delicate cut crystal glasses. Charles remembered the glasses from his undergraduate days when he and his fellow students had sat nervously in Sir Peter's study, treasuring the crystal glasses and hardly daring to put them down for fear of breakage. Sir Peter said the glasses dated from the eighteenth century, but Charles suspected they were from the Pound Shop. Milt thought the sherry tasted like it was from the Pound Shop as well.

So-called hypothetical conversations were a regular part of Rupert's life, and he always enjoyed them. He could never discuss them, of course, but the previous week, he had entertained the private secretary to Prince Charles, the Prince of Wales, who had asked what would happen if his son were to marry a Jewish girl. Apparently, Prince Harry was having another fling.

Milt took a sip from his small glass and tried not to grimace. He cleared his throat and began, "We have a hypothetical situation that I would like to put to you both in confidence."

He paused while both professors nodded their agreement and sipped their sherry. They both of course knew what Milt and Charles did, but officially they were just civil servants, so it was best not to ask too many questions or interrupt. Of course, Milt was a Cambridge man, but they didn't hold that against him.

Milt, of course, was aware that both these professors knew what he and Charles did, so he cut to the chase: "We have a man in custody who claims to be King Stephen, Stephen of Blois. If true, this man would be a thousand years old, and he looks about forty, but we have good reasons to suspect that it may be true."

Milt would not go as far as discussing anything about the silver man and the connection with the Americans.

Immediately, both professors were intrigued. People of Charles and Milt's intelligence and standing would not come to them with a fanciful tale of a madman in custody; this must have some plausibility.

Sir Peter put his glass down on a side table and took a well-thumbed volume from a shelf. He consulted an index and turned to a relevant section. Charles had briefed him (discreetly, of course), so had already read the text beforehand. He knew Milt would not have the patience to wait as the elderly academic fumbled around his extensive book shelves.

As Sir Peter began reading from the book in his hand, it was immediately obvious where Charles had picked up his habit of staccato speech: "Stephen, king of England, ascended to the throne on 26 December 1135 on the death of Henry I. He was born, ahh … that is disputed, but it was either in 1092 or 1096. That would make him …" He paused while he did the math in his head. "920 or 916 years old."

Sir Peter would have carried on reading, but Charles interrupted him politely, realizing that his boss was not in the mood for a history lesson. "Professor Soames, perhaps you could let us know the constitutional effects … if this is true."

Sir Peter sat back down with the volume still open on his lap and continued to read, while Rupert took a sip of his sherry and then began in his distinguished voice.

"Well, if true, there would be a major constitutional crisis. A monarch crowned and still living always takes precedent over a monarch who was crowned at a later date." He then added, as if to soften the brutal frankness of his opinion, "Of course, hypothetically speaking, it has never happened before or actually been tested in law.'

Milt and Charles exchanged glances, sitting in somewhat shocked silence.

To fill the void, Sir Peter tapped the volume with an index finger and said intriguingly, "Of course you could always exhume the late king's body."

He went on without being asked, "I thought I remembered something odd about his death; he is buried in Kent at Faversham Abbey. You could go dig him up and see if the clever science types can identify his DNA."

Milt and Charles shot Sir Peter a glance, and Rupert smiled.

MI6 kept several safe houses in and around London, where from time to time they "entertained" guests. The occupants were not exactly under house arrest, but were guests that MI6 liked to keep a close eye on.

The king had been taken to a safe house in Fulham in West London. It was a large Victorian house that was now split into two large flats. Two female housekeepers entertained the king around the clock in the spacious upstairs apartment, while an MI6 security detail managed the only exit in or out through the downstairs flat. The objective was to isolate Stephen from contact with the outside world.

It was obvious that the king enjoyed female company, and the ladies on the MI6 payroll were used to plying the selected guests of this flat with their expert hosting skills. This was not just limited to their sexual favors; they were also trained gourmet cooks and knew a fine bottle of wine when they saw one.

During his time there, Sir Peter traveled up to London from Oxford and went to dinner on a number of occasions in order to study this king in the flesh. Sometimes the dinners were with MI6 specialists such as psychologists, and sometimes with Charles. They talked to the king, who they respectfully called "King Stephen" or "Your Majesty," about his life and verified it in detail against historical records.

They built up a psychological profile and could find no detail that was inconsistent with him being the real King Stephen, who had lived in the twelfth century. In fact, every operative verified the story. Psychologically, medically, and historically, everything checked out.

They dug up the remains buried in Faversham Abbey and took a DNA sample. The historical records showed that the grave was the burial place of King Stephen in 1154. They dug up the remains in the middle of the night to avoid public scrutiny. Dame Ann confirmed that the DNA of the remains was similar to (but not the same as) the person in the Fulham safe house.

That night, over an excellent dinner of venison and an excellent pinot noir from Burgundy, the king told the story of his deception with his cousin. Up until that point, Sir Peter and Charles had held back from telling the king any of the historical facts they knew about his reign. They had not wanted to do this, for fear of the king using this information, rather than telling his version of events.

As the king did most nights, he drank wine as if it were water, and his words were soon slurred: "I changed places with my cousin, William of Blois, and he was to travel to Winchester in my place. This was to give me time to ride to Farnham to meet the archbishop. I wanted to persuade the archbishop to go to Rome and talk to the pope on my behalf and recognize my kingship, so those dastard barons could be brought onside. But then that bitch Greta appeared, and then the silver man."

As the story unfolded, Milt watched the king live on a large TV monitor inside the MI6 building near Waterloo Station. The hidden CCTV cameras in the dining room at the Fulham flat were broadcasting the meeting live over a secure link. As the conversation proceeded, he wrote instructions on a notepad and continually tore off the sheets, which he handed to MI6 operatives in the room, who carried out the written instructions to investigate facts and figures.

On one note he had written, *"Was William de Blois his cousin?"*

The operative brought the note back, where he had put a tick, and written *"Confirmed."*

A note was handed to him from one operative, which he asked to be texted immediately to Charles.

On the video screen, he could see Charles reach for his jacket pocket as his Blackberry buzzed. The message read, "DNA matches his cousin."

Charles skillfully steered the conversation, saying, "Your Majesty, you say that William was your cousin; how exactly are you related?"

The burgundy was having its effect on the king; his eyelids drooped slightly as he slurred, "My father had many lovers, and he enjoyed it. Probably where I get it from." He laughed and looked across the dining room to the kitchen, where one of the hostesses was keeping a discreet distance. "My mother said William's mother was a French maid, a tart that she dismissed. Anyway, we were brought up together."

Charles interjected, "So you weren't actually cousins, you were half-brothers?"

"I don't understand the term."

"You had the same father but different mothers."

"Yes."

Sir Peter turned the conversation to a different subject. As he did so, Charles's Blackberry buzzed again; the message read, "DNA half-brother's perfect match."

Weekly World News

Ancient King's Bodied Exhumed by Secret Service

> *The British Secret Service have dug up the body of an ancient king to test the DNA. Speculation is rife that this may result in a legal challenge to the throne of England ...*

Keith moved in with Ellen in Fleet. They ate out regularly, went to the theatre in London, and attended concerts and ballets together.

Keith's old clothes had largely stayed in his mother's house. Ellen had changed her man, taking him to Gieves & Hawkes so his new outfits emphasized his height and stature. She also bought selected clothes on-line because his size was difficult to find in the shops. He also hated shopping, so it was easier that way. She enjoyed fussing over him, dressing him, and turning him into the elegant man she wanted by her side. He had large feet, and she bought specially made shoes for him. To her pleasure, she found that everything was true about men with large feet.

She took him to an expensive barber in Covent Garden on his birthday, and they styled his hair and shaved his beard, making him look years younger (even though his bald patch was a little bigger).

When they were at home, they made love all over the house and garden. Ellen had a hot-tub installed in the back garden at a particular point on the celestial energy line, and that became their special place.

They stayed that night in the Dorchester, not in the grand suite they had stayed in when the *Daily Chronicle* was paying, but the room had a king-size bath. They sneaked in two bottles of wine they had bought in a supermarket to avoid paying Dorchester prices, enjoying them in the bath. They went to dinner at Roules, and Keith had his favorite, oysters, followed by steak and kidney pudding. Keith first ordered just six oysters, but Ellen insisted he have twelve. She said he would need them.

Keith's mother sort of liked Ellen. They were polite enough when they were together, but they were never going to be bosom pals. Speaking of which, the size of Ellen's breasts was something Keith's mother was vexed about. Ellen didn't have to be psychic to sense her real feelings.

Keith and Ellen went to his mother's house for the occasional lunch or dinner, but she would rarely come to them. The pretence she gave was she didn't want to leave the dog, and she couldn't bring him because of Ellen's cats.

They both loved Keith, but that was all they really had in common.

She did not approve of Ellen's profession, believing it to be a con. Keith did not approve of fortune telling; as a scientist, he was still skeptical, even though she told him things she couldn't possibly have known.

For example, she told him about a paper hidden in an old Bible in his father's study at his mother's house. It turned out to be a long-forgotten share certificate for Arsenal Football Club in London. His father had hidden the certificate before his death, because it was the pay-off from a friend over a gambling debt. Keith's father had kept his gambling away from his mother.

Keith took the share certificate to his bank, who made some discreet enquiries. Within a day, he had received two offers for the shares; the higher, from a businessman in Oman, was a little under £1 million.

The payment of £827,602, net of the bank's broker and legal fees, was deposited into his account the following week.

Keith handed in his notice at the Rutherford Appleton Laboratory and equipped himself a study in the spare room at Ellen's. He planned to publish scientific books on the paranormal. He was going to dedicate his life to a scientific study of Ellen's gift. She thought this a real turn-on, and they christened his new desk and his office chair in true style.

The following day, as he was setting up his new computer, his world turned on its head. Ellen came into the study, beaming, to announce her news; she already knew it would be a girl.

Dallas, Texas

Mohammad was the most unlikely CIA operative. He was originally from Bangalore, India, emigrated to the United States with Senita, his wife, in 1984, and settled in Dallas. He was a sheik, wore a turban, and was seriously overweight. His expanding waistline was the result of Senita's superb cooking. His wife excelled in classic Indian cooking, published cookbooks, and gave culinary lessons.

One day, he was sitting in his truck, eating the lunch Senita had prepared for him. She provided linen napkins and cutlery for each course. He savored each mouthful, knowing that when he got home, Senita would question him about the meal. It was a game they played. She tried to catch him out with delicate flavors, special ingredients, and subtle twists in the preparation.

His cell phone beeped, but he did not read the text message until he had enjoyed the last morsel of food. He carefully packed the dishes away, wiped his hands for a final time on the napkin, and neatly folded into the embroidered carrying bag Senita had made for her husband's lunch.

He looked at the text message on his iPhone. It was sent from an unregistered number and consisted of a code: "Dahl 2."

Dahl was one of his favorite dishes, but it was also his CIA code name. The number 2 meant that two packages had arrived.

Mohammed worked at the huge UPS distribution center at Dallas/Fort Worth International Airport. He was an expert operative and forger. Every so often, he would receive instructions to switch the contents of a package. He would receive the new contents through a rival delivery courier, Federal Express (an ironic touch never lost on him).

His hobby was keeping reptiles. He kept snakes and iguanas, which required a diet of insects and mice, some dead, but mostly very much alive. He subscribed to a daily service that delivered a varied diet of reptile food to his home address. Senita wanted nothing to do with the gruesome deliveries, so it guaranteed that the packages were never tampered with. The operative who dispatched the live locusts, grubs, worms, frogs, and rodents was another CIA agent. Occasionally, she dispatched a pre-wrapped package to Mohammed. This she did with efficiency. She made more from the CIA than she did from most of her reptile meals.

Mohammed's fees were paid into a secret bank account he had opened before leaving India in the 1980s. Payments came from a trust fund in the Seychelles, untraceable back to the CIA. Every year, an accounting firm in

Delhi filed his tax returns. He paid taxes on his income as a US consultant in gourmet Indian cuisine.

Today, his job was to open two packages and replace the contents inside. One was an electronic circuit board, and the other a tin of quinces from New Zealand. Both items were sealed in removable plastic cling film, so he could remove it at the last minute, leaving no trace of fingerprints.

He took the circuit board and canned quinces from a compartment behind the passenger seat and put the embroidered lunch bag back in its place.

Printed on each outer plastic wrapping was a UPS bar code.

He went into the building and used a bar code scanner to locate the secure bins where each target package was stored for onward shipment. He decided to replace the circuit board first. He unlocked the security door with his security key, found the pallet, then the package. It was a standard UPS shipping box, about the size of a small pizza box, but about twice as thick.

He was already wearing gloves. This was not unusual in this warehouse, because it was dusty inside. He knelt behind the pallets, where he was out of sight. The huge warehouse was a hive of activity, and no one would have given a second glance to a uniformed UPS employee kneeling next to a pallet of packages. It was a normal activity.

He was a big man, and he turned his back toward the open side of the cage, concealing his hand movements behind the bulk of his back. He carefully examined the package seal down two of the sides and slipped them open with a small pen knife attached to his key ring. He removed the circuit board inside, which was backed between layers of foam packaging and inside a plastic envelope. He removed the plastic envelope and replaced the circuit board inside with the one delivered with yesterday's reptile food. He then took a roll of thin tape from his pocket and stuck it carefully along the cut seal. He placed a magnifying glass over his right eye and examined the seal all the way along, pressing the tape home in places. He then removed the tape and examined the seal again through the glass. The colored resin set quickly and provided a perfect seal on the plastic outer packaging. For good measure, he took two UPS Security Shipment stickers from a roll and stuck them at random angles over the replaced seal.

He put the box back on the pallet and picked up the original circuit board, now in the UPS box he had carried in. He put the tape residue in the box, locked the cage door, and threw the package in a large trash bin, where it quickly sank out of sight underneath a pile of lightweight packaging plastic and bubble wrap. For good measure, he nudged the bin with his shoulder as he passed, settling the heavier contents in the lower part of the bin.

He repeated the replacement of tinned quinces in another storage area. The original tin went into another trash bin, along with the outer plastic wrapper. This time, he removed his gloves and threw them into the trash as well. The whole operation had taken less than five minutes.

Ensconced in the safe house in southwest London, the king had become increasingly difficult in recent weeks. His drinking was out of control, and he had been violent to the hostesses on more than one occasion. He had become very particular with his food, demanding foodstuffs that he knew from the past: roast swan, carp, pike, and quinces.

When the new food delivery arrived, he recognized the tin of quinces and demanded them at once. The hostess opened the tin and was about to pour them into a serving bowl when the king grabbed the open can and popped the quinces into his mouth, using his finger and ignoring the sharp edges of the opened can.

He was unshaved, and the sugary juices dripped down his chin. He wiped them away with the sleeve of his shirt, a shirt she had recently washed and freshly ironed for him that morning. The hostess left the kitchen, not wanting to watch the disgusting spectacle. It was not her place to reprimand this man on his manners, and frankly, she had seen worse.

The king leaned back against one of the worktops and continued eating the quinces from the can. He chewed with pleasure, but before the tin was empty, he fell to the floor, clutching his chest.

The security detail in the flat below watched the king slump to the floor. Unhurriedly, the officer in charge called Charles.

The hostess already had a bag packed. She stepped over the king's body as she left, as if it wasn't there. She was driven away in a waiting car.

Within hours, the flat had been thoroughly cleaned and sterilized, and all consumables were removed. The clothes, sheets, towels, half-eaten can of quinces, and anything else that might contain traces of the king's DNA or fingerprints were taken away and incinerated.

The next day, a Latvian mining engineer moved into the flat in Fulham, and one of the hostesses returned.

The king's body was taken back to the MI6 medical center at Paddington Green; Dr. Brightwell conducted the post-mortem. Her findings would have told anthropologists much about the way humans had developed in the last thousand years, but they were locked away at MI6, with a top security classification.

The king was cremated and his ashes scattered next to his cousin at Faversham. Charles thought that a nice touch; Milt thought it a waste of petrol.

The president accepted the resignations of both Sally Carmichael and General Alexander. After a period of time, they were free to further their careers—not as easy as you may think for the former head of the Whitehouse Press Office and the ex-director of the NSA. Neither had risen through the ranks without making enemies along the way. As the saying goes, you can't make an omelet without breaking eggs. They had both made some pretty big omelets in their careers.

They each published their memoirs, working with separate publishers and ghost writers. The books came out about the same time, but neither made it to the best seller list.

Sally was a master of self-publicity, of course, and it wasn't long before she was back in the papers in her own right. She joined one of the many lobbying firms in the Washington DC area but soon became bored with the constant round of breakfasts, lunches, and cocktail parties.

As she put it to a longtime girlfriend, "My job is to flirt with fat old men with bad breath, so other fat old men with bad breath get what they want."

Kevin Alexander had taken a consultancy job with QinetiQ, a UK-based defense contractor. QinetiQ's British CEO was in town, and the firm was hosting a cocktail party at the Four Seasons Hotel, just off

Pennsylvania Avenue. The general had hired Sally's lobbying firm to fill the room with interesting people from the Pentagon and Defense Department officials. The general wanted to make an impression on the CEO.

In the end, they had a reasonably successful evening. The CEO went away happy and took his entourage with him, all except Michel Devereau, the deputy director of ESA, who somehow got himself invited to the event. Sally towered over Michel in her high heels, which gave him an eye-level view of her cleavage in her low-cut cocktail dress. He had clearly not forgotten the favor he was owed for the press release about the asteroid and had conveniently taken a suite in the hotel for the night.

There were twenty or so people left in the room, apart from Michel and Sally, mostly pretty hostesses employed by the lobbying firm as introducers. Their job was to pour drinks and introduce the guests to each other so that the interesting people got to mix.

There were also some men and women in uniform. These were recently retired US military officers paid by the lobbying firm to attend these events and mix. The general was also there, resplendent in his dress uniform.

Sally was the most senior representative from the lobbying firm that night and was in charge of the event. The rule was no one went home until after the last guest had left. Everyone was waiting for Sally to finish talking to the short Belgian. They had all had enough to eat and drink; you can only eat so many small bites of smoked salmon with quail's eggs.

They all drank alcohol sparingly, so the guests felt they were not drinking alone, but most of their glasses of champagne were still full. The liquid inside had long since warmed to room temperature. The bubbles were no longer effervescent.

The staff were standing around in small groups, chatting amongst themselves and trying not to look at their watches or look in Sally's direction. Eventually, the general came to her rescue, butting into the conversation, much to Michel's annoyance.

"Michel," he said, holding out his right hand.

The Belgian had just accepted a fresh glass of champagne and changed the glass from his right to his left hand so he could shake the general's outstretched hand. General Alexander could feel the dampness of the chilled glass as he shook Michel's hand warmly.

"Michel, it has been wonderful to see you, and thank you so much for coming. I do hope to be able to see you in Europe next time I'm over."

"Likewise," said Sally.

And with that, the general deftly took the glass from Michel's left hand and, still gripping his right hand as if in a handshake, marched him to the door. Sally waved good-bye, and before Michel could protest, he shut the door to the suite and locked it from the inside. Sally mouthed a silent "Thank you."

Sally dismissed the staff. They all ignored the gentle tapping at the door, and Sally and the general took the service elevator downstairs, where they stepped into a waiting taxi. They couldn't help their laughter, even though they both knew how unprofessional it was.

That night in Sally's apartment, they decided to set up in business together.

The plan was simple, really; they both knew a lot of people. They could bring clients in to lobby and do media relations for them. Why work for someone else, when you could do it just as well for yourself?

Despite Sally's tiredness, they sat up til two o'clock, making their plans. The general slept on her couch that night.

Now three months on, Alexander Carmichael and Partners was boasting six clients. They had offices on Pennsylvania Avenue. The general's second wife had filed for divorce, and the general slept most nights in Sally's bed. Neither did anything to hide this amongst Washington society, and it kept their names in the papers. This was all good for business.

However, it had been a grueling few months, and they decided on a short vacation. So they left a wet and windy Washington DC for a week of sunshine in Jamaica.

They traveled on a scheduled flight to Orlando and then changed planes for the flight to Jamaica. A few heads had turned on the Orlando flight; they were reasonably well known faces, but on the Jamaica flight, they were treated like ordinary passengers.

Everyone on the flight seemed to be on vacation, and nobody was interested in talking politics, let alone Sally and the general. After they arrived, they drove their rental car to a guest house in Buff Bay: two totally anonymous American tourists. After a couple of welcoming rum punches and a swim in the pool, they were both a million miles from Washington and ready to relax.

Sally had chosen the guest house with care. They wanted anonymity, a place where other American tourists were unlikely to go and recognize them. Plus they had both had enough of the inside of luxury hotel chains like the Four Seasons. If they had stayed there or at a Marriott, they may as well have remained in Washington. The design and the decor of those hotels was so similar the world over.

The guest house served no-nonsense home-cooked food. Fresh fish and jerk chicken were the specialties. It had a bar and a pool, and good access to a sandy beach. But by the third day, they had had a little too much sun and decided to take the car to explore the island a little.

The general had lived his life by a plan and a routine, and on vacation, he liked to do the opposite. After breakfast, they decided to drive along the coast until deciding to turn around and come back. The rental car had an inbuilt sat-nav, so the general was not concerned about getting lost. They drove east along the coast toward Port Antonio.

The stopped for lunch, and the restaurant had free Wi-Fi. They both checked their emails on their smartphones and dealt with some minor business issues.

Sally pulled up Google maps and leaned contentedly into the general's shoulder as they looked at the small screen. Sally swiped her finger across the map to move it on her smartphone screen. As she did so, the names of towns and villages appeared. Then the name Williams Field appeared.

The name took the general back to another conversation several months previously, and he remembered the safe house where Jesus had stayed. He explained the significance to Sally, who looked at him curiously. They were both thinking the same thing: *Why not?* Neither had seen this creature from another world, and they were curious.

Just before they left the restaurant, the general went to the men's room and locked himself in the only cubicle. There were some things known only to himself, things he had not shared with Sally. During his time at the NSA, he had stored sensitive documents on a secure server. He had done this discreetly. In his job, he trusted no one. This was his insurance, should things ever become difficult.

The process to save the documents was easy. The NSA spent most of its resources monitoring Internet traffic and the vast amounts of data that moved around the world every day. The powerful computers were programmed to look for code words, phrases, and patterns. The general knew if he had emailed the documents to himself, there would have been a record that the NSA would have tracked.

To avoid being spied on themselves, the NSA often used memory sticks to exchange documents. These small devices or flash drives were about half the size of a packet of cigarette papers and would fit in almost any computer using a standard USB port. Nonetheless, the memory sticks contained vast amounts of data. The data on them was automatically encrypted and protected with a password. If the password was used incorrectly three times, the data on them was automatically erased.

The general kept dozens of these memory sticks in his office drawer, and if he had to take a document home to work on, an assistant would save it on a memory stick for him. He often added additional documents to these files. In this way, he sequestered vast amounts of data, including all of the highly classified Silver Testament and Silver Shield documents. He was now able to access them through an encrypted link between his smartphone and his files. He quickly found the details of the CIA safe house at Williams Field, including the records of the two agents assigned to guarding Jesus.

He committed the details to memory and deleted the downloaded information from his smartphone.

Their rental car was an Audi, and the air conditioning system was highly efficient. Despite the midafternoon heat, the car was cool.

The general deliberately drove past the sign to Williams Field, even though Sally pointed it out to him. He explained that he wanted to drive the back way around, because there would almost certainly be CCTV on the main gate.

From the main road, they could see nothing of the big house or the helipad. But before they took the next right after the Williams Field sign, they saw a helicopter rise into the sky. The helicopter was not close enough for them to see who was inside; it rapidly flew away, out to the open sea.

He didn't really know what he was doing here, but it was an adventure, and being this close to his old world of highly sensitive US secrets was stimulating. He slowed the car and pulled to the side of the road under some tall trees. There was a high wall but no obvious barbed wire or alarm systems. There was a faded sign on the wall saying "Jacobs Creek—Private."

Although the sun was shining, he could see rain clouds building in the gaps between the tree branches. It rained heavily most afternoons for fifteen minutes, and then the sun came out again. He said to Sally, "Let's wait in the car until it rains; it will give us better cover. We can then take a look over that wall."

Sally looked up at the gathering rain clouds and said, "Okay." She then got out her smartphone and began to browse. She began a monologue commenting on the information she found: "It's also raining in DC … Democrats want a vote on gay marriage … the German chancellor is in town."

He kept the engine running so the air conditioning continued to function, and although he was listening to Sally's monologue, he was also watching the wall for any sign of movement.

When the first oily drops of rain hit the windscreen, the general turned off the engine, and they both got out of the car. The heat hit them immediately, in spite of the rain. The general felt the perspiration start: part heat, part excitement. He loved the adrenalin rush of action.

He found a convenient tree and scaled to the top of the wall. He put a hand down, and Sally scrambled over after him. They crouched under some trees, sheltering from the worst of the rain. There appeared to be a path to their left; the general pointed it out, and they began to move toward it.

The general was startled to see a tall, handsome young black man staring down at them from the end of the path. His features were serene, as if perfectly chiseled from black marble. He had appeared from nowhere.

The general raised his arm to wave and was about to say they were tourists and were lost, when the high velocity bullet tore into him. He was dead before his body hit the ground.

It was a difficult shot through the trees and the rain, but Mat and Jessica had been selected for a reason. They were both excellent shots. The second bullet splattered most of Sally's head against the perimeter wall. The newly promoted NSA director, Admiral Smythe, had just left by helicopter, giving the agents specific instructions to shoot any intruders on sight.

Jesus continued to walk along the path until he came to the inert bodies. He couldn't believe why these people still inflicted such violence upon each other.

The two agents jogged up to the bodies and made sure they were both dead; Mat climbed over the perimeter wall and checked the unlocked rental car.

Only when Jessica rolled the general's body over to look at his face did she recognize him.

"Oh, shit," she said under her breath. But they had their orders: shoot intruders on sight. No information about the silver man must ever be allowed to leak out.

Later that evening, the silver spacecraft appeared from the night sky and hovered above the helicopter landing pad.

Jesus walked up the side steps and touched an invisible panel on the side of the craft. A door opened, and he stepped inside. The door closed behind him. After a moment, he emerged in his silver suit. No part of him was visible, but Mary could tell it was him by the way he moved and the set of his shoulders.

He waved to the small group of people below the launch pad, turned with the grace of a ballet dancer, and stepped inside the craft. It hovered for a few seconds just above the launch pad and then rose silently, rapidly disappearing into the night sky.

Mary waved to the craft, with Mat, Jessica, Jed, and Lisa; through her tears, she whispered to herself, "God bless you, Jesus."

Ali and Admiral Smythe stood to the side. They prayed that Jesus would succeed.

The admiral had returned once news of the shootings reached him. He could now focus on what to do about the bodies of his former boss and his partner, sealed in body bags in the basement below the helipad. He also had to decide what to do about Jed and Lisa; they had heard the shots.

Jesus took up a position just behind the elimination capsule. He could see it growing in size. The sensors indicated that the planned destruction of Earth was a hybrid approach: there was to be an impact, followed by the controlled release of an organic virus. It was uncertain how the planet would be affected by the large impact, so the organic virus capsules would be activated later to a greater or lesser degree.

He was feeling the effects of high-velocity space flight now. He felt a little light headed and found it difficult to focus. His sensitive and immature rebirth tissues should not have been subjected to those rigors until later in the cycle. This was a very dangerous thing he was doing.

The asteroid was growing in size through a constant realignment of the carbon molecules inside. The elimination capsules buried inside it had activated the carbon's growth. After the impact, the deadly organic virus would be released remotely if required. The impact would not release the virus; the capsules were designed to withstand these cataclysmic events.

His craft carried no weapons; what he had to do was reverse the growing process until the asteroid shrunk in size. He would then pick up the elimination capsule and fly it into the sun. Only the intense heat of a star could destroy the elimination capsules.

He used a high-frequency laser, similar to the one he had used to stun Greta, the king, and his two companions about a thousand Earth years before. However, this time, the laser was programmed to a different frequency. The effect was to reverse the chemical vapor disposition process that allowed the carbon atoms to multiply.

He was feeling the effects of the space sickness, and his calculations were challenging. He found it difficult to concentrate on the complex formula to calculate the exact laser frequency. He finally programmed the laser to the required frequency and fired it at the asteroid in three ten-second bursts. The powerful laser beam used a great deal of the stored energy on the craft.

The effect of the laser was delayed, because there was momentum within the asteroid. The asteroid would continue to grow for about one Earth hour before it would begin to shrink.

After an hour, the asteroid was still growing. He checked his calculations and realized he had made an error. He then reprogrammed the laser and fired it again. Three ten-second bursts.

Jesus slumped at the control console of his craft and ate some high-energy food. The effect of the space sickness was terrible. He realized he must get back to Earth to continue his rebirth, or he may never be able to fully regenerate again.

His instruments told him that the craft was now down below half of the stored energy reserves. He didn't want to think about the fact that if he had to fire the laser again, he would not have enough energy to fly the asteroid into the sun and return to Earth.

He felt alone and desperately wanted to talk to someone. He couldn't communicate with his own people; he desperately wanted to speak with Mary. But he couldn't risk opening a communication channel for fear of detection. So he waited, tears filling his eyes. It was a human emotion, he realized.

After another hour passed, the asteroid began to shrink. It would be a few hours before the object was small enough to be towed by the craft, but he busied himself connecting the towing structure.

He calculated the energy needed to tow the asteroid and then return to Earth. It was going to take the craft's energy reserves down to within dangerously low levels, so he decided to tow the asteroid at a slow speed to conserve energy. Unfortunately, this slower speed made him more easily detectable, both from his people and from astronomers on Earth.

The flight to the sun would normally have taken only a few minutes, but because he wanted to save energy and because of the weight of the asteroid, the journey took two days to complete. All this extra time in space, while his body tissues were not fully regenerated, took its toll on his strength.

He released the asteroid about halfway between the orbit of the smallest planet, Mercury, and the sun. A mixture of the momentum from the journey and the sun's massive gravitational pull accelerated the asteroid into the fiery heat of the Earth's closest star. He watched alone as the asteroid and the elimination capsules were consumed into the white-hot mass. He turned the craft back toward Earth and collapsed at the controls, exhausted.

The two nearest planets, which the humans called Mercury and Venus, had no water for refueling, so Jesus used the last of the craft's energy reserves to return to Earth at half-speed. After landing safely on the helicopter pad in Jamaica, he removed his silver suit. It was early morning, before anyone was up.

There was a golden sunrise. The birds were singing as he stepped naked into the pool. He closed his eyes and floated for a few seconds.

When he opened them, Mary came into view, carrying a clean robe. Her smile turned to concern as she saw his drawn and haggard features. She knew he had succeeded; NASA had tracked the asteroid. But she now saw at what cost to his health.

Jesus slept for the next eighteen hours, and when he awoke, he admitted to Mary that he thought the damage was permanent. He would not be able to be reborn again. They wept together.

At the exact moment that the elimination capsules were destroyed by the white-hot heat of the sun, Greta awoke.

She smiled to herself as she listened to JC's gentle snores; he lay next to her in the huge bed in their New York apartment. The gray uncertainty of her terrible vision had just vanished. Her certainty of seeing New York City in ruins, with thousands of dead people, had just disappeared. She didn't know why or how it had occurred, but she knew that she was free of the terrible burden of her vision a thousand years ago; the uncertainty of the future was gone.

She patted her stomach.

Although it was still the middle of the night in New York, it was morning in Fleet, England. Ellen had just awoken and was sitting up in bed, drinking her morning tea, while Keith sat next to her, reading the morning papers. These days, they took both the *Telegraph* and the *Daily Chronicle.* Cathy Murphy was now the deputy editor of the *Chronicle.*

Keith was reading a story in the *Telegraph* about an asteroid that appeared to be on a collision course with the sun. The spokesman from ESA, Michel Devereau, claimed it was not anything unusual.

Apparently, this had been anticipated, and in an unprecedented spirit of cooperation between the United States, Russia, and China, they had all sent deep exploration rockets to investigate. The operation had cost the United States $375 billion. Or as the headline put it:

US Wastes Third of a Trillion Dollars on Space Mission.

His friend from NASA, Dr. Ali Palaszwaski, was quoted denying a report in the *Weekly World News* that two Chinese astronauts had been sent on a suicide mission. Keith made a mental note to email Ali and see how he was doing.

There was a story on the front page of the *Daily Chronicle* about the double-murder in Jamaica of two former US government employees, apparently a drug-related incident.

All of a sudden, Ellen felt Greta's joy. The cats stirred in the bedroom, and she let out a small cheer, punching her fist in the air as if she had scored a goal.

Keith looked up, startled, thinking there was something wrong. "You okay?" he asked.

"Yes, I'm fine," she said, "just some good news from Greta."

Ellen took his hand and put it on her pregnant stomach. Ellen also felt Greta's comforting touch on her belly from her bed 3,500 miles away in New York. By now, Keith was used to the way Ellen was able to communicate with Greta, using some form of telepathy, and he accepted it without question.

Even though she was thousands of miles away, Greta could feel the new sister growing in Ellen's womb. She knew this child would be very special and wondered, now that the terrible burden of her vision had passed, could she also experience the elation of her own child? She began kissing the back of JC's neck.

Epilogue

The effects of Mohammad's actions at the UPS Warehouse in Dallas were twofold. The first was the death of the king; the second was a rocket exploding on a launch pad.

If King Stephen had been allowed to live, it would have created a major constitutional crisis in the British monarchy. It was, of course, unthinkable that the British MI6 could conduct regicide themselves. So over a coffee in a busy Starbucks, Charles had shown Wayne DiBello, the CIA operative in London, an image of a tin of quinces offered for sale on a New Zealand website.

The CIA labs had developed a two-step toxin that was undetectable in a post-mortem. There were twenty quinces in the tin. Half of the quinces in the tin were contaminated with toxin A, and the other ten with toxin B. Each toxin was odorless and tasteless. All the king had to do to trigger a fatal reaction was to eat two quinces in the correct order. Dr. Brightwell discovered the secret of the CIA's two-step toxin and began working on an antidote. Just in case.

The rocket that exploded on the launch pad was scheduled to take Bob Cabana into space on his last heroic mission. Bob had led the mission in Colorado when the baby Jesus had been reborn. He was an experienced NASA space shuttle pilot. The replacement circuit board that Mohammed switched had a revised firmware chip that caused the hydrogen fuel to ignite prematurely.

Bob Cabana had been diagnosed with leukemia, which was common amongst astronauts. When you left the protection of the Earth's magnetic field, the heightened radiation levels were sufficient to bring on the onset of deadly cancers. Most astronauts died young, a fact kept out of the press.

Bob had volunteered to go with Jesus. The UN had pulled together an international consensus for once. World leaders all agreed that diplomacy was essential; otherwise, more elimination capsules would follow.

Bob didn't want to leave his children and grandchildren. His wife of forty-seven years had died the previous year. But he knew he was dying, and so this was his chance to do something special.

He even had to lie to his children when he said good-bye.

But he had negotiated one condition with the US authorities. He had left a diary of the events leading up to his departure with a legal firm in Switzerland. If the planet still existed, in twenty-five years' time, the diary would be published. This was his immortality. He hoped his surviving children and grandchildren would forgive him. He had also left them personal messages.

They didn't know about the cancer in his blood; this fact was kept from the public. They thought he was going on one last mission.

The live TV pictures showed him strapped into the capsule of the Space X rocket, supposedly on a supply mission to the International Space Station. The vessel required just one pilot, and who better than a former shuttle commander?

In fact, the vessel was being flown by remote control, and the pictures were a recording. The Space X rocket exploded eleven seconds into its flight, providing spectacular TV footage. A prewritten obituary for Dr. Bob Cabana was released.

Just as the obituary was released on the press wires, Bob Cabana, dressed in a silver suit matching Jesus's, stepped into a spherical silver craft on a helicopter launch pad in a remote part of Jamaica. The craft floated over the launch pad for a few seconds and then, with unbelievable speed, silently shot out of sight.

On the launch pad was a small silver object. Ali climbed up to retrieve it: a silver glove. He looked to the heavens.

He realized that this was Bob's parting gift to mankind; if they could analyze the material of the glove, they could make huge progress. He took the glove to a tearful Mary and the waiting admiral.

To be continued …

List of Major Characters and Events

KING STEPHEN AND HIS COURTIERS

King Stephen of England, born 1092 or 1096, in Blois, France. Wife, Matilda. Reigned 22 Dec 1135 to April 1141. Father King Henry I of England.

William of Blois, King Stephen's half-brother.

Rupert of Ypres, protector of King Stephen, finest swordsman in England.

Henry of Gloucester, protector of King Stephen, finest bowman in England.

THE WITCHES

Greta the Witch, a powerful witch living in twelfth century in England. Soothsayer who is favored by Matilda (King Stephen's wife) and sent to spy on her husband.

Ellen the Witch, a powerful witch living in the modern day in Fleet, England.

Carla the Witch, Ellen's lesbian lover. Less powerful witch than Greta or Ellen.

THE BRITISH SCIENTISTS

Dr. Keith Maxwell, eccentric British space scientist working at secret UK government laboratory.

Professor Helen Collins, Dr. Keith Maxwell's supervisor.

Dr. David Thomas, head of PR at secret laboratory where Keith Maxwell works.

THE US NATIONAL SECURITY AGENCY AND THE WHITE HOUSE

The admiral, or Admiral Gerald Smythe, NSA security adviser and clever military operator. Access to the NSA Director and US president.

The general, or Army General Kevin Alexander, NSA Director, the admiral's boss.

Sally Carmichael, head of White House Press Office.

THE US SCIENTISTS

Dr. Ali Palaszwaski, senior NASA scientist collaborating with Dr. Keith Maxwell.

Dr. Mary Morrell, senior NASA scientist from Marshall Space Flight Center, a specialist in deep space particles.

Dr. Bob Cabana, shuttle pilot and head of NASA Kennedy Space Center. Selected to lead the postmortem of the silver man.

THREE SCIENTISTS WHO ACCOMPANY MARY MORRELL TO JAMAICA (ALSO IN COLORADO BUNKER):

Dr. Anne Davis, medical doctor specializing in children's medicine.

Dr. Brian Fellows, anthropologist.

Dr. Carl Lancaster, educational psychologist.

JACOBS CREEK, JAMAICA, AND THE CIA OPERATIVES

Jed and Lisa, Gardener and housekeeper at Jacobs Creek.

Mat and Jessica, CIA agents acting as married couple.

THE PRESS

Weekly World News, a sensational American magazine that prints the half-truths of the story through regular leaks from US military personnel and others.

Cathy Murphy, tenacious and attractive reporter from the British tabloid the *Daily Chronicle*.

Martha, Cathy Murphy's assistant at the *Daily Chronicle*.

JC, or John Constable, ex-British soldier and police officer who is chauffer and protector to Cathy and Martha at the *Daily Chronicle*.

MI6 AND CIA IN LONDON

Sir Geoffrey Milton, head of MI6 (known as Milt).

Charles, Milt's assistant, University of Oxford history graduate; talks in staccato.

Wayne DiBello, head of CIA in London.

NSA OPERATIONS AND CODE WORDS

Silver Shield, code name of operation to protect the baby Jesus from public disclosure.

Silver Testament, code name of operation to destroy the elimination capsules headed by the admiral and Dr. Ali Palaszwaski.

LAUNCHES

Bird 1: Russian unmanned with nuclear weapon, would reach the asteroid on time.

Bird 1R: backup Russian launch authorized by President Putin, also armed with nuclear weapons, but would not each asteroid on time.

Bird 2: US rocket, first to be launched with electromagnetic radiation (EMR) weapon.

Bird 2A: backup US rocket with EMR, would not reach asteroid in time.

Bird 3: Chinese manned rocked with aim to collect beacon and fly it into Jupiter to destroy it. Suicide mission.